"Here is a heroine as charming and clever as
Scarlett O'Hara and as ready for love as Forever Amber."

—Jacksonville Journal

NANTUCKET WOMAN

"A pulsating story . . . Diana Gaines's period
detail is rich and convincing . . . This is the
kind of adventure story in which it's the ad-
venturer that counts—and Kezia's a remarkable woman, earthy, intelligent, and the mistress of her soul."

—Publishers Weekly

Bantam Books by Diana Gaines

DANGEROUS CLIMATE
NANTUCKET WOMAN

Nantucket Woman

DIANA GAINES

BANTAM BOOKS
Toronto • New York • London

To Christopher Stewart Jaffe,
latest passenger on my bus,
may he ride easy and go far.

*This low-priced Bantam Book
has been completely reset in a type face
designed for easy reading, and was printed
from new plates. It contains the complete
text of the original hard-cover edition.*
NOT ONE WORD HAS BEEN OMITTED.

NANTUCKET WOMAN
*A Bantam Book / published by arrangement with
E. P. Dutton & Co., Inc.*

PRINTING HISTORY
E. P. Dutton edition published August 1976
Bantam edition / November 1977

ISBN 0-553-10499-3

Published simultaneously in the United States and Canada

---

*Bantam Books are published by Bantam Books, Inc. Its trade-
mark, consisting of the words "Bantam Books" and the portrayal of a bantam, is registered in the United States Patent
Office and in other countries. Marca Registrada. Bantam
Books, Inc., 666 Fifth Avenue, New York, New York 10019.*

PRINTED IN THE UNITED STATES OF AMERICA

The body in which we journey across the isthmus between two oceans is not a private carriage but an omnibus.

The Guardian Angel,
OLIVER WENDELL HOLMES

PART I

Puella

1723-1743

One

Kezia's last words were for her only begotten child who, in the way life has of playing jokes even upon the dying, was not present. Kezia had that one moment of lucid articulation in seventy comatose hours after a fall on Monday evening, March 26, 1798. Lit by an unwonted number of candles, the faces of her gathered kin evoked not a glimmer of recognition in the staring hickory nut eyes. The doctor came in and picked up her wrist. A sister leaned over and kissed her cheek. One of her grandsons whispered, "Gramama, come to." She felt nothing, saw nothing, heard nothing. And then toward nine o'clock a gust of wind shook the jamb of the closed window, riffling the candle flames and a few strands of dark hair which she had that week rinsed in indigo. Her eyelids flickered. She tried to raise her glance above her toes which a pair of hands gripped through the counterpane. She said quite clearly, "Daughter, thee is the proof that I have not been a bad woman."

An uninnocent statement to be sure, but what unloved child ever felt innocent? From the time Kezia was born, late December 1723, love-hunger consumed her—does it really start in the womb?—and jealousy warped her, a jealousy so painful that as soon as she was able to exercise any control over her emotions, she sublimated it completely and presumed she had none. Her mother, her father, her brother, her mother, her father, her brother—this was the refrain, the lifelong lament, these the early omnipotents, her first loves, the people she least resembled and never knew, nor they her.

The Folger house was small and the walls thin.

With ears ever on the prick for praise, Kezia early picked up the criticism.

"I don't know what to do with her," Abigail Folger complained in the dark fastness of the four-posted bed. "She's a sight harder to raise than Elisha ever was. Not as meek by half as a maid ought to be. And slow to learn, clumsy handed. If I didn't know how devilish smart she was—"

"Keep her more by thee that she may imitate thy graces," was Daniel Folger's drowsy reply. "She tags along with Elisha and me down to Straight wharf, the rope walk, the sail loft. They're no fitting school for maids."

It came as no surprise that her father did not want her with him; there were times when he couldn't even think of her name: "Um, lass, how um thee?" And if she made to kiss or touch him, he tacked hard away. But her whole body clenched in the trundle bed when she heard her mother sigh, "Ah, but it gives me respite. I've so many chores to do, and now with the infant Peter, I am sore fashed. I labored overlong with him, I've not yet got my strength back. 'Tis a great trial when the feet present themselves first."

To the three-year-old Kezia, feet first sounded right enough. The wrong was that he came out at all. Now she was not only not the eldest, not a boy, but not even the youngest. Displaced by a blotchy bald thing whose skin did not fit—it lay in wrinkles at the wrist and ankles and other places hastily covered from Kezia's sight—this was the prize around whose cradle one must tiptoe, his cry the first heeded, his mouth filled at the sweet fount now forbidden to Kezia, his length stroked and bundled against winter draughts, the soft top of his head untouchable by her but often kissed by them, his inane toothless smile coaxed with tickling and chuckings and bird imitations. It was disgusting. It was also frightening. If they preferred this wizened mite to her, of what earthly value was she? Was it possible she was of none? The cry that ripped out of Kezia when she poked her finger into Peter's eye was, "Nay!"

After that Abigail kept a closer watch on the infant. When she was called from home to assist at a childbirth or had to fetch flour from the mill, she called in a teen-aged cousin, Debbie Coffin, to mind him. Debbie was pretty with flashing dark eyes and as kind as she was lively. Not surprising that Kezia came to adore her. They had make-believe 'entertainments' with poppets of Debbie's—cattail bodies stuck with twigs for members, walnuts for heads, hair of dune grass. But Abigail's interpretation of the second commandment was so fanatical she wouldn't let Kezia keep them. "Graven images," she called them. Kezia wept and would not eat and had screaming tantrums but Abigail was unmoved. On the contrary, Kezia's rebellious carriage convinced her the lesson needed teaching.

When Debbie's twin, John Coffin, was not at sea, which was rarely, he and Debbie were inseparable, and it pleased them to take Kezia with them all over the island in the boxcart, on horseback, on shank's mare. She dug with them for quahogs on the south shore in sight of the Indian village. They taught her how to swim frog-fashion, though the legend was that Nantucket young were born web-footed. Her pipestem arms were too weak for hand-lining fish from a dory, but she baited hooks and untangled foul lines and said things that made them laugh. In the spring, they went on squantums to Quaise and Polpis. In the fall the girls trailed John to Coskata Pond where he bagged black duck. Winters they bellied down the Wannacomet Hills on the chebobbin. They even achieved a kind of iceboating by rigging the chebobbin with a piece of old sail. Speeding before the wind on a frozen-over pond, bracketed by their warm bodies, Kezia howled with delight, the air crisp as radishes in her open mouth. Who could sit quiet learning to stitch a sampler after being initiated into such heady pleasures of the wilds? Who needed a father or brother to take one voyaging? Certainly not Kezia who, asked at school to list the members of her immediate family, left out both. When

the omission was brought to her attention, she was genuinely surprised, as guileless of murder as a sleep-
walker. "They are so much at sea," she explained,
"they did slip my mind."

Debbie was an assistant teacher at the Quaker
School, and although Kezia was a bright and eager
scholar, there is no doubt that Debbie's attentions made
school homely for her, a home that like Debbie's own
or almost anyone's she vastly preferred to hers. Indeed, Abigail remarked somewhat acidly that if Kezia
went to Meeting as willingly as she went to school,
she'd be sure to get into heaven. After school, when the
days grew short, Debbie usually walked Kezia home.
At the stoop of the Folger homestall, Kezia would cling
like a limpet to her cousin's arm.

" 'Tis betimes. Not yet five o'clock! Do come in. Sit
a spell."

"A minute then. I've chores to do but I'll clip in
for a minute."

Sometimes they'd hold rods tipped with hissing
apples to the blue part of the blazing fire. And Debbie would dip into her fund of legend. How Nantucket
came to be: a stone shaken from the shoe of the Indian
giant, Maushope. What the name meant: sandy soil
that yields nothing (*nantuck*). Why there was fog:
Maushope smoking pokeweed in his pipe. How the
Forefathers bought the isle sixty-four years ago for
thirty pounds and two beaver hats, one for the seller
and one for his wife.

"Too cheap, a whole island," Kezia opined.

"Well, he kept a tenth share plus Quaise for himself. And two beaver hats. They last a lifetime!"

They'd sit toasty in the fireplace, intoning the
names of the clanheads which were the warp and the
weft of all Debbie's tales:

"Coffin, Macy, Folger, Swain/Gardner, Hussey,
Stahhh-buck/Pinkham, Russell, Bunker, Worth/Bar-
nard, Mitchell, Cole-man."

They'd chant it over and over, faster and louder,
bobbing their heads, rocking to the beat until they

rolled off their stools, bodies sprawled pell-mell on the warm hearth bricks, gasping out a primal excitement that went beyond laughter. Suddenly, dragonfly Debbie would jump up. "Time to make sail!" She'd grab her hat and cloak and fly out the door while Kezia's mouth still hung open on a harsh breath.

"Kezia, what does thee? On the floor like a pup!" Abigail would come out of the borning room adjusting her fichu, having just given suck. "Oh, has Debbie gone? I heard the to-do and hastened to greet her."

"She was late for home. She went out in a gale."

There was a kind of ballast in her mother's voice that got Kezia up on her feet, but she felt strangely disturbed as if she'd done an unclean thing. She thought of the thrust of Debbie's full, round breasts and wondered how long before she'd sprout a pair of her own.

"Well, don't stand adreaming. Rig the table board. Use the huckaback cloth."

Kezia would obey in a trance, so preoccupied that she'd drop things or break or spill until she won a reproof, with luck, a physical one—a slap or a box on the ears. The greater the loss of Abigail's restraint, the deeper Abigail's ensuing guilt which invariably evinced itself in a gesture of affection, a hug or a kiss or a tucking into bed. On a day in her sixth year, however, Kezia's mind wandered too far.

There was nothing in the break of that raw whippy day to mark it as a fateful one, though it did unfold an extraordinary series of mishaps. There was first off the dead rat in the rain barrel when Kezia broke the icy crust to wash. At breakfast, she overturned the sugar box. Abigail kept her temper through two scourings of the floor, which nevertheless remained sticky underfoot. Then toward noon, Kezia dropped the newest baby on her head. And, turning quickly from the pothook near the grate, she tore her frock, not her First Day one but nevertheless half of her winter wardrobe.

By four-thirty peace and harmony seemed to be restored. Judith was asleep in the cradle on her face,

the welt on the back of her head having been pressed
small with a cold knife. Abigail rested before the fire,
mending Kezia's petticoat. Kezia sat on a footstool
nearby, cleaning the prized set of two-tined forks. The
family cat, Jedidah, snoozed in a ball on the rag rug.
Mother and daughter were silent, each enclosed in her
own thoughts, the ticking of the clock and the logs'
cracklings unheard.

Presently, Kezia put down the cleaning rag. She
unreeled a long thread of yarn from her mother's ball
and tied one end of it to a fork. She stood upon her
stool, hurled the fork into Jedidah's rear end. Her
bloodcurding whoop was matched by the cat's screech
of pain as it leaped up and streaked out of the room.
Abigail screamed, jumped to her feet, clutching her
yarn.

"Pay out, pay out, Mother!" Kezia cried. "Give
her the line! The whale is sounding and I've only got
one iron into her!"

That was the breaking point for Abigail. She
grabbed Kezia's cloak, threw it and the child out the
door, yelled, "Get thee hence, imp of Satan, and do
not return until thee is housebroke!"

It was late and a nor'wester moaned like a woman in travail, trying to deliver rain. Kezia held the
hood of her mantle bunched tight under chin, bucked
the wind head down, pressed close to the bearberry
bushes. Would Debbie believe that she had seen not
Jedidah's rump but the streaming black hide of a
spermaceti? That, as steersman, she had but obeyed her
captain's distinct command: "Lance! Now! Give it to
her solid!" If Debbie did not, what would happen to
her?

She did not mind if the Friends set her aside. In
truth, she hated Meeting—the sad colors, the solemn
faces, the interminable silence during which she had to
sit still, hands folded like her mother's. (Did God know
that she never thought about her sins nor strove for the
Light, but went over the multiplication tables in her
head, doing the twos up to a hundred and the fives up

to further than that, singing them to herself like the bawdy verses of a tavern lay? Perhaps He did and was about venting His wrath.)

The Coffin keeping room, so-called because here the fire was always kept, was ruddy with light. Leaning from the front stoop, Kezia could see that Aunt Miriam and Uncle Samuel were entertaining the Starbucks. An occasion of some importance because the little handleless china cups from Canton were being used. Young Tristram Starbuck lounged against the mantel at the side of the fire, his gold head almost touching the ceiling. John's back was to Kezia, so near that if the window had been open she could have tapped him. Debbie, whose eye she prayed to catch, sat motionless, head bent over her cup as if her neck were broken. The candles glowed, the fire flames jigged, the hum of voices came as if piped through the far end of a telescope. The tears ran warm down Kezia's cheeks, dripped cold from her nose. Why were other families so serene, so civil, and hers so degrading? Oh, what was to come of her? If her mother told her father and he told the selectmen, what then? The stocks? Or flogged like an Indian while everybody watched? Sobs laddered in her chest, her nostrils sniffed convulsively. She slunk away, cousin only to Jedidah, into the shadows at the rear of the house. She walked the great live oak on cat steps, swiftly, paw over paw, up the trunk.

It was one of the few shade trees on the island, remarkable for never losing its leaves, and it grew straight up in spite of the wind that forced most island trees to bend south. Uncle Samuel's father had brought it from Spain, and she knew every crotch, every limb, every knot on every branch of it. She climbed until she was level with the sightless eye of the bedchamber which Debbie had to herself now that her older sister was gone—first married and then died. Bracing her back against a stout branch, she crossed the toes of her shoes in the vee where it joined the mother stalk and gazed with all her energy at the black opening in the silver shingles. She had a stone in her hand, ready to throw. She could easily move forward on the limb into the room via the window, if only it would yellow up, if only Debbie would grab her thought. It was astonishing how often they thought the same thing at the same time. Kezia concentrated. And prayed to the devil: "Oh, Satan, if indeed I be thy imp, empower me now. This once."

The room slept and the sky grew darker, and the wind shook her with dog's teeth that would not let go. She wondered if she had been gone long enough to be let back in. It seemed hours. Then she set her chattering jaw. No. She would not go home. She was not Jedidah. She was small but doughty, she could wait. Debbie had to go to bed *some*time. Let her mother fret about her whereabouts. Mayhap she'd send her father and Elisha to search her out. They'd go to the waterfront first, they'd think she'd drowned herself. It was a thought. Then they'd be sorry.

She was savoring her mother's tears frosting the narrow loaf she made under freshly turned earth when she heard a door slam and then the trudge of feet. A man's figure halted directly under her perch. It was John Coffin without hat or coat, his white shirt agleam in the dusk. He began to pace back and forth, his hands opening and closing behind his back. She could hear his heavy breathing and she made her own thin, and she stiffened against the tree limb to control her shivering.

Debbie came running with a beautiful paisley shawl—new, Kezia had not seen it before—over her head and shoulders. Debbie ran to John and grabbed his forearms and he shook her off and turned away.

"Dearest, please," Debbie begged in the wind, splaying her hand dark on his white back.

He wheeled to face her. "Thee cannot mean it. Thee cannot. We swore an oath to each other under this tree."

"It was wrong of us, John. Wrong to swear and

wrong to know each other carnally. We were possessed
by the devil. The maggots of remorse gnaw constantly
on my vitals. Oh, help me, Brother. I have been weak
but I have suffered much. I cannot abide the loneliness,
the waiting—not that and the awful guilt too. At least
thy life is full when we are apart. Thee is at sea, free
and natural, busy with the hunt. But, John, my lot is
emptiness. What would thee? That I be everybody's
aunt, a captive in our parents' house, with nothing
womanly of my own, no lover to declare, never a
chick or a child or a pot to call mine?"

In the long silence that followed, Kezia wanted to
cry out, "Thee has me, Debbie, thee ever has *me*.
How can thee say thy life is empty? All the things we
do, the good times we have, has thee forgotten? Does
thee not love me anymore? Did thee never?"

"Tristram Starbuck," John said heavily, stern as a
father. "My good friend. How can thee be so faithless?"

"Believe me, dear love, it is the better way. The
only way."

Kezia had never seen Debbie look beaten, sound
despairing. In what way had she betrayed John? Told
Tristram a secret? Done a bad thing? Something worse
than stabbing the cat? But Debbie was never bad,
never lied, never tattled, was beautiful, good, practical-
ly grown up.

"Does thee love him?"

Debbie bowed her head. John grabbed her shoulders and shook her until the shawl fell to the ground.
Debbie's cap came aloose and her hair spilled down.

"Answer me. Does thee? *Does thee?*" And he—
oh, God!—slapped Debbie's face, first one way and
then the other.

The mews became cries and then sobs.

Up in the tree, Kezia's hand clenched the stone,
tears rolled down her cheeks. She considered hurling
herself down on the brute, raining blows on his head.
Even Elisha would not so mishandle his sister. Oh,

she'd give him a beating, and if he knocked her off him she'd bite him in the leg! She braced herself for the jump.

"No, no, I love *thee*," Debbie was gasping. "Only thee, as long as there is breath in my body. God have mercy on us both!"

Kezia's foot halted in air. Did she mean it, or was she saying it so he'd stop hitting her? She pressed her fingers hard against her mouth as she watched the two come to grips. Oh, what was happening? It was deadly, but it was not combat. He heart began to pound and a strange heat came up in the cracked place between her legs as their faces fastened, mouth upon mouth, John's hand alternately stroking and clutching, up and down Debbie's back.

Debbie wrenched away. "Belay—someone will see!"

But John pulled her back to him. "I care not. I will not let thee go. Thee are me and I am thou, born of the same single seed. One. *One!* Before God, Debbie, would thee tear me asunder?"

Debbie's voice was hard and cold as a wave breaking over a rock. "We are torn as it is. Thee is gone, either gone from me or forbidden. I have a whole life to live. I want a home, babies suckling at my breasts. Tristram can give me them. Can thee?"

John's head went down. He groped her titties, lingered as if saying farewell to them, dropped his hands to his sides. "Forgive me, beloved. I would not stand in the way of thy happiness."

"Oh, John," Debbie wept, returning his hands to her breasts. "Thee is my happiness. Shall we be lost then? I am willing." She flung herself against him. He gently disengaged himself, returning her arms, crossing them on her bosom as if they had died.

"No, thee did right, Debbie. I lost my head—the shock of the announcement. I had no idea. But so be it. Hush, sweeting, do not cry."

It was too much, too bewildering—the backing and filling, now angry, now pleading. And besides, she *knew*. What they had done. Elisha had recently showed her two dogs bungholing. "Soon there'll be a litter," he said. " 'Tis a dirty thing but 'tis how babes are made. Us too." Almost, not quite understanding, she translated slowly. "Our mother and fa—?" He'd kicked her shin hard. "One word more—*one*—and God'll strike thee dead!"

Kezia felt very tired. The whine of the wind made her dizzy. The dizziness made her nauseated and faint. Hailstones fell in blobs on her face; one stung her eye. Her foot ran with needles, she moved it stealthily in the fork, but it wanted stamping. She didn't know this Debbie, this John, she wished they would go away. She tightened her fist on the edges of her cloak but she might have been wearing a fishnet for all the chill it shut out.

At last Debbie went into the house. She'd forgotten her shawl, which lay in sodden folds in the mud. John retrieved it and held it to his face and his shoulders began to shake. So it *was* a dirty thing, else would a grown man cry into his sister's garment? Sinned. Neither of them would ever be the same. Nor would she. She stood in her wind-torn ark and waited for the world to be washed away. Suddenly—of all voices! Her body quivered like an arrow shot into the limb of the tree.

"Has thee seen Kezia, Samuel? We have looked and looked!"

The stone missed the stoop and landed all but silently on turf as Abigail was made welcome, drawn inside.

The pneumonia Kezia contracted that night kept her abed for weeks, and her fevered dreams so blended memory with chimera and taboo that the encounter itself became blurred. Thereafter, however, the twins were as dynamically entwined about her soul as were her own parents.

Two

Twenty times she wakened during that June night—the breeze soft as wings, the light powdery with a neap tide three-quarter moon—yet at sunrise her sisters and the little brother were up and chirping while Kezia still slept under her hair.

Mary shook her arm, little Abbie tugged at her thumb, and Daniel tickled the arch of her foot.

"Kezia, wake up, 'tis sheep-day!"

Kezia's eyes flew open. She let out a yelp and leaped up. She swung over the sash of the window, teetering on her flat waist, her feet floating out behind her. Seventeen years old, a woman at last. Would he notice the vast change in her? If he did not, she must find a way to flaunt herself, make him see—.

Judith grabbed a bunch of her sister's nightdress. She was like her mother, fresh-faced, practical. "Thee'll fall—"

"Fie, Judy. Not today. Why, today if I had to, I could fly like a bird."

The young ones giggled, poking each other, stirred to the bottom of their empty bellies by their big sister's excitement and the possibility of her flying, which they believed.

"What a day, what a day!" She sighed in, sang out, stripping off her sleeping garment as Judy gasped and hurried little Daniel out of the room. Oblivious to the bustle behind her, Kezia gazed out at the slate-colored harbor and watched its rim begin to glow. The glow inched up over the totter-edge of the world, and gradually the water took light from the sky. Craning eastward, she saw the Coffin house set in coral. Was he

14

there? Or still aboard the *Deborah?* Or had he spent his first night in his bachelor house down by the wharf?

The room emptied of sisters while Kezia combed her hair. The comb stuck in the knots but gradually it came clear, and she pulled and stroked till it crackled. Out of the drawer in the candlestand by her side of the bed she took a red silk ribbon. She had had to give a kiss for it—just a little peck though she had been quite scared—to a bewhiskered sailor with a chewed-up ear and sour breath, but it was worth it. If her mother should gainsay it, she'd—she'd—well, what would she? Surrounded by water on four sides with ten shillings to her name, where could she run to? The Indians? And become a virtual slave as Shanapetuck was? Stow away on a sloop and be dumped at the first port, mistreated, perchance defiled, on the way? The shillings were a savings of ten years. Uncle Samuel gave her one on each birthday, had done ever since she was seven, and she had never yet found anything she would exchange them for.

She swept the handful of hair into a ponytail and tied the bright ribbon around it. It was a curious thing, she mused, that Shanapetuck had appeared at their door just when her mother so needed help with the infant Thomas.

"Thus doth the Good Lord provide," Abigail had said, looking heavenward as Shanapetuck expressed willingness to exchange her labor for bed and board. But Kezia would have been inclined to look downward for the source, considering Shana's cloven foot. Not that Kezia did not like Shana, nor that she feared her. She so resented her parents' religion, which to her was nothing but a tomb of nos, that except for the possibility of being burned later, so much later it might as well be never, she was not at all sure she preferred God to the devil. She believed in Shana's potions and predictions, but there had been something fishy about her story that her people had whipped her for picking gooseberries. The English, yes, that she could have believed, but the Indians often stole, the fruit of a bush as free as land or sea or air to them. Shana, lame, unkempt, raggedy, was yet an attractive girl, hot-eyed and buxom, and her trouble, Kezia surmised, was not with gooseberries but with a man. Shana always knew more than she told, she had a great stillness inside her, elf-shot, some said.

Kezia tilted her head at the hand mirror that she kept hidden under her garments because her mother disapproved of such instruments of vanity. John had given it to her on his return from a whaling voyage three years ago. At the time she would have preferred a crusty murex or, better still, one of his feathered lures for trolling, but since then a metamorphosis had taken place. Where she had had angles, she had curves, where she had been thick, she was thinned, as in the waist and upper thighs. Dark hair sprouted in a spongy triangle above the secret button that when rubbed produced a strange and powerful bliss. Baby-fine brown silk shadowed her armpits, her breasts were tight with budding, and she bled at each quarter moon. Oh, she had the proper fittings, 'twas just a matter now of getting the captain to sign on.

She examined her moles—one on the right side above the wane of her eyebrow and an even tinier blacker one on the left between the corner of her lip and chin. Had Debbie spoken true, did men verily find moles irresistible? In France, Debbie declared, they called them 'beauty patches.' But Nantucket was another kettle of fish. Still, John Coffin was no simple Nantucketer, he'd seen the world, France too.

"Kez-eye-err!"

She dropped the hand mirror. Luckily it did not break. She groaned softly to herself, pulling some short dark hairs from the center part down over her high forehead to make a bang. She tugged forward some hair from above her ears, roughed it between her fingers into curling wisps to 'soften' her face which because of its length was inclined to look coltish. Theirs was more square. Her eyes were their color, a dark luminous brown, more tilted than theirs. Her nose was neither Coffin-flat nor Folger-fleshy; it was her best feature. Their lips were Coffin lips, strongly molded, full in the underlip, whereas her mouth was rather thin; perhaps it would thicken as she did more kissing. She chewed it again and again, and then, spitting on her index fingers, forced her lashes upward. The lashes were grand—long and dark. But the fingernails were bitten.

"Kezia, come this minute or thee may spend the day in bed!"

Her mother's voice struck from tween-decks, each word a lash on her back. She grabbed up her slippers and ran down steps, burning her palm on the hempen handrail.

She had just bent her head to her porridge when the dread command came.

"Take off that bedizenment."

"What bedizenment, pray?"

"That which thy hand has flown to."

"Oh, Mother, it will not show. My bonnet will cover it."

"Then thee surely needs it not."

"But today—for the festival!"

"How came thee by it?"

"A tiny little red ribbon cannot offend—"

"I asked thee a question."

"I heard it not."

"The ribbon. I asked thee where—oops!" Abigail grabbed up the pudding whose edges had turned from brown to black. She put the bowl hastily down on the brick and sucked her finger.

"If I promise to wear it only today, never after?"

"Oh, pother, child, don't try me now. There is no time for argument, we shall be the last in Sherburne to set out as it is. Thy father and brother Peter left before daybreak to round up our sheep. We know not how many have perished in the spring storms for this is the

first thy father has found the time to count earmarks."
Still talking, she snatched an end of the hair ribbon
and before Kezia could exhale, it was curling in the
fire that had steamed the pudding. "Riddance to rubbish and thee got it from one of the world's people or
thee'd have answered me how. I know thy tricks."

The little stench the dying ribbon gave off was
brimstone to Kezia's nostrils. She let her tears drip into
her cold porridge and she slowly spooned their salt into
her down-jerking mouth.

"Think not that John Coffin may be landed by a
bit of red ribbon, my daughter. He is beyond thee in
every way, thirty-two years to thy seventeen—"

"Seventeen and a ha-alf—"

"—and rich and much admired by women. If
'twere marrying he was after, would he not have long
since found him a bride? Far better save thy calf eyes
for Samuel Starbuck."

Kezia's face twisted with rage. "That spindle-
shanked mildewed parsnip? I'd sooner be a thornback
like Aunt Hannah!"

"Leave my sister out of this, thee wanton jadehopper!"

Kezia jumped up from the narrow table plank,
upsetting the communal jug of milk.

"I saw thee in the lane after the clambake last
Sixth Day," Abigail went on, tossing a wiping cloth to
Kezia, "and thee was kissing that parsnip."

"I was not," Kezia choked from the floor, her face
puce.

"Durst call thy mother liar?"

"I—I—*let* him. I did not kiss back. 'Twas just
for the practice!"

"The prac—!" Abigail closed her eyes, took a
deep breath. "Cast off, Kezia. Cast off without delay.
I know what store thee sets upon this day and I would
not be so cruel as to deprive thee of attending. But if
thee is not out of my sight, I cannot promise—"

Kezia was out the door before her mother opened
her eyes.

The pond seethed like a cauldron of soap. The air throbbed with blather. Hoarse male shouts and soprano laughter burst like rockets into the balmy air. One could make out the elders in their flat-crowned broad-brimmed hats and long coats. They always came early to settle disputes about earmarks, which tended to become unclear after months of exposure to inclement weather. Here and there one could see the red jacket and tricorn of a king's man, a popinjay among sparrows. Behind the rickety sail awnings clustered the carts, and close by, horses cropped the grass around their hooves. In an agony of impatience Kezia ruffled the reins of the lagging horse. "Avast, Jerry. Keep thy stern awaggle!"

"Mind the potholes in the path. Jericho's not used to so long a haul, he might tumble us."

"I *have* been minding." Had in fact been secretly proud of her piloting but of course her mother never remarked her good performances, only her bad.

She would make straightaway for the Samuel Coffin booth, Kezia decided. Their cook, black Hepsy, and Hepsy's son Nathan might be glad of an extra hand whereas the Folger booth would have a plethora of help—the offspring of six uncles, to say nothing of Judith-dear. Besides, hadn't her mother expressly said to get out of her sight?

Aunt Hannah's spare frame stood abaft the tent. They all saw her but did not think to wave. Aunt Hannah was one of those persons who simply *are*—like beasts of the field or sponges in the sea. In addition to waiting upon her kin, she kept herself by making cloth and garments, quite literally a spinster.

"At last, Sister," said Aunt Hannah, as they pulled up. "I had begun to fear thee lay becalmed at home. A babe sick or some mischance. Welcome, children. Is it not a fine day for the washing?"

"Aye, and let us praise the Lord for it," said Abigail. "Doubtless the Congregationalists will take credit for its fineness and brag of it to the coofs as if they had decocted it in their own tryworks."

Hannah's only beau had been a Congregationalist, and since marriage outside the sect was strictly forbidden to Quakers, she had given him up. She said mildly, "Ah, well, Sister, we are all God's children." Then, turning her attention to the school of Folgers who surged around the cart, she directed the unloading of the food baskets and the jugs of birch beer and sugared water flavored with lemons. "Bide a moment, Mary, Dan'l, Abbie. First the cargo, then the crew, eh? Careful with those tarts, Judith dear. Thee may stand down, Kezia. Cousin Tristram will unbridle thy horse. Turn to, lad."

Unnoticed, two Folger rascals, tennish, winked at each other, sidled to the rear of the cart. As the last cannikin of goodies was handed down, each boy pulled out the hook on his side of the tailgate and unobtrusively leaned. Out tumbled the passengers in a heap. Daniel howled with glee, rolling about like a shoat in the dust, but Mary whose drawers were exposed began to cry. Little Abbie was furious. She bit a trousered leg. The bitten boy hopped away, baying. Judith righted herself, straightened her bonnet, and began to dust off her younger sisters. Kezia let out a guffaw before she remembered her seniority. She drawled to her mother while setting Danny upon his feet, "This is but a sample of what we may expect throughout the day. Bedlam. Pranksters. Strams. Oh, it's too vexatious."

"What's strams, Kezia?" Danny asked.

"Tykes like thee who run between the legs of their biggers!" And she sent Danny off with a light spank.

"Ah, well, 'tis a once-a-year day, and bedlam is the order of it." Abigail stretched toward the placid sky. "Thee need not tarry, Daughter. Thee's free to visit or to watch the washing."

Urged to skip, Kezia's gypsy foot turned leaden.

"I thought to help set out the victuals."

"No need. Aunt Hannah and I can manage. There are many willing hands."

"Mine are not unwilling."

"I meant no reproach, Kezia. Twist not a body's

words for ill meaning. Take thy leave as freely as 'tis given. Only, mind, we sup tonight with Grandmother Wilcox at sunset. We shall up-anchor at three of the clock to tidy ourselves. There will be many guests at Grandmother's table, including our renowned cousin Benjamin Franklin. We would not shame thy father's mother."

"I shall be there in good time. And tidy too." But she stalled.

Judith asked her mother where to stow the butter.

"Any good deep piece of shade, dear. Under the trestle's a good place."

"I wish thee good day," Kezia said, kicking dust.

"Good day, dear Kezia."

"Does thee go to gam with Debbie?" asked Judith.

"Debbie and divers others," Kezia replied airily. And still hung about. The "dear" was from Aunt Hannah, and so counted for nothing.

"Good day, my mother."

"Good day, child, good day, good *day*."

The bite of that sent her off too suddenly; she jostled her mother's hold on the bowl. Abigail stopped breathing and popped her eyes but she did not drop the pudding.

"I beg thy pardon," Kezia muttered, head down to hide the rush of tears, and she loped away, aboil with the unspoken: But it is thee who makes me clumsy, with others I am deft.

Running, her spirits lightened. She called back greetings to neighbors who were setting up their sail-shaded booths. She was breathless, holding the stitch in her side, when she reached the two grandmothers sunning on the crest of a hummock.

"Good morrow, Aunt Miriam. Mistress Starbuck. Where is everybody?"

They were a formidable pair. Aunt Miriam projected an authority of beauty that the cult of plainness could not vanquish, and she had an instinct for elegance—her garments silkier, her slippers daintier, her hands paler than anyone's. On this day she wore mitts and a light cotton face mask under her hat to ward off the tanning rays of the sun. Her extreme delicacy had held Captain Samuel in thrall these many years to the envy of more prosaic couples who cattily whispered that with Miriam Coffin it was Samuel first and children suck hind tit.

Dinah Starbuck, on the other hand, was a matriarch, big-boned and handsome, one of those born aristocrats whose clothing is irrelevant and whose conduct makes rules rather than follows. Her carriage was still majestic and her Grecian nose rode high above the seventy-year-old ruins. Under her scrutiny, Kezia's back straightened and she hid her nails in her palms.

"By everybody," observed Mistress Starbuck dryly, "I presume thee means Debbie."

"Nay, Kezia, do not blush," Aunt Miriam said. "Constancy is a most excellent virtue. Debbie's gone down along the hollow to the spring. Thee might take a vessel to fill, too. Ask Hepsy for one, there's a good girl."

Halfway down the hill, the kettle banging against her thigh, Kezia kicked off her shoes. She'd worn no stockings or undergarments on this warm day. She held up her skirt, taking pleasure from the slippery grass on the soles of her feet.

Debbie was lying on her back in a bed of buttercups. Seeing her thus, as if she had not a care, Kezia realized with a pang how much she had missed her. Almost constantly pregnant, Debbie swung ponderously from loom to sink to cradle to hearth, at chores early and late. And Tristram was more ubiquitous than most husbands, preferring not to roam but to hunt cod and an occasional whale offshore now that he had Debbie to come home to.

Kezia sat down in the curve of her friend's waist, hefting an escaped hank of Debbie's hair, so like in texture and color to her own. "How good it is to see thee taking thy ease. I can scarce believe my good fortune, finding thee alone and idle."

Debbie's kerchief lay tossed aside, her skirts pulled high over white thighs gone heavy, her bodice unstrung. The nipples were brown from having given suck. Kezia preferred her own smooth pink ones. Under their quiet exchanges, Kezia studied the face that was her destiny. This was the face where her heart was to live, crisscrossing halls of hope and memory, moving from chamber to chamber, from cellar to roof walk, in shadow and sunlight and abysmal dark, contracting in fear, expanding in strength, beating always and only with love—a kind of involuntary reaction that perhaps accounted for her indifference to other people's opinions. High broad brow bulging under an uneven dark hairline. Black eyebrows finely arched. Round sunken eyes, thick cream lids. But Debbie's eyes flashed no more, as mutely patient as a yellow-bagged cow's. John's had fearful glints, they judged and they mocked, they were never benevolent. The twins' mouths were once, Kezia remembered, identically sculpted, blood red at winter fires, glistening after mutton or milk. Now Debbie's rose had bloomed, it drooped, rueful, overripe, and where there was strength there was now only sweetness. John's man-mouth? She could not quite conjure it up. To try made her uneasy. But then it appeared—cruel, that thick underlip. And whereas Debbie's puckered instantly with affection or compassion, John's curled with contempt, and therein lay the challenge.

Wickedly, Kezia drew with her fingertip John's moustache between Debbie's nose and lip. "Thee looks like John."

"With good reason."

"I would that I were a twin."

"Why?"

"Then I should not know loneliness."

"I am often lonely."

"Even with a husband and children?"

"Even so."

"I doubt we mean the same thing by loneliness."

Debbie—sure, busy, needed, vivacious; what could she know of the black hold where Kezia spent long spells, sometimes self-consigned, sometimes pushed from behind by an unexpected hand?

"Methinks we do mean the same. Not solitude nor yet lonesomeness, but aloneness as dark and evil as the fight against certain death."

"Thee does know! I could wish thee did not."

"I trow we are among many who know it well. Though some, as in endurance of pain, are hardier to bear it than others."

Debbie closed her eyes.

Kezia flooded with love. There was no one she could talk to like this. How fortunate she was to have a friend of such understanding, such wisdom and candor.

A black dumbledor whizzed by. A patch of cold air wafted up from the bank, prickling the skin of her sun-dappled forearm.

"Debbie, be thee happy?"

"At this moment? Blissful."

"In thy marriage."

Debbie opened her eyes. "We can do without happiness, Kezia, and instead thereof find blessedness."

"Then thee has no regrets?"

In one of those swift changes of mood, Debbie bounded up. "What a question to put to a woman wed eleven years and mother to five! But now that thee mentions it," said Debbie, picking up the pail, "I do have one. A small one but a regret withal."

"Tell me. Thee knows thee can trust me. I would not breathe it."

"Very well. The truth is I regret and oft quite bitterly—" she hesitated.

"Say!"

"Kezia, didst ever wish thee had been born a man?"

Kezia laughed. "Oh, verily. They do have the best of it, of that there is not the smallest doubt. But I tell thee, Debbie, I mean to have a taste of the best before

I'm through. Travel, adventure, aye, and riches, too. I'll not pine away on this pimple in the sea, walking the top of my house, scanning the horizon for my man's ship till my hair turns gray as shingles."

"Thee would not marry?"

"I'll marry, too."

"What husband would allow thy flaxing about the world?"

"Shall I tell thee?"

"Thee *knows?*"

"Yes, I know."

"Kezia, little minx, who? 'Tis not—no, it cannot be—?"

"Who does thee think of?"

"Samuel Starbuck?"

"Oh, fie. He's but thirteen—a child."

"Then I have nary a clue."

"Thy brother John," Kezia said simply. "Save for thee, have I ever loved another?"

The bucket dropped.

"Thee jests."

"Indeed not."

"Thee are but a maid, he is nigh twice thine age!"

"Thy tongue could be in my mother's mouth. What has age to do with it? I am old for seventeen and he is hale and comely." Kezia giggled nervously. "Comely as thee."

"He has proposed marriage?"

"No, it is I who have chosen. He knows not my feeling for him as yet. I—I wanted thy blessing first."

The two sets of black eyes locked on a level.

"Debbie," whispered Kezia, the old knowledge, unstated, unstatable, stirring in her innards like snakes, "thee would ever be first in each of our hearts. I ask no more than to be second."

Debbie hurled the pail hard alee. They watched it bump and bounce, heard its wooden sides clack as it rolled down the slope. Kezia felt as if she had turned to solid salt, petrified, pillared as Lot's wife, and for the same reason: looking back. She should have held her tongue. Then she felt herself grabbed, her head held hard against the soft ample body.

"Thee has been our little sister for lo, these many years, Kezia. Let it remain so. I would not see thee hurt. John is already wed—to Neptune's daughter. His ship is his home and the sea his farm. I know him well. Thee knows him not. Please believe me."

Kezia pulled away. "But if he will have me?"

"I doubt we shall have to cross that bridge. We shall never come to it."

Kezia dug her toes into the grass. "Make me a straight answer."

Debbie looped a hank of hair, which immediately fell again. "If John should ask for thy hand in marriage, I should of course give my blessing. And forthwith pray for thee both, for I assure thee such a union would not be plain sailing. Now, no more of this chatter. There's the water to haul. The sun is overhead, the men will be foregathering."

In silence they filled their vessels at the spring and started back. But the constraint was lessening. A stone had been thrown into the well of love between them. A cloud of mud had risen, was settling; they were too devoted to be disturbed for long by ambivalences. Retrieving her shoes, Kezia said clemently, "Yesterday, when I heard the news cried in the streets that the *Deborah* was sighted, I ran all the way to the wharf. I searched among the swarm but did not see thee."

"I had many things to do," Debbie said. "And I knew there would be a gaggle of family on hand to hail her home."

"The breeze was fresh. She sailed into the harbor gallantly with a new mast flag—a black whale on a white ground. The menfolk waved their hats and we all cheered till we grew hoarse. Then the sailors climbed the shroud and they gave us a chorus of hallos. I thought I spied John on deck—'twas hard to distinguish faces at that distance and many of the men had grown beards. The command was given to take in sail, but I waited and waited—hours it seemed. My legs grew wobbly. Dusk fell and still John did not debark. Judith arrived on Mother's orders to fetch me home. I had no course but to obey. Is he well?"

"Yes, he is well but much fatigued. There were latterly storms and too they ran afoul of some fighting Irish. But no man hurt and the entire cargo brought home safe. Molasses and peppers as well as oil. And ambergris, a goodly piece. Worth its weight in gold. John came not to our father's house till nigh on to midnight. He was tuckered, too tired to eat. Instead, we toasted his return with Father's best brandy. He intended to lie abed this morn but he promised to come to the feast. Thee shall soon see him for thyself."

Young Christopher ran to them. "What thinks thee, Mother? A ram chased Father! Father ran till he was out of breath and then he turned about and spread his legs and the ram ran *through!* Father fell astraddle on his back and was took for a ride—till he was knocked off!"

Tristram came up grinning, and relieved the girls of their burdens which sloshed over as they laughed.

"Thee be not wounded, Husband?"

"Naught but my pride. The beast rent my aft sail. Thee'll have a patching chore."

"I'd give an eyetooth to have seen thee ride him!" Debbie, still laughing, brushed some lamb curls from her husband's thighs.

" 'Tis good to hear thee laugh, Mother. Thy smiles are common enough but thy merriment I seldom hear."

Debbie gave her son a sharp look. She threw her arm around him. "Have I been sluggish of late? Well, today I am in fine fettle. Come, let's race to the top of the hill."

Laughing and loose, the four ran up the hill. Kezia, proud of her fleetness, gave it her all, outstripping Christopher who burst into tears. It had not occurred to her to let him win before his parents. She clumped away, hiding her hard breathing, feeling like a plowhorse among deer.

At the Coffin campsite, preparations for dinner went apace. Puddings spiced the air, peat chunks smoked in their cross-tree pans. Hepsy slapped a starfish hand off the plate of small cakes cut in the shape of hearts and rounds. Grandfather Starbuck rebuked a quarrelsome child. Debbie and Kezia smiled at each other under moustaches of beer foam.

Into this halcyon nooning rode Captain John Coffin, accompanied by his youngest sister, Priscilla, and within moments family harmony erupted in civil war. One could pass a lifetime on the island and never see one man raise his hand against another. How then did violence break out between two Quakers over so small and by no means new a thing? There smiled the prodigal, standing up in the calash in his shore clothes, leather weskit tight across broad, muscled chest, one full homespun sleeve writing on the sky a salutation to all. Curls black as a crow's coat shone around his suntanned face and besides the moustache Kezia remembered there was now a beard. Her heart was so tight it hurt. Something in his bearing and expression set him apart from the rest of the island men, and she responded to it without being able to put a name to it— the inimitable insouciance of one who holds his life cheap and has tried again and again to spend the last cent of it.

Slightly behind him, his little sister held her chin high, her pride as stuffed as a festal turkey at making an entrance with the hero of the hour. She was Miriam Coffin's last child, no more than a month older than Debbie's first. It had been a source of abashment to mother and daughter to be lying-in at the same time, and although the intermarrying natives were accustomed to strange coincidences of birth they were not above quipping about them. Debbie's Christopher gradually knew himself to be the butt of a joke he did not comprehend and he had come to loathe Priscilla as a result. Less generally remarked was the antipathy between John and Tristram, which dated from Debbie's betrothal and which ran the deeper because of their close boyhood friendship. Unfortunately, as John looked over his clan, Tristram and his firstborn were side by side in the foreground and they pricked John's eye till he saw red.

"Good morrow, Brother Tristram, how thy tribe doth increase!" John said, and he made a fulsome bow. To Christopher he said, "Well, Nephew, don't stand there with thy teeth in thy head. Hand down thy Aunt Priscilla!"

In the ripple of laughter, Christopher turned red and stood fast.

"Didst hear me, lad? Or be thee deaf as well as doltish?"

Tristram swept his son behind him, spanned the little girl's waist, and whisked her over the side of the carriage, setting her down hard enough to snap her jaws on her tongue. She began to snivel. John dismounted. He and Tristram stood eye to eye, toe to toe.

" 'Twas Christopher I addressed, not thee."

"Thee be not captain here, John Coffin. 'Twas a poor greeting at best. The taunt is worn to a thread."

"I greet in my own way. Who is thee to censor me?"

"Father of the child thee term dolt is who I be. 'Twould seem the company of sailors has roughened thy manners as well as thy humor. I advise thee to stow thy gab."

"I'll stow thee, thee stinking landlubber!"

John's fist shot out. Tristram reared back, and the punch glanced off his jaw to his Adam's apple. Gulping the pain, Tristram threw his knuckles at John's mouth, drawing blood. John hurled his stocky body at Tristram's tall bulk. They went down in the dust, growling like mad dogs.

"Grandfather Coffin, Grandfather Starbuck, stop them!" Christopher screamed. "Make them stop!"

The two elders strode forward. John's younger

brothers ran past them, peeled the brawlers apart, swung John upright, pinioning his arms.

Nathaniel Starbuck bent creakily to pick up his son's hat and held it out. "For shame, Tristram. We are men of peace. The Meeting shall have dealings with thee both."

Samuel Coffin chided his own. "John, John," he mourned in a voice so grieved he might have been David crying to Absalom. "What has come over thee? To smite thine own kin!"

John spat black in the dust. He spoke quickly through his cut mouth. "I am sorry, Father. I—I know not what—"

Tristram fended off the rush of his children— Zaccheus and Christopher and the squealing girl twins. Debbie laid a hand on his shoulder.

"Be thee hurt, Tris?"

John jerked away from his brothers and stood alone on wide-spread legs, eyeing the man whose loved ones covered him like foliage. Kezia could not bear the envy on John's face. She tore off her neckerchief and ran to him, pressing against his side to wipe the bloody corner of his mouth. He accepted the ministrations without a glance to see who was doing him the kindness. Then, absently, he took the kerchief from her, himself stanched the flow, and waded as through water toward the little family tree. He dropped down on one knee in front of Christopher. "I made a half-wit jest, Nephew. I beg thy forbearance. Wilt thou give me quarter?"

"If my father would have me, sir."

The rebuke, albeit mannerly, was not lost on John. He stood up, meeting Tristram's blue glare. "He's master brave, thy lad is, Brother Tristram, and if there be dolt here, 'tis I. I heaved my grapples aboard thee without reason." He put out a square brown hand. "Will thee make it up?"

His old chum's lightning changes of mood, Debbie had them, too. They were of the same pod, these two, and, will or nill, Tristram found their charm irresistible. He took John's hand and clapped his shoulder. "Nobbut a summer squall, Brother John. Thee had the wind up, never mind why. Come, let's have a swig of my mother's punch. I'm spitting sand."

But it was not Tristram's pardon John needed. He said, "Sister Debbie, can thee muster a welcome for a roily sea monster?"

Debbie's smile flashed. "Come along and sup before the pooquaws taste like cordwain." She tucked her arm in his. "Let us hope thy torn mouth shan't spoil thy palate. How long has it been since thee tasted cherry pie?"

At his elbow, Kezia murmured, "A shearing bun, Captain?" and held a basket under his nose.

"By hakes," he roared, catching her to him, "is this the little wharf rat I used to fetch and carry? This lissome nut-brown damsel, is it truly Kezia? Come, give an old coz a kiss. Or is thee too grown to give them away?" His beard brushed her cheek, as he pulled her down on his knee and kept her there, making much of her, feeding her tidbits she could not taste, could scarcely swallow.

"Tell me, what has thee done whilst I have been gone? Can thee still boat a blue with thy bare hands, scorning the gaff? Or are thy recreations now ladylike? How does thee spend thy days?"

"I have taken Debbie's former place in the new school," Kezia replied demurely.

"Thee prefers schoolteaching to helping at home with the chores?"

"Oh, yes, and I favor the earning of money."

"How does thee feel about spending it?"

"I've not tried yet, but I think I should like it very much."

John's laughter roared out and Kezia was proud to have drawn it. A laughing man is not a bored one. But she was nervy from the strain of sitting on him. She hoped he could not see her heart pound; he did seem to be eyeing it.

It was her bosom, not her heart, that had John's

eye, since she was not wearing the neck gear usual to Quaker maids. Smooth little crab apples, and wouldn't he like to have a taste! It would take the nutmeat of green fruit to clear his palate of the overripe flesh he'd gorged on for the last three years. Three? Say, rather, more than a decade, and don't try to count the caverns he'd plunged his cock into, spilling his juices like so much bilge water in a vain effort to put out the forbidden fire. 'Cursed be he who lies with his sister.'

Well, no one could say he hadn't tried to forget her, from Boston to Biscay Bay, from the Banks to the Bahamas. There was the practiced Angelique who had taught him, among other things, that a silk kerchief not only shut milt out but the Venus Plague in. There was the marble-skinned Lady Anne Rhodes who drank a concoction of fox saliva and goat's blood to counteract her frigidity, and there was her raunchy maidservant Bridget, who could have used an opposite potion, she'd nearly killed him, that one, and after him, his first mate. There was the masochistic Doña Adriana who had taught him a new use for buggy whips. There was Jioni, the half-demented Martinique priestess, whose lust was oral, nigh cannibalistic. And there were the nameless whores of the most wretched ports on both sides of the Atlantic. Only dire emergency could persuade him to put into a decent town, for it took little to tempt the men to jump ship. Months of mortal danger, storms, backbreaking work or demoralizing idleness, filth, cramped quarters, salt-horse diet, uncertain wages. Why did they do it? Why did he? Asking the question was a cat-and-mouse game he played with himself. He knew the answer well, had he not painted it on the very hull of his prison? He had to run away and he had also to come back, tied to her as to a cross. Accursed he was, the devil's own. Now what on earth was this prim little poppet waiting for him to say? He liked her voice, it had a clear-water sound that refreshed him, but her words had passed him by.

"Hm, splendid," he murmured, "splendid."

"Splendid? That there be not enough paper for

sum books? Thee mocks, John. We likewise need boards for flooring. As late as First Month, the earthen floor was so cold, I sat teaching with my feet on a chair. I must be uncommon careful as I am given to colds."

"Is thee?" And to keep her by, playing her a bit before he threw her back as too little, he asked mundane questions. "Tell me, what subjects does thee teach?"

"Arithmetic and reading. I'm a dreadful poor speller." There, she'd made him laugh again.

"Thee's a true Nantucketer then, not a body on this island spells his own name the same way twice." Her floating rib felt fragile to the pressure of his palm. She was stick slim, her flesh neatly tailored to her slight frame. "And has thee yet picked a sweetheart? Likely half the spriggins in the town are trying to hook in with thee."

Kezia was not instinctively coquettish. "None but that nidget, Samuel Starbuck. He des not yet shave, his ears are overlarge—"

Debbie, sitting at John's side, reproved her. "Fie, Kezia, he's a good lad, a bit young's all. But there be eligibles, a mort of them, John, if she'd but accept their attentions with grace. She discounts any lad who'd spark her. And she's known for dander. Her own enemy, never pleased with herself. She'd admire to be like Damaris Worth and such niddy-noddles—the pink and white ones with glass-blue eyes who simper behind their hands. A man soon tires of a china doll, does he not, Brother?"

Kezia was one child he could share with his sister. He said with avuncular tenderness, "China doll thee is not nor ever shall be, but given a few more years and a few more tears, thee may well fetch up a beauty."

The praise was so heady, she had to decry it. "Thee should see me in winter when I'm sallow as a bass' belly." And grimaced horribly.

"Kezia!" Debbie gasped, but had to laugh at the face.

"There is a saying in Madrid," John said, running his calloused palm under Kezia's hanging sleeve: " 'Beware the woman who can be both beautiful and ugly for she is rare.' " He eyed Kezia thoughtfully and stood up abruptly, setting Kezia on her feet. "Well, I'm for the harbor. I cannot hope to keep enough local crew aboard to unload cargo until shearing is done. The watches are composed of foreigners, not one of them as trustworthy as our lads, so I am uneasy. Should thee be pleased to accompany me?"

Kezia's heart lurched, as much with dread as with desire. Alone with him all afternoon, might she not bore him, say a stupid thing, betray herself in some humiliating way? "I should dearly love to, Cousin John, but—"

"I knew it. Some pillicock awaits thee in the thicket!"

"Nay, John. Thee's the only man on the island I or anyone wishes to be with today and thee knows it."

He laughed. "A celebrity that will last until the next ship comes in, if that."

"Oh, no, John. Thee hath no peer. Thee's the rovingest whale-master of all!"

"Yet and still thee disdains to company me."

"I promised my mother I'd be home by four o'clock. Grandmother Wilcox is having a supper and I must tidy up first."

"I shall have thee back in good time."

Three

John rowed the dory, expertly threading his way among the varied craft. His hat lay between his feet and the salt breeze lifted his hair. Kezia pushed her bonnet back to feel its play on hers. She let her hand trail in the water, it cut a green wake.

Kezia had lain on the bosom of the mother earth this morning in the hollow. Now she gave herself up to the masculine current, let it carry her, unresisting as an infant. Her eyes narrowed against the flashes from the little knives of water. She exchanged a drowsy smile with John, while in fantasy she draped herself across his chest, felt his muscled thighs against her, and sucked his earlobe as her brother Dan'l sometimes suffered her to do.

"Soon it will be warm enough to bathe at Siasconset," she said. "Might we not go there one day as we used to do?"

"To be sure. My sloop needs paint and repairs and I have some trading matters to conduct, but before I leave for the mainland, I shall take a day off, a good hot one, and we shall fish and bathe and have our fortunes told by the old squaw, Cuddusue, if she's alive." And he told her of a swim he had enjoyed below Trinidad where the water was warm as tea. "When we go aboard, I'll show thee a shell from that beach. It is as white and smooth as thy skin, with a lining of red inside the lip. Thee shall have it. Or is thee too grown to value shells? I mind thee used to collect them. Thee had a name for the jingle shell, something droll—"

"Indian toenail." And when he laughed, she protested, "But they do look so. All different sizes, from the big toe to the little." She added impulsively, "Oh, John, 'tis good to have someone who remembers one's past."

"Aye. So it is."

"My parents care nothing for when I was small—"

His oar caught a crab, snagged in a wave.

"—they only mind me bad or sick. None save Debbie and thee mind me as good or droll or dear. It makes me feel—I know not how to say it—valuable, I ween."

He gave her a deep brown look. Yes, he supposed he must seem like a parent to her, he was closer to their age than to hers. Yet he had not been thinking of her as daughter, more as playmate or nymph, and for these few moments he had felt young again, the John Coffin of those careless yet caring days. What a fool he was to think she could regard him as a contemporary.

Kezia did not fathom his look but knew that it closed her out. Something she said? Too intimate? Too childish? She felt that sick inner lurch again and wished she had not come.

They were sighted. A ladder was thrown over the *Deborah*'s side. The instant her slippers touched planking the stink of decaying oil punched her nose. She held her nose, but the truth was at this moment she preferred it to attar of roses. She leaned on John's arm and indeed his every word as, house-proud, he pointed out this thing and that, from cargo hatch to booby hatch, from quarterdeck to hold.

"And now the captain's quarters," he said. "A privilege not often accorded ladies, I assure thee."

She followed him down the narrow stairs, hanging on to the side rails, her limbs loose and weak. With quick down-sweeps, she wiped first one and then the other sweaty palm on her petticoat. Would he kiss her? Should she resist or go limp? She heard his flow of talk as through a glass quarel, marveling at his unconstraint.

Casting a last look at the patch of blue at the

head of the companionway, she stepped over the threshold as she would have entered a wizard's den, a king's bedchamber, a cathedral. Indeed to her the dark little chamber projected an authority that was at once magical, kingly, ecclesiastical. Each piece in the room glowed richly as must, she imagined, the pope's ring, the crown jewels, the stars in an astrologer's hat, Lucifer's pitchfork in hell's firelight. The teak desk had chased bronze pulls. The brass bindings of the sea chest shone like gold. Over the master bed, which was suspended from gimbals to hold steady when the ship rocked, a compass had been polished till it blinked. On a half-grilled shelf affixed to the wall stood leathern volumes with names like necklaces tooled on their spines. Mathematics. Sermons. Agriculture. A pale hidebound book untitled stood alone between a silver tankard and a ship's clock. She took it. The flyleaf said, *The Perfumed Garden.* Written by a sheikh and but recently translated. It opened in the middle to a minutely colored illustration of two figures on a bench in a walled garden. When she could believe her eyes, she snapped it shut. Her hand had scarcely fallen from the replacement when she heard his voice.

"What thinks thee of my privy web?"

She started. Wheeled. "Oh, grand." She cleared the hoarseness. "Fit for a king."

Moving forward in a trance, she saw her reflection in the mahogany-framed mirror above pitcher and basin. Her hair was wind-blown, her cheeks aflame, her eyes luminous as lanthorns. Who was this girl? Could it be she, in the blow at last? She heard the bolt slip. Her mind raced back to the moment when Samuel's lips pressed hers and drew a blank. What was it her part to do? Oh, Lord, let me not seem untutored, light me the way, I would not lose him.

He came up behind her, encircled her waist, his beard prickling her neck and clavicle.

He spoke softly to the girl in the mirror. "I foretold wrongly, thee's pretty as a pearl without having shed a tear. Could I make thee cry, Kezia? Could I touch thy heart?" She stopped breathing as she watched his hand slip upward and close upon a hard little protuberance. "Ah, there, I have made thee tremble. I would not frighten thee, but only teach. Have I not proved a tender instructor in times past?"

He turned her around to him slowly. Heat melted her to a fine plumb line. As he drew her close, the enemy part of him pressed into her belly like a bunch of stone grapes, and then tremble was not the word, she shook like timbers in a hurricane, and the inside of her mouth went dry and hot as with ague. If only she wouldn't feel sick. Oh, dear God, all-powerful God, help me—*help!*

"Little cinnamon rose." His moustache tickled her ear. He smelled beery. Oh, God!

The rap of knuckles on the cabin door made her jump. She heard his teeth click as her forehead bumped his bearded jaw. He released her so roughly the washstand bit her back.

The knock came again, louder.

"Avast, damned carrion rogue! I'm not deaf."

His profanity mortified her. His rage was that of a thief caught in the act of looting. She reached back to the towel rack for support, sundered with relief, humiliation, disappointment. She had never known the Lord to work so speedily. She half-regretted calling upon Him.

From the doorway came gat-toothed phrases: "Ship's stores . . . dogwatch . . . parbuckle . . . haglet stewpie."

Then John was gripping her shoulders, enunciating as if she were the town idiot and she nodding like one. She was to make free with the contents in the top right-hand drawer of his desk. Playthings there, mementos. She must make herself comfortable, he'd be back in a trice. He tipped her chin up. "And let be, lass. Think not so hard on matters natural and instinctive. Look not so big at me, thee can see as well from cups as from saucers. 'Tis only I, John Coffin, thy same

old affectionate friend. Tarry at ease the while. I'll not
be long."

It was wonderful to be in his trig domain while
he was out of it. So many possessions. She spun about,
drunk as a bee in a summer garden. A logbook lay on
the blotting pad with a quill pen in shot nearby, and
an inkwell of crystal and brass. A set of engraving
tools in a round wooden rack, a miniature ivory of
King George II. She touched each thing, picked it up,
put it down. The top drawer of his desk contained
pipes and skrimshander, and farther back, a necklace
of black banana seeds and white cowries which she
donned and inspected in the mirror. If only her people permitted adornment. She laid it gently back.

The other drawers were locked, but as she tugged
at them, from somewhere dropped a small bronze key.
She tried it in the next drawer after a second's com-
punction. He'd *said* to. It unlocked easily and contained a jade vial of perfumed salve, a gull feather, a
knotted thong, and handkerchiefs made of the thinnest
silk she'd ever rolled between her fingertips. The rest of
the drawers were uninteresting—stuffed with papers.
Sheets of latitude and longitude calculations, invoices,
correspondence with the East Indian Company of London.

She sighed. How could a man of wealth and
learning take seriously a maid of seventeen who had
been nothing, done nothing, knew nothing? Her mother was right. Debbie, too. He might be willing to steal a
kiss of an afternoon or take her on a day's outing, but
marriage—that was stargazing, nothing more.

Suddenly dispirited, she threw herself upon his
bed. Beside it, rolled charts were stowed in slots under
a wide board that served as a study table. So organized,
so learned . . . worlds away . . . another country and he
the supreme ruler. She had never felt more worthless, more immature. She pulled her knees up and sank
into sleep.

John stepped across the threshold of his cabin.

He'd have been at the work still had not the change
in light reminded him of his promise to set Kezia
ashore in time for her family supper. The sight of her
raised his eyebrow and the corner of his mouth. She
was lying in the fetal position, the bottoms of her
crossed feet bare and dirty. Her skirts were bunched
around her waist. The little witch had not bothered
with smalls. The pouting vulva lay revealed to his eye
as did the rosy puckered mouth in its webbing of
brown silk. The white nates were perfect globes, eminently pinchable, spankable. He thought of the knotted
thong but the drawer was locked and he'd lost the
blasted key. He stood there considering the possibili-
ties, and an eyelid went down as his member went up.

One might start with the clitoris, parting the fat
little pair of trout to expose the single pink tongue up
front, titillating it with light flicks, then tantalizing
with steady friction until she writhed out of control,
beating against his palm in a try for climax. When she
was thus under his thumb, so to speak, he could force
entry for the deflowering. By good fortune the silk kerchiefs were still handy. No, damnation, they were
locked up, too. His head jerked from one end of the
deck to the other as if the key might suddenly appear
to his eye. He broke out in a light sweat. If he searched
for it now, he'd wake her certain sure. Hold on, Cap'n,
don't let go of the wheel, plenty of alternatives and no
cause for haste. The summer stretched ahead, two,
three months of it. Cruise about a bit, mayhap intro-
duce her to Latinate practices. Not, however, the first
time out. Much as he would like this very minute to
eat the rosebud right down to its hips, having learned
from the naughty Adriana to savor the slightly salty
taste of blood, he must not forget how young the girl
was, how innocent. The young needed the diversion of
mouth-to-mouth kissing while being handled below—
same idea as the twitching stick which kept a filly so
busy up front she didn't have time to concern herself
with the shoeing behind. Young ones were also averse
to new flavors, it might take time to teach her to swal-

low his juices. The vomiters were a sorry lot. Manipulation, that was the ticket for the maiden voyage. And since she was in for shock in any case, one might excite the anus as well as the clit so that later on she'd hold still for a bit of buggery. She'd be tight fore and aft for a while, but he could gradually stretch both her holes until she'd serve him as maid and boy. Like many a long-term seaman, he did have catholic tastes, drew the line at sheep though, as some he knew did not.

Slavering from a slack mouth, chest heaving, he moved forward on bags of salt. Her graces were doubtless known to her hand if not to young Starbuck's as well, she'd likely make no objection. And she was but a cooper's daughter. She'd seen a mort of farm animals, milked cows, surely she'd be willing to work him off manually, pity to ruin a fine desk. He eased down on the edge of the bed, not wishing to wake the shoat until he had it tied. He found the curve of her frail waist with one stealthy hand while the other, not without tremor, went toward her exposed parts.

Suddenly over his heavy breathing, the ship's clock chimed. Only two bells but she was instantly wide awake.

"Oh, John, five o'clock already! Mother will be so displeased! Thee promised—how could thee let me oversleep?" She leaped from the bed and scrabbled about the floor for her slippers. "Oh, what am I to do?"

He sought the kneehole of his desk to cover his tumescence, galled that she feared her mother more than her would-be seducer.

"Do? Nothing," he said crossly. "Thee is with me and I'll do the doing." From his top desk drawer, he took a skrimshander jagging wheel and, on second thought, also the letter knife. "I shall be a Greek bearing gifts when I deliver thee to the Wilcox door. I shall take the blame for thy tardiness. Thy mother shall find my offerings irresistible, I warrant thee. Now pull the drawer of the washstand. See there a tortoiseshell comb? And pour out some water to wash thy face. A wind has come up with the reflux. Thee may wear my reefer. If memory serves, thy grandmother's house is south of the wharves, is it not?" His eye fell on the lost bronze key. His steward had doubtless found it when sweeping the deck. He twiddled it absently, but it was late and she was agitated and his cock was dwindling.

"My tucker! It's bloodied. Thee dabbed thy cut mouth with it, it's in thy pocket!"

He could not have been more surprised if he'd pulled out a rabbit. He sighed and unlocked the second drawer. "Calm down, thee may have this silk one. I'd intended to give it thee under jollier circumstances."

" 'Tis too small."

"Then take two, tie them together."

She followed his suggestion, and it worked well, the two kerchiefs crossed on her bosom. "Thee are so kind, John, such fine silk, and I have been a trouble."

"Nonsense. Thy company pleasures me. I only wish we could have spent more time together."

"Oh, I am so glad thee is come home! There is little funning on this isle without thee. Where did I put my hat? Ah, here. How I do hate being in a swivet!"

"My dear," he said, holding the reefer for her to slip into, "the funning has yet to begin."

Coming in late, Kezia quickly surveyed the table —ladies on one side, men on the other. One and only one place was unoccupied, and it was on the men's side. A selectman, she later learned, had been laid low by a bad clam. She glanced questioningly at her grandmother who nodded permission. Thus she found herself above the salt cellar, next the honored guest, her second cousin Benjamin Franklin. She had not met him before, though she had heard much about him. He was personable in a homely way, with brown silky hair, high forehead, knowing eyes, and a mobile mouth that went from gravity to amusement with intriguing frequency. It was hard to credit that this plain unassuming man was famed throughout the colonies for his inventive mind, his industry, eloquence, sagacity, and thrift. Even more incredible was his spicy reputation within the bosom of the Folger family. Though they kotowed to him on his rare visits to the island, behind their hands his mother's relatives denounced him as a philanderer of women both high and low. It was well known that his first son was conceived out of wedlock, and his present common-law marriage was the more frowned upon because his wife had deserted her first and legal husband who was still at large. Four years ago the Franklins' second son had been lost to the pox, and there were those, Abigail Folger for one, who considered their bereavement a judgment of God.

What mattered to Kezia about her supper companion was, however, none of these things. He interested her solely because he was John Coffin's age and, like John, a man of the world. Fortified by several sips of his wine and those dark, listening eyes, she was moved to ask what chance of success he gave to a marriage between persons of widely disparate ages. " 'Tis a friend I ask for," she concluded, fingers crossed in her lap. "The girl is but seventeen and the man close to thee in years. Does thee surmise he'd fine her too childish to serve him well as wife?"

A quirky smile, eyelids at half-mast. "If the girl be such as you, my dear, the fellow should find her utterly enchanting."

"I thank you, Cousin. But those who know the girl and who are—uh—of mature mind consider the match ill-advised."

"Ah, the croakers. They abound in every country and they ever bode disaster and ruin. I should not heed them. If the man be worthy and of good nature and health, count not his years." He held his goblet of wine again to her lips. She gulped a mouthful as he murmured close enough to her ear to move her hair, "Forsooth, every partnership is a gamble." Then he took her hand, and she thought he would kiss it, but just then her mother called down the table.

"Kezia, do prattle less and let our good cousin enjoy the provender. The wine, I fear, has made thee garrulous. Thy face is flushed with it."

Kezia's hands flew to her cheeks. " 'Tis the heat of the fire," she said, abashed.

"The fault is mine, Cousin Abigail, I urged her to imbibe. I thought a drop or two would not be amiss on this festive occasion."

"Very well, but no more," said Abigail. "And do have a care to partake of the ox-cheek, Cousin Benjamin. Grandmother Wilcox prepared it especially for thee."

He chuckled. "You sound like my wife. I have ever preferred stimulating discourse to the pleasures of the palate. It drives her quite wild."

The vinous pink of Kezia's cheek deepened to hectic red. A champion, she had a champion! "Stimulating discourse." Hah! Let that chime in her mother's ear!

At the Samuel Coffin house that night there were also several guests, a bounteous supper, repeated pourings of wine and beer. To walk off their full stomachs and heavy heads, John and Debbie took a turn around the lane.

"Thee spent all the afternoon taking inventory?"

"I did. Nor concluded the list."

"And Kezia, how did she busy herself during this time?"

John grinned in the dark. Was it possible his sister was jealous? "Would thee believe she slept?"

"Thee is changed, John. Irreverent, cynical. I know not what to believe."

A wave of anger engulfed him. He could not bear criticism, least of all from her.

"It is as if," she went on, "thee cared for nothing and no one nor even thyself."

"Shall I value what thee threw overboard?"

"Oh, come, Brother. 'Tis eleven years agone. Thee surely has taken comfort in many a bed since then."

"I do not deny it. But numbers are cold comfort, they have chilled my marrow. I was not always cold-hearted."

Debbie sat down on the bench under the old Spanish oak. She pulled her mantle close. Stars and moon had vanished in a mist, and the wind had freshened.

John put a square-toed foot upon the bench. "Thee said thee had a thing to tell me. Out with it. 'Tis time we went back. Tristram will be looking for thy return."

"Aye. Well, then, does thee know that Kezia believes herself in love with thee? That she would marry with thee?"

He laughed. "Ridiculous. Sublime. How come thee by this intelligence?"

Debbie shuddered not from the wind but from the diamond-hardness of that laugh. "John, do not dally with her. She is not a pet hound, a mascot to be kept by when thee'd be distracted from the unquiet of thy soul. She is a near-woman, a veritable powder keg, yearning, curious, vulnerable, proud, ambitious. Unhappy at home, she is determined to find a husband, and soon. Thee makes things no easier for her by compromising her in the eyes of the townsfolk. *I* believe she slept alone in thy bed this afternoon but shall they?"

He kicked the bench. "What care I for their petty tattle! Conformers, reformers, informers! Scarce a day have I been here and already I feel boxed as a compass. I vow I have felt more at home on alien ground."

"I regret thee is in so poor a frame of mind. But thee can sail away whenever thee chooses. Thee's free to live in the place of thy choice, near or far. Kezia has no such escape hatches."

"What would thee, that I refuse to take her to Siasconset shores as she begged?"

"So there, she does have designs upon thee!"

"She enjoys being with me and going on jaunts. Where is the design in that? Has she not voyaged with

me since she was little? And who can blame me for
enjoying her company? She is the only one on this isle
who does not presume to improve me, who likes me
as I am."

"Spoke like a child, full of rage and self-pity.
Thee knows full well that we are vastly rejoiced by thy
homecoming. Thy hand has been pumped all the day
and will I daresay be pumped all the week. As for
Kezia, I was not suggesting total renunciation. I pray
thee, be not overly dramatic, John, 'twould make her
feel snubbed. I ask only that thee have a care not to
stain her spotless character. If thee carry her to Siasconset, ask a chaperon to accompany, some respected
matron—"

"Like thyself, for instance?"

"No need to shout thy sarcasm, it is thick enough
to walk upon. Aye, like me, if thou wilt. Thee may
impugn my motives, what care I, so long as I know
they are pure. I love Kezia. She is like a ward to me.
I would not have her virtue molested."

"Verily, thee is the limit of bluntness. I mislike it."

"And thee of petulance. I mislike *it*."

He strode off on hard heels and came back on
soft ones. "Quarreling before I have been home a day.
Is there no love left for me in thy crowded heart?"

Deborah gave him her hand but her voice was
weary. "Too much, I trow, or we'd not be quarreling.
Evidently, I am not as purified as I thought. Yet I too
have changed, John. I am a mother now, first and
foremost. 'Twas never thus with our mother, she loved
Father above all of us and he her. Small wonder that
we were turned in upon each other, thee and me,
twins." She sighed heavily and it came out a groan.
"I am fond of Tristram, he is a good man, uncommonly pleasing of mien and conduct, but he strikes no
sparks, there is no flint in him. His taint is the opposite of ours, he has had too much of mothering, it
has made him soft. Were I in love with Tristram, I
should be jealous of Mother Dinah's sway; as it is, I am
impervious. My children are become my life, John,

and I find it a most cleansing thing to take thought for others before myself. They give me reason for living and a measure of joy."

"Which thee hath given me." He kissed her hand. Wittingly or not, she had spoken to his torment, released him from it. Let her love her brats to any extraordinary degree, as long as she did not love another man. He did not wish her unhappiness. All he required was that she be faithful to their abjured passion. He would sooner see her in a nunnery than in the arms of a lover. "I have been churlish. It is never easy to come home, much as I long for it when I am at sea. But now we have had this reunion, I am at peace and so in thy debt."

"Then I ask this token payment, John: Lie not with Kezia. She too is one of my children. Wive her if thou must but—"

He laughed to the night sky. "Wive her! What on earth for? I need no mistress for my house, I am rarely in it. If I have caught her, Debbie, I assure thee I fished without bait. As for dalliance, there are juicier lays about. A roll in the hay is more easily come by on this island of grass widows and savages than in ancient Gomorrah on the Dead Sea."

"Then thee doth faithfully promise?"

"That I shall not eat a green gooseberry when I can have strawberries and cream? Certainly I promise." He swung her to her feet. He grabbed her backside and squeezed till she squealed, kissed her lustily. "Come, we shall have a nightcap at our father's fireside and then I must sack in. I swear I could sleep till the trompe of Judgment Day. Land air takes getting used to." He stretched and yawned, relaxed in every ligament and muscle, as eased as if he'd just humped a harlot, as purged as if he'd cacked a mixen.

Four

During the week after the shearing, Kezia saw little
of John Coffin. She told herself he was fashed with
work. He had to see the cargo unloaded and stored in
his warehouse, he had dealings with off-island agents,
there were the lays to be figured and disbursed. The
bruit that filtered from tavern and countinghouse was
that no Nantucket whaleship had ever come home with
such prize. Even the bonus piece of ambergris found
in one of the spermaceti's stomachs was outsize. Up-
wards of forty pounds in weight, they said, and bought
by the representative of a perfumery in Lyons, France,
for a fabulous price, five guineas the ounce, they said.
The families of the *Deborah*'s crew wore broad smiles
and paid up their debts, and there was a list of men
waiting to sign on the *Deborah*'s next voyage.

But the short shrift John gave her at First Day
Meeting could not be laid to busyness. He treated her
like any other, no special smile or look or word, no
hint of future trysting. She attended Fifth Day Meeting as well on the chance that he might come, but he
did not. And on the following First Day, he was
again impersonal. She suffered in silence. There was
no one she could unburden herself to, not even Debbie,
who had warned her off. She thought of nothing else.

When on the last night of Fourth Month (March
was counted as the first month until 1752 when it
was legally changed to January) Kezia heard that John
was sailing for the mainland on flood tide, she did
what she could to detain him. She put a black cat
under a caulderkin. This was supposed to create a head
wind that would make it impossible for a ship to set
out of Great Harbor. The night, however, passed wind-

less. There was a hush in the air and a tide-flat smell
that presaged storm, but the *Deborah* got underway before it broke.

To make things drearier, Shana vanished. Kezia
had to give up her schoolteaching to help out at home.
She was up at daydawn and she dropped like a rock
into bed every night, but not to rest. She tossed and
turned and dreamed and moaned aloud in her sleep.
When sleep eluded her and she feared to disturb her
sisters, she would kneel on the floor at the open window, searching the stars for perspective. But within
seconds she was lost to their cosmic message, sifting
over and over the handful of moments she and he
had had together, trying to remember some error, some
offense she might have given. She flinched at the
thought even though she could not imagine what it was.

In the summer's course, Kezia learned a remedy
for lovesickness. From her unwitting mother. At
breakfast one day Abigail remarked Kezia's peaked-
ness. "No wonder, for thee does not eat enough to
keep a titmouse alive. Be thee costive, Daughter?"

Her mother's preemption of her most private func-
tions mortified her. And the assumption that all suffering had a bodily source she found crass in the extreme.

"I am not hungry. That's all."

"I doubt it's all. Judith says thee's up and down
in the night. What ails thee, child?"

"I—I have been having some pains in the head."
An understatement. Her head at the moment was so
tightly bound she would not have been surprised if
the top of it split off. Her very hair felt heavy.

"Thee has headache now?"

"Yes, Mother. Oh, yes."

Abigail forthwith dosed her with a drink of bit-
tersweet medicated tea. In twenty minutes, the pain
was gone. Kezia was grateful and impressed. Previously her mother's drug cupboard had been just one more
article of furniture to dust. Now it would seem it held
better magic than any feather, tooth, bone, or claw
that Shana kept in the leathern bag under her bed.

Kezia forthwith expressed a desire to know what had cured her and how to prepare it.

Abigail was more than pleased to have an apprentice. She took Kezia with her on walks to gather the ingredients for various compounds, she let her assist with the brewing, and never were mother and daughter so compatible as when engaged in pharmacopoeial pursuit. For once it was Kezia, not Elisha, not Judith-dear, not the newest baby, who received Abigail's praise and attention. "Thee's a quick study," Abigail told Kezia when the list of plants to recognize went from impossible to long to beautiful. Vervain, sassafras, agrimony, broom, birthwort, peppermint, and sorrel. Wormwood, borage, betony, sage; celandine, loosestrife, and yarrow. Kezia called their names as nuns their beads and witches their spells. "Knowing the name of a thing gives one a power over it," said Abigail, and it felt true.

Basked in her mother's favor, daily relaxed with valerian and henbane, Kezia grew gentler, prettier, and by summer's wane she had not only Samuel Starbuck to walk her home from Meeting or take her to a chowder party or seek her in a "hiding-frolic," but other boys as well. Characteristically, once she could take her pick, she decided that Samuel was attractive after all and old for his age. He and she spent every leisure hour together and each parting, each return to the family's bosom, was for each a little death. If they'd been to Madaket for fiddlers or the spit for cottontails or the south shore for cod, they dawdled over the division of the catch, each urging upon the other the choice or lion's share. If they'd rambled the commons or the bogs, there were bayberry branches and stalks of liatris or cranberries to apportion. If the beaches, driftwood and shells. One day, having picked a patch of early whortleberries, they sat down on a hummock to rest and watch the sun go down over Shimmo shore.

"Thee may wish on the first berry, or any first fruit of the season. Did thee know that?" Samuel popped a berry into his mouth. He threw another into the air and caught it on his stained tongue. "Now thee do it," he said, and he tossed a plump purple one up into the air. She bobbed for it but missed and dusted it off and ate it.

"Did thee wish on't?"

"No. Did thee?"

"No, for it could not come to pass."

"If thee did wish, would it have to do with thee and another?"

"Aye."

"Who is the other?"

"Thee knows."

"Not I."

"Who else then?"

"Thee would marry with me, Samuel?"

"I have not the wherewithal to think of marrying yet."

"One need not wherewithal to *think*."

In the dense quiet Kezia was the one who leaned close and put berry-stained lips to his. No bee had ever found such honey. Kezia longed for his arms to enfold her, to crush her against his chest, but he did not. He handed her her pail and picked up his. All the way home they were silent, aboil with glory and shame. She feared she had been too bold, he cursed himself for not having been bold enough, and their mouths tingled with memory.

At her doorstep, he turned red. His eyes bulged with effort. "I—I do love thee, Kezia."

"Sandy-haired men are known to be faint-hearted." She whisked up the steps, head high. But faced with entering her house, she vaulted back down over the rail.

"Follow the leader!" she yelled, and raced up again.

They did somersaults over the railing, one after another, she in a froth of skirts and yelps.

"Voyage o' berries?" the young sister Mary called from an upstairs window. "Where from?"

They ignored her, fighting past each other on the steps, Kezia giggling breathlessly, Samuel's growls breaking like crockery. She grabbed his coat but he pulled away, beating her to the rail.

"Isn't thee, Daughter?" came the sharp mother-voice. "High time. Milk wants skimming."

Samuel flashed a blue look, loped off, shy as a fox.

"Thy berries!" Kezia screamed, but he kept on, a torn coattail hanging.

In the cool dark buttery, Kezia sat on the stone step, hugging her desperation. She had to get out of this house, but how? John Coffin was too old for her, Samuel Starbuck too young. She knew every man on the island and they were the only two she fancied. Her eyes, accustoming to the shadows, espied a ewer on the shelf that her mother had been looking for high and low. Going for it, she upset the pan of unskimmed milk. Tears rushed to her eyes but her jaws jammed on the sound of dismay. One word, one scolding word from her mother and she would pack up this very night, ship out on the first sail that made for the Port of Boston, hire out to the first apothecary, kind or mean. She had those birthday shillings, and Cousin Benjamin Coffin, the schoolmaster, owed her two pounds' back wages. And there were sloop-owners, friends and kin, who would give her free passage. If it came to it, she was not above forging a note of parental permission. Surely the Lord would condone a small transgression that purposed to maintain the health and well-being of his flock.

Five

He leaned against the pillows, sipping the arrack she had made for him. Tart yet sweet with a puckery lace of rum. No question about it, if one had to go to sea, this was the way to go. Not that he'd take a maid along on a whaling voyage, the crew knew they could trust him not to do that; but they could not expect a captain sound of mind and prime of body to give the heave-ho to a lusty piece who had stowed away on a summer's sail between the 'on' and the 'off.' More than a summer as things turned out. It was Tenth Month already.

Her head rested on his middle and the sidesweep of her coarse straight black hair covered him to the knee. Her eyes were closed, a smile lurked in the corners of her wide flat mouth. In repose she was quite beautiful. Ordinarily, she was too expressionless, her face as inscrutable as an Oriental's. He fondled her breast which was unusually full for a young one. Soon ripe, soon rotten. Squaws aged faster than whites or blacks, and died younger, except for a rare few. But no woman in his experience, not even the Lady Anne, had skin as fine as this. Once in the tropics he had rubbed a euphorbia leaf and found it so smooth he had had to crumple it. Shana's flesh had the same perfection; it made one want to mar it. Not that she seemed to object. May have been the very thing that enslaved her. Enslaved but not possessed, for Shana had an area of inviolable reserve, and this he respected since he had it too.

He was well pleased with his six months' labor. The arrangements his father had urged him to make for the transshipment of their whale oil to London were satisfactorily concluded. A Boston firm had agreed to buy their oil outright at the going market price minus twenty-five percent. Fair enough when you considered that there was, besides risk and freight costs, the London agent's commission and brokerage fees that would have to come out of the buyer's charge. Furthermore, payment had been made in hard cash, English pounds sterling, so he and his father were free to make the investments they contemplated: a share in the whaling sloop *Oriole;* one twelfth of Quaise which a sea captain's widow was offering to sell; and enough left over to build a tryinghouse near their warehouse on the Clean Shore. *Clean* Shore. He snorted at the misnomer—no dirtier beach on the entire island. The natives had a saying, "Let no man mock the black plume of the busy tryworks." Still, all that pollution and stink, there had to be a better way to turn blubber into whale oil. . . .

Latterly, he'd hove down to Mattapoisett for refitting. The *Deborah* was now trig again: scraped, caulked, pitched, painted, her sham gunports renewed, her sails and spars good as new. All shipshape except for one niggler; if only he had not dallied with that little trollop in Mattapoisett, Jane Stetson. Well, put it out of mind for the nonce. Enjoy this girl, this drink, this moment.

"What shall thee do, lass, now we are returned? Where shall thee go? How shall thee live?"

"Back to Mistress Folger."

"She's bound to have replaced thee by now."

"I think not."

"What shall thee say to her? What excuse shall thee make?"

"None. There be eight children and I work for keep. Cheap need not be sorry."

He saw her tuck her odd foot under the normal one. The unconscious gesture moved him. It was not a club foot nor remarkably misshapen, the abnormality lay in that the two large toes were undivided, but perhaps it gave her pain for she limped now and then. In

Salem such a blight might have cost her her life, but the Nantucketers were not witch-hunters. As islanders, they were acceptant of individual differences, and as intermarriers, they were not unaccustomed to congenital peculiarities. Nevertheless, they were a simple people bred in a primitive community, and they were literal in their interpretation of the Book. To them a 'forky' tongue, hoof, or palate was the touch of Satan, and, knowing Shana, John was inclined to agree. Not that he was one to be put off by the sign of damnation. Sharing with a female his mother's seed had from earliest memory made him feel halfsome where his brothers were wholesome. The act of incest had been the final androgyny. No, he and Shana, both off-island islanders, were not ill-mated. They read each other by touch like the blind. And whereas perfection aroused the despoiling beast in him, the mammonish foot had an opposite effect—he had all he could do not to take that poor foot in his hands and gentle it. He was used to suppressing his instinct of tenderness, it had little place in a whaling captain's life, and to Shana he dared not show the least sign of affection or he might find himself slave instead of master. She was no ordinary primitive, this one. In another time, another place, she might have been a priestess, an alchemist, a guider of the destinies of great men. Which came first, the twisted foot or the second sight? The broken commandment or the need to break? Was it a flaw in him that drew him to flawed women? Or was flaw the spice that raised mortal fare to ambrosia?

Shana had come to him the night of the shearing. He had overeaten during those two days of merry-making and sent Jean-Paul to Abigail Folger, requesting an aperient. But there had been other incontinent fools. Abigail sent his man back with the message that her supply was totally dispensed, that she would forthwith prepare a new batch. By the time Shanapetuck came with it, Jean-Paul had retired, so it was John himself who answered the door. From the flash of the Indian girl's eye and the swivel of her hips when he asked her to come in while he fetched a gratuity for her mistress, he knew he could take her to bed, and he did. She had not been a virgin though she could not have been yet twenty. They had some uncommonly good rolls and he was moved to gift the girl with a string of beads he'd picked up in Jamaica. After that, she came nightly of her own accord, and he was not sorry to find her stowed behind his sea chest after they hauled off for the Massachusetts Bay Colony.

He smoothed her black mane absently.

"What shall my master do if the daughter of Mister Stetson pursue him?"

"Oh, so thee knows of that, does thee?"

"Shana knows much, says little."

"Would that I were as controlled. I rue the night I first saw Jane Stetson at her father's house." Pretty as a wedding cake and clearly taken with him, touched his vanity, cully that he was. He intended to be but courtly. Some compliments, a kiss or two, presuming thus to speed the refitting and better the price of the job. How could he have foreseen that Jane, all simpers and smiles, all peaches and gold and cream, would be so easy and so dull? "Well, I'll not be made the scapegoat. I'll not pay the piper for another's tune. Little likelihood I was the one who got her with child. I took care. And the time's a bit short. Less than two months. They've no proof—"

"Mistress Stetson's maid lay hidden under bed. They have paid her well. She will give testimony."

"Pshaw. So they have the word of an Indian serving slut against the word of a Coffin."

"More than word. A handkerchief of fine silk, sewed with the letters of my master's name. *Unwashed.*"

"Why of all the filthy—" he threw his mug across the room, "rogue tricks!"

Shana strode with a slight unevenness to the towel rack. She wiped the splatter of juice that ran down the paneling. "Much tattle if that girl come to Nantucket."

"Why am I so plagued? Why me? A well-used

filly if ever I rode one. When I think of the lads who galloped her, with no more than a spank on the rump to send her home to the barn. Marry *her* after all I've dodged?"

She came back and lay down with him, an s curve beside a t square. She laid a copper hand lightly over his heart. Only his face and neck and the hairy backs of his hands matched her color. Her hand moved in rhythmic circles from the wiry black curls of his chest to the fine hairline that exactly bisected his flat, hard, livid belly.

He groaned, not from regret so much as with pleasure, and his voice grew quieter, at odds with his words. "I'll wager her sire knows naught of her looseness. He's a moral man. Ahhh!" He closed his eyes, the more keenly to realize her touch. "Coming here, thee says? To get me? And I thought I was escaping the whole sordid business by sneaking out of Buzzards Bay in the dark of the moon!" He pulled her up by the shoulders. "What am I to do? Thee knows so much—" He shook her hard. "Say me, say me!"

"Take a wife," Shana advised through clicking teeth. "A white man cannot have two wives. A married man be no use to Jane Stetson."

For a moment he felt bitten by a friendly dog. Surely this crippled savage did not aspire to—? No, no, she was too sensible for that. He rolled over on his front, rested his face on his fists. After a moment, he slid a glance at her. "Thee doubtless has the bride in mind?"

"Aye, master."

Again a spasm of outraged suspicion clenched him. "Who, pray?"

"Kezia."

"My cousin, Kezia Folger?"

Shana nodded.

"Well, I'll be switched!" He rolled over on his back. His voice cracked with amusement. "Uncanny, a conspiracy of fate. My little coz with breasts no bigger than her eyes. Thee's the second to propose her

to me." But his smile went inward as he thought of the
white buttocks and dirty feet. There was titillation in
the thought of bedding down with his sister's pet.

December brought slashing rains to Nantucket
and Shana to the Folger door. Abigail took the
drenched girl in, but vexation warred with relief when
she noticed her fine clothes. Instead of the customary
swaddling of worn homespun, Shana wore a hooded
mantle through which peeped a Scotch-plaid petticoat
puffed out with underskirts, and on her feet a pair of
good leathern squaretoes. She also carried a wooden
chest that by the look of its weight in her arms was
stuffed with loot. Been to the mainland, if not London.
Doubtless stowed under some sailor's bunk and doubtless oft laid on it. Mayhap even shared with his mates.
Wanton. Wicked. Shameless. Abigail would have had
her cat-striped in the marketplace if she had not sorely
needed assistance. By way of chastisement, she plied
the gillie with heavy tasks and felt flouted when she
found Kezia helping Shana scrape out the chicken run
before school.

On the fourth day of the nor'easter, Kezia woke
to gray light. She listened. The dripping outside was
thin and sporadic, only the rainspout ran steady. The
birds, barn swallow and purple marten, were congratulating each other wildly: plenty of breakfast for
all. As well as sounds, green scents came through a
broken windowpane. To breathe the dawn air was like
drinking from a spring. She felt a little leap of joy at
the thought of tonight's party: a wedding reception for
John's brother William, and John was home for it. Pity
she'd have to wear a patched frock. She'd caught it on
a bramblebush riding home the other day, hell-bent to
beat the rain. Would she could borrow Shana's purple
gown. 'Twas silk-warped but so dark her mother might
not cavil. Through the wall she could hear Shana
moving about. She was glad Shana was back, otherwise
the lighting of the cook fire would have fallen to her.
She smiled and went back to sleep.

Shana dressed quickly in the plaid dress her true master had given her and drew over her head the stole her soon-mistress, Kezia, had knitted for her. The sands had spoken. She would serve them both, of this life she asked no more. The manservant, Devil-on-a-Stick, did not concern her. He would not stay once there were women living in the house.

She ran soundlessly through the wet lanes. On Centre Street she saw an old woman and a boy filling jars with angleworms. She turned the corner toward the wharf and let herself in by his south door which he left open for her by agreement. She took the stairs two at a time, her limbs fluid with desire. Not until he had put out her fires did she speak a word. Then she said, "The Stetson ship lies grounded on the bar. The girl is come but she is ill."

John was pulling on his clothes. "What is the hour? Get hence, wench. I have much to do. Rouse Jean-Paul. Tell him to hustle up to the roof with a spyglass."

Shana did as he bade though he spoke with the voice of panic. The sky was too low for man's eyes to see a ship even with the aid of the glass.

John had intended to wear a new-bought shirt for his brother William's wedding. It had the ruffled cuffs that the Quakers scornfully termed "knuckle-dusters." Now he threw the shirt aside and chose one of homespun. He would wear nothing the elders could possibly object to. He ripped the silver buckles off his shoes and his breeches. He shaved off his beard, soaked his head, and brushed his hair out straight as candles. If it curled in the mist, well, that was the Lord's work, not his. Gray stockings, drab breeches, brown worsted waistcoat, and long coat. He took from his chest of drawers a fall of spotless white—Jean-Paul could launder if he could do nothing else—and the Friends, *mirabile dictu,* had no objection to immaculacy.

He heard Jean-Paul's hobble on the wooden stairs.

"Didst look to the harbor, man?"

"Rien. The air is thick like milk."

"Hm. Very well. Jean-Paul, I propose to bring a guest home to sleep. Put this goat's nest in good order."

"May I ask, *mon capitaine*—?"

"Nay, thee may not."

"Eh, bien, une femme."

"Meddle in thy own business, Jackalent! Now, skimp off. Lay the makings of a fire in the keeping room and my bedchamber. And put out my best port."

"Merde, alors, une nouvelle."

"That's enough out of thee. Be there victuals for the morrow's breakfast? No need to bother with cooking today, I shall be taking my meals out. Now jump to it, thee son of a biscuit-eater, there is much to be done!"

In the tilted pier glass that the first Tristram Coffin had brought from Devonshire, John bowed to his eminently conservative image. Let them try to find fault! He drew the corners of his mouth down and accused his reflection, searching out sin, as would those he should soon—with a bit of luck and God's grace— be facing. Luck? Grace? That was overstating it. The plan was not a happy one, merely expedient, the lesser of two evils. In truth, he was back of the rips, couldn't sail and couldn't sink. At least Kezia wouldn't put horns on him the minute he shipped out to sea. She was not a pig in a blanket, with her there'd be no nasty surprises. Leastways, not for a while. She was still a maid, one could but guess what manner of woman she would become. As for that, what cared he? He'd be seldom home.

Six

Daniel Folger wore a foxy smirk which was nothing more than acute embarrassment. "The maid hath no dower, Captain."

"That is of no concern to me, Cousin. I am well enough off."

Aye, a walking oil barrel, thought Daniel with envy.

"Thee have not been passed by Committee," noted Abigail, pouring coffee for the unexpected breakfast guest. "Oh, there, dear me, I have spilled on thy sleeve. Here, let me dab it with water. Thee's knocked the keel right out of me, John Coffin."

"The Committee is not likely to make obstacle," John assured her. "They have seen Kezia in my company since she was little. They know she is clean as new snow, her clearance is foregone. As for mine, it would take considerable more than a month to uncover my sins. I doubt they could do it in a year. I have been a knave, and saint I shall never be, but I submit that between knavery and virtue there is a line of acceptability. This line for Kezia's sake I shall henceforth try to walk.

"Besides, let us be hardheaded. The Starbucks who sit on the High Bench are my in-laws. And my father and mother are well respected in the Society of Friends. When I suggest to the Committee that a double wedding would be a pleasure to them who have long desired their eldest son settle down, I am certain exception shall be made. Thee perceives—why should not they?—that I would marry now because the *Deborah* sails within the month. We're already late on the weather. By the time I return, who knows but what some lad shall have purloined my girl."

Shana came into the hall, staggering under a load of firewood. John relieved her of the logs, filling the woodbox and throwing an extra few onto the fire.

"Tawpoot, Captain," murmured Shana, but she did not look at him and quickly absented herself.

"Hm. Well. My." Abigail sat down, studied her lap, smoothing her thighs with the flat of her hands. " 'Tis sudden in one way and in another 'tis not, as thee points out. That Kezia has loved thee and thy sister above all others is well known throughout Sherburne. I believe thy optimism is reasonable, John Coffin. I do surmise exception might be made in this case."

She cast him a pensive glance. His urgency perplexed her, but then, Debbie too had these moments of impetuosity, they were like in many ways. Surely, for all his gainsaying, the twin brother of so fine a woman must be a good man. As for her willful Kezia who knew so much less of human nature than she supposed, was it not Debbie she loved and so imputed love to the male twin as well? Abigail sighed. There was something amiss here, she could not put her finger on it. Still, no natural mother, certainly not a good Quaker, ought to count the teeth of a rich bridegroom. She smiled warily and extended her hand to John across the table. "Kezia shall not say nay to thee, John Coffin, of that I am certain. Therefore, no more do we."

Daniel Folger's shoulders sagged with relief. Where the girls were concerned, his wife had the say. "In my view, Cap'n, Kezia be a fortunate maid. I should die happy if all my daughters did as well. Blessings on thee and thy union."

But Kezia, when she was called down and told, burst into tears and ran back upstairs. The parents looked at each other, dumbfounded. John bounded up after her.

He found her sobbing on a rumpled bed in which lay three sleeping little girls. He picked her up and

stood with her for a moment on the landing not knowing where to go for privacy. Seeing the door of the
scuttle chamber ajar, he kicked it wide, set her down
on what was Shana's cot. He kicked the door closed
behind him and knelt at the bedside.

"I would not crimp thee, little friend. If thee
would not have me, thee need not. There is no cause
for tears."

"Would not—*have?*" Kezia bawled. *"Thee?*
When I have adored thee since I could *see?*"

"Then why—? What troubles thee?"

"How should I know?" Kezia snapped, flinging
his hand away. " 'Tis that—oh, jumping prophets, I
am a dumb fool, but I dreamed it different. Not all cut
and dried and laid out on the kitchen table like a catch
of cod. Hurried to the church like a girl who *has* to—
when thee has not so much as kissed—"

He bent and kissed her very tenderly on the forehead.

She cried the harder. "I—I *liked* the beard."

"I shall grow another."

"I have nothing suitable to wear." If only she had
a gown as fashionable as Shana's plum silk! Would her
mother permit—?

"The Friends love dowdiness next to virtue."

"Not an outset, nothing!"

"It matters not." He drew her to him, held her wet
puffed face in the palm of his hand. Very carefully he
pressed his lips to hers. They were salty, baby-thin.
Gently he worked her lips open with his, thickened
their presentation, touched the tip of her tongue with
his own.

She clung to him as to a raft. "Oh, John, I do so
love thee."

Between caresses, he murmured, "I shall make it
up to thee, the hastiness. Thee shall have chests of
gowns. And tonight when we are alone in my chamber
I shall make love to thee till thee cry mercy."

"Oh, John, John!" The dove notes seemed to escape from her star-lashed eyelids.

But kissing for its own sake was a child's game and he put her away from him. He handed her his pocket handkerchief. "Here, lass, swab thy deadlights and belay thy lamentations. This is one day we dare not be tardy to Meeting."

Marriage among the Friends was dispatched with simplicity. It was merely a nuncupative agreement between two individuals who wished henceforth to share bed, life, and with God's grace, children. There were no flowers, no music, no prayer books, no veils, no rings; and since marriage was God's joining, not man's, no minister. The schoolmaster, Benjamin Coffin, opened the meeting with the usual interrogatory, pausing after each question to give the congregation time to examine their consciences and make silent reply.

"Does thee love thy brethren as becomes a follower of Christ?

"Is thee careful of the reputation of others?

"When differences arise, does thee make earnest effort to end them speedily?

"Is thee truthful? Just in thy dealings? Punctual to thy promises?"

Friend Coffin peered sternly at the men. "Is thee paying thy debts and living within thy income?"

The broadbrims, so like those of Roman Catholic priests, nodded or showed their crowns.

The schoolmaster's head shifted north by northeast. "Has thee proper regard for the plainness of thy dress and decorum?"

The flatcrowns nodded, with here and there some downward jerks of riding hoods inside of which the ladies were snatching forty winks.

Benjamin Coffin resumed his seat on the High Bench. After a silence, no one having stood up to declare conviction, William Coffin, John's twenty-year-old brother, got up and laid his hat on his seat. The Friends were not hatdoffers—"if ye have respect to persons, ye commit sin," said Saint James—but when talking to God bareheadedness was admissible. William proceeded down the aisle, self-consciousness giving him a rolling gait though he was a farmer. A second later, Priscilla Paddack tripped over her mother's feet, joined William at the Facing Bench. They were a good pair—jollier than they were bright, more liked than admired. The solemnity of the occasion had robbed them of their natural ebullience, and they hurt each other's bones clutching hands.

William deepened his voice and recited the words he had often heard but never with such awe of their commitment. "Friends, thee are my witnesses that in the presence of thee I take this my friend, Priscilla Paddack, to be my wife, promising to be a loving and true husband to her and to live in good order of truth so long as it shall please God that we live together or until death."

There was a noticeable pause and he poked his affianced who reared up, startled. Twice she began her declaration, twice cleared her throat of frogs. She spoke in a halting contralto, and those behind her could hear that her words were spoken through a grin. "I desire thee—uh—to be my friends—"

William elbowed her savagely.

"Er, that is—my *wit*nesses—that I take this my friend William Coffin—ahm—to be my husband. I do promise—ahm—by the Lord's assistments to be unto him a true and living wife—forslongswebothshllove."

Priscilla's rolling eyes drew titters from the younger members as the couple walked back to their places. Mrs. Paddack had drawn her feet in but there was little she could do about her knees which her daughter fell upon, and this time the titters were followed by fierce shushes.

Priscilla's nervousness had a calming effect upon Kezia. Where Priscilla had been heifer, she would be gazelle. She stretched her neck, stepped toe to heel, looked neither to the right or the left. At the end of the perilous walk, there was the solid warmth of John's body. She leaned against his arm and died when he moved his hat from her weight to his other side. Why had he not left it at his seat, how could she have

known he'd take it? To clear the blur of faces above
and ahead, she fixed upon Dinah Starbuck who was,
thank God, not looking at her but at John.

"—and I hereby condemn myself for past sins
and profess to be sorry."

The Committee had forced him to self-condem-
nation? Why? What had he told them, what had he
done? What manner of man was he? Love him? She did
not even know him. A pang smote her at the lost fantasy of the apothecary shop on the mainland. That self-
reliant young woman in red vanished like a passenger
to whom one still waves though the ship itself has become a black speck. She inched away from the sinner
beside her, allowing herself to admit that he had never
spoken a word of love to her, not even this morning
when they had kissed. Yet he had been there before
her at the meetinghouse, waiting to hand her down
from her father's cart. She had, in her heart of hearts,
expected a jilt.

John was still making his testimony. He took her
hand and looked down at her, announcing with a for-
mality unmatched by the ironic glint in his eyes that
with the Lord's help he would strive to be a loving
husband "during the relation."

Kezia swung on the last phrase as from a dizzying
perch. It could be construed as a day, a week, a year.
It was anything but binding. Yet she had heard it
spoken before, it was not a clause he had invented for
his future convenience. What a lintpicker she was,
she'd break a finger splitting a caraway seed! This
was her moment of glory, a girl's finest hour. Why
could she not savor it?

"Psst!"

Mistress Starbuck's eyebrows went up in impera-
tive triangles. Kezia's hand stuck wetly to John's and
she heard her own voice as from a great distance, as
if her larynx were sealed in a cask. The words were
cobwebs, they stuck to the roof of her mouth, they had
sound but no meaning. Nor did she see the man she

faced. What she saw was a string of beads—white shells and black seeds—on the floor of the little wooden chest from which Shana had loaned her the plum moiré gown. Oh, Samuel Starbuck, thee of the huckleberry lips, thee whose sweat smells clean as pinesap, whose soul is pure, palpable as a conch, why am I not marrying with *thee?*

Sounds of a scuffle at the front of the meetinghouse drew all heads. A middle-aged man in world's garb was being restrained at the entry. Water ran from his hat. Kezia felt herself guided firmly by the arm down the aisle.

"Good day to thee, Friend Stetson. Unhand him, gentlemen. This is my shipwright, Charles Stetson of Mattapoisett. He has fetched the lumber for my brother William's new house. Thee has arrived in good time, Mr. Stetson. Our religious services are but now concluded. A gladsome day for the Coffins who have participated in a double wedding. May I present my wife, the erstwhile Kezia Folger?"

The man's face worked like a stutterer endeavoring to speak. His Adam's apple bobbed so arrestingly Kezia forgot to bow.

The congregation was up and shaking hands all around. Howm thee? How's thee do? In the welter of well-wishing, Mr. Stetson's face lost its sanguinity, turned livid.

"I invite thee to sup with us this evening, Mr. Stetson," John said. "At my father's house. A cordial feast is promised with plenty of booze to warm the gullet."

"I thank you, sir, but my humor does not incline to sociables."

"But thee cannot unload cargo in this downpour," John persisted. "Shall thee not need lodging? Thee is more than welcome to take shelter with us, is he not, my love?"

A guest in the house on their wedding night? Kezia nodded dumbly.

"I lodge aboard my ship," replied Mr. Stetson curtly. "With my daughter who accompanied me on this accursed journey."

"Aye, 'tis a stormy spell. A pity. How *is* thy charming daughter?"

"No better than she should be," Stetson snapped, fixing John with a piercing look. "Very much under the weather."

"Oh? I am sorry to hear it, sorry indeed. Seasickness can be the very devil. Shall thee not reconsider biding ashore till the weather betters? My house be small for two guests but I am sure my father would happily put thee up."

"Thank you, no. I would speak with you, sir. I am concerned for my daughter."

"We are fortunate in having two doctors on our isle. Would thee have one of them to see her? Quick, Wife, catch Dr. Tupper before he departs!"

"Stay, madam. My daughter requires no doctor." He took a deep breath. "What she does require 'tis now too late for, I observe. Kindly tell your father the lumber shall be delivered to the Coffin warehouse. That, sir, should conclude our dealings. Mistress Coffin, I wish you good luck and I dare say you'll need it."

Mister Stetson stomped out. Friends closed in upon the newly wedded, congratulating, teasing.

"Good fortune, Kezia, thee's hooked the big one."

"Robbing the cradle, eh, John?"

Samuel Starbuck shuffled up, mournfully wished her happiness.

"Goodness, I be not dead," laughed Kezia. She stood on tiptoe to kiss Samuel's downy cheek. She held her arms to her sides lest they circle the rangy body that dangled from his overbroad shoulders. The laughter went out of her, a sense of loss replaced the surge of confidence. She had a feeling for this lad, different from her feeling for John. John was father and master of whom she was deliciously afraid. Samuel was brother and playmate. 'Twas a pity she could not have both, she needed both. "May we not still go for walks? And thee'll come to sup, I hope?"

"With the captain's permission," said Samuel, but their eyes locked in renunciation.

Aunt Hannah broke their spell, throwing Kezia's cloak over her shoulders. "Thee left it inside. Thee must take cover."

Judith was hugging her waist. "Oh, Sister, I am glad for thee. Thee deserves no less than a captain." To John, "Cherish her, Brother, she may not be easy to live with but she be well worth the try."

John laughed. "I'll mind that. And I have gained another set of sisters it seems. 'Tis well I am fond of womenfolk or I should feel whelmed."

John and Kezia kept glancing over their shoulders. Where was Debbie? Both preferred her good wishes above the others. Had she slipped out the side door?

At last, Abigail took Kezia away. "John, do give her leave to come home with me now. She must pack her belongings and make herself presentable for the festivities this eve. Thee no doubt has personal matters to attend to."

"To be sure I have." And drawing Kezia to him, he whispered in her ear. "Catch a few winks of sleep if thee can. I shall give thee precious little to-night!"

Kezia recoiled. Her face screwed up. She sneezed.

Custom decreed that the birde's parents 'keep the wedding,' but at Hepsy's insistence and to everyone's pleasure (the brides were relatively poor) the reception was held at the Samuel Coffin house. Lit by a plethora of candles, the pine-paneled walls gleamed a ruddy satin, cast a rosy sheen on every countenance. Huge fires in the keeping room, dining room, and hall glowed and crackled. The beeswaxed floorboards shone treacherously around the red-and-blue-patterned rug from the Far East. Muslin draperies trimmed rich as fur with hand-knitted fringe shut out

the rain and the dark. Oh, the Coffins knew how to
live, they did, nor could they be faulted for ostentation
since most of the furnishings were heirlooms, lending
a traditional quality that did not aggrandize the host
so much as hearten the guest.

To all this—the fires, the candles, the whiskey,
the opulence—the company responded. Their voices
rose in conviviality, mixed like a patch-quilt with bursts
of color—a man's guffaw, a girl's lilt. The odors of
party food—spices, winey sauce, browning fish and
fowl—blended with the fragrance of burning bayberry and peat and logs and the unwonted captivating
smells of *men*—their body-heated woolens, their wet
leather boots, their tobacco.

"Go on, Kezia, eat summat," said her mother,
pushing her to the table. "All this grand food."

Kezia dutifully filled a dish but she dined on
Debbie's smile. She had feared Debbie might be cold
or dour, but Debbie was in a buoyant mood. John too
acted well-pleased though to her fluttery heart his
pleasure seemed more with himself than with her. She
kept comparing his comportment to that of William's.
Whether William and Priscilla stood sideside or
across the room, they exchanged doting looks and
stifled laughter. Whereas John was totally engaged with
the elders. Of course John was of greater maturity and
importance. But why did not some of his eminence
spill on to her now that they were man and wife? In
fact, no one paid her any special attention, she was
still of no account, either teased or ignored. The lack
of attention, she owned, might have been partly her
fault. She was so unstrung at the thought of what lay
ahead—"precious little sleep tonight"—she wandered
about in a dazzle, less than outgoing. She hid her plate
on a cupboard shelf lest she be chided for lack of
appetite. Of thirst she had no lack but when she tried
to bring the wine to her lips, her hand shook so she
feared to spill on Shana's gown, and when she set it
down the rattling seemed to come from her teeth.

After supper when the party gathered around the keeping room fire to swap yarns of whale battles and sea serpents and shipwrecks, Deborah drew Kezia to a nook under the stairs.

"I do notice thy abstraction, Kezia dear. Has thy mother not explicated the goings-on in the marriage bed? Does thee not know what to expect? Can this be thy perplexion?"

Kezia's face flamed. She clutched her friend's arm. "Oh, Debbie, 'tis a fact I am considerable worked up. John is so—uh—experienced. I fear he shall find me maladroit. I know what is done, of course, I have seen the animals, but I understand there is a topside mounting among humans."

Debbie suppressed a smile. "Then thy mother has talked to thee."

"Aye, this afternoon. But so masked that I scarce took her meaning. 'When his ship enters thy harbor,' she said, 'he may have a mite of trouble crossing thy bar. Should that be the case thee must bite thy lips but under no circumstance cry out.' I am decidedly unclear—my *bar?* Then her extreme agitation. I could not but wonder how fearsome the pain—"

"Very slight and only for a moment," Debbie said crisply. "No more than a pinprick."

"A pinprick! She knows I be hardier than that."

"Darkness, fear of the unknown, these things can make even a pinprick hurtful. But, dear Kezia, fear not. My brother, though lusty, is full loving of womanhood. He'll be gentle, I know he will. Only hurt not his pride. Bring him not to task, for though thee may think him experienced, yet he has a fragile esteem of himself. Like all skills, lovemaking takes practice. John has taught thee many things—to gaff a fish, to row a boat. And so shall he teach you to make love. Resist not, entrust thy body to him, and all shall go well no matter how strange the performance may seem. Thee's an apt pupil when thee puts aside thy fears."

"Oh, I shall try, Debbie, I shall try so hard."

"Zeal is not called for, child. Just let it happen. Faith, thee's not the first virgin nor the last."

That was a new and astonishing thought. "Did Tristram hurt thee, Debbie? Was thee affrighted on thy wedding night?"

"Nay, my earnest little coz. I was not virgin when we wed."

Kezia swayed on her heels, black-hearted with recollection. How could she have forgotten? Willed herself to. He'll be gentle, said his sister, and knew well whereof she spoke. Kezia's hands went to her hot, thickened cheeks.

"There, I've shocked thee," Debbie said, "but for thy good. We are none of us divine, child, though we strive to be. Now let us return, we are too long apart from the company. Think no more. Expect not. All will be well."

Debbie and Tristram were the first to leave. "Lyddie has a fever," Debbie explained to her mother. "And what Lyddie gets, Mary's quick to catch."

John followed his twin to the inner chamber where the wall pegs sagged with oilskins and peacoats and the bed was a haycock of mantles and pelisses.

"So, my sister. Now each of us is sewn in his shroud. Pray God, I endure my living death with as much grace as thee." He held out his tankard of rum. "Shall thee sip of my cup and kiss me farewell before I heave myself into the seas of matrimony?"

"Thee's raddled with drink already. I find thy words unseemly. I would have thee forget our childish past once and for all."

"Would thee? And thee, has thee forgot? I saw thee weep like a Catholic in full view of the congregation."

Debbie pushed him out of her way. "I cry at all unions, 'tis my sentimental nature. And at births and deaths as well. I warn thee, John, I'll hear no more of incestuous love. I promised Kezia thee'd be a kind and considerate husband. Thee shall answer to me if thee be any less."

John's face went purple. "Thee dares to threaten me?"

"Out of my road, Brother. When thee's cup-shot, there's no dealing with thee. I bid thee good night."

He stumbled back at the slam of her arm which caught him across the belly and made him break wind.

John Coffin's house sat narrow in a grassy close fronting on Centre Street to catch the sun on its face and to keep the wind at its back, separated from its only neighbor by a creek that ran down into Great Harbor. It was a two-storied lean-to, with wide shingles that were the color of lichen in fair weather and nearly black in a driving rain like this, as Kezia well knew. Time without number she had gone out of her way to walk past the place whether John was abroad or ashore, wanting something of him in her eye. Often and often, she had picked up a bit of the crushed clamshell that made a path to the sidewise flight of steps, kept it in her pocket as a touchstone.

Associating John as she did with grandeur—the house in which he'd been raised, his ship's quarters— she was unprepared for the squalor of his bachelor diggings. The house was musty and damp, cold as the grave, the furnishings humble and sparse as any south shore fishing shanty. In the dimness, she made out a hutch table with four straight chairs around it, one of which was ladder-backed with arms, and a pine settle whose high back barely escaped the ceiling and all but blocked entry. On the right, a steep winding stairway led doubtless—she swallowed—to the bedchamber. She turned resolutely to the left, cockbilling her skirts as she rounded the settle, seeking the warmth of the hearth. The blackened maw glowed feebly, a few coals on a mound of ash. Around and about stood or hung charred rusted utensils and a leathern bellows whose body was as cracked as an old shoe. The wind came up from between floorboards and through the chinked walls. Two flickering stumps in Betty holders cast eery shadows. One bit of candle was suspended from a trammel on the north wall near the door to the hall and the other spat onto the dining table.

Kezia pulled her cloak about her.

"Here, warm thyself." John put the armchair close to the embers and proceeded to build up the fire, cursing his manservant the while. "Not a proper houseman, d'ye see? Just an old sea dog I keep out of pity. Truly, Kezia, I am not so graceless as this pigsty might lead thee to think. But now thee's the mistress, things shall be different, eh? May I have thy cloak? 'Twill be cozy in two shakes of a lamb's tail. That's one good thing about a shallow grate in a small room."

"I shall keep my cloak, if thee—"

He disappeared through the ill-hung batten door. She quailed in the tilted chair, her eye on a thread-legged spider, her ear cocked to the scurrying above. Rats or mice? She measured the sound and concluded, mice.

He returned with a bottle, two goblets, and a dish of hardtack. The pop of the cork raised her a foot off her chair.

"Can't find the port. Champagne's as well. Better. Thee looks as if thee could do with some cheer."

"I be not uncheerful, I assure thee."

"Speak to me, then. We must share our thoughts now we are one."

" 'Twas just—well, I was thinking—this is the first night of my life ever spent away from my parents' home."

"Ah, is it indeed? Well, well."

"But I am cheerful, exceedingly cheerful, thee must not think I am not."

"Ah. To be sure."

The liquid bubbled in the scars of the table— he'd overpoured—and dripped from the goblet's base onto her lap. "Ah, soiled thy servant's robe, did I? I am sorry. A bridegroom's hand be not the steadiest."

She did not join in his laughter. Shana's gown. How had he known?

He sat opposite her on the settle and talked of the great spread Hepsy had put out, had Kezia tasted the eels? And how strained his mother had seemed, had she noticed? And what an amiable pair William and Priscilla made. He hoped Debbie's child Lyddie was not coming down with a serious ailment. Exactly the kind of gamming her mother and father indulged in after they had had guests in. In this case it was the husband who was the loquacious one and she as monosyllabic as her father, but married beyond a doubt, and how she wished they were not.

Kezia screwed up her courage. If she did not come out with it, she'd never be able to bed with him, wine or no wine.

"John, I do not wish to seem morose nor pry into thy affairs, but I confess there is a botheration on my mind. May I speak of it?" How stilted her words, how quavering her voice! She'd lost herself, even her name.

"Certainly. We must be free with one another. I would put thee at thy ease."

"Very well then." She inhaled and spoke above a cement wall of diaphragm. "This morning I saw in a small chest belonging to Shanapetuck, our Indian servant, the selfsame shell necklace that was in thy drawer in thy quarters on the *Deborah*. How did she come by it else thee gave it her? I did not know thee knew her. Yet thee quickly recognized her frock on me."

"My poor child. So this is what has stuck in thy craw. Why did thee not lug it up sooner? 'Tis easily explained. Thy mother's slave delivered a stomachic cure one night. I sent a gift to thy mother in gratitude, I no longer mind what, a jug of rum perhaps or a loaf of sugar, and to the savage I gave the little string of shells. 'Tis worth nothing, they abound in every tropical marketplace—"

"Oh, she is no savage, John. She is an extraordinary person with visionary powers. I should never have suspected thee of—of dalliance with a savage."

"Thee might have and been right. I have wenched with all colors, Kezia. Thee must face it, thee has not married a boy." He belched. "Nothing sorrier'n a chaste bridegroom."

She heard the slurring of his words and envied his drunken state. She finished the dregs of her wine. "Oh, I know that, John, nor do I expect—"

"Drop more?" John asked, pinching the neck of the bottle.

"No, no. But there is still to be answered—"

"Aye? Speak up, girl, can't bear mumblers."

"The gown?" she yelled.

"Ah, yes, the gown." He poured himself another glassful. "Change thy mind?" he asked, waving the bottle at her.

She shook her head.

He eyed the rising bubbles. "French wine shall never in man's time on earth be surpassed."

Kezia leaned forward, doggedly riffling her petticoat.

"Hm. That, yes, well, now Kezia, I hope thee'll keep mum about it, I'd not have Abigail hear. Thee's my wife now, thee'll not go running to her with tattle?"

"Oh, no, John, I have long kept my own counsel. I should never betray thee, or Shana, to anyone."

John made an effort to clear his head. He shook it, breathed deep, sat up straight, blinked his eyes. "The fact is, Shana did stow away on my ship. We were well out to sea when she was discovered and I was not inclined to put about on that account. She disappeared when we made port and I gave her no more thought. But when we stood to embark for home on a late night tide there was the copper penny again, begging to be carried back. 'Twas the least I could do for thy mother, I thought. We stashed her and her belongings in a spare cuddy. She appeared one day in the plum and the next in the plaid and I twitted her about her worldly garb. For answer she said she had worked in a wealthy Dartmouth home and her mistress had paid her off with hand-me-downs. Though, 'tis my guess she served a man, she's a well-stacked redskin, broad in the beam—" Shit, he was talking too much, overpro-testing. But Kezia had sprung out of her chair and was hugging his knees.

"Oh, Husband, can thee forgive me? I despise myself for my base thoughts. I am not worthy of thee."

He pushed back her cap and stroked her bent head. " 'Tis quite the other way round. Make no mis-take, Kezia, thee has married no Puritan. I've long been a seafaring man and I've seen the seamy side of many ports." And suddenly longed to be in one of them in a flea-bitten bed with a fat-arsed stinking na-tive.

"Nay, talk thyself down no more, John. 'Twas bad enough thee was eldered to public confession. Thee shall not be labored with in private, I promise it. Thy home shall be thy castle and thee my true king. All I wish is to make thee happy."

She went on at some length. He sighed. Herring and rum and bubbly—bad combination. Had the heartburn. He could sleep it off if he had not brought this child home with him. But if he told her he felt un-well, she'd think him old. What a pother, her head full of romantic notions, her mouth full of primer sentences. *Agnus balat,* the lamb blaiteth; *cicada stridet,* the grasshopper chirpeth; *mus mintrit,* the mouse squeak-eth. Damn it all, Shana had maneuvered him into this, her and her sand readings. He could have han-dled the Stetson affair with nothing more than glibness, he'd talked his way out of tighter spots more than once. Well, might as well get on with it. He stood up and pulled Kezia abruptly to her feet, kissed her with the fierceness of rage and frustration.

She thought it desire.

Remembering Debbie's advice, she did not flinch as he tore away her neckcloth and then rent her bodice so that the napkins that stuffed it flew out like pigeons and her peach-pit breasts were pitifully revealed. She would have been more humiliated by his laughter had

she not been so disturbed by the damage to the borrowed gown. Three brutal tugs stripped her of the
petticoat, and she stood docile in drawers according to
instruction. He grew angrier and angrier which she
interpreted as passion, and when he threw her stripped
and goose-bumped like a knapsack over his shoulder,
she thought: "Entrust thy body to his care and all will
be well no matter how strange the performance." He
was breathing like a dog as he ran with her up the
stairs, his arms like cables around her thighs, the buttons of his coat biting her belly while her hair fell
down his back and her nose bounced painfully off his
shoulder blades.

"Make answer to *her,* eh?" he was muttering,
"then by God, I'll have something to make answer for."

He threw her down on the low lumpy bed and
brought a candle over to study her. Her skin shriveled
under his stare, or it might have been the cold, but oh,
she did long to be covered. Debbie, my friend, where
is the tender teacher thee promised? Here is but a brute
enemy, cruel and panting with bared teeth, sour breath.

He undressed quickly, flinging each garment aside
as if it offended him. She got one glimpse of his neg-
ligible backside when he wheeled to face her and she
saw his cock pointed above her head. Her heart
stopped. Impossible. He might as well try to put it into
her navel, she'd crack amidships either way. She drew
her legs so tight together her anklebones hurt. She shut
her eyes and still saw the blue vein that ran the length
of his member.

"Open thy eyes!"

She closed them more tightly.

"Look at me, look at my cock! Damn thee, I say
look!"

She slitted one fluttering eyelid.

He waved it close to her face and she saw the
foreskin pulled back to reveal an angry red crown. And
oh, God, haired ballocks! The eye snapped shut.

"Open, I said!" But she would not, and he slapped
her cheek. When he saw her tears, he slapped her again,

back and forth, palm first and hard-knuckled back. "Cry on thy wedding night, what is thee, a cow-baby then?"

By tightening her teeth and clenching her toes, she managed to force her eyes open. Her will did not permit the tears to fall and they blurred her vision, giving an underwater quality to his ugly wattle-red flag.

"Spread thy legs!"

She wound them together like a corkscrew.

"Flout me, shall thee, sniveling little—"

She struggled with him, rising to her knees on the bed, her doubled fists flying at his arms, his chest, his chin. He laughed at her.

"That's better, a bit of pluck. Wanted marriage, did thee? Then work for it, cunny, thee's had it too easy."

Was it a game then, and fighting the preliminary? No. Something must be amiss, she could not imagine her mother and father thus engaged, not in the wildest dream.

He caught her flying wrists in one hand and pressed her nethers hard down on him. She tried to bite his nipple but, unable to get a purchase, came away with a gobbet of hair between her teeth.

"Vixen!" he cried, and fell on his back, taking her with him. His hand struck her backside, once, twice, three times, and with each stinging spank, she felt the thrust of his cock hard and mean and high, not quite in her nor quite out. She wriggled, helplessly impaled.

Punishment she had had aplenty at home but never a blow to her body. She wept with outrage, scratching, kicking, butting as she would have fought a man-eating beast. His grunts mocked the sounds of her efforts. His strength soon spent hers. She slumped in his hold, astraddle his hips, held, danced, jogged upon him like a floppy doll. Let him use her as he would, she could do no more.

He worked her pelvis back and forth over his cock, the tip of it no longer at her forward hatch but

sliding under her crack, soon striking familiar pleasur-
able fire. She hung on to his shoulders, her breath coming faster, her head lolling, the blood coursing through
her body like mulled rum. She felt his rough tongue
flick the tips of her breasts, and then his teeth taking
little bites, first of one and then the other, and at each
sharp pinch of the nipple, her back arched, her whole
body reared and came down on his cock again, again,
until finally she shuddered and moaned aloud in climax.

He was laughing, holding the collapsed heap of
her. "Aha, thee's pleasured, greedyguts, but what of
thy husband? Thee'll never breed sons this way. Give
over!"

He flopped her on her back, and now, when she
wanted to lock her legs over the ticking inside her,
he forced them wide. She felt the scratch of his thumbnails as he peeled apart the once-private place. Forehead to forehead, her mother had said. I love the kissing, Kezia had told Debbie. If they could but know.
She might have had her head tied up in a sack, he'd
not have noticed. He forced himself into her. A length
of ship's rail into a bung no bigger than a pine knot?
She could have told him it would not fit. She would rip,
had to. So be it. She heard his own cry loud above her
agonized mewing.

He plunged again, bewildered, maddened. He
stormed her like a battering ram and could not pene-
trate. Her screams were horrendous. He began to fear
the neighbors would hear. Wreck his reputation as well
as his tool. The fault was not his, surely, his erection
was stout as could be, but this was no membrane, this
was gristle if not bone. At length, foregoing all hope of
ejaculation, he rolled off her and fell across the foot of
the bed, his body slimed as with primeval ooze.

After a while, he felt some relief, the tumidity
slowly abating. She was sobbing steadily. The infant
crieth.

She heard him get up. She heard him grunt as
he pulled on his boots.

"Thee's got a mighty gate there, girl. I doubt the man lives who could crash it."

She heard his thumps down the stairs. The house door slammed so hard the bed shook.

Maybe if it had been a lesser horror, she'd have lain awake, but it was so calamitous, she slept. And woke to the sound of rain. Every bone in her body ached. Every sinew. The hair on her head, even her teeth and her skin hurt. It was as if a wagon had rolled over her and had dropped upon her from its tailgate barrel after barrel after barrel. And her mouth was dry as a beached fish's, all that wine.

She had no idea where she was. She turned her head toward the silver light of day and her neck rebelled, the cords stiff and sore. She pushed up on her elbows disturbing the shards of glass that stuffed her pelvis so that each motion caused their jagged edges to spike her innards. She made a brave effort to sit up. Her buttocks burned. She shifted from one cheek to the other and neither would bear her weight. She fell back, groaning. The memory of the night washed over her. She prayed to drown in it, never to surface again.

The future was too insane to contemplate, the past too obscene to remember. She firmly blanked both out of her mind, dealt exclusively with the present. He was not in the bed nor in the room. Below then? She listened, not quite sure whether she heard the clock downstairs or her own heart. And then she placed the sound just outside the door. Faint but regular. Sleeping on the landing? Oh, the poor bedeviled man. He would wake as ashamed of his drunken abuse of her as she was of her malformation. Misfits, both. Oh, John, John, what have we done to each other?

She squared her shoulders and forced the aching cords of her neck to hold up her head. She must help him bear it. Perhaps they could help each other. Mating was not the be-all and end-all. They could make an outward life together and their secret should bind them as tightly as love.

She pulled the coverlet about her destroyed body and shuffled across the cold floorboards. Yes, unmistakable—breathing. Before she opened the door, she looked into the water pitcher. Empty.

Shana lay curled on a dusty braided rug just over the threshold. Kezia poked her bare toes into the sleeping girl's ribs.

She watched Shana stir, open her eyes.

Shana jumped up and put her hands on Kezia's crossed arms. "Kezia, you sick!"

"No, I am well," said Kezia in a croaking voice that was not familiar to either of them. "What does thee here?"

"Captain John has brought sad news to your mother. She bids you come home."

The shards stirred in Kezia's bowels. If only she were numb to the pain, but she was not. Not yet. There was surely more to come, worse. John had surely told her mother that she was a freak of nature. That there had been no consummation. That no man, not even he with his vast experience, could cross her bar. He would annul the marriage. The secret would soon be out. She might remove from the island, but her life in any case was over.

"Help me to dress."

Shana, eyeing Kezia sharply, was moved to add, "Your mother grieves for Elisha."

"Elisha?"

"Nimrod went down in storm. Elisha washed overboard. Drownded."

Kezia put her face in her hands and sobbed. Later she would be ashamed that her tears were not of grief but of relief.

Seven

John was, as she had thought he might be, abject. He was also, as she had not expected, concerned for her welfare. He would not hear of her living in his squalid house. Nor, to her inexpressible gratitude, would he countenance her return, however temporary, to her girlhood status and venue. After the wedding night which he had so bungled, John feared that the gloom in the Folger ménage might be more than Kezia's reason could withstand. He installed her in his parents' home, left a hundred pounds on account for her with his father, and sailed away within the week.

This time Kezia had no wish to detain him. Out of the ashes of her maidenly hopes had come what she had always wanted, membership in the Samuel Coffin home, apex of light and warmth, epicenter of change and activity. Marriage had brought her security, affection, privilege, luxury, companionship—everything but a husband which at seventeen she was not ready for in any case. Some day she would assess the shocking intelligence that she was imperfectly made. Meanwhile she faced the new day with the guarded cheerfulness of the amnesiac and tinkered with alternatives to motherhood. Schoolmistress, doctress, shopkeeper? Perhaps John's house could be used for stocking and selling wares—pins, needles, pots, coffee, and the increasingly popular tea, a most bracing beverage, hot or cold. But when she suggested such a shop to John, he vetoed the notion.

"Tain't fitting for Cap'n Coffin's lady to be scrounging pennies. There's no want to money."

"I had not thought of that aspect, John. 'Tis only that I enjoy to muckle about in matters of business.

Ships and shops, travel and trading, they fire my blood as woman's work slows it. My father, who is not one of overpraise, has commented more than once that I have a head for ventures."

"I doubt it not. Thee's sharp as a needle, and I would not make of thee an Alice-sit-by-the-fire. The sea's my life and if we're not to have a family, thee must have thine, I perceive that. But for the nonce, while tongues are awag over the suddenness of our marriage, I would have thee stay in the quiet. Teaching is ample and seemly occupation, agreeable to thee. Why not continue it? 'Twere wise at this point to attract no special attention, does thee take my meaning? I cannot abide the prying that goes on in Sherburne. Thee must promise me, Kezia, thee'll not blab our—uh—marital condition. 'Tis nobody's fault and nobody's business. Thee must make the best of it, hear? If thee can't have cream, thee must bloody well learn to love thy saucer of milk!"

She backed away from the fury of his voice, sucking her fingers.

"Nay, be not afeared of me, lass. I'll never more lay hand on thee save in amity. Come to me."

She ran into his outstretched arms. He kissed the top of her head. "Ah, God, have I blighted thy life? 'Tis my way with women, my curse."

"Nay, I am proud to be thine. I love thee well. Kiss me, Husband, oh, kiss me."

His firm underlip thickened, clung to her top one, and his saliva tasted delicious. Her eyes closed in ecstasy, her legs ran like sand as she felt him harden against her. She fought down desire and then a tidal wave of despair. It could not be. Could never. Not with him nor any man. She slid out from under his arms, knelt to the sea chest. She reached up a hand. "The key."

He slapped about his hips and chest, growling. "Aye, the key. Here 'tis. Allow me." He knelt beside her, jammed the key in the lock, twisted it violently, and then several times banged the bent metal mouth with the heel of his fist until he drew his blood which he sucked. "What a coil we're in, my poor little wife. 'Tis a strife against nature. Thy nature in especial. Thee's fire and ice, girl, I know thy makeup. Thee's nobbut a babe, but babes grow up. Thee's quiet now, still reeling from shock, a transplanted seedling. But one day the vixen that sleeps in thy crotch will wake and feel hunger and want out."

"I shall keep it leashed."

"But leashing takes its toll—it builds a meanness." He pressed his forehead to the trunk. " 'Twould be better if we were devout like our parents. God seems to love some of His children above others."

She said over the loud cracking of her heart, "I would release thee, John, if thee do wish it."

He kicked the trunk and then sat down on it, pulling her to his lap. "Nay, nay, I am content. 'Tis thee I am concerned for. Thy path will be thorny and thee'll be walking it alone. People will watch and when thy belly gets no bigger, their ears will itch with curiosity."

"I'll not scratch them."

"Thee's stouthearted, ever was. Oh, Kezia, I would it were otherwise."

His voice broke and her head came up sharply. He was not crying, but the possibility remained. She said, "Do not grieve, John. I am happy in the bosom of thy family. I and thy sister Miriam are become the closest of friends."

"I have asked my father to accede to thy smallest wish. Whatever takes thy fancy—gowns, books, silver, household goods. For we'll have our own house, little wife. When I return we'll raze that old hovel to the ground and build another. 'Tis a good site my father has deeded me. Has a good prospect of the harbor, is handy to the tryhouse and the warehouse. And I like the creek on its bounds. We'll make it fine inside and out—staff it proper. Thy hands shall be smooth and white like my mother's, as becomes a captain's lady." He picked up her hand, chuckled softly. The knuckles were crusty from the cold and the exposed quicks black-rimmed. Ashamed, she tried to pull her hand away, but he kissed each dirty child's finger. "A gold sovereign for every full-grown nail upon my return."

She swallowed a dry sob.

"Thee'll write me letters?" he asked.

"I shall have one ready for every ship that departs the isle."

"I shall bring thee presents from every port. May-hap a necklace, costlier than the one of shells and seeds."

"Where could I wear it?"

"Under thy bodice by day and to bed by night."

"Then better bring me a sprig of lavender."

They laughed and hugged each other, holding cheek to cheek.

"I shall miss thy pert tongue, old peeper. And see thee keeps thy hair under thy cap. I'll not have thee seining adulterous hearts while I'm gone."

She grabbed his hand and held it to her cheek. "Oh, John, it's as well we be not lovers or I'd stow away with the stores afore I let thee go." She saw his eyes go bleak and she could have cropped her tongue. She teased lightly, "And how'd that be for ill luck—a chick frigate—worse than setting sail on a Sixth Day!"

There was the crunch of wooden wheels below.

"The calash," he said, lifting her off him. "Na-than's brought it."

"Brother!" called David from outside the door, "I come to fetch thy chest."

The hour of truth was ended. The world pressed in upon them. They did not look at each other again but moved about tensely, their voices matter-of-fact.

"Where in Tophet's my pipe?"

Kezia handed it to him and rushed for her hat.

"Abide here, Kezia. I detest farewells. I would have no one accompany me to the wharf." He took a tinder from the tin box that hung near the fireplace. The sparks flew and he blew, but the twist of linen would not catch fire. His grunts of disgust were fierce

as curses. Kezia grabbed up a rushlight, plunged it into
fire, held it to his bowl, John puffing away, and lo,
there was smoke.

Nathan and David took the chest away. Still holding her hat, Kezia closed her eyes, the better to savor
the tobacco that would be the last smell of a man in
her chamber for a long time. When she opened them,
John was looking out the window, puffing, puffing.
She longed to go to him, hug his waist, lay her cheek
between his shoulder blades, but she was closed out,
she could tell when she had ceased to exist for him.
He wheeled, grabbed up his ditty box and his hat, and
made for the door, slamming it after him.

She stared at the door, oppressed by its blankness.
She walked to it, put her hand on it. Upon contact, its
lifeless surface became a total distraction. I have lived
more than a hundred years, it said, and I will live for
hundreds more. You are merely one of many to whom
I stand up and seal off. She banged the door with her
fist and it shivered. She flung herself face down on the
scratchy crocheted bedspread and let the sobs come.
She wept for the long asexual life that stretched ahead.
She wept for the premature death of Elisha. For her
mother's stony bereavement. For John's terrible indulgence: "Whatever you fancy." No proper Nantucket
husband was ever moved to say that. It was more
heartbreaking in its nonconformity than any words of
love.

The knock on her door came at dusk. She leaned
upon an elbow, knuckled sleep from her swollen lids.
A stave of iron bound her head; without it her head
matter, white as a right whale's, would spill out, laying
the core of her naked, exposing her edible brain to the
raw air. Her throat felt sore, shredded as with a rake.
So. She was getting sick, how irksome. No, how good.
Give up. Rest. Let the outsiders take over, let others
keep her alive, she had not the will. Malaise poured
through her, wave after wave. Let it come. Surrender.

"Kezia?"

"Come."

Miriam came in, rosy, solid as an oak beam. Kezia watched her draw curtains, light candles, poke ash to coals on which three furry savin branches soon sparkled. As she moved about, picking up Kezia's hat, straightening the tinderbox, closing a drawer, Miriam talked in low intimate tones.

"The *Deborah*'s gone out on flood tide. Thee had better make thyself ready to sup, Sister dear, we set down at table in a quarter of an hour. Later than usual tonight for Mother and Father but lately returned from thy parents' house. They went to express their condolences. They said thy mother seems to take it well. Thy father be less stoical—he is much cast down. But it is ever thus in my opinion. Men are less accepting of fate than women, has thee noted it? At least it is so on this island, mayhap because with the men so much gone, the women must be flexible and strong." She glanced at Kezia to see if her oblique advice had found its mark. "Be not forlorn, my sister. I shall sleep beside thee tonight and we shall talk the sun up if we wish to—who's to know? Mercy, John left his pipe. The bowl is still warm."

"Let it be," Kezia decreed in a sepulchral voice. "I would not have it moved. He shall find it as he left it. And so shall he find me. My life has stopped."

But life went on, slow and narrow as the trail of a snail. Kezia's Aunt Kezia died and Kezia's niece Kezia was born—perfect in every way except for a misshapen foot. John's brother David married, and so did his sister. Abetted by Kezia, Miriam wooed and won the handsome Richard Pinkham, and Uncle Samuel deeded each of the couples a house and lot in Wesco, for which generosities he came to be called "King Sam." The town's pink and gold beauty, Damaris Worth, married Samuel Starbuck's brother Edward, who was squat and swart and gross and referred to behind his back as the Hairy Ape. Kezia grew three inches in height and her breasts went from peach pit to greening apple, but they still made a hard pillow for her nieces and nephews and if someone bumped them, she literally saw stars. And then one gray windless April noon, a boy came running with the news that the *Deborah* was spotted off Tom Never's Head and he collected a florin and an apple tart for his pains.

Kezia flurried about, wishing she had washed her hair, throwing on this frock, tearing it off, pulling on that. She emptied the tallboy drawers to make room for John's belongings, rushed around with armfuls of hers, wondering where to stow them, dropping them in a pile in the corner, then deciding the room looked untidy, and stuffing them back into the drawers. She could hear the news of the *Deborah*'s arrival being cried through the streets—hard music to dress to. Somehow she got herself together. What else to be done? She spun about. His pipe! It had become an accusing eye and she had tucked it away, but where? After five hot disheveling minutes she found it in a spare chamber pot. She set the pipe out on the lowboy, remembering when she and Miriam had made a shrine for it—yesterday, three years ago. If anyone that day had foretold to her she'd be petting in a cave with Samuel Starbuck!

Could her intimacies with Samuel be excused on the grounds that since her harbor, like Capaum, was closed to all ships, the fruits of adultery could not possibly accrue? What precisely constituted adultery? Samuel brought her to climax with his hand and he had emissions against her, but he said—and he was a devout believer—that there was no fornication without entry. However, if the seventh commandment was not relevant, perhaps the eighth was? Did kisses from a man other than one's husband constitute theft, or accessory to theft? Though in the Quaker faith marriage was not a sacrament, yet was it not a covenant, and did not morality require that covenants between man and man or man and woman or them and God be honored?

Plumping a pillow, smoothing the last wrinkle of

the bed, she thought of Miriam, her confidante, who knew all, forgave all, loved and admired her in spite of her juvenile infidelities. She made up her mind to fetch her and make her accompany her to the wharf. An arm to hang on to.

She called to Nathan to see to the kindling, then ran out, down the steps to the muddy street, her mantle flying behind her, her hands out in front of her for nail inspection—long, every last one—her feet whirring like a curlew's before a wave.

David Coffin fell into step beside her, punching his palm with excitement. And Richard Pinkham in his green work smock.

"I was going to get Miriam," Kezia gasped, holding her side.

"She's there," Richard assured her, apron flapping over pumping knees. "She's at the scene or I'm a February fly."

The throng of runners swelled. Chadwicks and Chases and Wyers and Howes, Woodburys, Stantons and Barnards and Ways, and the name of John's sloop ran with them, a torch firing the island. "The *Deborah*'s in! The *Deborah!*"

Miriam ran to meet them, red-cheeked, faun-eyed. "Smile, goose, thy husband at last!"

The crew waved from the lighters. The crowd waved back, cheering.

Debbie arrived with her brood. She kissed Kezia's cold cheek. "Where does thee keep thyself? I never see thee." She called greetings to her kinfolk. "I warn thee all, John will not disembark till the moon is down. I know his ways. I consented to come only because the children begged it."

A little snake of insight writhed in Kezia, showed a forked tongue. The *children,* Debbie?

The sun burned through the mist and the water turned from gray to blue. Some of the crew jumped out too soon and had to swim in, others waded at knee depth, laughing, shouting out names. They swept up their loved ones in strong arms, swinging them about

like acrobatic dancers. Every so often, a stranger or two
slunk away from the reunions. A huge Negro, a
'Portugee' with a loop in his ear, a Limehouse with
lobster-red skin. The foreigners made for the taverns
and the natives for home.

By gloaming only the Coffins huddled in sil-
houette against a bloody sky. The tarnished brass path
on the darkening blue water looked hard enough for
wagons. The *Deborah* was as lifeless as a ghost ship,
just a few penned lines. Sea gulls circled thick as flies
high above the afterglow, taking a last wheelabout before homing to Muskeget Isle where they slept standing
up. The little children began to whine and tug at
sleeves and coats. Kezia shivered in her cloak. Christopher growled he was hungry, and his father who had
come late and weary from the mill looked to his wife.
"Shall I row out, fetch him in the dory?"

"He'd mislike it," said Debbie, "wouldn't he,
Father?"

"Aye, he would," Uncle Samuel sighed. "He'll
sneak ashore when he's good and ready; he cannot endure the to-do. Let us to our homes now, but come to
sup on the morrow. That'll give him a day's rest, and
then he'll tell us of his exploits. I should not be surprised," he winked and dropped an arm about the
nearest grandchildren, "if there were not presents for
all."

There were close to thirty at the family supper.
The elders sat in chairs above the large silver center-
piece of salt, Captain John in the honored place between his father and Nathaniel Starbuck. In the middle
section of women, well below the salt but on a chair
of her own, sat Kezia, next her sister-in-law Miriam.
Below them, the younger children sat on wooden forms
and the bigger children stood. The latter ate from
trenchers which their relatives refilled upon request
from the bowls and platters on the table. In a high
chair close behind her grandfather, a little Kezia,
Debbie's youngest, laid about with a wooden spoon,

until Nathan removed her. At William's wife's breast sucked a swaddled infant, brought to be shown off to Uncle John.

After the repast there was the distribution of gifts. Madeira for the men, utensils and gloves for the women. For Christopher, a spyglass which the boy left behind. For the captain's wife, among other things, an Isabella grapevine in a tub.

"We'll plant it on the south wall, Kezia. The birds shall nest in it and we shall smell its perfume and eat of its fruit into our sunset days."

"Oh, John, shall we truly build then? A house of our own?"

"Aye, and at once. We'll gut the present one or mayhap tear it down, using the sound lumber and glass. What thinks thee, Father?"

"As thee and Kezia wish, Son. I gave thee the land, the house on't 'twas nothing much."

"And oversmall," said John.

Uncle Samuel shot a look of hope toward Kezia. Would they have need of another room? He said, "Has thee the wherewithal to build, Son?"

"Aye, 'twere a goodly haul."

"As good as the last?"

"Better by a hundred barrels. And bone."

Pressed for details of the voyage, John told of falling overboard too near a maddened bull whale, and he took off his shirt to show a hole in his shoulder you could put there fingers into. He told of the smallpox epidemic off the Western Islands. "I had to cancel leave for all hands. The men squawked, but we fueled and watered from lighters." And he told of a Portuguese grandee who tried to persuade him to make his home in the Azores and teach the natives the art of whaling.

"He made me a most generous offer," John said. "A villa on the isle of St. Michael, a lifetime subsidy, servants. In time, he said, he might wangle me a title from the king."

"What? Remove from Nantucket? To a foreign-tongued land? Take the bread out of the mouths of thy landsmen?" A father's cry, translating to, "Do not desert us, my son."

"Oh, John, thee wouldn't!" protested his mother. "Be they not black in the Azores? And followers of the pope?"

Kezia's mind moved quickly out of the new-built house to a castle on a hill with a full-circle view of the ocean. She queened it with an entourage of lackeys, chestfuls of damask gowns and silk slippers, attended court balls in London, Lisbon, Madrid. Palm trees, flowers, piquant foods, near-naked dances to the beat of drums! Her foot waggled under the table, but she did not speak out, too new to the role of John's wife to do more than listen at so large a family conclave.

"Stay, my parents, I did not for a moment consider it. I pass it on only as an anecdote of interest. 'Tis not every day a foreign nobleman offers land and livelihood to a simple American seaman."

Debbie laughed. "Simple American seaman! Is that the way thee sees thyself, Brother?"

Kezia thanked God she had held her tongue. What a child she'd have shown herself, taking seriously what the others, even John, regarded as beyond the pale. With a sigh, she relinquished the queen dream and returned, not unhappily, to the house in Wesco. Two-sided, with a parlor and a dining room on either side of a measured staircase, not one tread of which should squeak. Fringed draperies, British-made furniture, silver from Mr. Revere's smithy in Boston. A limestone like Miriam's for purifying water. A bake-oven built handily into the side of the oven instead of the center. And color in the rooms, bright fabrics and rugs, bowls of flowers and greenery all about. Upstairs, a guest chamber. "Dear Cousin Benjamin Franklin: My husband, Captain John Coffin, and I would greatly admire to have the honor of a visit from thee and thy wife at the next Shearing Festival." Maybe with her own house, her life would begin. A woman of means,

John had called her, but she had no money, not in
hand, not to spend. Even her clothes were ordered by
Aunt Miriam, made by Aunt Hannah, paid for by
Uncle Samuel; she but loaned her body for the fittings.
Nor had she any authority. In marrying, she had but
traded one set of parents for another, and John made
three.

After supper, friends and neighbors came to
call. They stayed till long after curfew, carrying sleeping children out in their arms. Kezia and John came
late upstairs with their candles. At the door of their
chamber, John kissed her forehead. "I had Hepsy fix
me a bed in north chamber. The wound in my shoulder
has left me with fitful sleep."

"I should not mind, Husband."

"I cry out, Kezia. Keep it twixt me and thee, but
my steward claims I howl like a very wolf. Nightmares, see?"

"Then I should gently rouse thee and stroke thee
down."

"Thee is a sweeting but 'tis asking too much. I
bid thee good night."

Alone behind her closed door, Kezia brushed her
hair. She wet her temples with flower essence, dressed
in a thrummed muslin nightgown, and a beribboned
cap. She took up her hand mirror and rubbed her lips
with the juice of an elderberry. Then she tiptoed to
north chamber. She rapped lightly with three of the
fingernails he had that morning paid for.

When he let her in she began unexpectedly to cry
against him and he drew her into the bed, covered
them both in the must-smelling fireless dark. She was
startled and pleased to find him naked. Her tears
wetted his furry chest, her cap ribbons tangled in his
hair.

"Now, now, sandpiper, 'tis not as bad as all that."

"It is, John, it is. I mean nothing to thee, how can
I? But to me thee's all the world, the light of my life,
the beat of my heart, the broth of my tears. I could
not wait till thee came home. I long for the taste of

thy lips, thy tongue, I need to feel thy skin on mine. 'Tis unmaidenly I know, but I care not. Oh, John—" She began to rain kisses all over him.

He sighed. He lit a candle. He wrapped the coverlet around his waist and went over to pour a glass of wine. "Here, it will ease thee. I shall have one, too."

"I do not want wine. I do not want my senses dulled. I want to be aware in every nerve of thy touch and thy kisses. John, husband, make love to me or I shall go mad. Is there nothing we can do?"

He set the candlestick down. He sat beside her on the bed and his eyes on her were blind as the nipples of his chest. "There are things we can do. Yes."

She carried his hand to the cleavage between her breasts, made him share the pounding of her heart. "Then instruct me, I beseech thee. I would do anything to please thee, only tell me first. I—one has—there is—a fear of the unknown."

He defined in three cool dry sentences *fellatio, cunnilingus,* and the combination that the French sailors called *soixante-neuf.* In spite of his tone, his erection made a hump in the coverlet, which she did not notice. She had let his hand go on the first sentence. Her breasts tightened like fists. Her calves knotted and she tried surreptitiously to wiggle her toes to relieve the cramp. She swallowed, concerned now with the large stone in her throat, known to doctors as *globus hystericus,* but it would not be dislodged. She forced her attention back to the matter at hand.

"And thy—er—blow?"

"What of it?"

"What do I do with it?"

"Thee swallows it, of course."

"What does it taste like?"

"I am told," he said, "slightly salty, otherwise tasteless."

"The amount," she said faintly, "it is not enough, I trow—that is—I mean—I could not choke?"

"I have never heard of such a demise."

She opened her eyes but did not look at him. She chewed the cuticle of her thumbnail, trying to save the nail.

"Look here, this is most embarrassing." He got up and began to pace. "Thee asked me and I told thee. Those things are not of my invention. They are age-old practices."

She said nothing, chewed, stared into space.

"Well, mistress?" His voice was glacial.

"I do not think it would please God."

"Yes, well—er—ah—um—just so. Now shall thee be good enough to return to thy bed? I could do with some rest."

She began to cry again.

He yanked the bed clothes off her. "Get out!"

"I'll not! I want to stay!"

"Keep thy voice down—would thee rouse the entire household? I caution thee, Kezia, tears shall avail thee nothing. Shed them if thee must on *thy* pillow, not on mine."

She bounded out of bed, clutched his legs, pressed her face to the patchwork sarong. "John, send me not away. Give me time. Could we not—but kiss and touch? Do it with hands?"

He picked her up firmly and shoved her in motion toward the door. "Thee has the boy Samuel Starbuck for that. It would not suit me."

She tethered Betsy to an evergreen a half-mile or so up the moor. The mare could crop thereabouts for the heather was tender with new growth, in the winter only sheep could chew it. "Rest here, old Bet, I'll not be long." She ran down the incline. Long before she came near enough to slide down the dune to the shore of the little cove, she could see his dory pulled up on the shore of the little cove. Their hideaway at Quaise. She doubted even the Indians knew of the tunnel that ran under her flying feet. She and Samuel had walked it upright a few rods inland and had not come to its end. They had groped their way along the inside of the palisade, scalps tight with the suspense of exploration. But then Kezia had touched a bat, or thought she had, and screamed. Her cry had echoed down the vault and they had turned and run for the sky. Afterward they had planted beach grass to disguise its mouth and had sworn in the mixed blood of their wrists to keep the secret of the place that they had come to call "Calcutta."

Now Kezia parted the reeds with a rustle and stood just inside the cave waiting for her eyes to accommodate. He spoke before she made him out.

"What kept thee? I've grown a green mold waiting."

"I am late by less than half an hour. I came the long way on horseback," she said, breathless from the run.

"The Coffins dine well and talk much. What's amiss? Why did thee send for me? 'Tis dangerous to meet when John's at home."

"Oh, Samuel. He knows. About us."

"Knows?" His voice tore like a piece of calico. "How?"

"Nantucket has more eyes than a field of potatoes."

"Did he berate thee? Didst tell him we did not fornicate?"

"He knows that, yet he is angered. He has much pride."

"And I thought he was accepting me as a likely hand! He just wanted to get me where he wants me, away from thee!"

"Away?" Her loss reverberated like a skipped stone that must finally sink.

"Aye, off to strike my whale. Oh, Kezia, I'm all agog!"

She could have slapped him. It did not occur to her that her need for his kisses and tinkerings was as selfish as his need to prove his mettle. She could scarcely breathe for anger. And envy. Men! Their marvelous freedom to walk out, seek adventure.

"Kezia? He would not—?" His voice broke again. "Be he a vengeful person?"

As man she could hate him, but not as boy. She reached out in fierce maternity and held him close. "Nay, he's too good a captain for that. Or so, I believe. But to play it safe, if go thee must, 'twere best thee took another ship."

"That I cannot. I have signed articles."

"Oh, Samuel, *when?*"

"Yesterday."

"But why? Why his ship?"

"The luck of the *Deborah* is fabulous," he said dejectedly. "And how could I dream—? We were so cautious."

She held him more tightly. "Then fear not, love, he'll treat thee kindly or make answer to me." Let him touch one hair of this dear head and she'd blab to all of Sherburne what John least wished them to know —that he could not get into his own wife. "I have a power over him—though it would break my word to use it."

He heard the grit in her voice. "Kezia, wouldst be free of him?"

"Nay."

"Dost love him?"

"With all my heart."

"And me?"

"A friend, a treasured friend."

"But thee loveth me not in that way?"

She took his hand and held it against her cheek. "Samuel, I love thee in every way."

"But not as well as he?"

She returned his hand. "Him more than both of us."

He walked out of the cave to the dory and she followed him. She watched him bail some water out of the bow with his hands.

"Shall we not remain friends, Samuel?"

"I shall have to think on't. I am much confused.

But of this I am sure, no more dalliance. I want no more of wedded women."

The term made her feel like a Jezebel, a not unpleasant feeling. On the contrary, a sweet melancholy, a touch of relief. She was tiring of their puerile relationship though till this moment she'd not known it.

He shoved off. Then she felt lorn. She made a cup of her hands and shouted, "Greasy luck!" But either he didn't hear or wouldn't turn, just kept on rowing.

When the doughty old *Deborah* sailed out of Great Harbor, Samuel Starbuck was her cabin boy, one of a crew of fourteen, with the hundred-and-tenth lay. On that same day the maidservant Shanapetuck again vanished from the island.

PART II

Femina

1751-1762

Eight

Up from below voices floated past her open window, waking the warm dun air.

"Now here's a fine house. I'll wager they've ships at sea."

"Aye. John Coffin, whaling master and trader. She's but half his age. Was a Folger, cousin to Benjamin Franklin."

"A good-sized house too. Many children, I expect."

"There you're wrong. Nary a one nor sign of one. Pity, but she puts a good face on't. Keeps a shop hereaway. Round the corner."

Kezia's brush slowed. Odd to hear oneself published, it gave another dimension to one's reality. And pleasant to hear the new house approved of for a change. The Friends, to whom alteration was ostentation, had had nothing good to say for it since the foundation was laid in stone instead of merely dug out. Heretofore, Sherburne folk had backed their homes to the winter gales, but Kezia and John faced them, wishing to catch their sails as they came in from the Sound, to see what stood at the bar without having to go up on the roof in foul weather. While they were about it they raised the ceilings—Kezia had grown tall, her shoulders higher than her husband's—and they had broken from the lean-to style to make a second-story apartment for Aunt Hannah. But most scandalous were their separate bedchambers. "Unheard of!" went the tongues. "No wonder they go childless."

The abundance of possessions was also noted and frowned upon by the Friends. 'Lay up not treasures of the earth.' Not only fine furniture and china and

103

silver, but all manner of contrivances—trivets, plate-warmers, Dutch oven, spice mill, even a dripping-stone like Miriam's which Hagar, the cook, never troubled to use. In a town of gray houses, Kezia's was garnet with a spanking white door, the front rooms paneled and painted apple-green, and all the cupboards painted robin's egg blue. Even the drawers came out blue at you.

The Friends complained to her mother. "Thy eldest daughter sets a nice example of opulence. Her keeping room's laid in oils and her bedchamber's every color in the Union Jack."

"Well, her aunt is given to mixing dyestuffs," Abigail defended lamely. "Kezia has made over the long room to my sister for her lifetime, 'tis so writ in a deed. If Hannah chooses to make her draperies in return, who's to say her nay?"

" 'Tis not all Hannah's work. Fame says Kezia has put her scholars to making her a comfort with tricolor patches—red, white, and blue. She sits by the fire and reads at them while they work on the quilting bars."

The fact is, a fine house is not endearing. It may cause people to curry favor but they will not wish you well. Miriam Pinkham now came into Kezia's house with a snapping eye and a quiverful of needles. "What does thee have new *this* week?", or, " 'Tis plain to see there are no babes in this dwelling, 'tis ever so tidy, some might say nasty-neat." Even Debbie, who was not covetous but who had other goads, would toss an occasional barb. "Houseproud is housebound. I mind when thee vowed to travel the world. Eleven years wed and thee's not as much as scooned to Boston."

"I was restless then, a chit—I knew not what I wanted. Now I am well content. 'Tis not only the house I enjoy. I have my school, my shop, and I'm dabbling in foreign trade. I find it all most diverting. When time hangs heavy's time enough to go traveling."

It was the truth. Competition with men was strong meat, it had given her the taste of blood. Miriam and Debbie's fare would no longer suit her. If people resented her difference, so be it, it was God who had set her on the solitary way. But the whole truth of her reluctance to travel was that in this day and age a lone woman on the high seas was much subject to rape. Oh, yes, it commonly happened. On a rum-soaked night when the glims were doused and the wake slicked over shipboard noises, it did happen, and she would rather be eternally damned than known for a female eunuch. Oh, she'd see something of the world before she was done. Old enough, no roisterer would think to mount her. With God's grace her old age would thus be enlivened with new sights, customs, people, things.

New, but not better, for surely there could be no more delightful spot on the globe than Nantucket of an August afternoon such as this, mingled breath of sweet fern and seaweed ablowing out the curtains. Oh, Shana, if thee could but see me now—my lady's hands, my grand house, the way the nabobs harken to my views and opinions. And John too, thee should see the admiring letters he writes me, I've a whole packet tied up with a red silk ribbon. Aye, I doubted thee, but thy prediction was sound, 'tis a marriage.

There were indeed more ways than one to become man and wife, and she no longer woke sweating in her bed from a nightmare in which John took another wife. He'd not desert her now. Never. They were wedded as surely as if their bodies could lock. Their game was filling their coffers and they played it together, attuned as they might never have been in sexual union. For even if she could have given it house, she'd have had to share his cock with girls from here to Hong Kong, 'twas the way he was grained. But what they had together now, no woman could take from her. The more money they made, the more they belonged to each other, multiplying not in sons but in real property.

Their conjugal partnership had begun seven years ago when the house was finished and John gave her permission to quit the schoolteaching and open a shop.

"I know I'll do well, John. 'Tis just a matter of getting folk to give over their money."

And he had laughed and said, "Then do it."

Typically, once permitted to, she was loath to part with her scholars. She still held morning classes for girls in her parlor during the slack midwinter months. Afternoons, she kept the shop. At first, sales had been alarmingly slow. She had sat disconsolate behind the counter, her heart curling to a black ash every time a person cruised upstreet without coming in to buy. She'd watch their dust out of sight with a rage that was just short of a curse on their backs. And when some did turn to, she hovered over them so oppressively that many a would-be purchaser left out of spite.

In due time, she learned. How to jolly not to browbeat them out of their coins. To let them browse and inquire, belittle and hag, pass the time of day. She learned when to talk a thing up and when to keep in the quiet. She learned when to extend credit and how not to while yet seeming to. When to be firm and when to give an inch or an ell. It was a challenge to her, heady as the charades they used to play around Uncle Samuel's hearth. Nor did the stakes make her cautious, for though she loved to win, she took a sour pleasure in losing. In this, she and John were alike, both daring the fates, accepting losses as part of the game.

Neither she nor John had had any idea of the difficulties that beset a shopkeeper. There were no banks, no brokers, no money changers—the shopkeeper had to fill all of these roles. As banker, due to a chronic shortage of cash, one always had a surfeit of notes and they were not easy to collect, since the law allowed debtors twelve months to pay. As money changer, one had to establish the value of such foreign coins as found their way to New England shores: pistareens, doubloons, reals, johannes, moidores, guineas, crowns French and crowns English, and Spanish pieces of eight. To make matters worse, currency values varied from state to state as did market prices, and barter was so common it was called 'commodity money.'

Now barter was no simple matter, the trades usually being at least triangular. A typical entry in Kezia's shop ledger read: "For 1 pd. tea, 1 quire foolscap paper, 1 pair glazed lamb gloves, received from Prudence Barney one coverlet. Sold same to Josiah Coffin to be paid for come Sheep Festival in 3 pds. wool." Nor was the barter always conveniently negotiable. To be paid in dried fish, firewood, whiskey, potatoes, grain, livestock, tools, or even a man's labor exerted no pressure—one could take one's time finding outlets. But payment in dairy products or produce or butchered meats was pothersome. One had to dispatch the stuff at once, often at a poor price, or eat it up. Kezia's frequent entertaining, which was laid to the loneliness of her life, was generally inspired by an oversupply of perishable food.

Then there was the currency muddle. In 1749, Massachusetts, whose paper money was hopelessly depreciated, decided to make a fresh start. A new unit was issued called 'lawful tenor' and Parliament sent over a large stock of silver to back it. From 1750 on, one pound of lawful or new tenor equaled roughly eight pounds of old tenor, and the American dollar was worth a fourth of a pound. But the changeover took time and meanwhile money was reckoned in many ways: 'old,' 'middle,' 'new,' 'sterling,' 'pay,' 'pay as money,' 'trust,' 'commodity.' It drove everybody crazy. Everybody except Kezia. She kept wading resolutely forward through the mess, taking chances, making remittances, buying pigs in pokes, but *buying,* trading constantly, and at the end of each fiscal year, having lost a little here and overcharged there, Kezia came out ahead.

Under the signboard that framed John's coat of arms, four bezants and five cross-crosslets, a painted riband said, "Ye Coffin House." No need to specify, everyone knew her stock in trade: tea, coffee, cutlery, stationery, chinaware, pins and needles and other millinery, plus whatever John was able to pick up at a good price in foreign ports in amounts small enough to pass as ship's stores or ballast—salt, oranges, raisins, wine from Spain. Nails and Bibles and hats from Britain. Hemp from Brazil, paper from Holland, molasses from the West Indies. If John had been lucky enough to fetch up at Surinam, the free port of Dutch Guiana, there'd be a rare variety—velvet, sweet oil, cambric, duck, cordage, gloves, broadcloth, laces. A cargo like this Kezia had had drummed through the streets. "New shipment of imports at the Coffin House!" the crier announced, between rolls on his drum, quite literally drumming up trade. "If goods don't suit, return and receive full money back!" And as Kezia had cannily suspected, the islanders came running at the sound of a money-back guarantee.

Kezia also learned it paid to advertise. Once when she had a surplus of bowls, a sign in the window fetched in custom:

> Quart bowls of different sizes,
> Ninepence apiece and different prices.

In this particular case she sold the lot, but ordinarily oversupply was a pitfall. It was not as if she lived in a large city such as Boston or Philadelphia. When each household had enough of an item, that was it; she had glutted her own market and she couldn't give the stuff away. Yet judicious buying was next to impossible. The British restriction of manufactures kept the colonists dependent upon England for the commonest necessaries. While they were at it, the colonists sent for homely things they missed—tricky importations such as seeds and bulbs and trees—and the follies of thoughtless packers were incredible. Once Kezia was shipped a load of lemons under a load of salt. She was so furious she assaulted an innocent crewman. And communications were anything but speedy. For example, a shipment of iron pots arrived months late so that the wholesale price was much dearer than Kezia had estimated and the amount of goods twice what she had ordered. "Regret had to double your request in order to induce this small vessel to accept your cargo," said the agent's covering letter. She still had plenty of those pots stacked in her father-in-law's warehouse, rusting away in the foggy dew.

Kezia looked forward to the time when they should have their own fleet so that they need not rely on securing space in the ships of others. And so that John could retire from whaling, which, as the years went by, he had come to hate. Meanwhile their first jointly owned ship, the *Gemini,* was abuilding at Hokanum. But a ship took as long as a baby to make. Constitutionally unable to stay beached any longer than a flounder, John had jumped at the chance to captain Joseph Rotch's brigantine, the *Love,* and they had bought a share in it. Joseph Rotch retained a full half. The John Coffins, Paul Starbuck, Abishai Folger, and Josiah Coffin owned an eighth each. It was the consent of these men to John's plan to bypass customs that she had to wangle today. "I rely upon thy clever cogency," John had written, "to assure our partners that all shall be effected with utmost tact and secrecy while remaining as ever we shall, loyal subjects of the king. Let them see it this way: if a parent be unduly strict, the child is naturally moved to disobey *sub rosa* without loving the parent a whit less."

Kezia tied the strings of her skimmer-dish. The hat had made a stir when she had first worn it because it was not black but of pale Panama straw; John had brought it her. She smiled in the looking glass. Wait till her partners went home and told their wives that she had shown up at the conference barearmed, having cut off her sleeves. She could just hear them. "What? Butcher a whole dress because of a heat spell?"

Hagar, tucking the linen between the feather beds, huffed as if she were hoisting a mainsail. No wonder— her flesh overflowed her garments like muffins in a tin.

Kezia leaned halfway out the side window. "Shongo? I am readied. Is the calash rigged?"

She watched the redskin rise up from the grass by the creek and streak for the barn. He was wearing but a loincloth, though she had insisted on breeches again and again. She ought to get rid of him, even as an outhouseman he was too savage.

"My reticule, Hagar, please." Hepsy's sister—hard to believe they sprang from the same loins. Hepsy, neat, straight and spare as a tree, whose presence in Samuel Coffin's house quietened every room and the souls of its tenants. *This* one could make her dissatisfactions felt through walls and up stairwells, they came at one around corners like draughts. But Hagar was a superb cook, and there were those who'd have stolen her if they could.

Hagar held out the reticule and a pair of linen gloves.

"Too hot, I do not want gloves," said Kezia. "Put them back."

"Coming on to rain. Sleeveless, you'll be glad to have them."

"Oh, very well," Kezia said, snatching the gloves up and stuffing them into the silk envelope. It was easier than arguing with Hagar's infallible bunion. Why did she let herself be bullied and fudged? Good treatment brazened them, they wanted mastering. She sighed. She did find it hard to rule them. Save for Obed the Indian houseboy, the servants were all older than she.

She took the time to walk back to the end of the corridor, poked her head into the long chamber. It was hung over with roves of white wool and thick skeins of blond flax. The post bed looked like an intruder among the looms and wheels and dyepots and tools—hetchel and carder, shears and swingle and swifts, baskets of wool balls with knitting needles poking out of them, a half-worked sampler aslant on a stand. By a window in this stalactite cave, Aunt Hannah sat spinning in her white cap and gray skirts, the treadle going up and down under her foot, the spindle flying round and round, her fingers nipping and releasing, making a hum that did not falter as now and then her fingers dipped into the gourd shell of water that hung on the wheel.

"Mind, we sup at Mother's house tonight, Aunt."

"Aye, I mind. Where's thee off to?"

"Downalong to a confabulation at the Rotch warehouse. I'll be home at four of the clock."

A growl of thunder seemed to billow the curtains. The darting eyes caught the cut-off sleeves. The nodding slowed, but the smile held. Kezia felt blessed.

"Shall Hagar fetch thee up some bannock?"

The clock-reel ticked. Aunt Hannah stopped to tie the knot. She wiped off a moustache of sweat with the tip of her neckerchief. "I had summat."

"There's the bananas Micajah Coffin brought us. They're cooling in the buttery."

"Turn black if they be kept overcool. Tell Hagar to keep them in the pantry. Hold still a minute, Kezia. Do I see through thy petticoat?"

" 'Tis too hot for undergarments, Aunt."

"Best not stand against the light then."

"I'll take care not to."

The faded signboard at the warehouse said, 'Joseph Rotch, marriener,' although Joseph Rotch had not commanded a vessel since 1746 when his wife's cousin was lost overboard his ship. He had been downcast long after the tragedy, but his natural ebullience finally overcame his melancholy and guilt, and working from shore, he'd become one of Nantucket's foremost and richest men. Kezia was fond of him, called him 'Uncle Joseph' though he was no kin. Everyone respected him. If he agreed to John's proposal, the others would fall in behind him.

The four men looked up as she flish-flashed into the cobwebbed room that stank of tobacco, of fetid whale oil trying out on the beach, of kelp decomposing in the heat, and the must that wood takes from salt water.

"Well, Kezia. Late on the tide."

"I regret I was unavoidably detained."

They had left her the wainscot chair so she sat higher than they. She wriggled about, dropped her reticule, patted her hair under the straw brim, made a fan of her hand. She saw them eye her bare arms. Old coots, all teeth and outwards. In revenge she noted the black-sweated armpits of Paul Starbuck's shirt, the haired mole on Abishai Folger's cheek, Josiah Coffin's sagging jowls and oozing pores. Abishai was her cousin, Josiah was John's, Paul Starbuck was Samuel's father, and not a jot or tittle of love lost among them. . . . Maybe the rift between Samuel and his father was healed now. Samuel had hooked his whale and a rich wife. Plain girl, eyebrowless. . . . The cambric handkerchief with which she dabbed her moist cheeks gave out a fragrance of verbena. This delicacy cooled her down a bit, enabled her to say almost complaisantly, "Pray go on. I would not interrupt."

"We were but gamming till you came," said Joseph Rotch. "Would you like some cold tea, my dear? My wife sent a pitcher of it."

"No, I thank thee, Uncle Joseph. I dined well at home." Too well. She pressed a hand to her taut diaphragm and swallowed a bubble of gas. By this time, she should know better than to eat dinner when she was choppy.

The men resumed their talk. Curious though they were to find out why she had called the meeting, their way was to skirt matters, loosen their tongues, warm up their manly pride. To go at once to the point would have given this cockapert maid too much status.

They were bemoaning the current depression—a favorite topic. Suddenly Joseph Rotch gave out with one of his famed sneezes, riffling the papers before him on the table. The men kept straight faces—maybe they did not find his sneezing ludicrous, but Kezia did, and the superiority of youth rose in her like cream. Her hands nested in her lap, her ankles crossed themselves, and she leaned back on a curved spine, waiting for an opening.

"The only booming business today is shipbuilding, of which we have none," Cousin Abishai was complaining. "Thank God for our oil or we'd be in straits."

Old curmudgeon had the right of it there. The disappointing peace treaty made with France over Canada—its ill-defined boundaries, the handing back of hard-won Louisburg—had damped trade. Ships and oil were the only two exports that were holding up. Last year in London John had got a good price for his cargo of spermaceti oil and had sold there the age-blasted *Deborah* as well, hitching a ride home. That money would pay for their new whaling ship. His salary as captain of the *Love,* which was four and a half pounds every month he was out, covered their living expenses. But they had several outstanding debts, they had nothing laid by, and the shop badly needed stocking. She must make Rotch see the light.

"Taxes, there's the rub," Joseph Rotch was saying. "Sight more troublesome than the currency mingle-mangle. Twenty percent tax on tea, and fame says it'll be worse before it's better. I do declare—"

There it was, the opening, and from the right man! Kezia went quite loose, waited out the sentence.

"—it becomes harder and harder to remain loyal."

"John says," she drawled, "setting the Lords of Trade over us is tantamount to sending wolves to protect the sheep."

"Ayestruth. We be most wretchedly exploited," agreed Rotch.

"And so must act in our own behalf," Kezia averred. "Which brings me to John's most recent letter. First off, he would inform thee that since thee empowered him as captain of the *Love* to rove and dispatch as he saw fit, he took the outward cargo directly to the West Indies instead of Madrid."

"Now why in tarn he change the course?"

"Because, en route he spoke the *Lydia* returning from Spain to Boston. Its captain came aboard to sup with him. He told John their cargo was similar to ours —cod, hogsheads, whale oil—and another, a Vineyard vessel, had dumped her load of the same, so the market price on all three products was currently down."

"Ah, I see, I see."

"So, John deliberates, where to go? To London? But all that duty! And who knows how the market holds *there*? Thinking on it, he minds the weak spot in the Entrepôt Trade Act. Enumerated articles wheresoever bound must be threaded through the needle's eye of British or Welsh customs, that we all know. But the act does not prohibit exporting to the *colonies* of European countries. So he decides to make for the port of St. Eustatius."

"Where's that?" asked Josiah Coffin, a landlubber.

"A small island in the West Indies," replied Kezia.

"Below Puerto Rico in the Leeward Isles," added Paul Starbuck, who'd done his share of sailing.

"Owned by Holland," said Rotch. "One of the few free markets in the Western Hemisphere."

"And therefore," Kezia continued, "out of all proportion in importance to its minute size. Now, John, as I and thee know, is a man who makes friends easily. He struck up a friendship with one Martin Godet who dwells on the island and through Godet's good offices, sold the entire cargo at a gross profit of nigh one hundred percent. All in pounds sterling and Dutch silver, my friends, not paper. We shall have cash, hard cash!"

"Hear, hear!"

"Well done!"

"Good fortune!"

The fat murmur went over and under her outpouring. She was unstoppable now, a sorcerer, a siren with sailors at her beck, a piper to children. This was the moment she loved, when she held them spellbound, winding them to her will.

"I mind not the oil prices he mentions but my head retains the cod. Including the twenty-four hogsheads in which it was packed, our investment in dried cod was something over a hundred pounds. They were sold for a hundred and eighty-six pounds, seven. Too bad, John says, that we did not also have wool and grain. The market for them is away up. But hindsight's blind sight. John writes that Godet has offered to act for us in future. The usual fee of three percent including brokerage. So now we have a knowledgeable and trustworthy agent and therefore—" She paused. "May I change my mind about the tea, Uncle Joseph?"

"Go on, Kezia, go on. We're all ears."

But she sipped thoughtfully of the tea before she went on to say, "Well, now the *Love* is empty. John would fill her hold with whatsoever goods Godet can procure at low prices. West Indian products such as molasses and sugar, but also Holland manufactures of which the colonists are so desirous—tea, canvas, tools, paper, so forth. He is certain he can make a straight wake for home without encounter. The seaways are singularly free of English customs ships, he says. The Royal Navy is evidently more concerned at this time with the founding of Halifax than with small traders. And once he nears our coast, he'll scud. He knows every bay and creek and port, though he has it on several authorities that there are no revenue cutters patrolling our Eastern seaboard."

"Do I properly take thy intended meaning? Does thee suggest what I think thee suggests?" Paul Starbuck asked.

There was a quizzical half-smile on his face that she could not interpret. Startled? Pleased? Confused? Disdainful? She held her tongue, but her heart began to beat with unpleasant heaviness.

"Thee plots a bold and dangerous course, Cousin," opined Abishai noncommittally, eyes on Rotch.

She dared not examine Rotch's face, but she could see his fingertips making a church steeple that opened and closed. Through its aperture, Kezia fell and fell. Were she and John renegades? Had she shocked these worthy men? Had she in fact delivered herself and John up to them? Her hand went to her eggshell middle to ease the rumbling. She stood up, her knees flimsy.

"If by the widest chance, a customs officer should

flag down the ship," she said, "John will say it was his intention to declare the cargo at the Port of Boston. His bills of lading will show he has come from a free port. If he is not halted, he will run for home and we'll have paid no duty on what should bring us rich profit. What say thee to that, gentlemen?" The appellation was plural but she looked to Rotch.

"I think it's a fair gamble," Rotch replied serenely.

Kezia swayed in the dizziness of relief. Then, as jubilation filled her sails, she thought, the old pirate, he's done it before. He's an old hand where John and I are just coming up through the hawsehole.

Paul Starbuck said, "Good enough for Joseph Rotch is good enough for me."

"I second that," said Abishai Folger.

"Good, I shall forthwith write John—"

"Not so fast, Kezia," said Josiah Coffin. "I take issue with this plan. I cannot go along with the rest. If John should be stopped before Boston—"

"But that's unlikely, he says!"

"Unlikely but not impossible. If he should be stopped, the cargo examined and no clearance papers to show, customs would be within their rights to confiscate the ship and every last barrel of cargo on it. What John's proposing is smuggling, pure and simple."

"Since injustice is neither pure nor simple, outwitting it cannot be," snapped Kezia, turning her back to look out at yellow clouds in a bronze sky.

" 'Tis not unjust to be taxed for protection, which is what the Royal Navy gives us, from pirates in every sea. Nor is there injustice in levying duties to regulate trade."

"Piffle. We're taxed to enrich the British merchants. Uncle Joseph said it. If thee does not know that, thee's a fool."

"Name-calling boots nothing, my girl. Sit down and hear me out."

He regarded her sternly until she sat.

"I happen to have a deep and abiding respect for law and order," lectured the island's respected court judge. "And I tell you smuggling is a crime that leads to other crimes. Bribery, perjury, divers unsavory practices. Ultimately, disrespect for the law breeds anarchy."

" 'Tis a long jump from smuggling to anarchy."

"It is one of the roads, and I am not willing to follow it. I like money as much as any but I will not breach the law of the land to acquire it. Solon said, 'wealth I would have but wealth by wrong procure, I would not because punishment follows.' And the Bible says, 'he that make haste to be rich shall not be innocent.' "

In spite of her frustration, Kezia felt a surge of admiration. It was somehow reassuring to know that a judge was incorruptible. It made one rather proud of the human race. And Josiah spoke well, should, he was a deacon in the Congregational Church. Her own tone came under control at his example. "But if the law be a bad one, if it brings no benefit to the colonists, interferes with his pursuance of livelihood, what then? If indeed its violation is taken for granted by most merchants—"

"Most merchants? Who, for instance?"

"Thomas Hancock of Boston, Israel Pemberton of Philadelphia, the Derbys of Salem, the Browns of Providence—." She could have reeled off more but he interrupted.

"Hancock may be self-serving, I have heard rumor of it. But Israel Pemberton? You go too far, Kezia. I know the man. I do not for a moment believe that Pemberton ever deprived the king of his duties."

" 'Tis common knowledge. There's been no real enforcement for years—"

"Where is the proof of these slanders?"

"I am not on trial, Cousin. I refuse to be examined. Thee has but to ask about—in the port countinghouses—"

"Hah! As I thought. Hearsay."

"If I did give thee proof, would it change thy view of John's proposal?"

"It would not."

"Then thee is unconditionally opposed to John's request for permission to load the *Love* as he sees fit?"

" 'Tis not the cargo I object to—"

"Then what?"

"Not *manifesting* the cargo."

"What would thee have him do?"

Rotch and Starbuck exchanged glances. She was forcing him into a corner, making him spell it out. The maid didn't know when to ease off.

"He can take the sugar to London and sell it there and he can buy manufactures there with the freight money. He can sell the manufactures in Boston or New York. The double sales will offset or at least lessen the duties and we shall have risked nothing."

Kezia chewed viciously at her thumbnail. Josiah's position was unassailable, conforming to the axiom, a bird in the hand is worth two in the bush. The profit would not be so rich but it would be sure. Yet John had written, "I am proceeding with all speed in the hope that they concur." Which meant he was rounding up cargo, mayhap had already bought and paid for it. She could not fail him, he had such faith in her, but it was not easy to be cogent when half of her, the head half, agreed with Josiah. The others, however, did not, they were on John's side, Rotch too, and Rotch's judgment was seasoned. She must take courage from that, face Josiah down with that.

"Is it on moral grounds that thee alone of all of us objects? Is thee alone of all of us a man of honor?"

"I—I would not sound holier than thou, but, as I have said, I respect and obey Parliament's prerogative. It is the law."

"Would thee admit that the law, this particular law, is unfair to the colonists?"

"I would say it is monstrous unfair."

"Then is not the colonist morally justified in avoiding its payment?"

"Only if he can do so legally." He shifted in his chair. "Find some loophole, say."

Loophole, hm. A quantitative morality then. Not absolutely incorruptible. "Well, the legal penalty is only monetary, is it not?"

"Aye, of course. Kezia, what dialectical game is this?"

"No game. I respect thy position, Cousin, but I would fully understand it. If the penalty is strictly monetary then thy objection can be only on monetary grounds, is that not so?"

Paul Starbuck and Rotch exchanged looks again. By hakes, she had him off soundings.

In his anger, Josiah Coffin had the look of an age- ing harlot—his cheeks overrouged, his eyes blue in pink beds. His shiny jowls shook. "I need the money from the sale of the cargo, I tell you! I am not letting hard cash slip through my fingers! Nor do I fancy forfeiting the pounds I paid for my eighth of the brig."

"That is all I wished to establish, Cousin. I should not have considered tampering with thy conscience, but now I may freely ask thee. Will thee go along with the plan if John and I assume thy share of the risk?"

There was a cold moist blast of wind, a blink of white light, a clap of thunder so close their scalps moved under their hats. It lasted less than a moment. Then they were boxed again, only the freshened air to vouch for a world outside. The juicy pop-pop of Joseph Rotch's pipe called the meeting back to order.

"Why not?" Josiah Coffin smiled. "I take no risk if you take it for me. 'Tis a rash promise, however, your husband not being present to validate it."

Kezia fished a folded paper from her reticule and handed it to Josiah. "My husband has assigned me the right to represent him."

Josiah looked around at the men before he bent his head to paper.

He mumbled aloud, " 'Know ye, that I, John Cof- fin, mariner and merchant, of the town of Sherburne in the island of Nantucket, colony of Massachusetts, com- monly called the Bay Colony, whereas I am about to depart for several seasons from the colony aforesaid do by these presents ordain, authorize, constitute, and appoint my lawful wife, Kezia, to be my true and lawful attorney to transact my business, carry on my trade, manage and dispose my estate, and also contract debts in my name.' "

Kezia's chin went up and her eyes down. Under John's signature was Aunt Hannah's and Samuel Coffin's as witnesses, and the date was of the *Love*'s last embarkation, "2nd, 7 mo., year of our Lord, 1751." She said, "The signature is, as thee can see, witnessed and notarized."

In the silence, a jackscrew chantey streamered in from the wharf.

> *Grog time of day, boys,*
> *Grog time of day,*
> *Huro, my jolly boys,*
> *Grog time of da-ay-ay.*

Josiah handed the paper back. "It's legal right enough. I confess I am surprised. Not like a Coffin to let a woman play ducks and drakes with his money."

Kezia let that one pass. "Shall we draw up articles? I am prepared to sign here and now."

"No need. A verbal contract, three witnesses, and the gingerbread's cut the right way for me." Josiah's smile was a mere baring of teeth. He did not yet realize he had won something, he *felt* like a loser. "Now if you'll excuse me, my mount is shy of tempests. I bid you good day."

They watched him exit. The men, one after another, shuffled up. Kezia was the last to rise, knees unhinged still, but strong in the core of her. Lover of law, hah! Elders were all the same; they said one thing and did another. 'Where there are animals, expect imperfection, where there are men, corruption.' Even her mother . . . nightly with her new husband, Daniel Pinkham, that big, old brown-toothed tailor in her father's bed. The rain tap-touched the sill, tentatively at first, then with a harder regular beating. She stroked the silken skin of her arms, rejoicing in her youth. Loathsome to have jowls and haired moles and whiskers, to sweat black, to sneeze like a Hun.

" 'Tis a very cloudburst. Would any of thee gentlemen be pleased to ride home? I have my gig."

A moment before the three men had loved her. She had been Joan of Arc bearing their flag. Now they felt hostile toward her, they did not know why. Her cousin Abishai said it took more than a summer shower to melt him down, he'd walk, but Paul Starbuck and Joseph Rotch accepted her invitation.

She had to run back for the paper she'd left—the power of attorney. When she came out, Rotch and Starbuck were each ensconced in a corner of the back seat. Shongo waited to give her a leg up. She went between the two men, sat down on Paul Starbuck's open palm, then started up as if branded. In shock, she raised one buttock, listing to Rotch, but when Starbuck did not remove his hand, she remembered his reputation and had to conclude it was no accident. (God punishing her for not wearing underclothes?) Wedged tight between their hipbones, she could not escape the finger that began to exert a sly pressure against her aft hatchway. Eyes front, face aflame, she resolutely ignored her plight.

"How fares your sister Judith and the new babe?" asked Rotch. "I understand it was a breech birth."

"Aye, a difficult one. Judith is recovered—hunh! —but the babe is pindling. She was mashed somewhat about the head."

"Let us hope and pray she will be well, though I know what a worry—. My wife and I have suffered more than our share of losses. Three living out of thirteen births. It is hard, very hard."

"I know—ow!" Her back arched, her teeth clamped. There were two fingers now and they stealthily explored her pudenda. No wonder Samuel disrespected his father, randy old scoundrel!

"This will do, right here, Shongo," directed Rotch. "I thank you, Kezia. Good day to you, Paul."

"And the same to you, Joseph. My respects to thy good wife," replied Starbuck, taking bold possession of her entire crotch.

Kezia leaped down on Rotch's heels. Her ankle twisted but she did not heed the pain. "Shongo, set aside. I've mind to see how the new bay handles."

Shongo handed over the reins impassively though the bay was not new. They rode in silence to the house where Samuel had been raised. Starbuck, murmuring thanks, had but set his foot on the fender when Kezia whipped the horse's rump. The man pitched forward spread-eagled on the wet ground. Shongo grabbed the reins to halt the calash. "Back, Mistress, he fell! In the mud!"

Kezia shook him off, kept the horse at a canter. To Shongo she growled, " 'Tis where he belongs, he's a pig." It was the worst but not the first time a man of business had snidely tried to remind her that she was but a woman. Henceforth—she swore it—she would fight back by fair means or foul.

When on a golden day in October John brought the *Love* and the duty-free cargo safe home, Kezia told him of how she had honeyfogled Josiah Coffin. He gave her a kiss clean as salt and tweaked her nose. "Watch out or thee'll make us so rich, I'll stay home and be a do-nothing. Underfoot and overweight till thee'll wish me back at sea."

It was the kind of badinage that had become their way. They were straight with each other only in matters of business. Yet they were ever affectionate, and was this not preferable, Kezia often reflected, to the ill humor that had so blighted her parents' relationship?

Their first jointly owned vessel, the *Gemini,* was completed the following month. John had insisted upon its design over the misgivings of the shipbuilder. When he brought it home from the Hokanum shipyards, the old salts poked fun at it.

"Hate to have to run from a privateer in that," they scoffed. "Be like a tortoise running from a hare."

Kezia took one look and could have cried. It was square-rigged, blunt-nosed, broad in the beam. Not only ugly but it had cost a pretty penny—three hundred pounds sterling. What could John have been thinking of? But when he asked her opinion, she was unwilling to incur his displeasure. "Well, it does beat the pattern," she said, a current island expression that made him laugh. And when she overheard him defend it to his father, she was glad she had said no more.

"She's not a racing filly," he said, "she's a plow-maid. She may not stir the prick in a sailor's trousers, but she's strong, I warrant thee. Her squared-off bow and stern present more sail area to the wind to move the weight of the ship. She's but ninety pounds burthen, yet in addition to gear and stores she'll hold five hundred butts and then some."

"But building a tryworks right into the middle of her main deck! The weight of the bricks, John. With oil in the kegs, she's got to founder, big's she is."

"Aye," replied John imperturbably. "I shall dump the structure on the homeward voyage."

"What? Waste good bricks? Has thee lost thy wits?"

"A sight cheaper to waste bricks than to risk putrefaction of the oil. I have never liked the race home with every catch, Father. I enjoy to range. Furthermore, the whale industry's agrowing. We shall soon have to find new grounds, like or no."

Later, Kezia ventured a question. "What of the fire hazard, John? Might not a fire big enough to heat such huge kettles burn the deck?"

"Well, there's a pan under and around the furnace that is to be kept filled with water during the rendering. I saw such a device on a French caravel. And if 'twill make thee happy I'll have a bucket brigade standing by to wet down the timbers should a fritter jump the pot."

"I must say it would seem thee has thought of everything. It's entirely possible, Husband, thee's a very genius." But even as his arm went around her shoulders she was figuring the cost of insurance for the *Gemini*'s maiden voyage. Better to pay at the rate of fifteen guineas than to risk the whole out of pocket.

The night before the *Gemini* put out to sea, John and Kezia shared mulled rum on the new tip-top table by the fire in their keeping room. Kezia was in her usual state at the prospect of his departure—glad for the respite of mental and physical torture, yet loath to lose him.

John's frame of mind was equally conflicted. He had but an hour ago bid his twin sister farewell and the taste of her tongue still thrilled like a brilliant wine. How many times could a man renounce his true love? He would miss Kezia, too—her intelligence, her humor, her consideration of his likes and dislikes. She was a sprightly friend and a good partner and there were many island husbands who did with less, leastways when ashore. Besides, he was late into his forties now, he liked the comforts of home and dreaded more each time, more than even Kezia guessed, the wet and the cold, the privations, the risk of limb and life, the loneliness, the boredom, the backbreaking labor, the awful responsibility for the lives of other men. His prime was waning, and he begrudged every moment of it spent out there between the endless circle of sky and ocean.

"Write to me, peep," he said. "Write me everything, the bad as well as the good. I shall have my first cruise of oil to Britain by First Month, *Deo volente*. Send all letters previous to that date to the agent in London. By Second Month and through the summer, I purpose to be in Newfoundland Seas—Belle Isle, the Davis Straits, the Grand Banks."

"Thee must write, too, John. Often. I live for thy letters."

He looked about. "I think of this room on dirty nights out there."

She sighed and stared at the fire.

He took her hand. "For pity's sake, don't go to the wharf on the morrow. There'll be a crowd. How I mislike being Godspeeded and farewelled! Turns me testy."

He could have saved his breath. For that midnight she chanced to see the boy Obed steal out of John's chamber frog-naked. Next morning she had the migraine headache. Double vision, nausea, the gamut. She could not have risen for the Second Coming.

Nine

The calash ran toward the house of lights across a carpet of new-fallen snow. The night was clear, cold, so still it seemed to be listening. The only voices were the brass bells that tinkled on the strip of leather attached to the halter and, once, the double hoot of an owl.

Aunt Hannah jounced in her charcoal woolens, her breath smoking from her quilted hood. Her black-gloved hands were folded in her lap, her anklebones touched through polished boots. She'd have worn her everyday broken ones, but Kezia had sent her back to change, and truth to tell, it was nice to have someone who cared, took her back to times when her parents told her what to wear. Reception should rightly be held at the Barnards', Samuel Coffin ought not let Hepsy run his ship, but she always had, even when his wife was alive. She stole a glance at Kezia's stony profile. Poor lass, going to a wedding entertainment in the same house where'd she'd had hers could but heighten the loneliness she gamely tried to drown in daily toil. Sight less trying to have no husband at all than to have one who was never home. The Barnards now, they were only too glad to get out of a do, all's they cared about was keeping their money in their pockets. The whole family of Coffins deferred to Hepsy's pride, ever had, and the way they coddled stupid, lead-arsed Nathan was a shame; what Nathan needed was to eat a piece of mad dog. Well, Samuel was getting on in years and waspish with gout; leastways the two blacks took good care of him, otherwise Kezia'd have him under her roof, that girl would gather up strays till the walls bulged. She glanced again at the features cut with a fine chisel and the mouth a downward slash. It'd turn up fast enough, soon's she mingled. There could be a pond of tears inside that girl and she'd spill nary a drop. Sat dry-eyed through the memorial service for her father and brother Peter who, like Elisha, went down in the vasty deeps, never to riz more.

The bay ran, tick-tock, tick-tock, and the bells sang, lingaling, lingaling. As he drove, Shongo looked up at the round white face scooning merrily across the Milky Way. With the moon, he shared a smile of secret knowledge, man to man. *They* knew why mistress was down of mouth. Each month she fell back two days, and this was the twenty-eighth day since the last onset of her flux. Tonight she would have the darkness of soul, tomorrow the red waters would flow over her dam, and the day after that she would be herself again. Click-clock, click-clock, tingaling, he was glad he was a man.

Kezia laid her dread of the evening to John's presumption of Christopher's ill will. John had had forebodings when Christopher asked to sign on the *Gemini,* but one could not very well refuse one's sister's son. Now John suspected the lad of having informed on them. When John was last home he'd told her that Christopher had proved a troublemaker among the crew and had been given a taste of the cat. To make things up to him toward the end of the voyage, John had taken him ashore for a night on the town in the Port of New York. "We were the only ones to take leave of the vessel and 'twas not I who blabbed. Yet there was the British customs ship lying in wait for us off No Man's Land. A search warrant was shown but pulled back afore I could see the names of the witnesses. If the revenue men set out forthwith and sailed a straight course, they were bound to head us off, we having tucked in and out of bays all the way to Sakonnet before making a run for the Vineyard.

"They took us into Boston where we stood condemned at a Court of Admiralty. The ship and its entire cargo confiscated. Coffee, sugar, fifty-six tierces of rum, ten chests of Holland tea—three hundred pounds to the chest—and an assortment of millinery picked up on the cheap for our shop, all packed tight as penned sheep. I was fortunate to be able to buy back the *Gemini* at its cost. The *Gemini II,* if we can scrape up the cash to redeem it, will be several months more abuilding, so had I not recovered the *Gemini* we'd be grounded. The affair lies heavy on my mind. Mischance or evil intent? I confess I am cockbilled. Could my nephew still bear a grudge for the drubbing I once gave his father?"

Kezia's way would have been to face Christopher down with it, but John had gainsaid this. "Keep my suspicionings from Debbie, they would but trouble her and change nothing. Act, I beseech thee, as if nothing were amiss." And so she had come with the rest to toast the young groom's future though she felt more like weeping at the past.

There is a variety of reasons why women cry at weddings. Debbie needed to so much she got drunk instead. She fell flat as a barn door before the supper. Her brothers William and David carried her up to bed. Mary Barnard, the bride, watched them do it with bale in her eye. Mary was older than Christopher, potato-faced, and large with no womanly curves at all. She hulked over Christopher who was built like his Uncle John, well-set but of middling height. Mary had to duck her head under the lintel, and seeing this, Debbie had bawled blearily, "Thee does not fit in this house!" And passed out.

Close to Kezia on the settle near the fire, Miriam Pinkham, big with her fourth, ate somewhat greedily from a trencher they both shared. Looking at the two, heads together, lips moving like boiling water, one would not guess they had lost affection for each other. All that remained to them was the habit of candor, a candor now hurtful. They envied each other's style of life. Each had got what she wanted but, as usually happens, too much of it. Kezia, who never admitted to jealousy, overadmired Miriam's towheads, chubby, rosy, wild as Tuckernuck steers. The Pinkham cottage teemed with immediacy—fights and pranks and tumbles and howls and piping laughter. In the summer it smelled of urine and in the winter of woodsmoke and soured milk, and at eventide in all seasons it opened its front door to its master. Every time Kezia went there, she felt diminished.

Miriam's jealousy was simpler because she was simpler, not given to hiding her feelings. She envied Kezia her freedom, her privacy, her elegance, her brazen equality with the magnates of the town. Kezia never did a stroke of housework while she, Miriam, born to luxury, now slaved from dawn to dark, washing clothes, scouring, milking, slopping livestock, glad to sit down to the spinning wheel or to suckle a babe. She who had reveled in pretty clothes went about in tattered frocks, her neck dirty, her hair lank as an Indian's, her hands red and cracked. For Richard the Smiler was feckless, the lemon of the Pinkham lot, though the town loved him as they did not love the Coffins and so blamed Miriam for 'mismanaging,' just as they'd criticized her mother for her 'cornstarch airs.'

"What a pleasure to eat victuals one has not had to cook," said Miriam, licking her fingers. "But thee'd not know, would thee, waited on hand and foot as thee is, and thy cook, Hepsy's sister Hagar, in possession of my mother's receipts. 'Tis a wonder thee keeps thy shape."

"Had I a husband to sup with nightly, I would gladly cook for him," Kezia said. "Tell me, Miriam, do thee and Richard still—that is—I mean to say—can thee do it without harming the child inside?"

"Of course, silly goose, the babe's safe in the bag of waters. Scarce a night goes by but Richard's all over me, and sometimes after a day of toil 'tis the last thing I desire. But the Pinkhams are famed for their passion, as thy mother who has married one can tell thee."

Kezia upset the trencher. Both jumped up, dabbing at their petticoats while Nathan dealt with the mess on the floor.

It was shortly after supper that Kezia's cramps

started. They were worse than usual—lobster claws opening and closing on her innards. She sought out Dr. Tupper. He was in the dining room where most of the men stood about in clusters. The talk she moved through, which she ordinarily preferred to women's, fell on pain-closed ears.

"Sold my body and my bone, but I'm waiting for a better offer for my head matter . . ."

"New fire engine due from Londontown any time now . . ."

"Skewered by a ram he was. Ought to be a law that neat creatures have their horns sawed off."

She plucked his sleeve. "Dr. Tupper?"

"Kezia, my dear, what's amiss? You're white as a sheet!"

He moved her off. He was an unprepossessing man, short, round, bald under the peruke he wore to parties, but his sausage fingers had a tender touch, and he was enormously kind in spite of his blunt speech. He was one of the few Presbyterians the Quakers favored.

"My monthly—" Kezia faltered. "The contractions are—oh, bad—like travail, I judge. The potion thee last gave me for the migraine worked so fine, would it also do for the cramping?"

"Oh, my, yes. Yes, indeedy. Come, lass, take my arm. Tipped womb, I should hazard the guess. One of these days, I shall put my hand up there and see. Nay, look not so frighted, not now while you're in pain. Wait here, I'll tell my wife and your Aunt Hannah. No need for *them* to leave the party."

Outside they looked about in vain for Shongo. In the hall no doubt, drinking up the dregs of the rumpots.

"Up with ye, then."

And up she went on the doctor's old roan stallion. She kept her face in his back, her arms clasped around his barrel middle. Every bounce was an agony. The wind they made nipped about inside her cloak like a gaggle of maddened geese. He lifted her down at his house. She sat huddled on the bench in his tiny cluttered office while he hurried hither and yon, lighting candles, mumbling. "What dosage did I measure out last time, I wonder? A grain, I daresay, but two'll never hurt you. Here, Kezia, knock this back. 'Tis in ardent liquor so you'll not mind the taste. 'Twill warm you to boot. Oh, won't the tongues wag over this, me nabbing a pretty maid like you away from the funning, whisking you to bed, your husband t'other side of the land. Come along, dearling, lean on me."

To one who called her 'dearling,' she'd ride to the gates of hell, but it took all her grit to remount the horse. The flow had not yet begun, there was that to be thankful for.

Obed let them in. Bless him, he knew exactly where she kept the napkins. He assisted her as well as any maid, slipped off her boots, unhooked and unlaced, fetched her night clothing, folded away her shed garments. Another mistress might have sent him away knowing what she did, but once the shock receded, she found it easier to bear than simple adultery. It reflected less upon her insufficiency as a woman and more on John's corrupt tastes. In any case, she had put the entire incident firmly out of mind.

Drowsing, drifting, Kezia smiled. " 'Tis working, dear Doctor. Ah, blessed easement. I do thank thee."

"Very well, then. I shall top by in the morning." He pulled the covers to her chin, outlined the length of her with the heels of his hand. When she woke a moment later, he had four fingers pressed to the pulse of her wrist.

"Well, slugabed, how are you today?"

From the deep billows, she smiled up at him. "Serene as a terrapin on a calm sea." Today? The sun streamed through the south window. Afternoon then. Was it possible? She had slept through school and dinner.

"And the menses?"

"Aflowing. That elixir is God's medicine."

"Might make you costive, but you know remedies for that."

"Aye. In future should I be similarly grabbed, may I have the laudanum again?"

"Oh, my, yes. No harm in it." He dug into his knapsack. "Here, I shall leave this flaskful. Keep it handy. And when you write to John, ask him to get you some at any London pharmacy. 'Tis dear in Boston. He may find the powdered opium easier to transport, takes up less space and less chance of breakage and spillage. You're familar with medicaments, just measure it out on your scales. A grain, at most two if the pain is severe. Best mix it in wine or coffee. They act as adjuvants to accelerate the effect and they kill the bitter taste. If pain persists, repeat the dose in, say, three to four hours. And while you're about it, you might ask John to get me a supply as well. I get shipments of it regularly, but I dole it out so freely, I am ever running short of it."

At first Kezia took it only for pain—menstrual cramps or headache. One grain usually did the trick. If it did not, she doubled the dose as directed. In extremity, she tripled it. But there came the night she watched Samuel Starbuck tenderly kiss his pregnant wife before a whole company, when she took it for escape. Without physical pain to sop up the effects of the drug, she experienced the full impact of its charm. It was a nepenthe particularly suited to her for, unlike alcoholists, who seek conviviality, or the hashish-eaters, who seek paradise, Kezia sought relief from inner tensions and this opium provided. Under its influence, even her sealed crotch became no more than a cosmic joke, and if the junket turned nasty, she found she could break it off by merely changing her place, say from the chair at the window to her bed. Oh, it was nice to be able to surrender and yet remain in control!

She planned her 'getaways' so that she should not' be missed. Seventh Nights were most feasible. In the town of lone women there were supper parties, quilting parties, 'sociables' on the slightest pretext, most of them at week's end when the week's chores were largely done. Kezia always came away from these 'gatherments' feeling curiously insecure, so it was a good time to partake of the laudanum whose solace was unfailing. It not only restored her confidence in herself, it gave her a sense of superiority. The night would pass in a dog-sleep which somehow rested her more than a sound one, and left an equable glow that lasted throughout First Day.

Now the meetinghouse was not just a place where she met with her people but where she met with her God. Previously the services had made her restive, now the silent time sped by as she communed with the Heavenly Father, impervious to heat or cold, to the hardness of the benches, the body odors and bad breath. Kezia brimmed with love for all, young and fresh, old and stinking, all were her brethren.

"Has thee noted Kezia's good attendance at worship of late?" Aunt Hannah remarked to Abigail.

"Aye, and her graciousness to the members of the congregation," Abigail said. "Ah, well, Kezia was never one to be pushed. She has come to God in her own time."

Is synchronicity more than chance? But for mistaking a news report, Kezia might have gone on imbibing only on Saturday nights. But in 1755, the Grand Banks claimed three Nantucket whale sloops and thirty-nine Nantucket men. Kezia heard the name of her husband cried in the streets as one of the lost. She locked herself up in her room, and as the shock and grief became insupportable, she poured herself a strong potion of oblivion. Later she found out it was not her John Coffin who drowned but another, a younger, son of Tristram, husband to Anna Coleman, Elihu's daughter. She conducted a service of fervent thanks to God that evening in her keeping room which the whole household attended. Afterward, still overwrought, she took a draught as a sedation. Thereafter, laudanum became a nightly indulgence. If peace of mind lay in a flask on the shelf, why not help oneself to it? Now, when there was a business meeting to cope with on the morrow, she made bold judgments without anxiety or egotism. Now, when she went to bed at day's end she no longer burned first with need for a man and then with shame for having masturbated. Actually, she rarely felt desire at all, and this in itself was a relief.

When John was home, she gave up the indulgence. She was afraid he might disrespect her for it, or worse, forbid it, and too, she had no wish to be 'floaty' in his presence. But the abstinence did put her under the weather. In those years, John would say, "Every time I come ashore, Kezia catches cold. I believe a deepwater skipper's more than she can tolerate." One of these nights, she was so uncomfortable, sneezing and sniffling, eyes streaming, she decided to have some after all and persuaded John to partake of it with her. All it did was put him to sleep. Next morning he said he preferred his own poisons—tobacco and rum.

"But rum addles the brain. And tobacco discolors the teeth," Kezia argued. "My stepfather, Daniel Pinkham, would be a handsome man were it not for his stained teeth. And Dr. Tupper says Nathaniel Starbuck's lip sore—which refuses to heal—is caused by the hot stem of his pipe. Whereas opium is harmless."

"Ah, well, the book's not closed on that, is it? Bound me up, it did. In England it's fed to the workers to keep them at their benches, for dysentery is rampant in London, a dirtier town never was. 'Tis said after a bit they can't live without it and it's a costly habit."

"Oh, well, I can forego it—if ever we need to practice economies," she said lightly. But she thought, so that's the cause of my constipation, and remembered that Tupper had warned of it. Oh, well, small odds, there was always calomel.

Her biggest problem was time. She was always chasing it, never catching it, never had enough of it, it slipped by her like sand through a fist. She bought herself a watch and looked at it often, but she still arrived late to appointments. For this her mother labored with her.

"Thee has ever had a disagreeable penchant for tardiness, Kezia, but 'tis become a vice. If thee says thee'll come at five of the clock, thee comes at seven. And thee is ever drowsy. Thee's pushing thyself too hard, girl. Why, thee's flushed and moist of cheek in the coldest of weather. Industry is laudable but, like thy Aunt Hannah, thee carries it too far. Keep up this pace, and like her thee'll be old before thy time. If thee must stay in trade and keep shop, though goodness knows thy husband provides thee a more than good living, if thee must ape the men as thee has ever been wont to do, at least close the school. The pay's not worth it—a penny a week and five shillings for firewood."

"Oh, I couldn't do that. I don't do it for the money. My apt little clerks, we are a family."

But close it up she did. Doing so was a wrench, but it was lovely to be able to lie abed mornings. Curiously though, she was as short of time as ever, she could not figure out why. The shop virtually ran itself. Or rather, Rachel Bunker ran it. With the clever and willing assistance of Obed. He could not read or write so he was no help with the books, but he was an engaging salesman. Between the two of them, they left Kezia free to devote her attention to the import and export business which involved endless letter-writing. This was what kept her from falling out of the world —orders, deals, bills of lading, contracts, correspondence. They made life worth living in spite of her gnawing grief at being an incomplete woman.

As Kezia's tolerance to the drug waxed, the benefits inevitably waned. She doubled the nightly dose and from double, triple is not far away. Unfortunately, her dreams came to be more terrible than wonderful, quite out of her control, utterly exhausting. She was obliged to increase the morning dose to bring her out of her lethargy and take her through the day. The vicious circle included the necessity for cathartics and clysters. Her stomach and intestines became so irritated, she took quantities of ammoniated tincture of valerian to quiet them. She had appetite but all manner of food upset her, so she virtually stopped eating. There was also the daily need for application of alum salt to her underarms, for the drug made her sweat; every gown she had was stained. At length, disgusted and angry with her dependency upon so many medications, she decided to give up laudanum altogether.

The first day of abstinence was long but not unbearable. She felt rather weak, too weak to go out to divert herself, too fidgety to wait on customers in the shop. She kept to her room and answered letters—one from her Cousin Benjamin Franklin which was two years old! It gave news of the earthquake in Lisbon and ventured the hope that her husband's ships had not been affected by the ensuing tidal wave.

In spite of a growing uneasiness, she went down to supper. She found Aunt Hannah's company excruciatingly tedious. She yawned so much that Aunt Hannah insisted she retire. Perhaps she did so too early in view of her inactive day for the night was interminable. She was up and down, pissing and farting, tossing from one side of her bed to the other until she could feel every spiteful bone, every rebellious muscle in her body.

Next day she was worse. She stayed in bed, thinking she had caught cold or the grippe or even pneumonia. She shivered and sweated and felt malaise in her bones. Her eyes and nose ran and her mouth kept filling up with watery mucus, an overwarm fluid, as if her mouth were hot with fever. The cold sweats made her hair stand on end; she could feel each follicle, even the hairs on her arms stood up, each in its own goose bump. Oh, it was so tiresome to be ill! And so badly timed, just when she wanted to give up laudanum and try to lead a regular life. But she had made up her mind to eschew it, and sick as she was, she was resolved to let the influenza take its course.

The yawning bothered her—she could not stop. Once she yawned so violently she dislocated her jaw, which threw her into panic. By frantically manipulating the jawbone, regardless of pain, she got it back into place.

By the end of the second day, she developed dysentery and vomiting. This convinced her that the illness had nothing to do with laudanum, but she still would not let herself take any. Grippe or influenza, even pneumonia, was self-limited. Let it burn itself out, she would fight it alone. But then the muscles of her arms began to cramp and jerk. She pulled up her nightgown and watched her abdomen corrugate and knot as if it housed eels. She passed ten large watery stools in the night and saw blood in her vomit.

She was not sure at just what point in her illness one or another member of her household came to attend her. She did not call for them, they simply came. They changed her soaked bedding, piled blankets on her, fed her tiny sips of sugared water. Shattered by the sight of her agony, each of them, unbeknownst to the other, begged her to tell them where the laudanum was hid. She doggedly refused.

After seventy-two hours, Kezia was a dreadful spectacle. Her face was pinched from dehydration, her eyes brown-circled and sunken, her lips a livid blue. Under the stacked coverlets, chills racked her body till her teeth chattered. Quantities of secretion poured from every orifice, every pore. She twitched, jerked, kicked involuntarily. Unable to lie still, too weak to move about, too nauseated to keep down even water, she felt her life-force ebbing. Her brain cleared at the thought and she began to entertain the possibility of dying. She felt neither fear nor regret nor bitterness, only a vague disappointment. Was this all? Was it not more for others? Did her name have a curse upon it? For Judith's Kezia had died at six months and Debbie's at eight years. Now her sister Mary had a Kezia, too. She made a pact with God: "I shall come now and willingly if Thee permit Mary's Kezia to live out her spate." And not quite trustingly clarified the contract: "Fourscore years."

She watched Obed get up and reach behind the books on the hanging oak shelf. With a laugh she was too exhausted to utter, she watched him count out into a sake cup seventy-five drops, three grams of laudanum. How had he learned her dosage? There was nothing that boy did not know. They all knew. If she sneezed in Quidnet, Aunt Hannah, Hagar, Shongo, Obed, and Rachel knew it in Sherburne. "Mistress," said Obed, proffering the little cup.

She closed her lips, turned her head away from the curious odor the wine he had added could not dispel.

He picked her head up. His eyes were black as dirt. "You may not die. Not your time."

She clenched her tired teeth.

He pinched her cheeks together making a fish mouth, his unrelenting thumbs separating her jaws, and he poured into her little by little the contents of the cup. She found herself swallowing more and more eagerly. Oh, God, was she killing Mary's Kezia?

Within the hour she was cured. Symptom-free except for debility. Her legs stopped jerking, her feet stopped kicking, her arms stopped cramping. Her nose and eyes stopped running. No nausea. No bowel contractions. No piss. No perspiration. She was limp as a rag as Obed washed her thoroughly, inside her ears, between her toes. She rested against his arm as he brushed out her long dark hair. He dressed her in clean garments, made her bed under her, sat her up against two pillows, put a third under her knees, set a ribboned cap on her head. He folded ten quilts away, some in her chest, some in John's. Then he waved gaily and ran down the stairs.

Aunt Hannah brought her duck soup and biscuits, and she drank and ate all. She smiled at the doorway full of Hagar.

"Hagar, I thank thee. 'Twas just the thing. Delicious."

Hagar shook her head, raised pink palms. "Praise God. Hallelujah!"

Three days later, Kezia was able to walk. She walked to the pier glass and was shocked, but not dismayed, not displeased. That kind of suffering, one wanted to be able to read the signature and postscript. She counted her ribs. Even her breasts had shrunk. What matter? There was no one to fondle them but herself, and like a mother, she loved them big or small.

She gave Hagar six peacock feathers and to Rachel an embroidered Spanish shawl. She had once withheld from a Boston consignment two 'mourning rings' which wealthy Presbyterians presented as mementos to those who attended their family funerals. These she gave to Shongo and Obed—why not? they were as good as married anyway. (Did Shongo know he was sometimes cuckolded by the master?) To Aunt Hannah she gave a single sentence that made the old maid rich for life: "Thee is more to me than my own mother, and I do believe I am more to thee."

Then she retired from the battlefield and moved back into her world of half-dream.

Ten

Because half of it *is* real. It takes ten years to get to the door but the door is real. The ceiling is ten miles away but the ceiling is real. The meals they bring to her are real. The laudanum rubies are real. Even the stuff of her nightmares is real, drawn from experience that she can often trace. She has forgotten nothing. Stuffed in the duffle bag of memory is every thought, every feeling, every experience she has had or heard of. Whatever once frightened or thrilled or saddened or revolted or sickened her comes back to her now, simplified, disguised, distorted, costumed, masked, exaggerated, but taprooted in her past.

Take the island custom of fertilizing the fields. Thrice nightly in planting season, it is permissible on Nantucket to run after penned sheep with torches, scaring the manure out of them. As a child Kezia would steal out of her bed to watch her father and Elisha perform these rites of spring. Etched on her brain are the devilish grins of the man and the boy as they ran hollering, and so are the long sad faces of the sheep and their piteous bleatings as their droppings fall smoking between their stick legs onto the hoed earth. Now in her dreams she is the ewe. She stands rooted, unable to run as her kin come at her with their fire. When she wakes, her bed is fouled and the fouled bed is real.

Deep-etched too is the time Elisha was sick abed with chicken pox. "Thee'd never dare kiss me on a pock, would thee?" So she kissed a pustule and was soon after covered with them but so were Judith and Mary who didn't. Now, in her opiate trance, a lover's lips break open and ooze with pus and she must needs

140

kiss them or be a coward. Sometimes the lover is John, sometimes Debbie, sometimes Christopher's ugly wife, Mary, sometimes a pirate with a ring in his ear. She has also kissed the fork-tailed devil, his lips are red and winy, and he has a goatee. She turns to water under the ecstasy of his kisses; she would belong to him but he never stays, he has other women, other places to go. She lies on the white sandy beach, her bones picked clean as an armature, sun-bleached. The last morsel of flesh is her pudend. Why did they leave it? Not nourishing, foul of taste or odor, taboo? The breaking waves lave and lick and beat her cunny till it throbs, and the throbbing is real.

From High Bench she barks and bays to a congregation of cows and donkeys and all the children are kittens. They moo and bray and meow back derisively. Looking down at herself to see what the yelling's about, she sees she is smeared with excrement and menstrual blood. Cats hanging upside down from twisted pine boughs, eye her balefully through bangs of chin whiskers, and when she turns tail they throw harpoons into her backside. Cattails grow out of her buried-alive body; she realizes her grave is unmarked and no matter how loud she cries, no one will hear and resurrect her. She wakes in holy terror to the placid blue eyes of Aunt Hannah who has brought her hot porridge and a mug of chocolate. To come from where she has been and to confront that benign innocence! She could weep with relief, but all she can manage is a sickly smile.

"Nigh on to noon," Aunt Hannah says. "Thee must eat some, child, rest is not enough. Here, just freshen thy face with this wrung-out cloth."

"Aunt, are there thieves about? I looked for the silver salver and found it not. Nor that set of twifflers that was John's mother's."

"Oh, my dear, has thee forgot? 'Twas nigh two years ago. The Friends, every last one of us, refused to pay that French-Indian war tax. So then the local tax-gatherer forced entry and distrained the equivalent of the tax in valuables. I get hot all over when I think on that helpless day. Thee sick abed upstairs and Captain John away. What could I do? He said 'twas the law.'"

When Aunt Hannah departs, evil closes in on her again. This time, while the porridge thickens and the chocolate forms a scum, bees thick as fur crawl into her mouth and nostrils, trample her eyes with their feet-legs, investigate her belly button, sting her arsehole, cause a stink between her toes. She cannot brush them away because she is tied to a lying-down cross. Of course, only the scum is real. She picks it off in one piece with the tip of the spoon and sips the tepid chocolate.

It is the last tie to sanity—this distinction between the real and the imagined. When she can no longer tell which is which, she will be mad. So it is important to her and she makes these tests hourly, often minute to minute, for time stretches and shrinks like a spyglass and sometimes it has no existence at all. The books she cannot read are real. She has no attention span, she cannot concentrate, the words die like wild flowers on the page. The letters she cannot write are real. If she brings herself to the point of putting pen to paper, the thread of thought breaks off impishly in the middle of a sentence. There was a place not so far away where it would have broken her heart not to be able to write a letter. Fortunately she has lost her ambition. The purpose had been to make money and thus raise herself in others' esteem. But people (real ones) no longer furnish her life, save those in her household who are bound to serve her, and what could she possibly do with more money? John provides her with food, clothing, fuel, shelter, medicine, and a mort of things she has no use for: horses, cloaks, boots, rain gear, even a rig that lies moored in Great Harbor, its sails furled, its crew long since dispersed.

Horses and ships, what for? There are voyages aplenty to be had at her window, she is too weary to bestir herself. Getting out of bed takes an act of will,

dressing is a feat. And there are other reasons for not
going abroad. She might forget and raise her arms in
company revealing the black wet moons that smell like
low-tide flats. She might fall—a step looks wider than
it is, a doorway larger, a table farther away. Just from
wandering her own house, mostly her own room, her
body is a fretwork of bruises and candleburns. If she
did spunk up and go out, she might be greeted by
angry faces saying, "Thee's late," or " 'Tis the wrong
night." Or if she said a queer thing they might laugh.
So she goes forth no more, not even to Meeting.

Who knoweth truth? asked Pontius Pilate. 'Tis not
inconceivable that God may *reward* her for her cruises
on the magic carpet of laudanum. The drug mayhap
was invented for and put in the way of certain of His
children—the chosen ones. To the clods, opium country
may remain *terra incognita,* but to the intrepid, its
citizenship has its worthwhile segments. She does not
always lie prostrate under the incubus of nightmare;
sometimes her dreams are in color and joyous. There
are periods of exquisite tranquillity and moments of
exaltation when she knows the freedom of renunciation of the world, even as Jesus preached it. The lows
outnumber the highs, but this is true of real life, and
just as well too, for who could bear happiness for long?
Either its poignancy would tax us to death or it would
become dull.

The loyal Rachel Bunker confronted Aunt Hannah one day with the suggestion that Debbie Starbuck
be asked to pay Kezia a visit. "There must be some
way to end her solitary confinement."

"Won't see her own mother. What makes thee
think she'll see a friend?"

"We'll not ask her. Nor tell her. Let her be took
unawares."

"Well, she has ever loved Debbie," said Aunt
Hannah dubiously.

Eleven

Kezia's elbow rested on the sill. Her weight had made a little groove in the pine, as on an oft-trod stair. She would have liked to open the window so that she could merge with the twilight, but the window was stuck, or at any rate, she couldn't raise it, she had no strength anymore. The framed scene went dark blue as candles were lit behind her. She turned her head a fraction and saw shadows on the wall. She heard the light step. A log thudded on the fire and pine needles caught their breath. She turned idly. It was not Aunt Hannah. That broad beam was unfamiliar. She wanted no unfamiliars in her house. Who let who in? The matronly rear straightened to hang the black vessel on the swinging crane. Debbie Starbuck! Go to, Debbie, off with thee, let me be, there are too many walls between us, I cannot talk through walls, nor hear, nor wish to.

"My, this is a cosy room, Kezia," said Debbie in a matter-of-fact voice as if they had chatted but yesterday. "Fancy having one's own supper hook in one's own bedchamber!"

Kezia cast a wary eye, said nothing.

Debbie's knees cracked as she straightened up. She gave Kezia a crooked smile. "Getting old," she said.

"I wish I were old."

"May I use the ewer? I would wash the soot off my hands."

Kezia watched her lave her hands, remembering as from another lifetime the shape of them. Squarish, capable hands, not unlike John's.

"I must look like I was struck by the dry wilt,"

144

Kezia said, touching her hair. Aunt Hannah, or Obed, had brushed it at daybreak. Today? Or last week?

"Thee looks good to me," Debbie said casually, reaching for the towel.

"Do not make sport of me, old friend, I am not yet witless."

"Who said thee was? I merely said thee looked good to me. 'Tis good to look upon thy face, thin and pale though thee be." Debbie held up a bottle of wine. "Shall we splice the main brace?"

"I don't indulge in ardent spirits," said Kezia with a mischievous primness.

"Then, with thy permission, I shall quaff alone. I like a spot before the evening meal."

Kezia shrugged, but the walls were crumbling. When you have loved someone, the qualities that moved you once, move you again and again. Debbie sat and sipped and watched the flight of the flames. Kezia observed her from a shadowy corner. Debbie's face was the least plump part of her, there is no ruining good bones. The black hair was salted, but the beautifully shaped brows were still black, blue shadows still smudged the socketed eyes. The nose was as ever a mite flat, the Coffin nose, but the cheekbones were high and rosy and smooth, and under the full loose red mouth, the chin was rounded as a girl's.

"Does thee mind how we used to chant the names of the Forefathers?" Kezia asked, pressing her vertebrae to the cold wall.

"I have sung it with each child. Coffin, Macy, Folger, Swain/Gardner, Hussey, Stahhh-buck." Debbie laughed. "And now thee is a Coffin and I am a Starbuck, and I am fat and thee is thin, and little did we know what was in store for us or we might not have been so gay."

There was another silence.

"Why did thee come? I see no one."

"Shall I take my leave?" Debbie asked amiably.

"Nay, set a spell." Kezia slid down the wall and

sat on the rug, hugging her knees. She stayed just outside of the light. "But what is thy purpose?"

"I came to treat with thee, Kezia. This self-
imposed exile must end."

Kezia smiled silkily, taking down her hair, shaking it free about her shoulders. "*Must*—an arrogant
little word. No one says that to me anymore."

"The word *I* heard was *exile*. Pray, speak to
that."

Kezia, when she replied, spoke dreamily.

"Not exile, removal. To another country, midway
between here and there. Where time and space have
variable limits and rhythms. A moment of bliss is an
eternity. An eye-gouging takes but a second and there
is no blood, one heals the instant one wakes. There is
music and color in this sphere and they play simultaneously, long after the instruments have been packed
away in their cases. I do not always like this land, but
I am learning the laws of it. Once learned, acceptance
follows. One takes the bitter with the sweet, the pain
with the pleasure, and in this, is not one island very
much like another?"

"No. Some support human life. This does not. It
is destroying thee. Thee is drugged, Kezia. Aunt Hannah has told me to what extent. Thee must give up
laudanum altogether."

"Forthright Debbie. That is another word no one
speaks to me anymore. The name of my lover. It is a
pleasure to hear it."

"I should rather see thee sign on with a man."

"So should I, 'twould be easier to cut bait. I tried
once. Did not Aunt Hannah tell thee that as well?"

"I shall help thee. And God shall shed His grace
and mercy upon our concerted effort."

"They helped, prayed, too, and then pleaded with
me to go back to it."

Debbie, looking troubled, refilled her glass and
poured a little for Kezia.

"A divertive poison?" Kezia asked. But she sipped
of it.

"There must be a way. Where there is will, there is way."

"How old be thee, Debbie?"

"Fifty last Sixth Month. I never thought to live a half century. It seems little more than the twink of an eye."

Kezia wondered how old *she* was. She could not remember the date of her birth nor indeed the number of this year, but even of Debbie whom nothing shocked one could not ask what *year* it was. Once her mother had said to her of John, "he is nigh twice thine age." Likely she was thirty-two, thereabouts. Ghastly not knowing one's age, bad as not knowing one's name. She said, "Centuries, aeons, minutes, weeks, they are but words to me. I do not count time anymore. It relieves one of much of the stress of day-to-day living. Thee says fifty years have passed in a twinkling. Might not time be an artifact? Are not all measurements, all calendars, man-made contracts? Look thee, until a few years ago, Nantucket counted March the First Month. Then out of the blue, England said nay and now the First Month is January even for Quakers."

Debbie dished up the chowder, and as Kezia went quiet, she spoke of her disappointment in her daughter-in-law. "I tell thee, Kezia, she's as ugly inside as she is out. She punishes me by not bringing the grandchildren, and if I come to see them, she is barely civil. Of course, if Christopher's there, she has to be courteous. So I try to come when I know he's at home. Oh, Kezia, a hateful daughter-in-law is a curse and a blight."

It was bracing to hear another's troubles, but Kezia was getting edgy. It was past time. Should she cut the dose in half? One gram would do nothing, three might make her drift. Twenty-five drops equaled one gram. What was half of twenty-five? The numbers danced in her head, changing partners, playing hide-and-seek. Fifty drops came to the black line on the sake cup. Half of that and then a little more. She glanced at the ruby-colored flask on the lowboy.

"Has the time come for thy draught? Have it then, thee needn't feel constricted before me. I did not expect to be able to institute a cure this very night. Does it truly have a soporific effect? Perhaps I should have some, too, the wine has saddened me. I've wearied thee with my troubles."

Wearied? Yes, but it was worth it. She said, "I am glad of thy company, dear friend. And I *shall* have a potion now. Here, if thee would try some, but I give thee a very little for, like spirits, one must develop a toleration. It will lighten thy heart, I guarantee it."

"What dear little cups! Thee and John have such lovely things, Kezia. Hm—it has an odd smell, does it not? Well, down the hatch!" She made smacks with her lips. "I taste nothing but spirits. How long before it goes to work?"

Aunt Hannah came in to bid them good night. The fire was hot but low, a bed of coals, and in the flickerings of but two candles she did not notice that Debbie's face was flushed and shiny. Debbie had had very little opium, the equivalent of half a grain, but facilitated by wine, it had gone to her head.

"I have put a lantern westerly of the front door below, Debbie," said Aunt Hannah, "should thee need it to light thy way home."

"Do not go home, Debbie, stay the night with me," begged Kezia, as she had done as a child.

"Tristram—the children—"

"They're not babies," said Aunt Hannah.

"And they know where to find me. They know I'm not gadding—"

"Oh, good, then thee'll stay!" said Kezia.

And, "Good," said Aunt Hannah, whose head was in the chest of drawers. "Here is a nightdress, Debbie. Someone made it for Kezia as a gift and I have not found time to alter it to her measure. There is a trundle bed under the four-poster, or if thee prefers, thee may use thy brother's chamber across the corridor. 'Twas aired but lately. Thee'll find plenty of coverlets in his chest. And now, girls, I give thee a good night." Girls, she called them, and so they seemed to her, though she was born the same year as Debbie.

The smouldering coals turned gray as they talked, wrapped in quilts. Thinned by the windowpanes came the first cheepings of the sparrows.

Debbie yawned. "The laudanum, or p'raps the wine, has done me in," she said, propping up her eyelids.

"Sleep with me in my bed, Debbie. The trundle is narrow and John's room has had no fire."

"Very well, I mislike to sleep alone. When Tristram goes fishing off Siasconsett, I take the cat to bed."

"Shall thee be put off if I sleep without cap or gown? It has become my custom."

Debbie yawned. "Why should I mind? There's a mort of quilts to keep us warm. I'll do likewise, 'twill save washing the new gown."

Made drowsy by the wine and the laudanum, Debbie began to doze off as soon as she stretched out, but she roused as Kezia backed her buttocks into the cushion of her belly, and drew her arm around Kezia's concave middle. How spare the girl was! She covered Kezia's icy toes with her own warm padded feet. We have each failed her, thought Debbie, her dead father, her remarried mother, gypsy-footed John, I, even Miriam. No wonder she turned in upon herself, no wonder she sought anesthesia. Who can live without love?

"Little friend, despair not," whispered Debbie. "God willing, thee shall soon be well and strong again. I shall help thee. I promise it."

Kezia turned about and threw her arms around Debbie's neck, pressed her fined body into Debbie's ample one. "Help me now, Debbie, quench me now. Oh, am I clemmed with hunger for the taste and touch of human flesh!" She covered Debbie's throat and shoulders with kisses, buried her face in the pillowy bosom.

Of all the island women, no one was earthier than Debbie, perhaps in resistance to her mother who had

been of air and water and so insufficiently nourishing
to her young. Forbidden to pleasure her body with the
beloved, Debbie had vouchsafed it to her husband to
make what use of it he would. Through it had come
girls, boys, a set of twins, until she had come to think
of it more as a way station than a citadel or even a
private estate. Perhaps because she was the split half
of a hermaphroditic seed, she made little distinction
between God's creatures, loving all who showed their
need. Along with her firstborn she had suckled a ewe
lamb whose mother had been blown out to sea in a
March storm, and had once hatched a clutch of eggs
that turned out to be snakes. Years ago, when she'd
found her second son committing sodomy in a sheepfold, she had mildly explained that this was against
God's law and thought no more of it. Now, as Kezia
cried out her longing, she felt nothing but compassion
and a concomitant urge, natural as maternity, to assuage it.

She held Kezia close, murmuring endearments,
full of pity for the frail back studded as with nailheads.
Presently, their skins did the talking. She turned Kezia
on her back and caressed the quivering form. The
small, hard upthrusting breasts reminded her of Little
Debbie's which she had never dared to touch. As
mothers do, she had restricted tactile expression of love
of her children and grandchildren fearing to arouse
their sexuality unnaturally. Now she vented yearnings
she had long denied herself. The mouth that had not
tasted the honeyed lips, the silk-haired armpits, the
pink nipples of her sons and daughters, the fingertips
that had not learned their miniature privates, nor all
those downy bellies dimpled by her cord, she laid now
upon Kezia, and in so doing, deeply received. Under
her fondling, Kezia played like a sistrum, gave out
sounds more stirring than music. Hearing them, Debbie heard again across the canyon of years her own
cries under her brother and realized for the first time
the sense of power he must have taken from them.

Once Kezia's body had been reopened, her heart

flew out. Her tears sluiced down, slowly at first like blood from stigmata, and then in great racking sobs.

Debbie held her tightly as if to squeeze the effluvium to a stop. "Oh, my poor love, there, there. Give over, do, or thee'll tear us both up."

"I have—made thee sin—against God," Kezia got out between hiccups.

"Nay, nay. I have sinned long ere this and of my own free will. If God chooses to punish me, I am willing. Other foxes have lost their tails, if one lives, one loses. Now hush, enough of tears. Time for straight talk." Debbie set her away, held her shoulders in both hands, looked her in the eye. "Tell me, is this the reason for the drug? Thee prefers making love with a woman and fears the sin. Is that it?"

"I—I think not, Debbie. But I cannot be sure. I have known no man."

"What! Thee cannot mean it! Thy marriage is unconsummated?"

"Aye, but I assure thee, the fault is my own."

"Thee would not submit?"

Kezia began to cry again.

Debbie tipped Kezia's chin up, pinched it hard. "Now, belay. Thee's cried a two-gallon jugful. I want the truth. Why has John not mounted thee?" And to herself: And what was all that carrying on with Samuel Starbuck?

"I have no entry. My harbor is locked by a bar." Kezia spoke again to Debbie's puzzled frown. "My maidenhead is impenetrable. John declared it to be solid bone."

"So that's why thee has not fruited! Why did thee not tell me? *Some*one!"

"John forbade it. Thee knows what a proud and private man he be. And now I have broken my pledge to him. I've told the secret."

"Oh, nonsense, thee's not told it, thee's confided it, there's a difference. Sometimes I do wonder whether loyalty is a virtue or a folly. Oh, Kezia, what a waste! What an unforgivable waste! Well, no use crying over spilt milk. We must look forward, not back, and thank the Lord 'tis not too late, thee's still a young woman. Solid bone, indeed, the great booby! Oh, I blame John, I do. He's not unpracticed, he ought to know better. Could he be right? Well, if solid bone it is, Zaccheus Macy shall hack it out. I'll bring him by at eventide. Thee stay sober, hear?"

Tell a blind man he shall see, tell a deaf one he shall hear, and ask him to stay sober? Kezia paced, bit her nails, prayed, had incredible conversations and encounters with John. At length she went for the ruby flask. It fell from her hand. She watched the floor bleed to the rug. The rug drank and she considered getting down and joining it, licking the ichor like a dog. She picked up a large shard, sucking it carefully.

Obed put his head in the door. "What broke?"

"My mettle. Come in, lad. Clean up this mess afore I cut my tongue."

Zaccheus Macy was a carpenter and a miller by trade, a bonesetter and surgeon by hobby. He had performed more surgery on the islanders than even Nantucket's two doctors with whom he got along very well, perhaps because he maintained an amateur status, accepting no fees. He requested that Debbie and Aunt Hannah remain in the room as he stretched Kezia out on her back, flipped her dressing gown over her head, spread her legs, and reassured her as he probed, ignoring her muffled sounds. "All's I need's a minute to get the lay of the land. Mind, I be father to seven daughters and brought them all, so the territory's familiar. Ah, good, 'tis as I suspected, no more'n the cartilage in a turkey joint." He put Kezia's robe down, pulled up a chair to her bedside, took her hand in his. "Now, harken, lass. Thy maidenhead is indeed uncommon thick but not so thick it can't be reft by a single stroke of the surgeon's knife. 'Twill cause thee no pain and very little loss of blood, not more'n a few drops. However, I must tell thee I am of no inclination to perform this operation unless and until thee's off the poppy sauce. There is every likelihood thee'll conceive when John comes home, and a mother who's three sheets in the wind's no help to a growing child. Children need more help than they ever get under the best of circumstances. In all conscience, I cannot free thy womb until thee's firmed thy will."

Kezia was loath to take her hand away from that large cool firm dry pair. She reached under her pillow for a handkerchief. She blew her hose, wiped her cheeks, swallowed and swallowed the thin juices that flowed from her jaws. Her head was so stuffed up her earnest assurance sounded less than tragic. "Dear fred, without the wod I have do use for t'other. This tibe I shall fight to by last breath."

He smiled, patted her well-covered knee. "Thee'll not come to that. Trust me. Put thyself in my hands."

Another father! Kezia could not have enough of them. She clutched his hands. "Oh, I do, I do."

Kezia had declared herself willing to suffer the tortures of the damned, and for two weeks she did. She slept some of the time because they gave her sedatives, but mostly she rolled her hurting bones across the mattresses. It was as if the bed itself hated her. The battle between them was personal, spiteful, interminable, and she resolved that the first thing she would do when she was well was burn it. It and the knitted hug-me-tight that Zaccheus Macy made her wear constantly lest the fluid that poured from her swollen sinuses settle in her chest and cause pleurisy or consumption.

Zaccheus came once a day and sometimes read to her from *Plutarch's Lives*. "These public processions of the maidens and their appearing naked in their exercises and dancings were incitements to marriage," he read in his low quiet voice, and she could hardly wait for the knife. "In their marriages the husband carried off his bride by a sort of force. Nor were their brides ever small and of tender years but in their full bloom and ripeness." Then he would glance over the book at her—a piercing gem-blue stare—and sniveling and jumpy and belly-knotted as she was, she would know he was reassuring her that there was prime time in store.

"How shall I tell—uh—explain to my husband?"

"Send him to me. I'll pipe him aboard."

When the time came for him to leave, there was someone in the corridor waiting to take over the watch, either Debbie or Aunt Hannah or one of Kezia's staff. They labored with her in prayer. They supported her chin when her yawns grew violent, they held her head when she vomited. When she sobbed, they rocked her in their arms. When she jerked, they walked her about the room or sat on her legs. And over and again, Debbie would remind her of the light at the end of the tunnel. "Bear in mind what thee is suffering *for*."

Her mother came and fed her revolting things. Sow bugs to 'draw out the fever from her brain.' Burdock tea to 'thicken her body water.' For her cramps, ginger and rhubarb syrup. For her kidneys, raw sea fowl's eggs in stale ale. For her liver, the powder of red squirrel baked alive. And quantities of milk, cow's, goat's, even whale's, which doubtless washed out the poisons of the other remedies.

When she gained strength, Macy prescribed labor, hard labor in the house and in the field. It took her through the terrible emptiness of those first ambulatory opiumless days. With Hagar, she pressed cheeses, churned butter, ground forcemeat and spices and coffee beans, made cider. With Obed, she cleaned pewter and trimmed wicks, swept rafters, beat rugs. She balked only when it came to plucking geese, a cruel dirty business at which she feared being pecked. She preferred the outdoor activities with Shongo: sowing seed, milking cows, riding the commons to view her fences or the earmarks of her sheep. Nights after Bible-reading, Aunt Hannah set her to weaving tapes and ferrets and inkles on the small gallus frame, or she might sit in the fireplace and cut up sugar or sharpen the knives. They did not let her up to bed till she was fighting sleep.

Before long, they were advised by Macy to let her work alone if she wanted to. She was even allowed to replenish her medical stores. "Time now," he said, "that she be her own disciplinarian. If she have not the will, policing won't give it to her."

She had all the will she needed, what she lacked was appetite. "I fear John shall find me scrawny," she fretted to Debbie. "Verily it is hard to eat for fat. The very sight of a heaped plate and I am full." She looked down at her two arrowheads where there should have been 'twin fauns of a gazelle.' "Such poundage I have managed to accrue goes not where I would have it."

"Fret not," said Debbie. "Getting with child will fix that."

So it was that after a brief and unloved childhood, a prolonged and tormented girlhood, Kezia pitched up on the beach of womanhood. She had been wed eighteen years. She was thirty-five, a virgin, and by the time her husband came home in early April of that year, 1758, 'in full bloom and ripeness.'

Twelve

The morning his ship was sighted off Sankaty Head, Kezia raced around like a cuckoo. The warming pans, the firewood, the tinderbox. His bed—was it aired? His shore clothes—laundered? Supper—he liked pickled eels. Pipe tobacco, brandy?

Aunt Hannah put her hands on Kezia's shoulder. "Ease off, child. Go aloft and pretty thyself. Leave the rest to Hagar and me."

She slid the bolt on her chamber door and proceeded to make the toilette of her life. She scrubbed and oiled and perfumed her body from stem to stern. She washed her hair and brushed it and dressed it and redressed it. She rubbed her nails on the hearth brick till each finger was tipped by a smooth oval. She used lemon rinds on her elbows and pumice stone on her heels. In accordance with that remarkable manual *The Perfumed Garden,* long filched from John's store of books, she applied a mixture of antimony and resin to her armpits to keep them dry and odor-free. Lest she be guilty of that 'third of greatest evils,' a wide vagina —what *were* the proper measurements?—she washed her graces with a solution of alum and pear tree bark. And she dressed in new clothes from the skin out. Aunt Hannah had even made her a sack-back frock which was the rage in London and Paris. She was inspecting her moles when she heard Debbie's voice in the entry below. She grabbed up her capuchin cloak and ran downstairs.

Debbie had stopped by solely to urge her not to go to the wharf. "No point standing about till thee's fin out. Thee's still crowd shy. And he'll not fetch up till past dark, thee knows that."

"Debbie, I'm agoing. If for no other reason than to show the town I'm myself again."

Kezia was surprised at the number of people who came up to her. People whose names she had forgotten, faces no longer familiar. How could she sweat and tremble so? They but wished her well.

"Pert again? God be praised. What *was* thy illness, Kezia?"

" 'Tis not known for certain. Aunt Hannah blames an overdose of a medicine prescribed by Dr. Tupper. It left me with a most stubborn poisoning." And jabbed at Debbie who stifled laughter.

The name of his ship was unknown to her. The *Johana*. A Dutch woman? Was it too late? She prayed fervently, keyed up with interior images, attuned to impossible conversations. "Prettier women, I'm sure thee's had. Younger, more skilled in the arts of love. But *sons,* John Coffin. Only I—"

"Well, what says thee, Kezia?" asked Debbie, "Shall we not give up? We're the last. And Father's hurting. He's leaning on his cane."

Kezia felt the life seep out of her. Nothing had changed. All was as before. The wild preparation, the infectious excitement of the crowd, the conviction, bone deep, that this time, this once, he'd come ashore with the rest. This ship, like so many other of his ships, stood blacklimned beyond the bar. The dock was deserted, the same three remained: his father, his sister, his wife. The waters that had been silver and then milk in a red cup were now mauve, losing color as she lost hope. Landward, house and tree were black, the brush on the hills soft as animal fur. Windows that had blinked pink now showed tiger-eyes, and from the chimneys came pale curls of smoke. The pungency of other people's home fires induced a sadness so old it was like a friend. She suddenly felt an overwhelming desire for the heart's ease that only laudanum could give.

"Come, girls," Uncle Sanuel said. "Here's Nathan with the calash. I'll ride thee home."

"We have our horses, Father," said Debbie, alert to Kezia's dangerous mood. "Kezia's coming home with me to sup."

"Nay, come to my house," said Kezia. "Thee, too, Uncle, I beg it. Hagar has cooked up a tempest, I cannot face her. Debbie, send for Tristram and thy Zaccheus. 'Twould be a kindness."

Samuel Coffin had been looking forward to putting his gouty foot up, sipping his tot of preprandial brandy, and eating a bowl of supawn before a quiet fire, but he felt Debbie's pinch, and he said, "I'd be pleased."

Of the feast Kezia neither ate nor drank, nor did she contribute to the rather sluggish conversation. Uncle Samuel left immediately after the repast. The Starbucks stuck it out till curfew. Departing, Debbie whispered to Aunt Hannah, "Watch over her, she's in the doldrums." Aunt Hannah's squint dropped and eyes sharp as knife points made the promise.

But Debbie could not shake off the fantods. When Tristram snored beside her, she got up, dressed, and rode to the waterfront. She dismounted, slipped the fustian blanket from under the horse's saddle, wrapped herself in it, and settled down to wait. She set the lantern down harborside, hiding it from land's eyes. Her head dropped, she dozed. She started when the timbers shivered. There was only a high fingernail moon and a few dim stars—she could see nothing—but she heard a low exchange of male voices. She rose stiffly, her bones creaking like a weak bridge.

"—caution thee. Keep a good watch. . . . Fortune in nails alone . . . breathe easier when we're unloaded."

Her horse's sleepy whinny was lost in the splash of push-off. The oars squeaked in their bracelets, dipped and dripped, dipped and dripped. The man approached slowly, his stride lagging, his head down. In truth, she had seen husbands more eager to be home. She threw the blanket over the horse, picked up the lantern.

"Welcome ashore, Brother."

"Debbie! Is't thee? Hey, what's amiss? Father?"

"Nay, nay, he's cranky with gout, but otherwise sound."

"Ah, good. Gave me a turn. But thee smiles so 'tis nothing serious that brings thee here so late."

They looked at each other in the kindly light. John was thicker of face and waist, and showed a grizzled beard.

"Thee's coming around to portliness, old Bro."

"No more than thee, my dumpling."

They embraced each other. Arm in arm, they trod the dock boards.

"Now then, what's the word?"

"I bring news of thy wife," she said, her voice going grave with the importance of what she had to tell. "I thought thee should be forewarned."

"I know, my dear, I know. She's barmy with laudanum. I've known for years."

"Barmy no longer. Cured, John! Not only of the drug and all its ghastly symptoms but of the reason for succumbing to it! She's *altered,* does thee take my meaning? Thee can mount her now to thy mutual benefit and, with God's grace, increase."

"*What?*" He stopped dead, jerked away from her.

"Zaccheus Macy did the cutting, but that was the least of it. The cure of the drug, breaking her of the habit, that was the strenuous part. It required our most conscientious efforts and vigilance. But praise God, Kezia is herself again, well and healed, and so eager to wive thee, John, 'tis touching to see."

"The devil thee says!"

"What—*angry?* Where*fore?* I thought thee'd rejoice! I thought—"

"Thee thought, thee thought. With what? With a head like a whip syllabub, that's what! Eighteen years. Eighteen years, woman, and thee comes prancing up like a bloody fairy to tell me there's been some wand-waving and everyone's to live happily ever after. A tale for children. Thee witless meddler—blast thy folly! Blast and damn, I say!"

When his yelling stopped, the world died. Her breathing and the lapping of the water buried it.

"She told thee, the little blabbermouth!" he said, kicking sand. "And she gave her solemn word. I should have known. Once she became a hophead, 'twas but a matter of time before she blew the gaff. I suppose all of Sherburne is agog?"

"Nay, John, nay. I can count on my hand those who know. Father, Abigail, Hannah. Macy. He would not gossip, he's a most honorable man. Rachel Bunker and the servants who would die on the rack for her."

"I never heard of a secret kept," he growled, "not on this tight little island."

"This one has been kept. Even I did not suspect. I was brought into the picture apurpose. They thought I might help. And I did, and I was so happy to be able —we all were. Oh, John, thy rage is stunning to me. I am completely taken aback." Suddenly she thought of his ship. "The *Johana!* So that's it—thee's got a new woman!"

"New, old. All kinds and colors. Like many a salty seadog, I like a wild fowl flavor and red meat on the gamy side."

"Oh, thou wicked—libertine—cullion—!"

He deflected the hand that swung to his mouth, grinning evilly into her face.

Clearly but thinned by distance, a half-mile or so away, the night watch cried, "Twelve of the clock and all's well!" The extraneous voice gave John perspective. "Poor Debbie, forgive me. I am grown rough-tongued. Thee intended but good. Thee thought to give me and thy ward a great gift. Well, look, no real harm done. A touchy situation but nothing I cannot cope with. A double life's no new thing to me. Let's say a fillip has been added. Aye, by Harry, my visits to Nantucket may prove the more amusing for't."

She punched his shoulder. "Lout! I cannot bear it when thee talks so—base and cynical. Fillip? If this is all it means to thee, I'll see her sewed up again. She's thy wife, thee roustabout! A tender innocent virgin, eager to take love and to give life. How can thee be so—so cruel, so unfeeling?"

He took her threshing hands in his. "I'm sorry, Sister, calm thyself. I shall treat Kezia with consideration, I promise it. In truth, I am heartily glad she's off the sauce. Now she's herself again, she can return to trade. She's more cunning than I by half, and the sooner she lays up a supply of capital, the sooner I can quit whaling. God knows I have earned the respite. I see thee wears the shawl I once gave thee. Thee's due for a new one, I shouldn't wonder. Now, come, look here, there's nothing to cry about, thee great goosey."

"Quit whaling? Thee's like a lad about the sea, 'tis thy life's pleasure," she said, gabbling in an effort to control her tears.

"Anyone goes to sea for pleasure'd go to hell for pastime," he said, and he dried her cheeks with his pocket handkerchief. "Here, have a good blow."

She blew. "I was stupid, John, I see it now. I thought only of Kezia, not of thee. She was so lost, so ill."

"I know, thee'd mother the world if thee could. Might be all to the good. I've a low boiling point, thee knows that. Hate to be jolted, unnerves me. But now I'm over the shock, I can see advantage. I shall get a son of her and his name shall be John Coffin. A man wants to perpetuate his name. Praise God, there's still brine enough in me pickle for that."

The part of her that was womb-joined to him spoke slowly, groping through labyrinths. "That means thee has sons but they have not thy name." And there came to her now a limerick the jack-tars sang to speed their labors:

> *Cap'n Coffin, red-meat-eater,*
> *Took a wife and he did beat 'er.*
> *Took aboard an Injun gel*
> *And her he treated very well.*

So many Captain Coffins, she'd never associated. . . .
Yet Shana had quit the island twice, each time on a
day when a vessel of John's had sailed forth. Oh, she
had been dense! "And the woman, God shame thee,
a piece of her tail is emblazoned on thy ship. And
thee atop her, the first three letters of thy name, then
three of hers. Oh, thou brazen—!" She began to cough,
choking on jealousy. The women he had had—she
could bear the thought when they had no name, no face.
Kezia she could bear, a changeling who belonged to
both of them, the child they shared. But that a lasci-
vious Indian wench should have had the sweet strong
manhood of him while she pined in a too-soft marriage bed, went gross with motherhood, lost juice and
shape and bounce! Her voice was gravelly with phlegm
and bitterness. "A savage, an ignorant servinggirl
bonded to Abigail Folger! I should have thought thee'd
have more pride, better opportunity—"

"Opportunity I had aplenty and took each and
every one!" he spat out, stung as only she could sting
him. " 'Twas I who chose Shanapetuck above them all,
and rightly for she has been a good wife to me, blast
thy snobbery. And let me put thee wise to something:
her mother was not too savage for thy husband's uncle,
Jethro Starbuck. Shana's his half-breed daughter."

"A likely story."

"Does thee mind the cloven foot of thy deceased
daughter? 'Tis in their blood strain. Our boys, hers
and mine, are soundmembered, thank God. 'Tis said
the blight passes solely to females just as baldness af-
fects but the male. Well, I be not privy to the mys-
teries of heritage. But this I know, Shana is a queen
among women and is so treated where we abide."

"And where is that, pray? Some southerly island
of heathen blacks?"

"An island, aye, but not of blacks nor heathens.
We live in a sumptuous *quinta* on St. Michael's in the
Azores. The holding was granted me by a man high up
in court. Both Shana and I are received by the king."

"And doth the king also receive thy bastards?"

"They are not bastards, woman. Shana and I are handfasted in marriage."

"Thee cannot have two wives."

"Under English law, no. But under God's—*quen sabe?* To my way of thinking, 'tis the will of God that I have three fine sons. And so would thee think if thee could but see them, Debbie. Comely young men and strong, noble of character and of bearing."

"Yet thee gave them not thy name."

"For obvious reasons. I would not chance shaming Kezia nor our kin on this isle. They have taken their mother's surname—Cook. If thee goes by the law, she is the daughter of Titus Cook, descendant of Nicanoose. It is a custom in Spanish countries for the children to take their mother's name." Which was the truth, but not the whole truth—the custom was to take the mother's name and the father's, in that order.

"What does thee call them?" she asked more softly.

"Libni, Samuel, and John. Libni, the eldest, is seventeen. Samuel is fifteen and a half, but he has already passed me in size. I have wondered if the lush climate does not hasten human growth as well as that of fruit and flowers. Even the girls there ripen early, and the flowers grow in profusion, large as thy head. John is the baby, thirteen, his voice just now beginning to break, yet he has struck his whale."

She had little interest in his paternal pride. She heard an earlier sound—the sobbing of a grief-stricken lad at the untimely death of their elder brother Libni. "Thee still grieves him." She gripped his arm. "Oh, my beloved, how did it all go awry? For we were good, John, we were."

He shook her off. "For God's sake, unhand me. Let me heal. I do when I'm let!"

"Is that why thee named thy firstborn Libni? Because thee was healed? Was my hand on thee then?"

"God help us, Debbie, we are alone ten minutes and we growl like sick dogs. Oh, we know where the raws are and we flick and flick. We are pitiless."

She knew he was saying "we," meaning "thee." She said forlornly, "I came not to harass thee but to safeguard."

"Well, then, enough. 'Tis past midnight. I have been up since first light, working like a prime minister. I am groggy without a drop of grog. Let us to our homes."

"Shall we meet on the morrow?" Tristram's tenderness was no match for this kind of agony. Semen is pale sherry compared to the whiskey of blood.

"Doubtless we shall. And rest easy about Kezia, I shall be kindness itself." He kissed her hand and put her up on her horse. "Here's thy lanthorn."

"Thee keep it. My horse is surefooted and knows the way."

"Am I not as clever as thy horse? Take it, I say."

She wept all the way home, her tears stiffening her cheeks to buckram. Why was she in a state? Nothing had transpired, had it? Shana, the sons—but nothing was essentially changed, was it? He had kissed her goodnight. She would see him tomorrow. Maybe it was the changelessness that was upsetting. In the garbled scheme of things, she was on her way home to couple with Tristram and he to Kezia. Life would plod down the same ruts at the same pace to the same people and places, and once every three years or so, she would hold him for a moment in her arms or he would hold her and with the grace of God one of them would die so. More than half their lives spent, the best years, with less and less to look forward to. Mayhap no one won. Mayhap for everyone it merely ended. Two homes, two families (no wonder he had to work so hard), two tries for meaning, and he had no more answers than she. The lantern slipped from her grasp. She rode on, not even considering it.

He, on the other hand, walked home in fine fettle. He dodged the crier, playing criminal and constable, growing younger with each step. He thought on Kezia's 'alteration' until his gait grew loose as a drunken sailor's. Why, she'd be untutored as a nymph whereas

Shana had grown critical of late, so listless he believed she might have taken a lover. She had quickly adopted the foreign ways, and Latins for all their confessions (maybe because of them) were more easygoing than the English. Or maybe her boozing had killed her desire, though it had ever had the opposite effect on him. A virgin, eager to be wived. Hm ...

The latch string was out. A fire in the keeping room illuminated a tray of biscuits and cold roast fowl and a bottle of wine. He smiled at the hospitable array and then took the stairs two at a time.

The room was warm from the low fire and he stripped quickly. He almost fell headlong over a chair but he righted it and himself without fining his erection. The bed was warm with the heat of her body, though she was playing dead. Not a twitch, not a breath, but the small fist against her side gave her away. She was buttoned to the chin. His hasty fingers caught in a net of ribbons. Yards of cloth leaped and melted, bandaged his hands, swaddled his knees.

"Be ye *sewed* into this sack?"

She sat up and whipped off the garment. Then she curled to him, in and about him, her bones tenacious as ivy. Her hair fell across his ear and his mouth. He shuddered with delight. She was satin-flanked, hard-arsed, her breasts no riper than green walnuts; she was as he remembered her eighteen years ago, unchanged. Accustomed as he was to the malodorous folds of Shana, this wife was sweet as forbidden fruit, and the vigor of early manhood infused him. He buried his face in the damp hair of her delicate armpit, purring.

"Thee smells like a peach from Alçobaca." He would not let her wince away, but held her ticklish ear to his lips as he whispered, "And tastes like a plum, I could eat thee, every inch." She sighed and let him lick the ridges of her shallow navel. Her belly, smooth and flat, put him in mind of Shana again, that pendulous pile of blubber, and he could have wept that God was being so good to him. His head went lower to suck the honey from the bud under the springy bush when

—snap!—her legs crossed. Her knees might have been soldered, her insteps welded bone to bone.

The old John would have pried her open as ruthlessly as a pearl thief wedges an oyster shell, but this was not the old John, this was John growing old. Uncertain, cautious, he slipped upward and patiently began the seduction all over again. He put her face to his wounded shoulder—never yet a woman whose pity could resist that gouge—and stroking her spine, he whispered the things that women love to hear, an inventory of her charms, reiteration of his need. And was rewarded—she nestled, her mouth sought his. The kiss, ah, yes, he'd grown unused to kissing. Shana's breath was too strong. But Kezia's mouth was clean as a kitten's. His tongue swung around her smooth little teeth, lengthened into her throat, while at the same time his hand trailed the crease of her buttocks. But when he would have minded the fault, she locked again, pliable no more.

Greater than his frustration was his pride in his staying power. He exulted in his control, grew obsessed with the testing of it, so that when her legs again opened to him, he ignored the target she offered up, lightly scratching her inner thighs, lightly pulling the pubic hairs. Her head lolled, her belly heaved, but every time she would come, he moved off until he was standing on the floor and she panting on her back, her legs hanging loose over the bed. It was she who grabbed and put him inside her.

She was tight as a tick. He exploded almost at once. She was still struggling for climax, her pelvis high, her legs holding him fast when the shrunken key slipped the lock.

She lay silent alongside him, and he whispered, "Thee's small, love, but thee'll give. Be not disappointed, 'twill get better, thee'll see. Like anything else, takes a bit of doing." It was too fulsome an apology and unwarranted, dammit all, his premature climax was due to her constriction. Furthermore, his ejaculation had had abundance and force, a potency that should make a baby, if not a pair of them.

"I'm not disappointed, dearest." Kezia lied. "I know I want use and experience. We shall soon give each other great pleasure, I am confident of it."

Long after John's breathing had become regular, even a bit juicy, Kezia lay wide-eyed in the dark as burning of mind as of crotch. *The Perfumed Garden* had led her to expect too much. Perhaps it was written for that purpose—to inflame, not a treatise at all but the recorded fancies of a dirty mind. Or perhaps Arabian men were different from Nantucketers? The hot climate, the lazy life—?

"But John, what of the cargo? Thee's not been down to the wharf nor the warehouse nor the counting-house. Ought thee not oversee—?"

She opened her mouth wider for the porridge he would spoon into it. It was the third morning he had brought her breakfast, and now he insisted upon feeding her, calling her 'sandpiper,' fussing like a new mother.

"The devil with it. A pox on all houses—counting-houses, warehouses, every last one. What's a first mate for? And the crew's an industrious lot. Watch out now, 'tis hot. Here, let me blow upon it." He sat back and gazed at her. "I vow I could look upon thy countenance for a thousand years and not tire of it. Those delicate fly-away brows—"

"Thine are identical, as are Debbie's."

"Nay, thine are more delicately drawn. And the shape of the eyes, two perfect almonds. Do not tell me we have those. Nor that fine aristocratic nose, we are plank-nosed, we Coffins. And those provocative moles!" He kissed each. "I mind them not, did they spring up sudden?"

"I've had them long's I can remember."

He touched the one on her chin as if it were a snowflake and would melt. "Ah, precious bane."

She took the porringer tipping from his hand and set it on the candlestand. "I'd go to the wharf with thee, 'twould take but an hour or so, and the day is fair."

"Look, fretbox, I've told thee, my first mate's the best nanny a cargo could have."

"The *Mercury*'s just arrived from Portugal via the West Indies. There might be a letter from Godet."

"If there is, someone will deliver it."

He scooped her to him with one arm. They kissed and snuggled and nibbled. Gradually, the mood changed. They grew intent, a conqueror and his prisoner of war. The prisoner escaped, to the chest for stockings, to the wall hook for a dress. Another day in this chamber and she'd go out of her mind. As for human touch, she'd had enough in the last three days to last her three years. The tip of her tongue had a blue lump, her breasts were huckleberry marked, her crotch raw, the muscles in her neck sore from straining for climax. Indeed, except that she hoped to get with child, she found no great satisfaction in being entered, particularly the times she had to roll over to her knees like a good little dog (so debasing) or when he screwed her atop him, she waving about like a flag in the wind (so lonely). What of the sheikh and his fanciful Moslem poetry?

> . . . *a heavy crupper, a slowly coming*
> *emission,*
> *a lightsome chest, as it were floating*
> *upon them;*
> *The spermal ejaculation slow to arrive,*
> *so as*
> *To furnish a long drawn-out enjoyment.*
> *His member soon to be prone again*
> *for erection,*
> *To ply the plane again and again and*
> *again on their vulvas,*
> *Such is the man whose cult gives*
> *pleasure to woman*
> *And who will ever stand high in their*
> *esteem.*

Far from having a heavy crupper, John's bottom was as small as her own, and as white. He was shorter than she, stocky, thick-waisted. In a word, resistible. In bed, as in life, he came too soon. What if all this sexual exercise was for naught? What if his seed were no longer viable? Mayhap this Johana was as old as he and so, less demanding. Or very young and so, easily pleased.

"Is there a Johana, John? I mean to say, besides thy vessel?"

"On my honor, there is not."

She knew him to lie easily but she was inclined to believe him this time. For however short he fell of her hopes, he was certainly finding no fault with her.

Out of boredom she said, "We ought to give an entertainment, John. We cannot keep turning callers back. Folk would gam with thee, hear the news of thy travels, thy jousts with the whale, the changing prices of things, politics. Thee's not even seen thy sister Debbie."

He jumped up from the bed, began to poke viciously at the fire. "No true lover ever wanted company."

"Bear in mind, dear, I am not, have not, been as sociable as most. I've spent overmuch time in this chamber. Indeed part of my cure has been exercise and fresh air. Shall we not venture forth for some small diversion—a ride to Squam, have our fortunes told?"

"I have no interest in the future. The present suits me well."

"Thee *said* my wish, my every velleity, was thy command."

He came hurrying back, picked up her hair, and kissed her nape. "And so it is! Whatever thee'd have! The moon? I'll pluck it down for thee. A shindy? The very thing. Let all see how dear is my wife, how beautiful. Thee'd know our fortune? Then know thee shall. Fetch a hat, we'll ride out to the Indian village now!" He threw open the window. "Shongo, put a mare to the boxcart! Stir thy stumps, man!"

John threw some coppers in the old squaw's lap. Cuddusue blinked with turtle eyes. Little white flowers of spittle formed in the dark corners of her mouth, but she made no move to take the money. John pulled two sixpences out of his pocket and added them to the pennies. Cuddusue laid her pipe aside. Her thumb fed the coins one by one into her fist like a frog snapping at flies. They disappeared into the folds of her skirt. She looked from one to the other. Kezia nudged John who had promised to go first. He looked annoyed, blew threw his lips, raised his chin. Then he thrust out his hand, palm up.

Cuddusue stretched her neck over it and frowned. She chomped out, "A woman shall be born and a woman shall die."

Kezia gasped, clutched John's arm. "I shall die bearing thee a daughter!"

"Nonsense! She's an old charlatan! Not a word of truth in it."

"Oh, woe, woe is me," Kezia moaned.

Cuddusue caught Kezia's hand and turned it up. Her mouth opened twice by dropping the chin. "Long life."

"There! What did I say? Come, the stink in here's worse than trying blubber."

John ducked out of the sail flap, but Kezia stayed, wheedling questions. Would she conceive? Would she have a girl or a boy? Would the child be sound? Who was the woman who would die?

Cuddusue waved a brown gnarled hand, whether at the smoke or Kezia was not clear.

"Is it a woman named Johana? Thee has but to nod or shake thy head."

"The captain waits," Cuddusue reminded, showing toothless gums.

Kezia ground her heels into the earthen floor, put her hands on her hips. "And I—on thee."

Cuddusue knew of this English, of her willfulness. Everyone on the island in one way or another was known. And this one was kind to the dark-skinned.

"Come to me when the snow falls. Come alone. Bring rum."

Jogging homeward in the cart, Kezia wondered aloud why the gift of foretelling the future was more prevalent among Indians than whites. "Shana had it, too, elf-struck she was. Does thee ever encounter her in thy travels to foreign ports?"

"Who?"

"Shanapetuck."

"Aye."

"When did thee? Where?"

"Strange places."

"Such as?"

"In a sangaree when I stir it. In a whirlpool, an eddy of leaves or of water or dust."

He puffed on his pipe. Unlike Cuddusue's, his tobacco was aromatic in the damp air. She took it from his mouth and puffed and made a face and put it back. "Horrid."

He smiled.

"What does thee mean? Whirlpool. Eddy of leaves."

"Shana once said that in the center of every whirlwind was a little god. She claimed she was such a god. She said I should know her to be near whenever I saw one."

A man by the old mill waved and John lazily saluted.

"*Thee* gave her the wedding gown I wore, did thee not?"

"Aye."

He guided the cart around a belled cow.

"Dost love her still?"

"Nay."

"Dost love me?"

She ought not have asked—it was a sign of weakness—but somehow his laconic pipe, his strong jaw, the image of him lying with another, made her want to surrender her power. She let her head fall on his shoulder though they were clattering down Centre

Street, part of the 'pass' that folk surveyed from their front windows at this rest hour between chores and supper.

Shongo was waiting to take the horses. Aunt Hannah was sitting on the front stoop, watching the to-do at the wharf. A whaling sloop was in. John and Kezia stretched their necks to the harbor.

"Captain Bocott is already on the dock," Kezia observed. "Not like someone I know who ever comes ashore by dark so that none may say welcome."

"Aye, I see him. 'Tis only up close my eyesight's failing. If thee should find thy spectacles gone one day, Aunt Hannah, thee'll know the thief."

Eyes going? Well, of course, he was as old as Aunt Hannah. Half a century! Shocking thought. She dodged it by remarking the sunset. "That sky, did thee ever see such color? No wonder they call it royal blue. I vow I could bow to it, worship it!"

"Kezia!" Aunt Hannah reproved the paganism, but John thought of a sapphire ring he'd given Shana that Kezia should rightly have. How mixed up life was, how proud he'd be to show this wife off to the king instead of that fat colored bousy witch. Soon ripe, soon rotten, the old sayings held, and now he was one of them: no fool like an old fool.

The wind blew pear blossoms that caught in their clothes. Kezia picked and ate two petals off his sleeve, and tried to make first John and then Aunt Hannah taste some.

Captain Bocott at the helm of a teeming boxcart hove to at their house. He reached into his pea jacket and brought out a white square. "Piece of mail, Cap'n Coffin."

John shook hands with the young captain. "I thank 'ee and bid thee welcome ashore. From what I can see without the glass, thy vessel's setting well down in the water. Greasy voyage, eh? Good to be home, I'll warrant. Quite a school of herrings thee's got there."

After supper that evening, Mary and William Starbuck dropped in to visit with John, as did Tristram and Debbie. Mary was expecting. Kezia put both hands on her sister's belly.

"The kicks are uncommon strong," Kezia noted. "Does that signify a boy? Do they hurt?" She was not certain sure, but she thought she was late for her period.

"Nay, but the hiccups do. They go on and on, sometimes for an hour. That tries me sorely."

Aunt Hannah and Kezia and Mary talked woman talk. William told Tristram about the difficulties of making shingles and Tristram told William about the trials of fulling, and John and Debbie talked earnestly under the stairs. So it was not until bedtime that Kezia thought to ask about the letter.

"I intended to show it thee," John said. "I must have left it downstairs."

"What a pleasant day this has been!" Kezia sighed. "Was the letter from—" she saw John step out of his trousers and the name sank slow as two pearls in the sea,—"Godet?" The member she had hitherto seen was long and thin with a blue pulsing vein. This one was totally unfamiliar, thick and empurpled, and it slanted upward. As if her vulva had eyes, she felt a blush between her legs.

"Aye. Prices and such," he said, donning a nightshirt.

There was a time, as recently as that day's morning, when Kezia would have been curious about "prices and such." Now she was not even faintly interested. She held her hair up and felt her breasts melting. "Ah, well, time enough on the morrow."

"Aye."

They spoke little, eyeing each other covertly, moving warily, stepping high and slow on the balls of their feet. An imminence like a sea change hovered in the room. The blue and white drapes had an alien look. Even her hands and feet looked strange to her.

John took a few swigs of the Madeira he'd set up on the hob. "Sup?" he asked, holding out the flagon.

From its color it might have been laudanum. If

it had been, she'd have drunk it because he offered it.
She swallowed the burn, and when her mouth acci-
dentally brushed his thumb, the hairs on her spine
rose.

"Get into bed. Hear the rain?"

She obeyed and watched him from under the
covers. He threw some savins on the back log. They
flared and he stepped back quickly, his face and chest
blazing like an Indian's. He was in a mood, there was
anger in him, but not at her; she could not evoke this
intensity of feeling, she was never more than a toy or
a tool to him, she knew that all too well. Yet she was
grateful to be the beneficiary of his rage. Thus far as a
lover he'd been rather silly, besotted with her but un-
satisfying. Passion, even obliquely aroused, was preferable to dotage. He blew out the candle and she lost
her breath. The shaft of air as he lifted the coverlet
raised goose bumps on her skin.

The minute he drew her to him, she surrendered
rather than submitted, willing—nay, eager—to be mis-
handled. Does not an herb want bruising for release of
its fragrance, does not a fruit give juice when nicked?
But he did not mishandle her. Whatever had vented
his spleen (something Debbie had said to him under
the stairs?), had also made her dearer to him and had
empowered him sexually. Gaining confidence, she
plaited with him, active, sinuous. It was not unlike
merging with the ocean when drugged, rolling with the
swells, increasing with the tide, running headlong to
shore. Drugged, the crash never came but simply faded
into uneasy oblivion. Now she was party to a rising
violence, insistent upon climax. Good destroyer, omnip-
otent father, forbidden brother, take me, break me,
stop my breath, grind my bones. She went down in a
vortex of unendurable rapture and her cries mixed
with his raucous gasps.

Pressed to the crack in the long chamber door,
Aunt Hannah slid to the floor in a dead faint. Obed
hissed in the corridor, rose from the floor in one feline
stretch and sought Shongo in the loft. The lovers

heard no sound. Fitted as one, they attended only to Kezia's honey-cove which throbbed gravidly nine times. Spent, he did not leave her. Drained, he yet filled her, even the mouth in her head felt full though their lips no longer conjoined. And, oh, he was lightsome on her chest. "Praise be given to God," as Sheikh Nefzaoui had written, "who has placed man's greatest pleasure in the natural parts of woman, and has destined the natural parts of man to afford the greatest enjoyment to woman."

Thirteen

They were an entity, an island within an island, time and people flowed about them without touching their high ground. One day they lay under a tarpaulin in the box wagon, waiting out a shower, and the next they made love in a bed of daisies at Siasconsett. Sometimes they were good together, often they were not, and if they were not, the poignancy of their love oddly intensified. Neither asked perfection of their bodies, only that they be in constant touch. Like the lilies of the field, where they spent a good deal of their time, they accepted the necessaries of life—meat and drink and shelter—from others with the preoccupation of lords.

The general feeling on the island was that they had waited long enough for this moment of happiness. The sternest of Quakers were inclined to indulge their fecklessness and obvious lust, counting upon them for nothing, poking fun, spying, gossiping, but letting them be.

"Didst catch a glimpse of the Lovers when thee put in at her shop?"

"Nay, but I did hear them larking about in the upstairs chamber."

"Did? Do tell!"

"Oh, scuffling and laughter and kissy sounds that humbirds make. Midafternoon, mind, enough to make a trollop blush! Must say, don't seem to hurt their trade none. Custom was three deep at the counter and Rachel Bunker sold me the last packet of pins."

So went the tattle over dooryard fences, at the town pump, in the marketplace. And down at the wharves the jack-tars sang the pair into folklore. On slow days at sea, whittling skrimshander or sewing sail, they had long sung a favorite:

> *The hat of Quaker John Coffin*
> *Is strictly for wearing not doffin'*
> *Not so with his breeches*
> *He doffs 'em to bitches*
> *And fame says he doffs 'em quite often.*

Now there was a new one to add to the legend:

> *The vogue tells of Mistress Kezia*
> *Whose hole went so high and no higher*
> *She had nobbut a clitor*
> *Till the Doctor did slit her*
> *And now she sets pizzles afire.*

And in the ordinaries and the countinghouses, family men put their oars in.

"Oh, he's come about a proper landsman, he has. Offered to take his turn at the night watch. Told him no, Kezia had more need of him nights than the town did. Offered to appoint him hogreeve though, that scared him some."

"Laugh, old lubbers, but were my woman as toothsome as Kezia, I'd never get up out of bed."

"Aye, sweet piece of tail, that. Never surmise she'd been ill so long. 'Tis like she riz up from a long spell of sleep, smooth-faced as a baby's bottom. Don't look thirty."

"When she expecting?"

"First Month as I heard it."

"Didn't waste time once Macy opened her hatch."

"Zaccheus Macy?"

"Aye."

"*Cut* her? "*Where?*"

"Where d'ye think, dunderhead?"

"Born battened? You don't say."

"All manner of queerness hereabouts. Comes from marrying close kin."

"Pity they didn't call Macy sooner. Mite late for a first lambing."

When the Lovers, as they were called, came to Meeting, a rustle went up even before heads turned. If they came to an entertainment—the last to arrive and the first to leave—the air would rarefy as invisibly as fur on a cat's back. They were aware of the stir they created, but, two against the world, they enjoyed it. They were never apart. When Kezia attended the delivery of her sister Mary's child, John hung about outside until the women called him in to share the caudle cup. During Sheep Festival, she washed lambs with him, the only girl among the men and boys, and when she fell into the pond, he carried her out piggyback and sprawled alongside her in the sun till her hair was dried.

It was not only the human populace they interested. Rabbits peered at them out of thickets; fauns came to drink at the brooks where they lolled; birds took crumbs from their hands; fish—when they ran out of bait—swallowed their bare hooks. Miracles became commonplace to them. Take the time they stayed overnight in an untenanted stage on the south shore. The day had been bright and warm but a thunderstorm came up suddenly, and, too, the horse was a bit lame from having picked up a thorn in his foot. Kisses and wild strawberries and leftover pilot biscuit would have been supper enough. Instead, awaiting them on a shelf in the hut was a smoked ham, a wheel of cheese, and half a pipe of hard cider. Some Indian who'd helped himself to his employer's stores would know he'd had visitors when he came to pick up his loot. But they returned thanks to one of his tribe: On Swain's Neck, they came upon a magpie cache—silver buttons and gold coins, some medals and a seed-pearl brooch. They brought it in its bed of dried grass, feathers, and lime to Reuben Swain's house, thus saving the accused Indian servinggirl from being whipped as an incorrigible pilferer. It was all in a day's ramble. Afterward, they splashed about in the upper harbor, picnicked at

Quaise, drank from the Shawkemo spring, made love in a sunny hollow which some sheep vacated for them. It was better on hard ground. Learning this, Kezia privily bade Obed slip a thick plank between John's feather beds. To Shongo, Obed gloomed, "Pray she don't kill our old master with all that humping. I know his back's hurting, he has asked for a board in his bed."

Quaise commons was their favorite grounds. She'd have shown John the cave on the beach but for her childish promise to Samuel Starbuck. Mixing bloods, what a cockle-brained waif she'd been.

"A good piece of Quaise will come to us," she said to him. " 'Tis so writ in thy father's will."

"Told thee that, did he? More'n he told me. Well then, mayhap we'll build us a country seat. Why not? Our children gamboling the meadows. And I shall teach them to swim as I taught thee."

"Them?"

"Of course. Twins. They run in the family. We must make up for lost time."

She grabbed his hand, held it to her cheek. "Oh, John, I am so happy. We are a natural couple at last."

But they were not a natural couple and they both knew it. 'For thy thoughts are not my thoughts, nor thy ways my ways.' Now that she'd fought her way back to it, she was a celebrant of life; she cared, hoped, strove, waiting breathlessly for it to begin. Whereas he seemed to have a deep weariness of it, self-serving because he felt himself damned and would wrest a few rewards during his brief stay this side of hell. She no longer believed his love of Debbie stood between them, rather, his love of doom. What made him so? Mayhap he was born in the small end of the egg, very often one twin had the best of it. He seemed to lack heart, and that lack held her fast; she had an imbedded need to be unloved. He made love with a caprice born of torment, neither giving nor taking fulfillment but only surcease. He used her now as she had used laudanum. For reasons she did not grasp the dosage was increased, but as with all addictions, its efficacy would be temporary. It was a matter of time till he sought new and stronger pain-killers.

"Oh, if this honeymoon would never end!" she cried, breaking from his kiss. "If thee would fare by my side!"

"I purpose to."

She measured her stride to his. "Or if go thee must, take me with thee?"

"Aye."

"The babe too?"

"The babe too."

"Liar, liar! If thee counted upon a future here, thee'd not yes my every whim, thee'd pave the way for an easy fatherhood. I was but testing thee."

On the bed, he runs his finger down her from the tip of her nose to King Solomon's line. He tells her the story of why she is thus divided and it is as if she has heard it for the first time. Always before she has identified with the child in the allegory; now she is the mother, and she avers dreamily, "I should do the same were it our son," and kisses his ungouged shoulder, saying, "Thy flesh is smooth as a stripling's. Could it be the whale oil with which thee is ever copiously anointed?"

"Thy flesh is not only smooth but flawless," he returns, kissing hers. "There is not a mark upon thee. Why am I so blessed? God must indeed love a sinner."

She thinks of the recent bruises and bumps, black, blue, evil green. "I believe He does." And after a bit, "Thee does not find me too thin?"

"Nay, all others fat. Thee is a hyacinth among thistles."

"I do have breasts now."

"Thee may thank me for them."

"And for the queasy stomach."

"That'll pass. Then thee'll get cravings, an appetite for all manner of strange foods—pickled limes, sauerkraut—"

"What knows thee of a pregnant woman's cravings?"

"Why—er—ahm—everyone knows. Even the Bible tells of it: 'Speak to me of apples, stay me with raisin cakes for I am sick of love.' "

"Tell me true, John. Has thee ever—does thee have any children?"

"From sea to sea, I should think. Now, sleep fast, old lady, for at suncoming we ride pillion the length and breadth of this porkchop. I have always wanted to do it. I may make a map."

And at suncoming they do. But from one end of the island to the other, she bids him farewell.

"When thee leaves, I die."

"Then prepare to live forever."

"Thee's faithless to the core, and well I know it."

"Was. Now, thee's spellbound me. Look, worrywart, I am at the rainbow's end, smack dab in the center of the universe with my love beside me. Now why should I leave?"

"How can I believe thee?"

"Dost call me liar?"

"The most practiced one ever I met."

"Doubting Thomas! Did I not send my first mate to the main to refit the *Johana*? Why, I've not even been down to overlook the brickworks they're fashioning for the deck."

"But refitting for what? For a journey, that's what, not for rocking idly in the bay surely. If thee must go awhaling, John, I pray thee set not thy foot in the longboats. Stay on the mother ship. Were thee not the owner of the vessel, thee'd be grounded or restricted to cod fishery. Not a man over forty is signed on to a whaler."

"Thee finds me old."

"Not I, dearest, but thee's earned a rest. Let some other master the *Johana* while thee bides home at least till the babe is born."

" 'Tis a thought."

"Then thee'll do it?"

"I shall think on't. Now hang on to me, sweeting, we're for home and breakbroth. If thee does not eat some, thee'll soon be qualmish."

Under his spurring heel, the horse breaks into an easy canter.

"Faster, John, faster, I want to feel the wind!"

But there is no outdistancing her anxieties. They lurk and pounce, at once the taint and the piquancy of every word, kiss, touch. When? When will he 'take the wings of the morn and dwell in the uttermost parts of the sea'?

The date of his departure was actually set the night the lighthouse caught fire. They had supper guests that night, Kezia's cousins, the Timothy Folgers, Timothy having just returned from a voyage. Afterward in the keeping room there was light enough without candles for the ladies to knit by. It was a warm evening, and the windows were open to catch the soft-blowing trades.

John, handsome in a new amber-colored frock coat, lit his and Timothy's pipe with some tongs that held a coal from the cook fire.

"By George, I forgot," said Timothy, hand sliding into his coat pocket. "I have this letter for thee. 'Twas given me when we took on wood and water at Fayal. Some Portuguese fellow sent it up by lighter."

"Permit me," John said, slitting it open.

Timothy noted John's scowl. "Bad tidings?"

Kezia twisted about to see her husband. "John?"

"Another missive from Godet is all. But there is a piece of business involved, a bit sticky. If thee'll excuse me a moment."

"Can it not wait till later? It's been a long time on the road," Kezia said mildly.

John was already on the stair. "Be down directly."

Timothy was knocking out his pipe, his wife, Abial, was counting stitches, and Kezia was lighting candles when the hue came in from the street.

"Fire! Fire!"

They rushed to the windows.

Timothy flung open the front door. "Where? Ho, warden! What burns?"

"The lighthouse, Brant Point!" trumpeted the town fire warden. "Grab a bucket, spread the word! I'm to the watchhouse for the fire engine!" The exhilaration in his voice could have rallied an army.

"My God," Timothy said. "My ship's moored thereaway. We've not brought in the cargo."

William Coffin, running by, shouted to John who was hanging out of the upstairs window. "Get a move on, Brother, thy ship's off the point. Thee'd best upanchor. Thee too, Timothy!"

Aunt Hannah, wet-handed from the hall sink, peered over Kezia's shoulder. "The lighthouse, eh? Pray God, it ends there. Which way's the wind blowing?" She held up a finger. "I make it a west wind, and freshening."

John came running down, tugging on worn duck trousers. "Timothy, take one of our fire buckets. Where's Shongo? Go run to him, Obed. Tell him to tackle up the horses. Fetch the ladder and the hooked pole. And then make haste, lad. Find Mister Worth, my first mate. Have him round up my crew. Our ship is perilously nigh the fire and we've bricks and casks on the beach."

"I'm coming too!" Kezia was tying on her hat.

"Nay, stay here out of harm's way." John shoved her back from the door.

"Thy shirt, John, thee's naked!"

"No need, 'twill be hot enough without!"

"Abial, get thee home," ordered Timothy. "If the wind should change, wet down the roof and the east wall."

"Take care, Husband," said Abial, standing on tiptoe to kiss him. "Thee's more to me than any vessel."

"A full cargo," Timothy moaned as he ran. "And the duty paid!"

The men swung up on their horses.

Kezia ran after them, caught John's rein. "Wait, John, hoist me up!"

"Kezia, I forbid it! Risk a miscarriage? Aunt, lock her in!" As he yelled, he smoothed his horse down, and just before he dug his heels into its flank, he caught Kezia a stinging blow on her upraised hand with a looped rein. "Back, I said!"

Kezia stood with Hagar and Aunt Hannah on the stoop, sucking her palm, glumly watching the madding pass. Not only men, but women and children. Blast him, the old fuddy-duddy, old enough to be her father and acting like one. The baby? It wasn't even a bulge yet. If *he* had to carry it—and oh, would that he did —she could see *him* staying home from a fire—in a pig's eye! She pounded the railing. "I want to go!"

Aunt Hannah put a hand on her arm. "Best not disobey. Captain of men all these years, he's not apt to take crossing from a woman. Besides, be sensible, what could thee do? Thee daren't lift a bucket of water."

"I'd *be* there! See the to-do!"

"There's some has got to go to a fire," opined Hagar sagely. "Firebugs."

"If the lighthouse goes," said Aunt Hannah, "the cooperage goes. And the brick manufactory and the sail loft. There's as much now at Brant Point as down along Straight Wharf."

"The new cobbler shop!" cried Kezia, for her sisters' husbands had parted company with the feckless Richard Pinkham and had started anew at Brant Point.

"Oh, my poor nieces," groaned Aunt Hannah. "Pray God, there's no oil casks about. Oil burns like brandy."

Kezia caught sight of Zaccheus Macy, alone in his cart, flicking loose reins. Now there was a man who'd not say no to her.

"Hold on, Zaccheus, I need a hitch!"

She started to leap the rail, remembered the baby, and took the steps.

Macy slowed for her, bent to lift her in, clucked up his horse again. "See the glow in yonder sky?" he yelled. "Terrible, ain't it? I'm behind hand because I stopped at the meetinghouse for the hooks and ladder. Mind the trolling bucket!"

"I can smell the smoke!" Kezia yelled back. "Wind's up! Gee the nag, man, or they'll have put it out afore we get there!"

Benjamin Coffin ran after them, ringing the school bell, calling, "All men to Brant Point! Citizens turn out! Bring hooks and buckets! Fire at the lighthouse!"

Kezia leaned over the tailgate, took Cousin Benjamin's hooked pole into the cart, freeing him to run less awkwardly.

The town side of the Brant Point fence was crowded with carts and tethered horses, a half-mile of them, and latecomers had a long way to run. The lighthouse was ablaze to its waist in a sky ruddy as an autumn sunset. Stripes of burning oil festooned the beach and a small field of harbor water bloomed solid with it. Kezia could feel heat on her face and breasts and thighs while the wind cooled her shoulder blades. Her breath came short and she held the pain in her side. "Hunker down," she told the baby. "We go where Dada goes. Get that straight right now!"

There were two lines of men—arms out like paper dolls—that stretched from the lighthouse to the shore. The tide was in and the furthermost wobbled in foam. The buckets went from hand to hand, up one line to the fire, down the other to the water, keeping the string of dolls wavery in the wind. Closer on, she could see John's brother William, white-shirted, reaching up from the top of a ladder to a figure outlined like a black star in a golden window. Closer still, she saw it was her John who was the star, standing atop the fire engine that was pulled up close to squirt the blaze. Hatted, shirtless, he held the iron pipe hard upon the darting tongues of flame. Below them, the fire warden and Zaccheus Macy worked the pump handle with such vigor that if John had not the iron nozzle to hang on to, he'd have been thrown to the ground. Behind the pumpers stood a second pair, waiting to spell the first.

Kezia's anxiety focused on the fire engine. She had heard grumbles about it being too small, but she had never seen it in use. Eighteen pounds sterling, this ridiculous English *toy*, no bigger than a boxcart. The wooden wheels wiggled with every jolt. How long could the crosspin hold? And the platform smaller than a crow's nest. Not even rigged for horses—the men had to drag it wherever the fire was, which in this case was over two miles of rutted highway. How could the elders have accepted this chicken coop? Why hadn't they sent it back, the slommacks!

She crawled through the spread legs of a link in the 'dry lane.'

"Hey there, get back!" cried the man above her. "Whipperginnie! Thee'll bake to a puddin and serve thee right!"

She ran to the fire engine, warding off the men who tried to grab her. She pounded on the sidewall of the engine. "John, the wheels ain't steady, take care thee don't heave overboard!"

In spite of the flames and the hard-hitting surf, her keening rose to him. He looked down and yelled toward the 'wet lane.' "Shongo, get her away! Take her home at once!"

Shongo broke from his line. She struggled with him and lost her hat. He poured the contents of his bucket over her bared head, and in one graceful armloop hurled the empty to Obed who ran with it— giving wide berth to a burning cask—to the ocean end of the line. Then Shongo flipped her over his shoulder, his arm holding her skirts closed around her, and ran to the fence.

"Let me down. I'll have thee whipped!" screamed Kezia, her fists slipping off his naked back. "Thee and thy catamite!"

Shongo threw her across the front of the saddle of someone's horse and mounting held her down while she shrieked and kicked and pummeled and finally bit him on the arm. No warrior, he cried out like a boy, but he kept on galloping. In the street at her house front, he set her down hard on her heels. She had a steamy whiff of horsehide and then a taste of dust.

"Red pig!" she yelled after him. "Savage! Buggerer!"

The wind whipped her wet skirts, blew cold on her damp hair. Out of consideration for the child within her, lest she take a chill, she went to her bedchamber, stripped and donned dry night garments, fuming aloud the while. Then she sought Aunt Hannah to rail against men. But the house was totally deserted. Aunt Hannah's bed had not been lain upon. Hagar was gone. Only she was put away, out of the thick of things, alone. It occurred to her it was the first time she'd had the house to herself since the 'cure.' And there was laudanum in the house too; she'd seen some in John's black leather shipbox which she'd gone through out of curiosity to see what was considered indispensable by seamen. The mischievous thought died at birth. Not her. Not now. There was the babe to think of, a reason for living above all others. Tenderness and gratitude engulfed her. John was perfectly right. She had no business at a fire. The dear man, she should not have flouted him. When he returned, she'd apologize, she'd promise not to behave so unseemly in future.

Through his open chamber door she caught a glimpse of his amber coat lying in a heap on the floor. She went in to fold it and lay it with loving hands in his chest. Then, she remembered the letter Timothy had delivered. The fashionable new coats had no outside flap pockets, only an inside one in the lining, empty save for a clove. 'Sticky' piece of business. What might that be? She looked about, but the letter was in none of the likely places. She began earnestly to look in unlikely ones and found it, stuffed under the seat cushion of his wing chair.

The stationery, noted the shopkeep in her, was top quality. Hm, was Godet's percentage of profit grown so high that he could afford Holland vellum? She took the letter to her room and held it by the candle. The script went steeply uphill, the hand studiously rounded with none of Godet's arrogant illegibility. Perhaps the missive had been copied more than once for though there were two blots, there were no crossouts.

> LaQuinta
> Punta Delgado
> Sao Miguel
> Azores, Portugal
> March 31, anno domini,
> 1758

Honour'd Sir:

My preevjus letter must did not reech you. In it I writ how our little mother was very ill. Doctor decreed the aylemint been of the livver. Now is dead the little mother. Qué tristeza, qué pena! But she met her God very pure. For one week preevjus she ate onlee white foods: Batata, peito de galinha, pão, flesh of apple, flesh of pear, white of egg, etc. Drank cow milk mixed with vinho branco—no Rum. Lencol branco, caixão branco according to her last wishes. The Count hee sent a pony cart full of lirios da ressurreicão. The bells of the church were wrung and many candles lighted.

Samuel and João remember their love to you. We intreet your return. There is many thing we do not know to do. Con sua licença I would take as wife the same Menina Ana de Mendez Rojas.

Wether fair after heavy rains and tides.

> I am with best respects, dear sir,
> Yr. Dutiful son,
> Libni

She let the letter flutter down from her hands, a leaf the tree is done with. Her heart began to thud and then to pound and then to palpitate so wildly she could think of nothing else but it; only peripherally did she play with the identity of the mother. Some grandee's daughter, dark-haired, olive-skinned, a foreign replica of herself to assuage his frustration? She held her cheeks and listened to her heart. She felt no pain, mental or physical, merely intense surprise. No, not surprise, shock. There might, of course, be pain later. But right now her heartbeats utterly absorbed her. Was this what was meant by a heart attack, an attack on one by one's heart? But heart attacks were supposed to be painful. This attack was so fascinating as to be diverting. And her cheeks were hot. In heart attack did not one go livid?

She walked to the mirror, taking deep breaths, not only for herself but for the babe. She observed herself. Her eyes were shining and huge and her cheeks were red. Fever or the fire? The *fire!* Was that tonight? It seemed miles and weeks away. How strangely relative and discrete were public events. Strained through the fabric of private crisis, they lost sand. She grimaced and popped her eyes, punishing, making fun of her reflection. Oh, how adorable, how beloved she had fancied herself! This is the way of life, stupid gawk, she told the clown in the mirror, high time thee faced it, shall thee never stop trying to spin flax into gold?

She lay in crucified position on her bed in the dark. She heard Aunt Hannah come up and listen at her door and then close her own. John too would think her asleep and be glad of it, tired after the firefighting. How simple he must find her, he with so many lives she knew nothing of! Ugh, the humiliation! Her very skin shriveled with lack of esteem. Her heart lunged—he must not find the letter gone, not tonight, the morrow was soon enough for confrontation. She swung out of bed, tiptoed to his chamber, stuffed it into the chair's upholstery.

Back in bed, she lay with her eyes wide open. She became ashamed of the triviality of her thoughts, but they were all she had, not a feeling to bless herself

with. Thoughts, for example, on the names of his sons.
Libni was his dead brother, that name they could
have and welcome, but 'Samuel' and 'John'—with those
used up what remained for her? There was no one of
her kin she would perpetuate. She liked her young
brother Daniel, but his name was the same as her hateful father's, also her rather oafish stepfather's. 'Zaccheus'—for the good doctor who made it possible? But
people would ask why, the child would wonder.
'Adam,' since like God's it would be her firstborn? Or
was Jesus to be counted His first, and why did Quakers
never name their children Jesus? Thoughts like that.
Overriding the event that provoked them.

When she heard his footsteps on the stairs, the
palpitations started up again. Her breathing came so
shallow and fast, she pressed the quilt to her mouth.
When she realized he was not coming in, she pulled
the quilt down and coughed quite loudly. His move-
ments sounded lurching, she heard him fall and curse.
Tired or drunk? There was always a tappit hen of whiskey passed around after community efforts like firefighting or house-raising. She heard him snore and then
the birds' tentative wakings stirred her.

She lit a candle and took it down the stairs. In the
pungent cuddy off the hall, on a shelf with her own
potions and simples, John's leathern ship box was
stored. It was beautifully made, a foreign importation,
the brass catch embossed with the initials *S.C.* His
father's before it was his. One of the things, rightfully
her son's, that would go to Libni? Each compartment
was fitted with a corked glass bottle and each bottle
was marked with a sticker, its contents named in John's
neat hand. The third cubbyhole from the right. The
knowledge that it was there to resist had given her a
good feeling these months. But now she could not trust
herself. She took it through the back door and poured
it out on to the black grass. Would he miss it? If he
did, she'd tell him she had dumped it out, and she'd tell
him why. And he wouldn't give a tinker's damn. No
more than she cared that the sky was dark now over

Brant Point. No more than the psalm singers in the cart that rolled quite nearby.

"Shut your traps, you libertines, good folk be trying to sleep!" some woman yelled.

"Tush, witchling! But for us libertines thy house might now be afire!"

The singing did not resume. The quiet was stabbed twice by laughter, and the wheels clattered off.

She had breakfasted and stood gazing out at the harbor when she felt his arms around her, his mouth on her neck. She hunched up. "Who was the woman— the 'little mother?' "

His hands dropped from her breasts. He moved away and she knew without turning her head that he was at the east window, staring out, seeing as little as she. She repeated the question, her voice gritty.

When he told her, she felt punched. She had expected—what? An exotic myth, a Negro princess, a *grande dame,* a titled cynosure, a mermaid, nothing imaginable. Anything but an Indian cripple who had emptied chamber pots in the poor home of her girlhood. Outcast, heathen, Jezebel—this he had chosen as her surrogate, mother to his sons? Yet underneath her outrage and disgust (the word *jealousy* was not permitted in her vocabulary) she knew these social labels to be false. Shana was universal, supernal, authentic, belonging nowhere, the equal of anyone.

"If I had known—had dared to hope that some day thee'd be a proper woman—" John faltered.

"Who on our isle knows?"

"Only my sister Debbie. I told her when she met me at the wharf the night I arrived."

"She went there after she left here. To tell thee of my alteration."

"Aye."

So that was how he had known, and come straight to bed! Dear Debbie, oft-tried, ever-loving friend. Gone to smooth the road, to warn, to protect. Tears tore at her throat. She swallowed them whole. Her jaws clenched so hard the muscles of her throat quivered but she would not cry, she would not. Her hands went to her belly and there grew quiet. Her throat unlocked.

"The previous letter thee had of Bocott. It was not from Godet. It was from Libni telling she was ill. And thee did not go to her."

He was on her in a flash, his hands, his lips, turning her, clutching her to him, shutting off her breath. "Kezia, I beg thee, try to understand! Try to see my side. How could I leave thee then? Our love—newfound, such happiness! How could I risk the loss? How could I hurt thee so?"

She fought him away. Her tears were of anger now, not soft ones of pity for herself or of gratitude to Debbie but hard as stones. They coursed down her cheeks no more stoppable than blood from a cut finger, no hotter either. "Hurt? Love? What does thee know of love? What would thee love *with?* Thee's got no more heart than a scarecrow. Oh, I see thy side, right enough. I see that were I sick unto death and thee lying with a woman, thee'd not stir out of the bed. Thee is the selfishest man God ever made. Thee loves only thyself. And Debbie. Her thee loves also. I have known that since I saw thee weep into her shawl. I was up in the live oak tree. But now I know why thee found her irresistible—because thee is her counterfeit."

His eyes went beady as a snake's and his voice was soft with venom. "Is that not why thee loves her?"

"The other way around," she might have truthfully said. "And once we were lovers." Oh, that would hurt him, but then he would hate her as he hated Tristram. For the sake of the child, she held her tongue. She knew the pain of fatherlessness too well. She said, "Let us speak no more of love. My heart's leaping days are over. I cannot blame thee altogether, ours has been an unnatural past. I perceive thee must sail for home to attend to thy bereft sons and matters of property. I wish thee Godspeed. But I would have our child fathered too, sir. If thee does not make this house thy only home, if thee be not here when thy lawful child is born, I vow I shall be wife to thee no more."

"Very well, madam. Then thee may fuck thy *self.*"

Oh, how quickly the dignity of her ultimatum ebbed! How she longed for him to apologize, cajole, regret, touch, plead, grab her to his bosom! But he turned and left without bothering to slam the door and stomped down the stairs. She broke for the window. He was striding toward Old Wharf. She ran to get the spyglass and came back to see him push off in a dory. She watched him row out, focusing and refocusing frantically. She ought not to have threatened, no one commanded Captain John Coffin, one could not hold such as he with a grappling hook. To close a fist on him was to force him out the other side, he was quicksilver, irretrievable. Don't hurt his pride, Debbie had warned, don't box him. Oh, God, send him back, I'll forgive—!

Aimless, despairing, drawn to Brant Point, she saw it milling with people. Besides the unloading of Timothy's ship and the loading of John's (the *Johana,* of course, she saw it now. Dutch woman indeed!), there were a number of repairers and curiosity seekers. The shoe manufactory was untouched by the fire except for some dirt streaks on the Sound side, whereas the cooperage and the rigging loft and the lighthouse were burned to the ground. She ran past the hoops of casks that lay blackened without a sign of their staves. She stood up to her ankles in surf, waving to John who stood on his deck, supervising the hoisting of barrels. No voyage, not even one occasioned by a death in the family, went without cargo. Between the shore and the *Johana,* John's First Mate Worth, in the center of a penned raft of sheep, waved back.

She turned when she was spoken to.

"Ahoy, Kezia. John's shoving off, is he?"

"Oh, William. I congratulate thee. There is little loss to thee and Caleb, as far as I can see."

"Virtually none. Providence is kind."

"To some," she said darkly. Mary has William, Judith has Caleb, everybody two by two as in the Ark, why am I the only one to walk alone? Give him back, God, I don't care if he's good or bad, I want him, we need him, the babe and I. Make him wave, a *sign*. I know he saw. Mister Worth saw, so he saw. Is he resolved never to speak me again?

"—owe the town a debt of thanks. Neither Caleb nor I were in town. By the time we came home—"

"Where were thee? They cried it in the street."

"I just told thee—Polpis with the children. 'Twas Mary's first junket since the birth. From the look of things, there must have been a furious strength to the flames."

What an idyl her sisters lived: babies, junkets to the country! She said tightly, "People exaggerate. 'Twas a fire like any other. I was here, I saw it."

"Happen thee left before the wind came up. Look about thee, see the ground? Swept uncommon clean as though by some agency far more nice than fire. Folk say the gale subsided as sudden as it come up. Folk saw clinkers this morning clear down to the skirts of No-Bottom Pond."

Kezia shivered in the sun.

Late that night John returned to a dark house. He stood at her bedside and his dark smoke-smelling presence assaulted every nerve in her body, a shock to her blood, a change in her pores as if she'd been suddenly immersed in water. Even in fantasy she had never felt such desire. Her arms stretched up and he filled them quickly, groaning. She gulped his kiss as if she were swallowing brandy. She clawed at his trousers. He tore them open and entered her at once, and she was moist, ready. They ground and pumped each other with a violence that only anguish can inspire, flying higher and higher. But he came betimes and left her drenched in their sweat, hot and thick and untapped. He lay on his back, done in, done for, breathing ever quieter while she burned. Listening to the signs of his ease, frustration raked her, turned to dusty hate, thirsted for revenge. So much to give Shana, to sons, to whales, to kin, to crew, to public emergency, with never a thought to saving a drop of himself for her, his lawful wedded wife. Well, she'd show him, she'd commit adultery soon's he was gone with the first man who'd have her, she cared not who or how many. Burning in hell could be no worse than burning on earth, and what was life if not an eternity?

As her body gradually let her down from the peak of tension, her wrath paled to crossness and she found it possible to give her husband a grudging bit of compassion. He was past his meridian, on the wane. Her mother had forewarned of this, but she had not grasped her meaning. How could she, a mere, ignorant maid? She stiffened—was he *cry*ing? And relaxed again in skepticism. She always thought he was crying, men didn't, not this one certainly, she gave him too much heart. Wrong again. Turning to her, he laid scalding wet tears on her breast. She held his head, feeling infinitely older than he. Oh, but this was a man strangely mixed; all these years and she knew him not, familiarity is not understanding.

"There, love, don't take it so hard. Thee's frazzled with exertion. Thee's overtaxed thyself. Rest now, sleep, dear one, there's always tomorrow."

"Oh, Kezia, I am sorry. Thee's been shortchanged over and again whilst I—I pay too dear for everything."

She thought he referred to this night. Too proud to admit inadequacy, he was trying to merge it with things past and things to come, giving their sexual failures a predetermined pattern over which he had no control and therefore could take no blame for. She stroked his head, sprinkled dry cool kisses on his face. "Do not fret thyself, Husband. Thee was drained from the day's labors. And I am well at ease, truly I am. We have had many beautiful times, bear them in mind.

Dwell not on this single—uh—" censoring the word
fiasco as too strong, she substituted, "mistiming. Thee
plagues thyself for a minuscule nothing."

But of course it came out, she might have known,
he wept not for her but for himself.

"I should have gone to her sooner, soon's ever I
heard. I should have been with her when she died.
That's what she wanted and, before God, deserved.
Now she'll hound me to hell."

A marriage has many endings. It runs on and on
in circles long after its head has been cut off. When
day came, they awoke like children, rested, mollified,
cleansed. They laughed at each other's black-streaked
faces, pointed gleefully at the dirty linen. The smell of
smoke was acrid in the room, it drew their passion like
musk, and soon they were tumbling each other in
fierce brief rapture. The marriage bed—private as a
chamber in a nautilus shell, primordial as a tideflat,
meetingplace of hunger and satiety, of disappointment
and fulfillment, battleground of victory and surrender
and compromise, salted with tears and semen, with
blood, vomit, piss, pus, with womb water and body
sweat. She wallowed in it for hours after the *Johana*
sailed, burying her face from time to time in his
smudged pillow.

Next morning she resolutely put him out of her
mind and prepared to resume her job as chatelaine.
There were decisions to be made, orders to be dispatched, laxities to be brought up short. Distracted
though she'd been by the hay rollings and the rantum
skoots with her lover-husband, yet her weather eye had
spotted spiderwebs and tarnished silver. There were
fences to be mended and the chicken keep stank whilst
Shongo was abroad rounding up helpers from Occa-
waw, his village, for the pulling and the spreading of
their flax. Summer herbs and berries could die on the
stem before Hagar would bestir her bulk out of the
hall to collect them. Aunt Hannah could be counted on
to see the clothing-stuffs 'y-teazelled and y-touked and

y-tented,' but winter could come and go before she'd do anything about the glass pane that was splintered in her chamber window. And that remarkably efficient Rachel Bunker could provide her employer with lists of supplies needed for shopkeeping, but she could not write the letters that would chaffer for and fetch them from the trading ports.

To symbolize the new regime, Kezia washed all of John off of her with strong soap, head to foot. Next she stripped the linen from the bed where they had made love, made it up clean. But the pillow she stowed aloft on a high shelf of John's chamber closet. As her belly grew, she took it out, finding in its fading stench the reassurance of his return.

In the fall when the heath was a richly woven carpet of reds and golds and purple-browns, and again in Twelfth Month when the carpet was dull and thread-bare, she made pilgrimages to Altar Rock where she prayed God to send John home for the borning. And with the catholic fervor of the true heretic, she called also upon Shana: *Let him go, 'tis my turn now.* But if he should not return, if he failed her yet again—? There'd be the child, yes, but did she really want to devote herself to a new life when she had not yet led her own?

Fourteen

Childbirth was a common enough event but because Kezia could do nothing in the ordinary way, there was much talk of her confinement.

"You'd think the captain would warp in for the blessed event. 'Tis years awaited."

"Nothing new to him. I'll warrant he's laid his eggs in many a basket."

"Never knew pains to start so early."

"Mayhap false labor."

"Nay, they say she's been dilated four days. Whole whang of women sitting around her hall. They ply back and forth between her house and their own."

"All them goodwives feasting there, day after day. Must cost a pretty penny."

"Kezia runs a bountiful house, same's *his* mother did. Fame says Hagar's extravagant as Hepsy. Says they been eating oysters till there be none left for export. And ten kinds of wine besides cider, beer, and porter."

"Muscles at her age bound to be morbidly firm. Should think she's more for stewing than fry-panning. Wouldn't be surprised if one or t'other don't come through the ordeal."

"God's will. Her mother's a practiced midwife. Can't pull her own daughter through, who can?"

"She's got more'n her mother. There's a big enough bee there to make quilts. Debbie and her sisters and Aunt Hannah and Rachel Bunker and Hagar—"

"Fat lot of good Rachel Bunker be at a birthing. She may know sums, but pshaw, her pie crust'd break a cart wheel."

198

The laughter petered out. Calamity was more gripping than levity. Like meat more than custard, it stuck to the ribs.

"This much travail, there'll be renting and bleeding. Hannah had better have her darning needle handy."

"When do they estimate the dropping?"

"This night at turn of tide."

"Aye, we die when the tide goes out and mothers let go between the flux and the reflux of the ocean."

Back at the John Coffin house, the mystique of life-giving was mulled and remulled. Perhaps if life were more easily created, we might take it too lightly. The whang had exhausted their first-hand tales, they were on to hearsay.

"—babe presented itself shoulder first, laying acrost. I'll have some sugar for my tea, Hagar, I thank thee kindly. Worse by far than a breech. Spot of rum? Well, I don't mind if I do. The babe had to be dug out with a crochet. The babe cried out in the womb—"

Rachel Bunker could stomach no more. She corkscrewed up out of her chair. "What ghoulish bilge! The lungs of a fetus *in utero* are in a state of collapse and the body surrounded by a fluid heavier than water. So how's it possible for it to cry? Say me that!"

"I grant thee 'tis uncommon," enunciated Mistress Macy. "Which is precisely why 'twas reported in the *London Health Gazette* to which my Zaccheus subscribes and the which he reads from cover to cover."

"Fiddle-faddle," raged Rachel. "Fish stories! Not a word of truth to them!"

Mistress Macy rose uncertainly. "I'll not stay to be insulted."

"Fine! One less mouth to feed," snapped Rachel.

"Stay, Mistress Macy, have a piece of pie!" urged Hagar.

"And thee, Rachel," said Aunt Hannah, "some coffee. Strong and black. Thee's half seas over."

Perhaps there would have been less backbiting

and drunkenness if they'd been closer to the realities of the moment, but Kezia's bedchamber was never intended for borning and so was upstairs, far from the hall. Inside that room, vanities had long since gone by the board.

Debbie wiped Kezia's pinched face with a damp towel. "Hold fast to me, lovey. Mind, we've all been there and we've all come safely back."

Abigail had been fighting off a sore throat since First Day when Kezia was taken with the pains. Everyone scoffed at her theory that one rheum begot another, but she'd seen it go through her house like fire in a wind, and to be on the safe side, she stayed at the delivery end of the bed as much as possible.

"Mama!" Kezia maundered weakly, clutching the bedclothes. "Oh, Mama!"

"Quiet, child. Call upon the Lord to help thee bear the pain." But to Debbie Abigail fretted in whispers. "She's losing strength. I believe it might speed matters if I broke her bag of waters. What say thee, Debbie? I'd know if 'tweren't my own but my heart is wrenched past reasoning."

Kezia's ears caught enough to moan, "Nay, nay, 'twill hurt me more! I can stand no more."

"Thee'll stand what thee must," said her mother, reaching up into the pelvis and closing her fingers hard upon the bag.

Kezia screamed, not with pain but with surprise. The rush of warm water soaked her legs and the bed. With it ran out her last drop of human dignity. At least 'twas not John to see her shame but only mothers. On this thought she rested between spasms. But the next pain was excruciating, a change in kind, crazing her with fear. Thus far her body had been making war upon itself. Now the dam was broken and a creature with its own way to make butted and kicked, cared not if it destroyed the cage. With one hand Kezia clung to Debbie's strong arm, with the other she gripped the bedpost, grunting involuntarily like a wild beast, and at the same time, felt feces pour out of her rear end, stinking, filthy. Oh, the ignominy!

"Never mind," said Abigail, "we'll clean thee. Thee just bear down—do thy part, darling. Where does it all come from? She's scarcely eaten, or I'd have given another clyster."

Even in Kezia's extremity, the endearment reached her. She inhaled, pushed and blew, inhaled, pushed and blew, as Debbie had earlier instructed her. Then she fell back, sweating cold as rain. She had mustered her last breath, her last push, her last scream. From now on it was in God's hands. God and these mothers and the creature itself, she could do no more. Their voices wafted back to her as through a wall.

"Mary, fetch the gentian water."

"If thee drowse her, she can't help."

"I need no help."

"If it's twins?"

"I can take two's easy as one."

"Won't it harm the babe?"

Mary saw Kezia stiffen in throe, and but mew. She ran.

When she came back with the potion, there was a red bundle tied up with a blue cord between her sister's white legs, and her mother was shouting like a fisherman over a strike.

"What is it?"

"I think—aye—a maid!"

"Thee's certain sure?"

"See for thyself. A maid, praise God, and sound, the sweeting! Now breathe, lovey, give us a kick and a holler, let us know thee's come to stay!"

Mary watched her mother slap the thing—once, twice. It was of good size but blue. Suffocated? Dearest Lord, be kind to my sister, maketh this babe to breathe. Amen.

Dead, Kezia decided wearily. Born dead without gentian water, so it was not her fault. Well, it was the babe or her, God had made the choice.

But there came a sound, minute as the breaking of a bubble. And then a whimper—tiny, piteous—and then a howl, and then a series of pulsating protests, lusty, gusty, full of rage. Kezia smiled under her heavy lids.

"Proud of thee, Kezia, so proud," Debbie was whispering into her ear.

A snattering broke out below, rose up. The whang. And then Kezia heard the second most wonderful sound in the world—her mother laughing.

"A maid!" announced Abigail triumphantly from the head of the stairs. "A one-headed, two-legged, five-fingered maid no biggern a bass! And lung enough for a boatswain. Hark at her! Ho-ho, she knows even now what a cruel world she's come into, don't thee, lovey girl? Thy grandmother gave thee a sound hiding and it hurts, eh?"

The women shrieked and swooped like gulls over chum. When the sound of them died below stairs, Kezia slept. Later, she heard a noise and peeped through her lids. By the fire, Hagar's cavernous mouth gleamed white and red at the mite it could have eaten in a single bite. Kezia would have liked to see the child straight on but she had not the strength to ask. Hagar was bathing her in—of all things—the powdering tub, the one they used for salting and sousing meat. All that baby equipment, collected over the months from bonnets to booties, and Hagar used the powdering tub! Zaccheus Macy had made a beautiful little cradle of rifted oak with a hood on it, but Hagar would doubtless lay her down in a chest drawer. Dear good kind Hagar, crazy as a bedbug, they all were, herself too. She fell asleep sealed up inside a bag of watery laughter.

They ate and slept and observed each other. Or so it seemed to Kezia; Aunt Hannah said the baby couldn't see. The baby's eyes, what could be seen of them inside the puffy lids, were black as a hat. The nose was flat, the cheeks creased and blotched. Besides the fingernails, the only perfect visible feature was a pink silk mouth that had split both her nipples, drawing blood instead of milk. There came finally a trickle of white, Kezia saw it dribble out of the side of the pink bow, and she gave instant fervent thanks to God. She whispered to the child. "Tear them up, sweeting, thee has the right. Make them to nourish thee that thee may grow big and strong." At that, the wight smiled. A lopsided smile to be sure, such as one occasionally saw on a dog or a horse or a cup-sot, but a smile. Kezia was moved then to unwind the swaddling clothes to make sure her mother had not made a mistake. The feet were alarmingly blue but it was a maid right enough, cracked in twain. Ah, well, John already had sons, here was something Shana had not given him, and considering the four-day mashing, not uncomely. Absently massaging the babe's feet, she tried to remember the pains so that she could describe them to other women at other births.

Suddenly, she became a manufactory of tears—less miraculous than the milk she was producing, but no less surprising. *Why?* Because John wasn't here to praise and pet and stroke? Because the baby was too much of a miracle, more than she had the energy to rise to? She sucked on her thumb, bending the nail-tip back and forth between her teeth. The baby began to cry. She looked at it resentfully. "If I cry no one turns his head," she told it aloud, "but one peep out of thee and zip-zap, sick or well, I must come running." She flipped the little tyrant over her shoulder, pressed and patted it. Its back was no wider than a bread loaf, but the belch could have come from a plowman. Kezia laid her away, covered her smoothly, looked down, rocking the cradle. Her own life had scarcely begun and already this one made demands upon it. Was this the way her mother had felt about her? I promise thee, little one, so trusting and mild in thy full-bellied sleep, that even if I cannot love thee sufficient, no one shall ever guess it, least of all thee. But who is thee?

Until I give thee a name, thee's no more than a mouse
or a weasel, a rabbit, a pup, a kitten, a squirrel. A
name, a name. Not *his* mother's because she misliked
Miriam Pinkham. Not *her* mother's because Abigail
was not a pretty name, and she misliked her sister
Abbie. Not Debbie because Judith and Mary might be
hurt, they too had named girls for her. . . .

On the third day following parturition, Kezia
did not have to summon up old pain, she had a new
one in her side so severe that she could not lie prone.
Even during the night, she was obliged to lean upright against the pillows. She dozed and managed to
get up to feed the child, but it took great self-sacrifice.
    At sun-an-hour, Aunt Hannah came in and flung
up the windows.
    "Kezia, this room stinks. Thee's ill. I must take
the babe away, fetch the doctor for thee."
    Kezia felt nothing but a listless relief. "Who'll feed
the poor thing?"
    "Mary will," said Aunt Hannah. "She's nursing
her Phebe, she's got enough for two. The Lord provides."
    The anger that burst inside Kezia found a target
—John. Where was he when she needed him? She was
worse off than a thornback, he cared nothing for her,
that cat-and-mouse villain, not even concerned enough
to come home to see his offspring, let alone his wife,
and she about to die of the two of them. Die? She had
not yet lived, not a ha'penny's worth. She'd wind up
in heaven out of default. Sick as Aunt Hannah said,
she'd be there sooner than she could bear to think. Her
head began to ache. Tears burned in her eyes. If she'd
been a Presbyterian, there'd at least be a headstone,
her name and her dates. Perhaps even a legend for future visitors: *Memento Mori, Fugit Hora.* Beloved
daughter, wife, mother. Now she'd disappear like a
pebble tossed into No Bottom Pond. It was unjust. All
the time she'd *tried*—forced smiles, loaned money,
pondered God's word, did a kindness, delivered sim-

ples, wrote letters—what for? Elisha, Peter, Father,
here come I. Shall thee not greet me? Shall I knock upon the pearly gates unwelcomed? Shana, wilt thou be
my friend for I too die alone?

Holding her side, Kezia watched her aunt wrap
the cooing infant in gift blankets of flannel and wool.
"Have them write down in the Friends' Book that the
maid doth bear her mother's name. That way I shall
not die dead," Kezia told her harshly. "And harken,
Aunt Hannah, I would have *thee* rear her, no one
else—not my mother, promise me. And should her
no-good, uncaring father trod Old Nan's soil one of
these fine days, tell him my last request was this: She
is to have all my belongings save the spinning wheels
which I bequeath thee. Tell him she is to have an
outset and dowry befitting the daughter of a Coffin and
a sea captain. Also any legacy that should come rightfully to me from Grandmother Wilcox or my mother
or any Folger kin shall be duly transferred to her."

Aunt Hannah quenched the fierce flameup of
pride at Kezia's trust in her. "I shall look out for her,
never fret, but this is early for testaments, Kezia.
Thee's bitter as a Narrow Creek eel. Such a frame of
mind is a sickness in itself. I'll nurse thee to the uttermost but if thee would recover, thee must exert thy
mind toward the Light and relinquish past grievance.
There is no better medicine. Be of good cheer and a
humble heart. If not for thy sake, then for the babe's."
She held the well-wrapped infant out for a kiss. "Say
'God be with ye' to thy mother, Little Kezia. Tell her
thee'll be back in her arms very soon."

Kezia put her parched lips to the incredibly delicate cheek. "Begone, the two of thee, or I shall find it
impossible to let her from me. My bitterness *is* for her
sake. I know what it is to lack fathering, I would not
deprive her of mothering as well. I am determined to
pull through. If God give me the smallest succor—"

"Pray for it. Implore it in deep humility, Kezia.
Open the windows of thy heart. Only thus shall the
power of the spirit purge thy bodily poisons."

Accordingly Kezia prayed. "Dear Lord, my spirit doth delight to do no evil nor to revenge any wrong, but to endure all things, in hope to enjoy its own in the end. . . . As it bears no evil in itself so it conceives none in thoughts to any other: If it be betrayed, it bears if; for its ground and springs is the mercies and forgiveness of God. . . ."

And she purged. She forced herself to remember the good moments with John. When he fed her from his plate, when he pronounced her flawlessly beautiful. When they laughed over the bountiful supper they discovered in the fishing shanty. And she minded his tender concern: "Was it good for thee? Verily?" And when her faith in prayer and in John faltered, she comforted herself with old Cuddusue's prophecy.

Big-bellied, Kezia had driven the box wagon to Squam alone during the first snow flurries of Twelfth Month. She brought a jugful of rum and dropped coins into the dusty serge lap, reminding her as she did so, "Last time thee spoke of a death."

Cuddusue's fist ate up the coins. "Not for you. For you long life. Likewise for the papoose you carry which is a girl child."

Disappointed, Kezia challenged, "How does thee know that?"

"God is the knower. I am but his drum."

"Shall I live to be as old as thee, Grandmother?"

"I cannot say. I know not how many years I have had." She shook the coins in her fist. "Come again soon. Bring more rum."

"Rum's not allowed Indians."

"No rum, no drum," said Cuddusue, and her cackles chased Kezia through the door-flap.

The seeress had since died but the prophecy lived. 'Long life.' Maybe so. She *had* been right about the babe's gender. . . .

Zaccheus Macy refused Aunt Hannah's urgent request. "I'm but a simple carpenter, Hannah. Bones or boards—they're all the same to me. I can fit the pieces of a broken arm as sound as I can fit ship's knees to a miter joint. But that's the extent of my chirurgery."

"Thee was of wondrous aid to her when she nearly died of drug. Thee's a natural-born healer."

But Zaccheus was adamant. He had an uncommonly jealous wife, a very mind reader, and she'd laid down the law about Kezia.

The physician, Samuel Gelston, proved to be in Chatham, giving smallpox inoculations. Abigail was down with the influenza. Aunt Hannah had no choice.

"But thee must promise there'll be no dosing with laudanum even though she be near death," Aunt Hannah stipulated firmly.

"Still blaming me for the girl's addiction, are you?" grumbled Dr. Tupper. "I tell you I take it myself—daily, three grains after breakfast. And so do more folks than you think, some of your own Sisterhood. Doesn't hurt us none. Kezia overindulged. Took more'n I prescribed. 'Tweren't my fault she poisoned her system."

And so Kezia fell once more under Dr. Tupper's intrepid care. He dosed her with turpentine taken internally over a period of ten days. The treatment produced severe hemorrhoids, the pain of which was relieved by leeches. Once when after a leeching the 'emerods' would not stop bleeding. Aunt Hannah on Abigail's advice rolled up some hat fur into a small hard ball and pushed it up with a bodkin into the hole made by the bite. An additional remedy applied daily to the vaginal cavity was the "Seneca Oil," later known as petroleum, which Shongo had procured from an Allegheny Indian sailor who claimed it had great healing powers for 'outward griefs.' Despite these bizarre curatives, Kezia gained strength daily. Such is the will to live.

Yet once recovered Kezia did not find motherhood a satisfying occupation. As she privily confided to Rachel Bunker, "Little Kezia's a dear, but a bore. A bit young for me. Besides, Aunt Hannah is ever at the cradle first, she outraces me at the slightest puling. I can't very well tear the mite from her arms." Soon Kezia was back at 'merchanting.' And since John neither came home nor sent word, it was inevitable, even in that moral climate, that Kezia should take a lover.

Fifteen

Their paths recrossed in June 1762.

The town shearing had taken place the previous week at the Washing Pond. This second one was called by the Swain clan, who asked over a hundred families to Polpis to help them fleece their flocks. The day turned out to be a 'weather-breeder'—perfect. Clear, calm, blue sky, water the same, and full sunshine, with a lady's wind blowing through the reeds, wafting wild rose petals and perfume.

After a bounteous supper served on trestles in the new-raised barn, the men participated in an 'Olympiad.' They threw the bar, hurled stones, footraced, threw the discus, using wooden chargers for disks. There were of course no awards—the contests were not for self-exhibition but for healthful exercise—but folks cheered their favorites, and the normally tranquil eventide was rife with shouting. Samuel Starbuck came off the hero of the day, winning all but the footrace which went to his young cousin. Christopher Starbuck, Debbie's firstborn. As Kezia brought Christopher a mug of rum-spiked lemonade, she jocularly recalled that bygone race he'd lost to her. "And now thee's the fleetest man about and I can't walk uphill without puffing."

Christopher turned away without reply.

Kezia looked after him, biting her lip, chilled by the lad's rudeness. In fact, he was no longer a lad, being a father twice over, a competent whaling master, a sometime trader. The years ran faster than footraces. She did the sums in her head. Christopher was thirty-two, Samuel was thirty-six then—and she forty. Was it possible—*forty* years old? She felt like a girl still, and it wasn't true she puffed on a hill, she'd but said it to be a sociable. Suddenly she felt a girl's longing for her old boyfriend and she went over to Samuel Starbuck with the drink.

He was hatless, coatless, his bared forearms fuzzy as a bee's legs that have been in squash blossoms, and from the vee of his open shirt a thatch of gold hair sprang out. The smell of his sweat was clean as pith, it made her breath catch. His gentian eyes twinkled with impersonal good humor. He clearly did not recognize her. Had she changed so much then? Oh, Samuel, Samuel, I mind when thy chest and arms were as smooth as my own. Thy face has grown big enough for thy ears and for thy handsome Starbuck nose but there was a time when both were overlarge and black-pored. I can see thy forlorn shoulders moving away from me out to sea—and now thee knows me not.

"Well, Samuel Starbuck, so thee's the champion," she said briskly. "See it don't spoil thee. 'Tis right heady being best."

Now who in tarn? Suddenly his brow cleared. "Well, I'm blowed—*Kezia!*" Of the maid he'd fondled —sharp-faced, sharp-tongued, sharp-elbowed, sharp-breasted—there was not a trace. Nor of the sickly girl he had encountered some five or six years ago in somebody's keeping room. That night she had had no word for him, nor for anyone, her stork-legs tucked under her, her eyes mottled and flat as calamander. Later, he gave his wife a rare humping, so grateful was he to be cured of his dangerous boyhood fancy.

Well, whatever had ailed Kezia, ailed her no more, that was plain to see. Gad, the sauciness of that smile, the flare of those nostrils, the glint of dark eye. No neckpiece covered her creamy bosom, and her waist—why, the span of his hands would overlap it by half.

"Thee's fetched up right womanly, Kezia."

"And thou, Samuel, hath turned to gold. I mind thy hair mousebrown."

His fingers sprang to comb his thick blond-striped hair. "Comes from walking the decks without a hat, I ween."

"Would thee like some refreshment?"

"I'd share with thee."

They drank, and she asked after his wife.

"She stayed home not to risk the long ride. She's in perilous waters now—three months from term. She's a miscarrier. We've had but one son in seven goes. This be the eighth."

"Oh, my. I wish this one safe harbor. How old's thy boy now?"

"Dan'l's eleven. And thee's had a daughter, I'm told."

"Aye, my one and only, I fear. I was grievous ill with the fever after. So scarred by it, the doctor has since declared me barren." Now why on earth was she telling him *that?* She rushed on. "But I cannot truly complain. I believe I am naturally cut to the jib of trader. Buying and selling, chaffer and correspondence fill my days most engrossingly."

He recorded the intelligence and the sudden loss of poise, remembering how easily she foundered on unexpected shoals. He liked that in a woman. His Abigail now, she was unwavering as the Rock of Ages, a man could dash his brains out trying to move her.

"Aye, aye, thee always did have a head for business. I find it absorbing too, more so than whaling. Long's I'm abroad. I'm neither for kettle halyards nor yet for bloody harpoons. Now thee mentions it, Benjamin Tupper was saying last night thee'd had a rough go after a thwarted delivery. He was at the family supper honoring my homecoming. He married my brother John's widow—him that was lost at sea."

"So he did. May I welcome thee home as well?"

"Ah, yes, 'tis good to be back." His eyes went to her bosom as his voice trailed off. "All the dear familiar faces—"

"—and thy voyage? Profitable, I hope."

"Very. I carried oil to London and with the cash for the sale was enabled to bring back a load of manufacture which I traded in Bostontown, all to good profit."

"How did thee find the price for oil?"

"Uncommon high. Though other prices be sinking, oil's on the rise and nothing answers but sperm oil, which we carried. The common brown stuff is twenty-three pounds the ton. The white is twenty-five."

"My, that *is* dear! How does thee account for the rise?"

"Short fishery. Increasing consumption. More lamps, more machinery, more timepieces."

"I wonder, should I not buy up some sperm oil from incoming whalers for shipment to London at summer's end? I know that autumn is the time of demand."

"What of thy husband? Has he none to sell?"

"I don't know where John is. He's been long gone, and I've had no word of him." Mixed anxieties of love and money made her frown. "Aye, I believe I shall make the purchase."

"I misdoubt sperm oil's easy come by. I have it from my brother-in-law William Rotch that Captain Folger and his partner are laying hands on what they can. Word is they're affiliated with Thomas Hancock who's sharper'n tacks."

"Well, I be not dull. I can buy Nantucket oil as fast as any Folger or Bostoner. Does thee think the price of oil will hold?"

"I do. The French and Indian War has hampered American whaling. England's had but poor supply during it. The demand is now strong. I dare say we shall soon be exploiting new fisheries along the St. Lawrence, now Canada's scalp swings from the king's belt. But the shortage must persist a while yet. Meanwhile, consumption of oil far exceeds the supply."

"I've a new ship abuilding. She's a hundred tons burthen. Not even named yet. She could be utilized for—"

Suddenly her tongue clove to the roof of her

mouth. His eyes probed hers. Like two logs untouching, flames leaped up between them.

He said urgently, "Calcutta. Tonight. Now."

His voice had lowered but even so she looked about. "Durst we?"

"My dearest—"

"Thy wife—"

She could not know that he was alone at the shearing because he and his wife had had a serious quarrel. He had come home after five months of celibacy eager to couple with Abigail, only to be told that the doctor had forbade it until the babe came and was six weeks old. He took the deprivation so illy that Abigail broke the full news: he was henceforth banned from her bed.

"For good and aye?" Samuel had asked, incredulous.

"That's what I'm saying," affirmed Abigail with the doggedness of the meek who have come to the end of the tether. "And not for lack of love, Husband, though I own that lust has become anathema to me. Six nearly fatal hemorrhages, not to mention the grief each time. I cannot go through it more. I am burnt out before my time."

"And I am come full into mine. What am I to do?"

"What thee wills. What thy conscience permits. Forgive me, Samuel, but my mind is made. If God grants us this child in my womb, then we shall have our family. Two good children are better than ten bad as have some."

"Well. Very well. I'll not force myself on any woman," Samuel said, but he felt reduced to boy's size as he added, "Where shall I bide?"

"In north chamber. 'Tis ready and waiting but for the tester and the window coverings. They'll be off the tenterhooks on the morrow. Thee arrived earlier than I expected."

"Then I'll sleep aboard my ship till the morrow."

Kezia was staring at him. He saw the quick rise

and fall of her breasts and he was so overset he could
not speak. Then when he would, his brother-in-law
was beside them.

"Shall we call it a day, Samuel?" said Will Rotch.
"My wife and I are for home. Where's thy aunt, Kezia?
May we carry thee home?"

Not only marriages are made in heaven. Illicit
unions are made there too, or so it sometimes seems.
Kezia spoke through Will to Samuel. "Nay, I thank
thee. Aunt Hannah did not feel up to the rollick, she's
but middling. I rode out alone and I'll enjoy a canter
home along the strand. Tide's out and 'tis a rare warm
night."

"And thee, Samuel?"

"Oh, I shall escort Kezia as far as Quaise Harbor.
I've a dory tied up there. As I told Abigail, I shall
berth on my vessel this night. The cargo's not put off
and I must rise betimes to get the men agoing. Where's
thy mount, Kezia? I'll give thee a hoist."

They dawdled till the last 'Godspeed' had died
away and the last cart had rumbled off after the last
outriders to the inland highway. Then they guided
their horses down the palisade at an ambling pace.
When they hit the hard road of wet sand, they broke
into a gallop.

The stars bloomed in summer profusion. A third
quarter moon silvered beach and dune and threw a
path of gold shale on the water, making the night as
friendly as day. The air as it rushed by them was
soft, salt-moist, grass-sweet. And all this beauty was
wasted upon them, as unreceived as the sound of a
falling tree in a deserted wood, for she trembled with
fear that she would not please him, and he trembled
too but not with fear.

He had no trouble finding the place, but the person—ah, had he forgotten how balky Kezia could be?
Her scarred conscience dismounted with her. She must
pay entrance fee even at the gates of Paradise.

"We can't tether the horses out of door," she said

crossly. "They might be seen by a night wanderer. An Indian who'd steal them. And blackmail us."

"Well, they bloody well shan't come inside. They've cropped all day long. I'll not chance a stink."

"Samuel!" Her face thickened with the rush of blood, she could feel it. Adulthood had turned him gross. He would offend her. And disappoint. A day of grappling lambs, all those Olympic games, his dasher was bound to be pindling. Glumly she watched him tie the two sets of reins to a driftwood log. They'd never get away with it. They'd be seen, tattled on. They'd pay and it wouldn't be worth the price.

Inside the cave, he hastily stripped himself and then tried to undress her. "If we swing for it, we shall be skin to skin as we were not in our youth." She gave him no help, no encouragement. *Swing* for it?

When he got her down to the buff, she was reluctant to stretch out on the dirt floor.

"There might be bat-do. Or snakes."

"Thee may lie upon me. I'll lie upon the snakes."

"I pray thee, love, outside. Under the moon."

" 'Twas thee who recommended caution, and rightly," he said, exasperated. "Thee stay a moment. I'll fetch the saddle blanket." Were all women so hangback or just the ones he chose? By heaven, the next time he'd take a woman of the streets. He would have had a harlot long before this if he hadn't feared the French pox they all carried in their purses.

Once they lay in each other's arms, their nerves eased. Learned responses were displaced by simple instinct, and they were as they had been with each other a long time ago—natural, childlike. Their sexual personalities, so different with their mates, quickly adapted to one another. With John, there was thrill from the first touch. She made him hard and he expected her ready in short order, demanding, "Now? Now?" so that she'd learned to heat up fast. They came almost at once, not necessarily simultaneously, but quickly, the climax brief, agonized, the catharsis less from pleasure than from an end of unbearable tension. Samuel's pattern with Abigail was likewise full of strain. She was always cold and loglike at the outset, had to be overcome like a hostage, and since aggression was distasteful to him—possibly because his father had been a lecher and his brother Edward was a brute—he lost a good deal of his power in his encounters with her.

As lovers, Kezia and Samuel discovered themselves to be voluptuaries, concinnous, unhurried, unself-conscious, measuring this conspiracy not only against their mates but against their past knowledge of each other. The hands she remembered from their childhood had been exploratory, tentative, sly as thieves. These hands were landlords, possessive, insistent, and she gratefully gave herself up to them.

"Ah, Kezia, thee's the same sweet piece."

But even as he said it he was thinking of her differences. The scent of her skin was muskier, her breasts fuller and heavy nippled, her belly softer, her bottom ripe for plucking.

There was no question of readying, he simply entered her in due time, taking full charge, making her fast to him, belly to belly, bone to bone. He remained strong and thrusting long after her orgasm. She had three before she began to weary. And to worry. Had he come? Would he not? Why not? Was he odd? Was she at fault? But then he came in a burst of sighs. Lightsome—he was lightsome on her breast! It was a long time since she'd thought of the Sheikh's treatise. Rolling off, he kissed the tip of an erect nipple which she quickly covered with her hand and then her belly button which she also covered, no longer wanting to be touched anywhere, by anyone. He gave a low chuckle, the farewell kisses had been but teasing. Yet this too was a difference. With John she wanted more and more, never satisfied.

"Would thee not like to come back on the blanket? What about bat-do?"

She realized then that she was lying in the dirt.

She rolled to him, pummeling his chest. He caught her fists, laughing.

"Come," he ordered. "Up with ye. We'll have a bathe in the sea if we hang for it."

This time the possibility inspired no fear. She welcomed the risk, felt a daredevil, indestructible.

They ran across the moon-whitened sand into the cold milky bay. Asserting independence, they struck out on their own, swimming frog-fashion past the sandbar. She passed him but then he caught her and pulled her back to the shallows. "Thee goes too far. 'Tis not a night for drowning."

They were now as cool as the water, flesh of its flesh, texture of its texture. Unwilling to leave it, they floated close to shore, their white feet pointing up fin-like, their loose bodies aroll with the incoming tide. He was pushed by a stronger wave back across the sand ridges, and he took her with him by her wet ponytail and dandled her on his lap, his mouth between her shoulder blades, her salt on his tongue.

She played idly with his cock until it was thick as a pillion grip, and dripping, hand in hand, they ran back to the cave.

They talked so long afterward her hair dried, and daylight stretched a long gray powdery arm into their nest.

"But, Samuel, thee's a stallion!"

"I surprised myself. I am not used to loving a woman who wants to be loved."

"Thy wife does not?"

"Nay, she has suffered me."

"But others?"

"There have been no others. The port trulls are diseased—even in London, one never knows, even in high society. There is a kind of shield, but I would not make love in armor. I never bought one."

She mulled that over. John was a womanizer long before she married him, and there was no reason to believe that marriage had changed him. Nor was he one

to take precaution. Did he never fear catching the
claps? Did he have some natural resistance to the
distemper or was he just lucky? Or had he been cured
of it, perhaps more than once? Was he indeed not a
risky bedmate each time he came home from a voyage?

"But if thee don't use it, thee lose it, as the saying
goes. 'Tis a muscle like any other," Samuel said. "And
now I am banished from her bed. She fears another
pregnancy."

"Good. I would not share thee."

"Nor I thee. Doth love John still?"

"Like the dagger that spills lifeblood when pulled
out."

"So be it. Let him be thy pain. I'll be thy pleasure."

"Oh, Samuel, it will not be easy. We shall have to
be ever on guard, committed to hiding and skulking."

"Aye. We'll have to love by our wits as we used to
do. We'll have to have eyes in the back of our heads.
Like bandits we'll be tied to each other, dedicated to a
single cause, attuned in thought to utilize every opportunity. And if need be, we'll lie, may God forgive
us."

She felt her heart fail. She had not the courage.
She was anything but a gay deceiver. How could she
tell him she would settle for this night and tempt fate no
further?

He went on, keyed up at the challenge of a double
life. "Taboo shall keep us ever young. Danger shall
keep us limber. Narrow escape shall keep us merry.
There are no such excitements in marriage."

"Samuel, I am afraid. I am cold at the thought."

He drew her close. "I'll keep thee warm. There's
naught to fear. God has put us in the way of each
other, and not once but twice. Our love is ordained."

She laughed nervously. "Would I had thy faith,
laddie. What if we're seen going home this day?"

"We shan't be. I shall take my leave of thee now.
I'll row out to my ship and send a hand back for the
horse. As Abigail thinks I sleep on my ship, so the men
think I sleep at home. The only one who might be

suspicious in the least is Will—and I happen to know he's going to help weed his father's flax field today; he'll be nowhere near the harbor. As for thee, listen close. Rest here awhile till the night watch ends. When the sun's well up, roam about the commons for some fence-viewing, or purchase a goat from some farmer. Aye, that's the thing—a nanny to give milk to thy little girl, doctor's orders. When thee rides into town, thee'll give the appearance of coming home from an early morning errand."

She shuddered. "Very well. If thee say so."

They kissed at length, but she was anxious. "And in future? We cannot risk this place often. Mind, last time John was told."

He thought on that. "I have it. London."

"*Lon*don?"

"Aye. Thee'll go on thy new ship with a cargo of oil and I'll sail out on mine. 'Tis a vast city, no frog puddle like Sherburne—lovers can easily get lost in it. I have friends there and kin. We'll put up in separate domiciles—I'll arrange everything."

London? Why not? Her reason for self-confinement no longer existed. Was it possible she was going to begin living at last?

He painted London with a lavish hand. The shops, the balls, the plays, the country seats, perhaps a fox-hunt. The dreamier her smile, the more he laid on color. But her smile was not the smile of a lotus-eater. We could corner the market on sperm oil, she was thinking, we could beat out Folger and Hancock by offering to pay cash and paying a few more pounds per ton. With a virtual monopoly of the British market we could boost the selling price to cover the extra outlay. This was but Sixth Month, there was all the summer to acquire the cargo. . . .

"I must go, my sweeting. Shall thee miss me?"

"Oh, Samuel, I shall think of thee every moment."

She got up with him, and they hooked arms, stood at the door of the cave, gazing at the mild, still dark ocean.

"Not a word, mind, not a look. We must be prudent, patient. Ever so," he warned.

"When shall we meet again?"

"Thee'll know. I'll let thee know. Keep calm but alert, and thee'll get my sign."

At the last, she called him back. "I know what I shall name my new vessel."

"What?"

"Calcutta."

He laughed. "No tellname, that!" They hugged. It was strange to her to be small against a man. John was of a height with her, never so enfolding. They kissed the sun up.

"I must go, love," he said. "I must."

"Wait—I've a business matter to put to thee."

"Not now. I'm late on the tide. We'll talk of it later. We've all the summer." He laughed to the sky and squeezed her to him. "For once money shall make love and love make money—we'll wear business like a cloak. Get inside now."

"Does thee love me the best, Samuel? Above everyone? I need to be first. I've not been."

"Thee has with me. Now and forever."

"And shall we speak truth to each other—tell everything straight out—no lies, no secrets?"

"I have no secret but one and thee's it."

They gripped hands on the covenant, even as she was choosing which gobbets of truth he must never know—her long-suffered deformity, her bout with laudanum, John's carnal knowledge of Debbie, hers. The smuggling, yes, he should know that and soon for she hoped he'd want to throw in with them. She'd tell him in London, that was time enough. *London!*

Sixteen

London, 10thm. 4d., 1762

My dear Debbie:

I am difficulted to credit that I have stayed in Londontown nigh two months. I had intended to leave my Little Kezia but a month at the outside and indeed concluded my business here in short and sound order, but the days fly by in a round of social engagements and I continue to postpone my departure. The weather on the whole hath been prettily sunny but when there is fog it is porridgy. Last week violent east winds blew away the pall of smoke under which the most of London lies, tainting the very vegetables grown here for the markets of Covent Garden. Where I reside however, Rhodes House in St. James Square, the air is somewhat better due doubtless to the greenery of the park.

Lady Anne Rhodes is cousin to Samuel Starbuck who peradventure arrived at Gravesend (via Spain) the very day I did. No sooner were we introduced than she insisted I cancel the lodgings I had procured at The Black Lion and bide under her roof. She is most Gracious and Diverting and we are become great friends. Now she and Lord Rhodes are pressing me to remain at least through Fifth Month at the end of which all retire to a country seat. I am of two minds about it. I miss my dear little daughter, but I am solidifying my position with agents and merchants here as well as learning how vast and wondrous is the European world. Vast yet small, too. Would thee credit that Lady Anne knew our John well in years agone? Writing of John, my heart grows heavy for I am certain he has fallen into severe hardship, or worse. Four years passed

221

and nary a word, not even an inquiry re the child.
If evil chance had not found him surely some
ships captain would have brought tidings if not
from him then of him. We did part in anger but
it is inconceivable to me that he would harbor. . . . .

Her mind snapped shut as it did now whenever
John gained entry. Her eyes wandered to the mullioned
window in the frame of which the leaves of a vener-
able oak turned slowly like so many glasses of different
liquors held up to the light. Champagne, sherry, perry,
claret, muscatel. She savored each color as if she were
tasting it, until gradually her mind eased. Her eyes
softened. At home the commons were rife with these
same spiritous hues and the mauve grasses were ablowing on the hummocks. Two oak leaves, the color of ale,
blinked at her, grave and forgiving as her daughter's
eyes. Little Kezia, born an old soul. She petted the
barbicels of the quill pen and felt instead the silken
brown hairs of the little one's head. Abruptly, she
turned from the window. Get gone from me, Little
Kezia! Nantucket, back off! Thee's bush-sized, thy wine
comes in sips, thee's paltry for me, I would drink my
fill at last, the morning after comes soon enough.

Her thrist was for men—their touch, their praise,
their smiles, their favors. Old and young, bloods and
stableboys, they all noticed her and they all liked what
they saw. It was an overnight miracle! Not one but
gave her a second look, a leer, a wink, a pinch, a whis-
tle. They murmured over her hand, they caught her
waist in the nooks, they pulled chairs for her. They
shouted overloud when she was about, galloped their
mounts too fast, drank too much, swashbuckled,
boasted. They slapped their thighs and flipped their
ruffles and stole looks to see if she saw. Lords and
dukes sent her fans and invitations. The gardeners
brought her chrysanthemums and roses, the cook's boy
left her sweetmeats, the groom fondled her ankle in the

stirrup, the undergroom left notes sticking out of her saddle: "Gor bles yore."

Was it something in *her* eye? Surely not, for even her host palmed her breast or dusted her thigh when he handed her down from a horse or a carriage, and she thought him physically revolting, a descendant of beagles, with jowls, sad drooping eyes, short legs. A sloppy feeder, too, due perhaps to his withered hands; in his fag days at Eton where the sadism of the older boys was renowned he'd been forced to make toast by holding the bread in his fingers. Then there was Charles Chetwynd, the steward, who waylaid her at every turn. He was comely and virile, but he was Lady Anne's man, she'd spotted that right off, and poach she would not. Need not. Samuel Starbuck was all the lover a woman could want, and a business aid to boot. No, the attentions were unsolicited, ever-surprising, heavenly—though as usual her brushes with heaven were ironic. That all this should come not when she was dew-sprent and yearning but when she had reached an age where most women were patching sail, shoring up slack! Every time she looked in the mirror, she was stunned. If she'd looked like this at twenty she'd never have bothered her head about merchanting, she'd have sat back like any Dolly-noddle and let men drop prizes in her lap. A latebloomer, Samuel called her.

She sucked the tip of the quill, waved it back and forth with her tongue. Unfortunately, Samuel was jealouser than a husband, and she was never as kind and considerate as he deserved. She could not resist passing on to him the daily proofs of her desirability. She supposed thus to make him love her the more, but instead it made him hate her admirers to whom he was thereafter rude. He even resented her popularity in mixed company and frowned when she drew laughter. For just as these darling English had pronounced her attractive, so they had proclaimed her a wag, and lo, she was!

This was what she'd have liked to write Debbie, but she feared to sound vainglorious, and as a result crumpled pieces of stationery bloomed like cabbages around her feet.

Ah, Debbie, 'tis as if I'd spent my life inside a cradleshell. I vow I did not know myself till now. I forget I am forty, I feel and look twenty, my heart's in a froth, I'm a syllabub, I fly. But I am often inordinately low as well. I sink unaccountably at a whisper or a frown, fearing insanely that the doors that have suddenly opened to me will as suddenly close. If my natural insecurity does not wing me, then anxiety about John does. It underlies my every waking moment and keeps me tossing at night. I have the strong conviction that he lives, that I should know it if he did not. But I do fear for him. So spake her thoughts but they would not voyage from her head through the pen to paper.

Perhaps she should stick to events. The dinner at Lord Bute's, for example. Fancy it, Debbie, me a cooper's daughter, a guest in the home of the prime minister. I was particularly drawn to his mother, Lady Mary Montague, who is still beautiful, though badly pockmarked. I regretted not being able to talk to her more sensibly for while at table my left thigh was pressed by the current actor-idol David Garrick and my right knee by the Duke of Queensbury. Promiscuous seating, alternating male and female, is the new fashion here. A pity that old goat Paul Starbuck did not live to enjoy it!

Kezia got up and picked a red pear from the basket of fruit the Frenchman had sent her. It tasted as it smelled—of perfume, juicy and succulent—so doubtless it had come from the château country as he claimed; the English pears were woody and bland. She walked about, eating the dripping fruit, eyeing the gold-framed paintings on the damask-paneled walls, running her free hand over the satin half-quilt folded at the bottom of her draped bed.

I wish thee could see the luxury in which these metropolites live, Debbie, could know the time and the money they spend upon their houses and their persons. Why, my mother's hair would turn to snakes if she could see the excess of artifice to which both men and women resort before going forth in broad day. Eye-blackener, face-whitener, freckle creams, herbal washes, depilatories, pomatums, lipsalves, cheek rouges, colognes and astringents, and, would thee credit, *hair-powdering* machines? Toothpick cases, snuffboxes, patch boxes (Yes, thee was right, they do stick moles to their faces, so I am by nature *à la mode* in this respect), eyebrow pluckers, headscratchers (for the scalp under the wig), and, harken to this, *false teeth!* Lady Anne pointed out a set in the mouth of an earl. Imported, she said, made out of pebbles taken from the Nile, I might carry a set home to my stepfather if I could get white ones. Of the Egyptian brown variety he hath his own aplenty.

It doth boggle the mind what people here would rather have than hard cash, and at the outset I fell in with this mania. Tippets, aigrettes, stomachers, periwigs, earrings, brooches—I knew not which to purchase first. Even the little girls wear bone bodices and panniers, and the little boys sport embroidered waistcoats and red heels like the king's. I felt myself to be a hayseed, a very dowd, and during the first week went hog-wild in the shops. Or so I thought till I attended a fancy dress ball. There, in spite of a totally unmanageable hoopskirt and craped hair, I was still the plainest of Janes. For I will not paint and powder and I cannot bring myself to overload a well-cut gown with furbelows. Yet there are those who are attracted by my simplicity: the jaded ones like Lord Eglinton and a young French coxcomb named Duvall. The latter is a member of the peace party here to negotiate a treaty. Likely he was chosen in spite of his youth because he speaks English without a trace of accent and is an excellent player of a popular indoor sport called tennis, pursued here by grown men as enthusiastically as if it were a livelihood. Duvall is a glossy whippet who insists he has fallen in love with me. At a recent party, he presented me with a nosegay and publicly toasted my *simplesse refraichissante.* I tapped him soundly on the head with my fan and reminded him I was old enough to be his mother, but instead of being abashed, he said I must dine with him at Watier's Club and pressed me for a date.

Elbows on the windowsill, Kezia mused about Duvall. A more worldly woman might know how to ward off his attentions. She however was intimidated, made graceless by them. It was as if he were using her to mock womankind. She found him sinister, and Samuel had no more use for the popinjay than she. Duvall kept after her to shop with him. He knew, he said, out-of-the-way wefthouses, silversmiths, cordwainers, milliners, tailors, who offered quality at reasonable prices. She suspected he might get a rake-off for bringing in trade. Anyway, she had temporarily lost her taste for material things, one could not move from desert to jungle without quickly developing a hatred of green. Samuel teased her about her contrariness. "Thee's a born off-islander, Kezia. When in Rome, thee does as the Greeks do. I've no doubt that when thee gets back to Sherburne, thee'll powder thy hair." It was true, there was perversity in her. Even if with but one foot, a toe, she must step outside the circle, be eccentric. Why? Debbie once said, "Thee not only goes out on a limb, Kezia, thee takes the saw along." Did she so dread criticism that she must court it, so quake at the possibility of humiliation that she must flaunt it? Was not this rush to self-exposure the soul of what the Londoners deemed her wit?

Take for proof of her quirky need that incident in Piccadilly when between coach and tavern a bucket of offal came down upon her from an upstairs bay. She nearly swooned with disgust—could swoon just thinking about it—yet it was not an outlandish occurrence, residents in all neighborhoods of London tossed slops into the streets. On this occasion, she was wearing a new Bergère hat which caught the most of it and she forthwith pitched the hat into the gutter. When asked why she was supping in her cap, she replied in such detail the whole company chimed with laughter, and the sound was so gratifying she did bless the shit that ruined her hat. In truth, the pleasure of making laughter was second only to making love. Who could be expected to forsake these enjoyments for the pudgy handclap of a baby girl?

And, oh, Debbie, what would thee say to the night I went to the Cockpit dressed as a blade? Women do not attend these shows, none but strumpets, but I teased Samuel into taking me.

Kezia threw herself across the bed and lay smiling up at the arabesques and grotesques that lived on her ceiling in tinted relief.

"What a pretty sir!" a coxcomb had remarked of her that night, and Samuel had jerked her close, glaring. Whereupon the coxcomb had winked at *him*. Samuel gasped. "God in heaven, he takes thee for my catamite!"

The masquerade outing was meant to be a lark, but somehow it went deeper, she had nightmares about it. All the pushing and shoving and cursing and cheering. The tension of the betting. The stink of rain-soaked wool and hide, of tobacco and male sweat. All those close-packed bodies, gentry and toughs shoulder to shoulder like so many butcher's apprentices in an abattoir, bloodlust oozing out of their shiny cheeks, slavering their mouths, twinking in their narrowed eyes. Down below, not far enough down, in a small-lit glebe, a pair of cocks pecked and clawed and spurred each other to the death. An elegant vicious performance, infused with acrimony as of some ancient family grudge. The first pair went forty-five minutes. Watching, one forgot they were birds; they were caricatures of man, extensions of oneself, at once releasing and satirizing the violence and brotherly hatred that lurks in us all. It fascinated her. But then revulsion set in. She felt menaced by this love-death of cock and man. She looked at Samuel's rapt profile and hated him. He should never have let her come, it was no place for a Christian woman. The air was foul, moist, close, and the crotch of her borrowed smalls was too high in the rise.

She tugged at his sleeve. "Samuel, I have had enough. I can take no more of this mangling. I am quite ill of it. I would go."

"But there are more bouts to come!"

"I care not. I wish to leave now."

"Oh, come, sweetheart. Be sporting, eh?"

The local adjective sounded affected in a Nantucket mouth. "What care I for a cruelty the English term sport? 'Tis disgusting."

"There, there, ducks."

Ducks. Another bit of English coin. "Take me out now," she ordered. "This minute. Samuel, I insist."

"Now, Kezia," he patted her absently, "be not pestiferous. Just a bit more. Only a bit."

She considered leaving alone. But she was afraid to. Dressed as she was—in this crowd of brutes and villains—and then outside was pouring rain. Would she find a hack? All those beggars in the street, the cut-purses—

He had taken her hand and was holding it in a bone-crushing grip. "Lookee there, that brown one, ain't he master brave?" And he yelled in his quarter-deck voice, "Go, Brownie, get his neck!"

"Samuel!" She was surprised to hear her mother's voice.

He smiled sheepishly without taking his eyes from the cocks. "Have to cheer him on, I've a wager on him."

"Thee never!"

"Not much."

"How much?"

"Oh, not more'n'd buy our supper." And forgot her.

By the end, she'd ripped the sleeve of his new plush frock coat and chewed off both her thumbnails. Afterward in his lodgings, they had a beastly row and then made love like beasts. The violence of the show had stirred them to atavism, there was no degradation she would not have submitted to. When he took her home at one o'clock of the new day, he laid her again in the hansom. And fetched her around eleven, shaven and groomed and smelling of Hungary water, to carry her to a Quaker meeting.

"I needed to sleep," she complained, lumpish beside him in the hackney coach.

"Need to go to Meeting more. We both do. Cleanse our consciences. And not a bad thing to show the Rhodes household that thy landsman takes thee to church as well as to suppers and sights."

"Household? Lady Anne never rises till noon, she'll not know. Nor will the steward who lies abed with her. As for the lord, he's walking in the park or riding some bridle path. He goes every morning, he's dead set on keeping fit."

" 'Twill be reported. 'Tis a far more organized house than meets the eye, take my word on't. Come now, honey, thy face is as long as Jacob's courtship. Meeting'll be good for us both. Does thee not feel a soreness of soul after our—uh—debauchery?"

"What I feel," growled Kezia, "is a soreness of cunt."

He laughed aloud and patted her hand. "There's a remedy for that. Abstinence."

She slid him a side-glance. "No need. I heal quick."

He threw an arm around her. "How quick?"

"Directly after the pudding."

He roared. "Oh, Kezia, thee's a good wench. Well, tallyho! We'll to my digs soon's we've et. And afterward, we'll take a turn about St. Paul's. Folks say 'tis well worth seeing. Thee can then tell Lady Anne where we spent the afternoon without speaking a falsehood."

"Omission's as lying as commission." She wished he wouldn't say tallyho.

He nibbled her ear. " 'Tis only for protection, love. We must think of our children." But that was the last thing on their minds as he turned her to him and kissed

her till they were breathless. His hand was well up
her skirt, parting her thighs, her labia. Never mind his
anglicisms, what a way he had, how tender and sure!
She moaned softly, wondering could she hold off till
after dinner.

"Lombard Street, sir!" called the coachman.

They broke in two. They straightened their fronts,
their hats, opened the curtains at each side of the cab,
breathing hectically. Samuel got out and lifted her over
the gutter which ran with the muck of last night's
rain. In the sedate group outside the meetinghouse,
they greeted the Reynoldses, Samuel's kin, parents of
Lady Anne. By the time they had walked through
God's doors, their exteriors at least were in good order.

Might she not tell Debbie she'd been to Meeting
with Samuel? No, better not mention Samuel's name
again. Once was to launder gossip, twice would iron it.
Dare she write of the opera and plays at Drury Lane
and Covent Garden? No wonder the Friends forbade
theatricals, they were more moving than any Quarterly
Meeting. How she had wept at Mr. Barry's portrayal of
Othello, identifying with Desdemona because Samuel
was so jealous-hearted. And then laughed herself sick
at the afterpiece. But no, better not, Debbie might in-
advertently mention it to her mother. Yet there was
this to be said for her mother and all the Friends at
home, never would they have countenanced such pov-
erty as existed in London. Restrained they might be
where pleasure was the condition, but where there was
hardship, they were generous. She could not get over
the inhumanity of the London-towners. Gentry and
rabble lined the streets to jeer at the wretches who were
being carted off to jail or gallows. And, while the man
in the street literally starved to death and drank gin to
kill the hunger pains, the rich ate for social pastime,
even the women were trenchermen.

Not that the food was all that good or even always wholesome. When Kezia was new come, she'd
suffered heartburn, nausea, and diarrhea, until she put
herself on a strict diet: no fish, particularly oysters, no

milk, which was often soured or watered; and certainly no white bread, for the London bakers to whiten the flour, said Lord Eglinton, mixed in bone ash from charnel houses. He may have been pulling her leg, but her gorge rose now at the sight of a piece of breakfast toast. She generally avoided meat, for this nation of beefeaters hung it too long, and she passed up the fancy sweets. Elaborate cake molds were in vogue, such as the hedgehog (a specialty of Rhodes House) with almond quills and currant eyes and dirty fingerprints on the frosting.

At a dinner for the king and queen, eight liveried men had rolled in a seven-foot-high chariot of marchpane. "I'd sooner ride in it than eat of it," Kezia had remarked, setting up a shock wave of titters. Even the beer was risky. Lord Eglinton said that dishonest brewers, faced by the competition of tea, watered the beer and faked a wallop by adding Coculus India Berry, which was a poison. So Kezia ate and drank sparingly—primarily fowl and cheese; cereals, fruits, and nuts; and tea or coffee or wine. But every time her full plate was taken away virtually untouched she thought of the hordes who lay dying of malnourishment in the tenements across town and of the hundreds imprisoned in Newgate for stealing bread.

A knocking at her chamber door made her start.

"Mistress Coffin?"

"Is't thee so soon, Bridget?"

She jumped up from the little bureau and opened the door to a stout old woman in apron and mobcap. Snowy curls bobbed around the pink face as the lady's maid bent a knee.

" 'Tis on to one o'clock, Mistress Coffin. My lady has risen and would be pleased to have your company."

Kezia hurriedly bent to gather the balled discards. "No, no, don't bother to help. I've been trying to write a letter home. Can't seem to collect my thoughts. I'll just save these sheets and finish later. Thanks to thee, Bridget, but I bid thee go. I must dress. No, no, I manage better by myself. Not used to being waited upon. Thee may tell thy mistress I'll be there directly."

As soon as the maid was gone, Kezia threw the rejected papers into the fire. Samuel had warned her to be on guard in Rhodes House.

"My cousin's a practiced spyer, they don't come any nosier. I've been a guest there myself and I know for a fact the porter steams envelopes, incoming and outgoing, without leaving a trace. 'Tis said there are peepholes in every chamber. Don't trust Bridget either, for all her curtsies and smiles. They've been thick as thieves since they were girls. She was the daughter of the diary maid where Anne was reared in Denham Park, and she'd put her hand in hot fat for her mistress. Giles, the hairdresser, is another spy. She trains them to it. Pays them overwell too, I don't doubt. Aye, the bargains under that roof be long struck and strong kept. Don't trust a one of them, not even a scullery maid."

Even so, Kezia was enchanted by her hostess and this hour of chitchat each nooning was one of the high points of the visit. Anne Reynolds had been a celebrated beauty, all peaches and gold and Devonshire cream, with eyes as blue as Oriental turquoises. One could still see what Lord Rhodes had been willing to trade a title for, and in spite of his ugliness, Lady Anne had done her part, giving him three sons. The eldest, an officer in the Footguards, Kezia had met when he was drilling in St. James Park and had liked his looks very much. In fact, a thought had crossed her mind but she had tossed it overboard. 'Twas said there were only seven faces in the world and there were many lovely Englishwomen, John could not have slept with them all.

Now, when she must prop her waning looks, Lady Anne had become expert at the art, and Kezia loved to watch the careful lengthy toilette, loved to go through the jewel box, sample the perfumes, set the music boxes atinkling, help choose the dinner gown, hear closet talk about the people she'd met and had yet to. It tickled

her perspective to hear about England's upper crust,
and it was reassuring to see how unpunished in the age-
old Motherland went adultery, gaming, gluttony, sloth,
vanity, and chicanery of all kinds.

For her part, Lady Anne was delighted to have an
attractive younger companion. What better confidante
than one who'd be gone with the spring winds, posing
no serious threat of competition or betrayal? Gone? Oh
dear, she would miss Kezia. She who had become accustomed to arid boredom would not soon forget the
oasis afforded by this bright, complex girl-woman who
sat at her knee and watched her apply eye shadow as
a novice might a priestess, who could take a joke as
well as crack one, who could complement a disparate
personality without losing an iota of her own. Yes, she
could understand why the elusive John Coffin had
chosen this one for marriage.

Thus an intimacy was sprung up between the two
women, an intimacy based as much on what they
kept from each other as what they told. Kezia gave no
hint of Chetwynd's backdoor wooing and Lady Anne
breathed no word of John's infidelity. Oh, yes, that
triangular affair with Bridget as their sexual minion
had continued well after his marriage. Before it ended
it had unlocked her ladyship's womb so that she was
able to produce an heir, and afterward conceived twice
by her proper lord, though the touch of those burned
hands was not easy to endure. How complicated lives
became, and for the simplest reasons! It had even occurred to Lady Anne that there might be something
going on between her cousin Samuel Starbuck and
Kezia, but she rejected the possibility on two counts.
One, Samuel was too straitlaced, a devout Quaker.
And two, they were not covert enough in their comings
and goings for a pair who had something to hide. But
would it not be the cream of the jest for John Coffin to
be wearing horns instead of giving them?

On to one? How had it got so late? Kezia fos-
sicked here and there. Her hair, a lace fichu, the green
moiré slippers, the gold brooch Lady Anne had given

her. Tsk—inkstains on her fingers! And those wretched thumbnails, would they never grow out? She washed briefly in the bowl, wiped most of the ink off on the towel, threw the towel on the floor. Too neat, the maids didn't think one a gentlewoman.

Charles Chetwynd was leaving Lady Anne's apartments as Kezia came flying down the corridor and slid to a stop, off-balance as always in his presence. In his one hand a sheaf of papers, in the other a ring of keys. Had the visit been as businesslike as these indicated? There were fresh wet comb tracks in his brindle hair.

"Good day to thee, Mister Chetwynd. Is it not a fine day?"

" 'Tis now that I've laid eyes on you, mistress. Did anyone ever tell you you've a smile that could ripen cucumbers?"

Kezia blushed. *"Vous me flattez, monsieur."*

He frowned. "Is that molly, Duvall, teaching you French? I'd not hang about with him if I were you, he's not a gentleman. Well, I must be off. Your servant." He took her hand, bowed formally over it. Then quickly he turned it palm up and planted there a sucking kiss. "You are adorable," he whispered, and stalked off. His heels were long gone before she stopped trembling.

Lady Anne's sitting room smelled as usual of jessamine, an odor Kezia found urinous, but by the time one crossed to the bedchamber it was lost in a potpourri of cosmetics and salves and lotions. The apartment was overpoweringly feminine, jam-packed with cupids and rosebuds and tasseled pillows and colors as lambent as a rainbow. A man had no place here save in the bed—a seven-foot square that Lady Anne laughingly referred to as her workbench. The marble fireplaces were small but there were two in each room, kept morning and night, so it was always a shade overwarm. The furniture was painted or gilt or inlaid wood, what could be seen of it under the tossed hats and camisoles and gloves and stockings, all re-

flected and re-reflected in a profusion of *rocaille* mir-
rors.

Lady Anne sat at a kneehole dressing table, *en
négligé*. One smooth white breast confessed to the
triptych mirror an olive nipple, an inch below peak
ripeness. Against the mirror stood a row of "fashion
babies," Parisian dolls imported to show the latest
French styles of hair and garb. Giles, the resident hairdresser, was combing Lady Anne's gold hair, which
was fine as a crane-fly's legs, into clumps of fuzz.

"Tease it more, ducks. *Moutonné* is the rage."

"Heads bigger than one's body are ugly," the
hairdresser protested.

"What a gloomy boy you are! Do it my way today. Tomorrow you may have yours. Now do stop
pouting. Kezia, what's made you rosy? You've a blush
on your cheek!"

Under the cobalt scrutiny, Kezia's color deepened.
"I slept uncommon well."

"—and stole your breath?"

"I hurried here."

"Why hurried? How've you spent the morn?"

"Writing letters. I cannot seem to find time—"

"Higher on the left, Giles. That bloody cowlick.
Aye, that's got it. Now be a good chap and make haste.
You're late for Monsieur Duvall. Would you believe,
Kezia, the bad luck I had with that Frenchman of
yours? I wagered that a certain duchess—you don't
know her but he does, he knows everyone, the scamp
—I wagered she was merely grown fat, not *enceinte*.
A reasonable assumption since her husband has been
in America for over a year fighting the French and the
Indians. Well, I lose. Though I still think the lady's
maid was fibbing, I think Duvall got to her first with a
small tip, considerably smaller of course than the
wager. He's not to be trusted, you know. Oh, he can be
charming and he's quite off his head about you, but I
doubt he's ever really off his head. He's paid very little
by his government and he has improvident habits so he
must use his wits to get by. Very well, Giles, be off.

And mind what you just overheard. Duvall is money-grubbing. See you get paid for anything else you do for him, I only paid for *wigs!*" She examined her head from all sides with a hand mirror. "Do you agree with him, Kezia? Is it teased too high? I don't want to look ugly, it's quite bad enough to look *old*."

"To my view, it looks fluffy and nice."

"Ah, my dear. Well, and which gown shall it be? Something elegant, those coming are either very rich or very wellborn or high in the king's favor. And their women are buffleheads. You and I should have a quite merry time of it."

"The celery, the one you wore to Lady Mary Montague's. Thy skin is like Meissen in that color."

"Very well, the celery. Bridget, did you get the wine stain out of the skirt?"

"And how seems London to the eyes of a Quakeress?"

Kezia was pleased to find herself seated next the famed Jew, Samuel Gideon. Merchant princes were far more interesting than the idle, effeminate princes of the blood. They knew the world markets, and from one who had made his own fortune, there were pointers to be picked up. "Sir, this Quaker's eyes falter at the luxury and opulence. Ostentation here is as much a virtue as at home 'tis a sin. I speak not in criticism but in comparison. So much richness, so much waste!"

"Quite right, quite right. We English are living in a most prodigal era. A time of great excess and great privation. Why, I understand it costs fifteen pounds a night in candles to illuminate Houghton Hall. 'Tis a wonder thy people who deal in spermaceti oil have not come to making candles of it."

"Hm. That is worth a ponder. We've not a single chandlery on our isle."

His gooseberry eyes fastened upon her tuckered bosom.

"No question spermaceti candles are superior. They burn whiter, brighter, longer."

"Aye. Well, seems to me I've heard there's some secret to the refining. The Brown brothers of Providence buy the raw material from us. Fame says they suffer no one to enter their manufactory. 'Tis all very hush-hush."

"Well, now, where's your enterprising spirit, gel? Others discovered the secret, so could you. Dressed more richly, a jewel or two, I vow you'd outshine every woman here. They're but Jenny Wrens under their finery. All it takes is money and now I've told you how to get it." He leaned close, said softly, "When the time comes, my dear, I could put you in touch with some friends of mine in Newport, Rhode Island, who ship substantial quantities of candles."

The old dear, likely close with a dollar but here he was, thinking her poor, offering her a way to get rich. "I am most grateful, sir. I shall look into it upon my return."

But she was less indulgent of the Duchess of Queensbury who inattentively addressed her as 'Mistress Grave.'

"Casket, your grace."

"Ah, of course. Mistress Casket, how stupid of me."

Lady Anne gasped. The duchess was cousin to Queen Anne. She stood up, signaling the ladies. The men, by custom, sat on, twiddling their brandies, waiting to relieve their bladders, the dinner having gone on from two o'clock to after five. The sideboard contained, besides urns for cold drinking water and hot water for washing the flat silver between courses, a cellarette in which was kept a chamber pot for the gentlemen's use after the ladies had withdrawn.

Since the day was fine, some of the ladies took this interlude to walk to the Necessary House at the back of the grounds. Kezia found herself strolling alongside the Duchess of Queensbury. The duchess asked her, as did everyone, how she found London, and this time, regretting her rudeness, Kezia replied politely: Ranelagh. Vauxhall Gardens. Marylebone.

"Psittacisms!" hissed the duchess. "Tell me what you don't like. What's horrid about us?"

Kezia thought of the day Samuel had carried her to the Tower Zoo for she'd never seen a lion or a monkey. Outside the tower for a copper, a man took vipers out of his bag, played with them, and then stuffed one into his mouth. But free at Charing Cross on the way home was the spectacle of two beggars in pillory being stoned by a crowd. Nearby a little girl of about nine or ten holding a doll was about to be dropped from a gibbet.

The coachman had commented over his shoulder, "Young for a pickpocket, ain't she?" Samuel urged him to get quickly through the mob for Kezia had hid her face in his shoulder. The coachman laid about with his whip, cutting a path through the people. At that Kezia cried out, "I hate this city! I had rather be a lion or a tiger, they are cleaner, nobler beasts!"

She said now to the duchess, "Well, as thee asks, thy cruelty. I don't mean to cocks and bulls and bears, but to each other. And it's not a matter of class. The poor are no more merciful to each other than the rich are to them. They attend hangings as gleefully as they would a play. Is it a national characteristic, this cold-heartedness, I wonder, or is it a universal stamp of the city? I know not the ways of American city folk. I have not yet visited Boston or New York or Philadelphia, though I hope to soon. But on our island no one is permitted to go hungry, and the jail is usually empty but for a stray sheep or cow. At Nantucket torture as a punishment is rarely carried out. Oh, now and then against a rumpot Indian, but fines are generally the rule."

"And indenture for those who cannot pay?" drawled the duchess.

"Aye, that is a fearful abuse, I own it. Yet I think the Friends are kind overall. And though we live primitively yet there is an insistence upon good manners that I see not here. We are more restrained, more—" She broke off. The duchess's eyes were narrowed, her chin high. Was it the light of the dying sun or did she feel affronted? "I'm sorry to sound smug or subversive. In a way I admire the lack of constraint here, it's freer. And I assure thee I consider myself English, a loyal subject of the king. I suppose generalities are silly."

They both ignored the sudden rumble and stink from the privy.

"No," said the duchess, "they are impressions, and impressions do reflect the national temper. But this changes according to the times and the reigning king, so I don't think—"

Their turn had come. Kezia fell back a step in deference to age and rank. The duchess tucked up her petticoat. She smiled. "My dear Mistress *Coffin,* we must talk further. I'd be pleased to have you dine with us on the morrow. The Rhodeses too, naturally. I shall speak to Lady Anne. Not a large dinner. Twelve only, my maximum for conversational exchange. I do hope you can come."

So it went—one social triumph after another. She might have ridden the culm of the wave well into springtime had not Chetwynd toppled her. Aye, toppled was the word for it, no mistake. It happened that Lady Anne could not accept the invitation to Queensbury House, she was promised elsewhere, but Kezia could and did. Afterward, having spent her energy in a stimulating company that had included poets, playwrights, and such intellects as Lord Elibank and Dr. Samuel Johnson, she begged leave of her host to sup in her chambers and go early to bed. Around nine, she was at the bureau by the fire in her nightcap, trying to put an ending to the letter to Debbie, when there came a knock at her door. She opened it to the steward who stepped in quickly. For a moment he said nothing, only leaned against the closed door, listening with his eyes.

"Mister Chetwynd! What's amiss?"

He was on her in a leap. She could not believe his strength. "Kezia, Kezia, I am maddened! You've bewitched me till I cannot work—sleep—eat. I do naught but think of you, yearn for you. I must have you. Fear not—the coast is clear, I assure you. Oh, sweet love—"

She was struggling, beating at him. "Belay! Thee's daft, sir!"

"Dammit, I beg you, don't fight me, girl. You are not cold to me, I've seen it. I'm not a boy, nor you a virgin. What's to be lost, tell me that? I'll give you such pleasure, Kezia. Only let me—"

She ducked her head from his hot breathy kisses. For pounding his chest she had no leverage, he'd pinned her elbows in his coil. Both her legs were locked in his, she could not get a knee up. All she could do was half-kick, but she was barefoot and he wore boots. He smelled of fog and horse and brandy—he must have come in from the outside—and his cock pressed her thigh, plump and lively as a summer rabbit. It turned her languid, slowing her blood, swelling her breasts, tingling her nipples. Her head fell back and her eyes closed as he kissed her throat, bit her shoulder. He began to undress her. She muttered through slack lips of 'danger' and 'folly.' He picked her up and threw her on the bed. A whizzing sound—his belt?—roused her. Had she too gone mad? A guest in—! She jumped up and would have slipped past him but he caught her, one-armed, yanked open his breeches, and took her on the settee with his boots on. He ejaculated instantly. She lay violated, high and dry.

His breathing rasped the dark.

"Feeling better?" she asked bitterly.

" 'Twas your trying to get away. Fox'n hound, you know. Wrought me up. Be quiet a while. It will be good, I promise you."

The little fireplace sent giant shadows leaping on the dim wall. The only other light was the candle flame on the desk. Though the top of his boot was cutting into her leg and his bulk grew painful to support, she went flashy with desire, careless, insistent. Oh, damn, was he going to turn out to be another John, all blow and no show? But she waited as she'd been bid, patient as a cat. At length he carried her again to the bed, covered her to the neck, and soon joined her, naked, between the silks. She lay limp in his arms as he stroked her, until he was hard. Only then did she dare to enjoy. He fondled her expertly, every crevice, every orifice. At his whispered command, "Don't hold back, there'll be more," she let herself go, crying out behind stretched lips, as his tongue and whiskers brought her to clitoral climax. Then he was the one who must be patient and he was and he was and he was until both went down in a spiral of sensation, pelvises grinding rapturously to a halt. He remained mounted, resting on his elbows, and urged her to several quick high alarms.

The ormolu clock on the mantel triple-timed her own vaginal throb, and she thought, I ought to have known, Lady Anne's a demanding woman. And he was affectionate too, holding her hand in the quiet under the quilt.

After a bit, he got up. She raised her lids with some reluctance. He brought the candle from the bureau to the table by the settee. He picked up his smalls, but stood ruminatively, making no attempt to don them. She looked closer. His tool had packed off. A single drop of dew hung from the slit in the rosebud in a nest of black hair. With the tip of her finger she wiped the drop away. He grabbed her hand and kissed it. The gesture had a simple finality. She yawned, stretched—sleepy. Watching him dress, she was glad that she was the one to stay, she'd have hated to stir from the warm snug bed, the halls were cold. Her arms lay bent on the pillow above her loose hair, and the blood purled like syrup under her velvet skin.

Dressed, he made a tent over her.

"Gor blind me," she said in the voice of the undergroom. " 'Tis quite a ride ye give, sire."

He grinned down at her. "My pleasure."

"Is it true there are peepholes?"

"Yes, but this is her whist night. They're all out or tucked. Giles, the little fly, is bumfiddling with his new chum, Duvall."

"So he definitely—?"

"Duvall? Of course. And the porter's in Bethnal Green with his sick mum. As for the lord, he sleeps like a polar bear. And Bridget's snoring her frowzy head off—I gave her a tankard of Irish without water to take to bed with her. Told her she looked to be coming down with a cold."

She smoothed the hairs on his ridgepole hand. She accepted his light kiss on her forehead as a street girl might accept money, faintly smiling.

"You bear no grudge then?" he asked. "I am not shamed in your eyes?"

"Nay, nay. But shall I be ashamed of myself on the morrow?"

"Why? You're blameless. I raped you. Good God, what if I seeded you?"

"No chance of that. And it was seduction only. Thee's a good and tender man. And ever so well-hung," she teased. "Thy lady's a lucky woman. Don't cloud over. She'll never know, so we've not done her a harm."

"Perchance a help. You see, I was losing my powers. I suppose that's what drove me berserk—no reflection, ma'am, on your charms. But dammit, a woman must not rule the rooster as well as the roost—it foils nature. I thought I was done for. Now I know better, I'll not bother you more. Too chancy."

"So thee does have fear!"

"Oh, fear. I've a belly full. One comes to the end of it. I'd sooner die a rooster than a capon."

"How old be thee, Charles?"

"Thirty-eight. She's forty-six. Leastwise that's what she admits to, she may be a good deal more. But oh, she was once fair, so fair! Anyway, she's frantic. She's come to the change, d'ye see?"

"I shall be forty at Christmastide."

"Gad. You could be her sucklebrat. Clean air's what does it. London's foul in winter. And the rich living. Well, the hour grows late. I'll be off. Give me one more smile of forgiveness for the road."

They smiled at each other, two comrades who

have met lightly and part the same. Into the quiet
there dropped a single small alien sound, no more than
the squelch of a kelp bead. He was gone like a shadow. She never even heard the door close though she
was listening for it. But she did not fret. He knew the
household, forsooth, he ran it, and he had reassured
her. She fell soundly asleep without another thought.

The next morning she woke and remembered and
tested her feelings. No remorse. No attachment at all.
They were but ships that had spoken each other in the
night and sailed on. Was this a sign of maturity? Taking life as it came and not browbeating it to death?
High time, then. And how nice.

The maidservant had left her tea in a cozy, buttered scones under a silver bell, and a scrawled note on
crested stationery: Lady Anne saying that she was
feeling under the weather and would not be visited this
noon. Another message from Lord Rhodes hoping
that since they'd both had a long night's sleep she
would ride in the park with him this morning. She
pulled a bell rope to call the maid to deliver her regrets
to her host. She breakfasted with relish, rolled over,
and went back, luxuriously, to sleep.

She woke to a plank of yellow sunshine across the
foot of her bed and a knocking at the door. Bridget
with word that Monsieur Duvall waited upon her in
the parlor downstairs to take her to the shops. What a
good day for it! She bounded up and dressed quickly.
Beside some oddments of clothing, she wanted a set
of three-tined forks and some plate cast with the Coffin
crest. If Duvall got a commission behind her back,
what of it?

They were both in a state of exuberance, giggly as
girls together, the first time she'd felt easy with him.
He helped her select two gowns and a hat, she saw him
fitted for a flowered waistcoat. The cutlery they put off
till after they'd had a bite to eat at Slaughter's where
she'd often supped after theater and where the *crème
brûlée au caramel* was nothing short of ambrosia.

She said, scraping the dish with the tip of her spoon, "I came with a swept hold, did I not? I wish I knew the receipt for this custard. D'ye think they'd give it? I've a clever cook. Mmm. Makes me rather sympathetic to cannibals—tastes like baby skin lightly baked in caramel."

He laughed, and after a moment said casually, "I'm afraid last night's indiscretion will cost you a hundred pounds, *cherie*. I do hope it was worth it, though I suppose to a woman of your means a hundred pounds is hardly—"

Her spoon fell with a clatter that made the waiter look.

He went on in the same dulcet tone, "Have I shocked you, *ma pauvre?* Oh, I do hate myself for this. We were having such a happy time!"

Kezia gave him an aqueous smile, unable to break her incredulous stare. "Thee prattles, Duvall—whatever of?" But her voice, like her mouth, shook.

"Of money, *ma chère amie,* the root of all evil and source of all good. I am vastly underpaid, but I will live in the Haute Monde and so am forced to scrounge. You were seen, *comprends?* By my little friend Giles."

She was all water now, running hot and cold under a goose-bumped skin that scarcely covered the nerve ends. She saw the bumps on her lower forearms below the lace-frilled three-quarter sleeves. She covered them with long firm hands. "What does he say he saw?"

"Madame, pray, do not make me spell it out, there's no time for quibbling. I promised Lady Anne I'd have you back in time to dress for the performance of *Hamlet* tonight. I hope our little *tête-à-tête* does not leave, as they say, a bad taste in the mouth. Such a waste of good crème."

"Lady Anne's ill abed today, that's how well informed thee is."

"A ruse, *chérie.* So that you and I could get our—ahm—business done. I am bidden to tell you your stay at Rhodes House has come untimely to an end. *Fini.*" His hands sliced air.

Kezia sat, shafted. Booted out? By her friend? Via this corrupt little fox-faced foreigner? But how did she find out? Who saw? That sound—? Of all the wild questions that went whirling through her mind, she could not find a safe one to ask. She was again a little girl, trying to maintain her balance in the crotch of the live oak with the wind and the dark webbing her about. She drew her mantle close. "Am I stupid or is thee addled? I make no sense of this."

"You're addled, and who could blame you? Were I in your shoes, I'd be the same. Oh, *ma pauvre petite*, don't scrutinize me, I'm easy enough to read—a black-guard who's short of funds, *c'est tout.*"

"And Lady Anne? Is she too short of funds?"

"Jamais, chérie. She paid me well. Part of it must go for this meal, *tant pis.* But the rest—well, I do need a new waistcoat, one sees the same people wherever one goes, one simply can't wear the same things, night after night."

If only her head would stop spinning! It was like being drugged without the body float. "Why did Lady Anne not pay Giles instead of thee?"

"Oh, she did, she did. Giles reported first to her. Always does. But the dear boy knows I am put to my shifts with not only tailoring bills, but card debts. I tell you, I'd do anything for money—short of kill, I'm not a violent chap, just weak—so he suggested to Lady Anne that she let me be the liason. Easier on both of you, *n'est-ce pas?* I am a diplomat, you know. This hasn't been too nasty, has it? Now, be a good girl and come across without further shilly-shally. *Mon dieu,* what's a measly hundred pounds to a woman with ships in every sea?"

She watched, huddled in her mantle, while Duvall counted out the dinner money three times. His forehead knotted as he figured aloud the smallest gratuity he could decently leave. He chided her good-humored-ly about the dessert charge. "Most women, even English ones, find the beefsteak sufficient." The old waiter had edged closer and was eyeing the count. It was evidently suitable for he thanked the Frenchman, not warmly but not surlily either, and padded off.

"Eh bien? Shall we not conclude this—ah—little matter?"

"What precisely am I to 'come across' for?"

"Rogering with the steward."

The swallow of tepid tea sprayed from her mouth.

"I am sorry to be vulgar, but you would make me say it."

"It's not vulgarity I mind," said Kezia, over the first shock, somewhat recovered, "it's the flummery. If Lady Anne has been told such a thing, true or false, then the mischief is done, isn't that so? Why should I pay thee hush money? Does thee think to tell my husband? Thee'd have to catch him first. I'd pay thee a hundred pounds to find him."

"Not your husband. Don't take me for a dolt."

Kezia sat back, genuinely mystified.

"Your lover, Monsieur Starbuck. Is a very jealous man, is he not?"

She picked up a glove, began to pull it on. Anger blew through her, rising, freshening, clearing the cobwebs from her brain as a wet nor'easter sweeps out a barn loft. "Her ladyship has indeed a most competent spy ring. I had heard of it. 'Tis a pity her talents for intrigue are wasted on such small beer. She should be working in the government service."

He grimaced with impatience. "No, no, *no!* You've got it all wrong. Lady Anne has no concern with your amours, nor Monsieur Starbuck's. *She's* only interested in the steward. It is I, *comprends?* I am a professional blackmailer. A lady of your beauty, and pardon, your age, far away from home—she is apt to play a bit, no? Even a Quaker lady. For to be Godfearing is not to say one does not sin, only that one trembles more when one does. Well, then. First I discover you have a lover. I follow you. I inquire. The charwoman at Monsieur Starbuck's lodgings is helpful, she wants money, who does not? But then I find your husband is lost at sea. *Quel dommage! Mais* a lady who cheats on her husband, she will also *peut-être* cheat on her lover. You see, Duvall has the experience, also the intuition. I follow you when you are out, and Giles, my little slave, he watches within. It seemed possible that you and Lord Rhodes—" He sighed ruefully. "The lord is rich, very rich. It would have meant a great deal to me and nothing to Lady Anne. She'd never kick you out if you were servicing the lord. *Au contraire.*"

He blinked as she picked up her reticule and stood.

"Thee may report thy mission accomplished. I shall leave Rhodes House on the morrow. Odd, I had this feeling about thee from the first—female intuition, I have it too. There was this curious smell of scum about thee, I know it from our ponds, the stagnant ones."

Ah, that was better, she'd been altogether too cool, he'd almost kissed the money off. "I am accustomed to insults, dear. There remains only the—" He smiled, rubbed his forefinger with his thumb.

"Thee's mistook me, Duvall. I am mine own woman. I answer to no one. Not a farthing shall thee get from me."

"Oh, if you're going to be like that, I shall have to call upon Monsieur Starbuck."

"Do. He'll bash thy head in and thee'll be none the richer."

"That remains to be seen. He has a wife and children at home. And he is a man who cares about appearances." He stood up, correcting the tilt of his tricorn.

She pushed him down. "Sit still, whippersnapper, I'll bring my own hack to."

And she did, having swept out without a backward glance. But once inside the carriage, she began to shake and pound all over. And to burn, her skin dry and hot. Getting sick? Oh, dear Lord, not now, when she had neither bed nor roof. Stop it. Self-pity's all.

There are plenty of places to sleep, Samuel's bed, for instance, till he could find her a berth on a departing ship, or she could let rooms in a private home or The Black Lion. But oh, she'd hope he found a vessel soon, she could not wait to get out of London. And oh, it would be dreadful to board a ship already ill; the sea made a hard enough pillow for a poor sailor.

"Where to, mum?" asked the coachman.

"What? Oh. I don't know. I'm not sure." How she wanted to give in to the shakes and the fever, just let go, lie down, be sick. Then he'd be concerned for her, fuss over her, no matter what. Her true love Samuel might not be, but he was all the world to her now. Was God punishing her? Dear Lord, I cannot do without Samuel, don't rob me, I beg—

The coachman coughed, showed a jowl thready with burst blood vessels.

"Drive a bit. I want air."

"Very well, mum."

She had an impulse to go back and find Duvall. Should she have downed her pride and bought him off? If it had been anyone but the steward! Oh, what a trial was a suspicious man! Not her fault—rape, after all. She'd fought like a tigress, and afterward—well, once the fat was in the fire, why not eat of it? A man, any reasonable man, ought to be able to see that. But Samuel was not reasonable. And he did care about appearances, his public image was important to him.

She looked out the window and saw a couple kissing in a doorway, the man's hand on the girl's backside. She felt suddenly raunchy. She thought of Samuel's burly body. She gave the coachman Samuel's address.

She intended to plan a strategy, something to discredit Duvall's story should he peach to Samuel. Instead she found herself thinking of Chetwynd. At least he had been honest with her, for a moment there she'd thought Lady Anne had put him to stud to raise cash. The coach stopped, and there they were in Old Bond Street. Samuel's upstairs sitting-room window was open. Was he at home betimes then? Her heart began to thud. Fear or desire?

She let herself in with her key. He was not at home. She paced the small rooms, mere staterooms compared to her quarters. She picked up a sampler that had fallen from its nail to the floor. It said in cross-stitches, "To thine own self be true." She put it up so belligerently, the nail came out and this time she let it stay floored.

"Kezia?" Samuel called. He came in and took her in his arms. "I thought thee gone to a play. Is thee fed? Can thee stay?" He put her in the wing chair. "Thee's cold-handed. How can thee be cold in Tenth Month? How'll thee stand the winter? I must get thee a cloak lined with fur. What would thee, ermine or sable? Here, I'll strike a light to the fire. Blast that char, she doesn't even know how to lay a few logs. She's not been in today at all. I know because that sampler fell this morning before I left."

"Thee should sack her," said Keiza, shivering.

"I can't, she belongs to the landlord. Came with the house."

"Well, tell him then how badly she's done—or write him."

"I shall. I've been with my Uncle Reynolds at the coffeehouse in Bow Street to read the news and get the 'changes. He told me Lady Anne was carrying thee with a party to the theater." He got up from his knees, the fire caught, and decanted brandy into two glasses. "The fact is the main business of the life of man is the getting of money, just as the main business of sheep and cows is to crop grass. Now, my deary, here's a snifter. To us! Down the hatch. Something's amiss, I can see it, but don't tell me till thee's warmed thy insides." He sat down in the chair opposite her.

"I don't want any. I've come from Slaughter's—a spit from where thee sat in Bow Street—and I've had food and drink up to here. London too and all its inhabitants *and* its visitors. I've been with that loathsome little flitter, Duvall, and oh, Samuel, thee'll not credit the trumpery he tried to blackmail me for."

She got up and flung down into Samuel's lap, joggling his glass. He dabbed at the brandy down his front. "Dearest, do buck up. Thee's taut as a harp string."

She put her cheek to his. "Oh, Samuel, be my snug harbor, hold me close. I do so need thee."

The Windsor creaked under their combined weights. He set the brandy down and holding her about, moved to the wing chair.

"So. The French peacock found out about us, did he? Someone was bound to, thee must have known that."

"That's not the crux of it. He's a professional rook. He followed us here, bribed the charwoman."

"Well, who'll he tell? John? He'd have to put a note in a bottle, throw it out to sea, and trust to the tides. As for my wife, she told me to do the best I could for myself." He squeezed Kezia's waist. "And so I have. The best. So who's there to tell? Lady Anne? I know too much about her peccadilloes to fear her tongue. She's never been faithful to her lord, not for a day."

"Will thee but listen, Know-it-all? He's not threatening to tell Lady Anne. That was *my* first thought. He says she couldn't care less about us. Nay, it's Chetwynd's wooing of me he'd tell her. By this time, *has.*"

His arm fell away. He moved out from under her, fetched his brandy with a shaking hand.

"Chetwynd's had *thee?*" he choked at the ceiling, giving her his back.

"Blast thee, Samuel, for being so predictable! Of course he has not. How can thee ask?"

"The story's of whole cloth?"

"To the last ell."

"Then why's thee so roiled?" He whirled, peered into her face like a barrister. "Tell me that, eh? Why?"

"At being gulled—it infuriates me. A hundred pounds he wants to keep mum."

"A hu—? But that's absurd!"

"I could've struck him. No, don't light the candles, I prefer the dusk."

"But Lady Anne's thy friend! She'd not take the word of a cheap foreigner."

"Oh, what thee does not know about women! Chetwynd is to her what thee is to me," he winced at her bluntness but she was too intent to notice, "and she's so afraid of ageing—all her life she's relied upon her beauty and now it's slipping away. She's terrified she'll lose him to someone younger. She's right too, she will, she'll drive him away by trying to hold him too fast. Anyway, her mere suspicioning would besmirch our friendship—there'd always be the nagging doubt. Worse, Giles, her hairdresser, is in on the lie. He's become Duvall's *lady*—oh, isn't it a pretty web!—and he knows Duvall's hard-pressed for money and wants to help him. He's prepared to swear he saw Chetwynd and me through one of those fiendish peepholes thee told me of."

"Then Chetwynd may swear the opposite and put an end to it."

She pressed her hand to her accelerating heart. The path she'd chosen—half-truth—was strewn with pitfalls, she had to dodge about. Now she realized she'd missed a turning, had best backtrack. "The fact is, Giles has already tattled and she does believe. She's sent me packing. My term at Rhodes House is 'untimely ended,' I am told."

"What? She said this?"

"Nay, Duvall relayed the message, over *crème brûlée*. She directed him to. Paid him to act as liaison to save us abashment."

Samuel put his empty glass down firmly. "Then we shall go to her. Together we shall face her down. I'll not have thee treated thus shabbily. Sending thee forth like a common wench on the word of a sodomite servant, 'tis a gross outrage. I'll make her sorry."

"Wait, Samuel, cool down. I'd not stay in any case. And I wish no confrontment."

"Wherefore? Has thee lied to me, Kezia?" He grabbed her wrist, twisted it. "Speak now! I'll have the truth or we are finished, thee and I, once and for all time."

She glared at him, tears filling her eyes though he was not hurting her that much. Selfish prig. How desperately she needed to speak truth, for her own sake. Not for absolution but for purge, not for redemption but for evaluation. She had so little feeling for the steward, scarcely knew him nor wished to. Was she a courtesan at heart as her mother had always believed? "Wanton jadehopper." Hitherto when she'd loved— John, Debbie, Samuel—she had cared profoundly, the bodily pleasure originating in brain and heart. But Charles was a passing stranger before and after. Was she losing fiber? Was her character gradually denaturing till one day she'd be as without honor as Duvall himself? What did God think of her? Was He consigning her to the devil? If not, why this dreadful aftermath of an essentially superficial experience? With Debbie she could have expressed all this. Between them they'd have talked it out. But this brother-face, this father-voice—damn the man, what she needed was a friend, not a Recording Angel. She'd pledged him no troth. What gave him the right to sound off like a lawful husband?

He flung her wrist down, and, rubbing it, she thought of Lady Anne's counsel during one of their confabs: "Never tell a man the truth. I don't care what he is to you. There's not a man flexible enough to accept it. The weakest woman is twice as strong and half as vain as any man this side of the grave."

She licked her lips. "Very well. He did come maddened to my door—"

"Chetwynd did?" Samuel began nervously to light candles, striking flint, cupping flames till they flowered. He poked the fire, left the poker unhung, stumbled over it twice, unseeing.

She plunged on. "Last night when all in the

household were asleep or abroad. I'd supped in my
rooms. I was fatigued from a dinner party at Queensbury House. I intended early retirement and was closing a letter to Debbie when someone knocked. I opened
the door and he whipped inside before I could—he was
importunate—drunk, I dare say. I fought him off. Oh,
I said some sharp things and soon brought him to
senses. He's a decent man at heart, he was just temporarily beside himself. He left—uh—before—without—
with profuse apologies and no harm done. Giles can
make something of it, but that's the long and short of
it."

Samuel picked up his brandy glass and hurled it
into the fire. "So now it comes out. Why didn't thee tell
me in the first place? Leading me down the garden
path—" He pulled her out of the chair and shook her.
"Blast thee, woman, thee'd madden a monk! Thee's a
very witch—flirtatious—soulless—no wonder thee's
attacked! I shouldn't have housed thee with my cousin.
First, her husband, easy prey, poor old cuckold, and
now her cocksman."

She slapped his face. His fair skin came up mottled with four fingers before he struck her back, knocking her down. She felt a sharp pain at the back of her
head—the crooked finger of the poker—and then no
pain at all, only a surprised interest in the gushing of
her blood. She sat up and touched the side of her face,
she stared at the fingers which came away wet, sticky,
bright red.

"Oh, God forgive me, what've I done to thee?
Torn open thy precious head. Oh, my love, my sweet!"
He picked her up and carried her into the galley, set
her on the table. He poured water from the kettle onto
dish towels and mopped her, while curses and love-
words leaked from his mouth.

"Get a knife," she ordered calmly. "Press it to the
wound, edges together." She saw how his hands shook.
"Samuel, dear boy, for heaven's sake, don't take on. I
feel no pain. What, not *crying?* Thou great booby, I'll

be right in a jiffy if thee but holds steady. Oh, look at us—blood all over, we might be sticking pigs. Get the brandy, lovey. Pour some on the wound. Hold on, not he whole decanter, just enough to cauterize. Now then, more pressure. Blowed if I'll bleed to death over a pimp, a steward, and a hundred pounds. Oh, I do need a plaster. Has thee not *some*thing? What does thee use when thee cuts thyself shaving? How big is the gape? Can thee see it through the hair?"

"Oh, Kezia, I do so love thee. 'Tis a torture to me I can't make thee mine. Not big," he said, grunting over the knife. "Tiny for all this spill."

"Not too hard. Ow! easy, laddie. The scalp's the bleedingest part of the body. Mother used to tell me that. I know, a pity, thee was born to be a husband. Is there any brandy left? To drink, I mean. I could do with a gulp. There, now, I do believe it's stopping. Oh, would thee look at this kitchen? Let's not wipe up a drop—give the charwoman a turn!"

"I might have killed thee."

"I die hard, friend."

"Never lost my head before. I ought to repent publicly in Meeting—"

"The very thing. Why should Lady Anne be the only one to know?"

He laughed and hugged her, absolved by the drollery. He carried her to the bedroom, kissing her neck, her nose, her brandied hair, the blood spot on her bodice. "Should we not have a doctor? Hang the scandal, it's out anyway. He might take a stitch or two."

"Nay. No need."

"Certain thee's not giddy? All that blood—?" He laid her down as if she were a Ming vase.

"A bit thirsty," she said, her eyes glittery, and when he would leave to fetch her a drink, she held him and kissed his cock. "For thy juices."

First they made love and then they made plans.

"I've another set of kin. The Alfred Starbucks, off Downing Street. They'll be glad to put thee up."

"Nay, dear heart, I've quite lost my taste for London. I'm for home. Isn't it a vexation, my ship's but a few days gone?"

"Captain Leverett sails for the Vineyard on the morrow. I encountered him this day in the coffeehouse. He'll carry thee if I ask him, and from the Vineyard it's nothing to hitch a ride home.

"I'll take thee to Rhodes House after we've supped and then I'll arrange with Leverett for a berth. Thee get a good night's sleep. Time enough to pack in the morning, thee's had enough for one day. I shall come by for thee and thy traveling coffers at noon."

"Will not this captain be loath to take a woman aboard?"

"He owes me a favor. Anyway 'tis a merchant ship, not a whaler. 'Tis the whalemasters who are skittish. Only trouble is—"

"Aye?"

"Nothing. Nothing."

"Well, there's something. Tell me."

"Leverett's a fair and stalwart young man, smooth-spoken with the ladies. Thee'd best not play me false or—"

"Thee'll break my head."

They laughed. She roughed his streaked blond hair. She said gaily, "And how do I know thee won't go wenching while I'm tucked in a sailing berth? Though if thee did, I doubt not thee'd do it in good conscience. What's fair for the gander's not for the goose."

"And thee would it were?"

"Oh, stop, enough. Really, Samuel!"

"Very well. Now, let's see. I can sail as soon as I lay in stores. My cargo's bought, there's just the loading of the tea. If the weather's right and God's willing, I should arrive home close upon thy heels. But, oh, sweetheart, I'll miss thee sorely."

"And I thee."

Still smarting from her equation of him with the steward, he said quietly, "Kezia, my jealous railings be not whimsical, they spring from torment. I have thee and I have thee not. Thee'll never love me as I love thee, I know it, and I try to come to terms with it. But I promise this, no man on earth will ever love thee better. Thee once said thee'd never been first in anyone's heart. God knows thee's not an easy woman, but thee's first in mine. Ever hath been, ever shall be. Nothing thee might do can change that."

"Dear Samuel, that's quite the nicest speech I've ever been made. 'Twill warm me on many a cold night when thee's from my side."

But she did not vouchsafe an equivalent avowal, and the pain of not hearing it enslaved him the more.

Kezia slept but an hour of the good night Samuel urged her to have: from three to four, after her clothes were sorted—she was leaving behind for Bridget garments too frivolous for colony wear—and her chests packed full. In that hour she had a dream. The dream drew from the anguish she had felt as a youngster when her mother used her pet goose, Jane, as a chimney sweep. Over Kezia's protest, her mother sent the goose flying up the central chimney again and again until the exhausted bird limped out into the backyard, folded her sooty wings, and slept though the sun was high. Kezia wept to see her pet so besmirched, and when the bird woke, she carried her to a pond, crooning her sympathy and feeding her bits of breadcrusts and sunflower seeds on the way. Then she sat dolefully on the bank and watched Jane cleanse herself, splatting and honking and ducking, till she'd prinked herself white again. In the dream, Kezia was both the goose and the weeper, and she woke before she betook herself to the pond.

She breakfasted with the lord, who seemed genuinely disappointed to hear she'd been called home on a sudden. He kissed her farewell on the mouth, holding her close, feeling her up and down through a lengthy Godspeed.

She knew she was not expected to pay Lady Anne

a last visit—and yet was. Her hostess would have cleared the decks, dreading the confrontation, hoping against it, yet keyed up for it. It would not do to let the lady down. Besides, not to come might be interpreted as cowardice and guilt. Kezia was looking for her gloves when she heard the rumble of carriage wheels. She leaned out of her bedroom window and waved her kerchief at Samuel alighting. "Five minutes. My boxes lie strapped below." He put up his palms in a gesture that said no need for haste.

Her gloves magically appeared in full view on the bed. She straightened her hat in the mirror. To her surprise, she looked rested, fresh, aglow.

Bridget admitted her to her ladyship's apartments. "Have a good journey, mistress. I thank you again for all the fine garments. I've a niece what'll fit them to a T." And left them.

Lady Anne lay tiny in a landslide of pillows. She looked strange and common without makeup, her eyes so swollen that just a slat of blue showed in each, her face pink and puffy. Her pale hair, uncombed, stood up in a stubble of cobs. The backs of her hands, lifeless on the silken cover, were blighted with liver spots. Mettlesome, she'd been an oligarch. Piteous, she was a contagious disease. Kezia made her manners from the center of the room in formal clichés. The only effort involved was keeping the sarcasm down to a tinge.

". . . Cannot thank thee sufficient . . . gracious hospitality . . . if thee should ever need a *pied-à-terre* in America . . ."

Lady Anne turned her face aside, interrupted harshly, "I've not slept a wink all night. I pray you may never know this kind of humiliation." She turned again to face Kezia, and her voice took on a plaintive note. "Oh, Kezia, Kezia, I shall miss you. I cannot afford you, but I shall miss you. Would you kiss me?"

"Forgive me. I would not. Fare thee well."

In the carriage, stroking her gloved hand, Samuel said, "Kezia, is thy pride averse to swearing?"

"Nay, for thee, anything. What to?"

"That nothing happened between thee and the steward?"

She replied as fiercely and falsely as she did three months hence when he asked the same about Captain Leverett. "I swear it."

Seventeen

"Sons of Liberty indeed! Sons of Perdition, more like. Muskets, adzes, scythes, are these the tools with which Englishmen solve financial disagreements? For make no mistake, that's what this quarrel's about—money. Nobody likes to be taxed, but there's a proper way to amend taxation—repeal. The trouble's with power-hungry revolutionaries like Sam Adams who can't wait for due process—"

She yawned. They were stretched out on hides on the floor of the cave, their underground bedchamber at Quaise. Samuel was so conjugal, no sooner had they climaxed than he lay with his arm about her, talking of politics. She pinched the skin over her knuckles and watched it slowly return, estimating the loss of elasticity. It was bound to come—the slackness. She was, after all, fifty-one, he her junior by four years, and how she wished it the other way round. She put a hand on her concave belly. Nerves kept her thin. But Debbie claimed the same cause for her gain. Debbie was grown monstrous, worrying about John. And grown old too. Kezia had bathed with her at Siasconsett and seen her pussy hair gray!

She snuggled deeper against Samuel, afraid of the violence and bloodshed to come. "Think thee there'll be a revolution for certain sure? Think thee there'll be a civil war?"

"I pray not, but Boston's a tinderbox. One or two more incidents is all—"

"Oh, well, let Rome burn. Myself, I'm for a bit of fiddling." She slipped her arms around his neck, kissed his mouth slowly and voluptuously. "Oh, I have missed thee, my sweet Samuel."

"And I thee. I cannot say how much, there are no words for't." He grumbled as he nuzzled her ear and neck, "Blast, why can we not be in the open? Why must we ever skulk about, stow away in this dark nostril of earth?"

But rage and deprivation are not inimical to passion, not nearly as inimical as marriage. His cock went up again without the touch of her hand, and she cooed at his teasing entry. When he settled into strong pumping, her cries echoed down their hollow purlieu, overflowed onto the beach, stopping a rabbit in his tracks and sending him into a briar patch.

" 'Tis nigh daydawn. Oh, Samuel, we are rash to meet like this; 'tis not like London nor even Boston. Last night I dreamed I was dragged to the marketplace and whipped!"

"Nonsense, thee's not an Indian who cannot pay the fine. Besides there's not a selectman nor an elder doesn't have shares in one of thy ships or mine." He stroked her head. "Never fear, love, I'd not let them harm a hair." He stroked her back, diverted her with a piece of news. "By the bye, I meant to tell thee I heard that Lady Anne Rhodes died."

"Unnnh!" She inhaled steeply, her body stiffened like wax, thumb-printed head to toe with memory. Her brain seethed, a congeries of mixed emotion. In one apartment, relief: most convenient to have one's secret under sod. In another, humility: that power should be no more enduring than a chick's egg tooth. In a small twilit cubicle, sadness. There had been those lovely moments—intimate, gay, vital, the kind she and Miriam Pinkham once shared.

Oh, the passing of love and friendship, the lists of the dead! Uncle Samuel. Aunt Hannah. The faithful Obed and indeed more than two hundred of his people, killed off by distemper, some said kinepox, some said measles, yellow fever; no one knew for certain. The only Indians spared were those at sea or those like Shongo and her maidservant Patience who were in Sherburne and the mysterious few who survive everything but old age. The English proved immune, leaving no doubt in the minds of the land disputers as to whose side God was on. Kezia had nursed Indians from midsummer to late winter, as had her mother, her sisters, Hagar, several other women, but they only relieved the stricken, cured none. Gone too was the genial Dan'l Pinkham, leaving her mother widowed again, and many of the island men had sunk to the bottom of the sea. Suddenly, in the house of the heart, a beam of sunshine lit a very private closet: But I—I am here, I remain, prosper, according to God's will.

"How did it happen?"

"She was on her way to a play, with friends. The night was dense with fog. Her carriage turned over. No one else was seriously hurt. But her spine broke. She died within an hour."

"Not the worst way to go. Quickly, painlessly, with dignity. I'd sign those articles right now."

She had spoken through Samuel to God. Thus shriven, she stood on the far shore shoulder to shoulder with Lady Anne. They waited together in their winding-sheets. Which side would claim them, the up or the down? The land about them was vast, silent, white, cold. The wind turned vicious, whined and whistled, penetrating their earthly shrouds. Instead of a Receiving Angel, Shana appeared, limping badly. Where was the promised serenity? Shana's face was contorted and she was wringing her hands. Was it hell then? Why? They'd not been good women, but surely not that bad?

She felt the jab in her ribs, heard his voice, and returned, shaken, humble with relief. She could have kissed the dirt floor. Was it a sin to be so glad to be alive?

"John?" she echoed uncertainly, groping back for Samuel's question. Ah, the association became clear: Speaking of death, has thee heard from John? She replied that she had not.

"I think often on shipwreck or capture—the way our men go unarmed into piratical waters, lambs to the slaughter! But captured don't necessarily mean dead. And it's curious, I have the distinct conviction he lives. I should know it in my bones were John dead, I sense him."

It was his turn to yawn. She had said all this before, but he knew it gave her release. At length he got up and looked out of the cavern. "Morning star's out."

She watched him dress with loving eyes, already missing him. In the half-light, she could see the huckleberry lad, though at forty-seven he was dusty as a miller and his muscles had gone lardy. "So, my sandy parsnip, 'tis farewell again. 'Tis almost better to do without. Thee comes home and wakes up my graces and then they burn."

"Good, I like them hot. Come tonight."

"Dare we push our luck?"

"Why not?"

"Very well, tonight then. Oh, good, good!" She grabbed his hand and kissed it.

He was so pleased, he spoke sternly. "Keep an eye to windward as thee comes. Caution be the better part of valor."

She almost laughed. That marvelous sense of rectitude. They committed adultery, they smuggled, chaffered sharply, overinsured their ships, practiced usury, lied when it suited their purposes—yet Samuel could make Shakespeare sound like Scripture, and whereas she ever ran from the devil, he walked hand in hand with his God.

Little Kezia, when she got home, was gone to the schoolhouse where now, at fifteen, *she* was assistant to the schoolmaster. The others of the household were at their chores, no one even saw her come in. Upstairs in her chamber the morning fires were lit, running busily up-chimney. She stripped off her filthy clothing, poured hot water from the kettle into the basin, and soaped away dirt and sweat and semen. The fire glowed and danced. Her body tingled. She was dressing to go down and have a bite to eat when a sudden wind screamed at her windows, banged doors, knocked over a bucket or a stool somewhere below. A downdraft of soot blackened the hearth floor.

"Patience," she called, fixing her bib as she left her chamber. "Come tidy my—"

She stopped dead on the landing when she heard his name cried in the street. Hagar's bulk darkened the open front doorway. The outside air was cold but quiet. Hadn't there been a blow? That soot on her dropped towel? The voice of the crier was a boy's, rasping, croaking hoarsely. "Wreck at Brant Point!" But there'd been no storm. She raced to the keeping room where on the mantel in the right-hand one of a pair of Eton china vases she kept the silver dollar against his return. Part of her resisted: not this morning, not after a night of illicit coitus. But her heart was thumping a contrapuntal sentiment: I knew it, I knew he lived, I knew it, I knew it, I knew it.

An agendum of the Nantucket Town Meeting Records dated March 23, 1774, reads: "It was voted that the Town build a lighthouse on Brant Point . . . as High as the former one that blew down lately." A footnote to this copied record in Alexander Starbuck's *History of Nantucket* reads: "The *New Bedford Mercury* had a letter from Nantucket dated March 1, 1774, which told of a great gust of wind at 8 A.M. It lasted about a minute, but destroyed the lighthouse, several shops, barns, etc. Had it continued 15 minutes no more than half the buildings in its track would have stood."

In the lee of that wind a longboat washed ashore and crashed its timbers, cracked an oar in two, splintered its staves and thwarts, scattering two bodies. One, identified as Jeremiah Bickford by his widow and Dr. Tupper, was toothless and lacked an arm and leg. The other, unconscious but only half-dead, was John Coffin.

Spring came in like a lamb that year and stayed lambish. The hills breathed out the scent of trailing pink and white arbutus. Violets pushed through the crusted loam making way for the chickweed that fed the robins who mated early and sang their hearts out. Coatue had a bumper crop of rabbits and enough plantain to feed them. By June the stick-legged calves were trampling scatter rugs of roses and broom. Beach-plum frothed the dunes like surf. The Great Harbor sparkled blue, abristle with masts of all heights, sloop and shallop, pink and snow, whaler and brig, come for another Shearing Breakfast. The wharves were ahum with activity: the shops hammered, workmen hollered to each other, sailors sang chanteys under the squawking gulls. A spilled cargo of sandalwood baked by the sun spiced the days of a week, no one in a hurry to sweep up what smelled so good. Old men snoozed by their fishracks, goodwives went off in their jaunting-carts to visit, children strayed the beaches for drift-wood and played tag and dressed their kittens and strung daisy chains. Nantucket, in a word, was at her smiling best and Kezia could not stand it another minute.

It was not the nursing she minded, that was a glory to her, not only because it was John but because she was good at it. He was mending under her eye and this was a deep fulfillment, very different from the hopeless care she'd given Obed. She was pleased with the way his sores had healed, having treated them with a remedy of her own: sassafras bark powdered and mixed with fresh pork fat. And particularly relieved that his hair was growing back. To delouse him, she had had to shave his head and chest, and he had wept all during the cutting. She kept assuring him it would come in again, and it was—peppery on his head, silver at his temples, white on his jaws and chest. His chin whiskers would soon be a beard for he could not shave regularly, the slightest nick formed pus. He was smaller than he'd been, gaunt, trembly of hand and lip, but he was again recognizable.

She fed him six times a day because his stomach was shrunk and he could eat but small portions at a time. Citrus fruits, potatoes, cooked fresh vegetables, raw greens in sugared vinegar-oil, beef broth and calves' foot jelly to replenish the marrow of his bones; kidneys and brains and liver for his blood; custards and sweetmeats and breads for fat and vim. Fowl and meat she minced to pulp, for scurvy had made his gums spongy, they bled at the slightest pressure. He was lucky to have retained his teeth.

He could walk a mile without stopping but no one could induce him to mount a horse, and even now in wild strawberry time, out of doors he wore his father's greatcoat. Shongo took him in the springcart to the cornfields and he'd sit in the sun while they hoed and planted. On Meeting days when kin and friends came up to him, asking questions about his capture and incarceration, he'd look at them blandly and repeat things the field hands said. "Don't skip a row in planting or someone close to thee will die." And, "Don't cut hay on the day of an underground moon."

At night she rocked him to sleep in a hammock slung from the rafters of his chamber. From bathing him while he was in coma, she knew he'd been castrated as well as whipped with a cat-o-nine-tails. She doubted he knew she knew for since coming to himself, he allowed no one to see him undressed, not even Shongo whom he sometimes called Obed, but slept— as he went about by day—in his old shore clothes, his hat, and his shoes. She kept her door ajar, alert to his smallest outcry. She'd run in the set him aswing, mayhap stroke his hand or pick up his hat and put it back on his head. If he woke, she gave him spiced milk punch or hot buttered rum and now in the balmy season, a sweet sangaree laced with gin. If he got the shivers, she couldn't quiet him under a dozen quilts. Likely he'd eaten of human flesh and drunk of human blood, for his sleep talk was shot with the horror of cannibalism.

Dr. Tupper looked in on John two, three times a week. Early on, there was a stream of callers, the house was like a tavern, but it slacked off because John was so unsociable. To Bickford's widow he said only, "We were taken by a Spanish sloop and a brig

—privateers sailing under English colors, which proved to be false." When she pressed him for more he said, "Dragonflies ride on each other's backs for the pure fun of it," and went upstairs. With others, even his brothers, he clammed up or dropped off. With older biddies, her mother or selectmen's wives, he was shocking. If they made a pleasant remark of the weather, he might reply, "In Spain the balls of the bull are considered a delicacy. They fry them. They are called *los cojones,* the *j* pronounced as *h*." With Kezia, he was obedient as a child, timid, withdrawn. Only in the presence of Debbie and Little Kezia did he brighten. Jealousy was not in Kezia's vocabulary. The word itself made her bristle. She was not so small-minded that she begrudged his brief self-recoveries, no matter who induced them. What discomfited her was that he seemed to be afraid of her. She tried harking back to their good times, not to repossess him but to remind him that they had once taken joy in one another.

"Oh, John, does thee mind the day we found a magpie nest with gold and silver in't?"

He stared at the squared-off tips of his shoes and said, "Shongo sings to the corn, says it helps it to grow."

She had to lean forward to catch the stringy tune:

> *If whiskey was a river and I could swim*
> *I'd say heave-ho and dive right in.*

"And afterward, we lunched on a rock while the birds scolded?"

His lips scarcely moved, the refrain whined through his nostrils:

> *If whiskey was a river and I was a duck*
> *I'd—*

"When we walked away," she enunciated as to a lip-reader, "twenty sparrows or more came down. High-stepping, aflutter, apecking away. One of them rose in the sky with a strip of ham hanging like a worm from his beak."

"Hands planted beans and squash between the corn hills. Going to call that place Succotash Hill." He sneaked a look at her, willing to smile, rubbing his knees, rocking back and forth on the chair's straight legs.

"Oh, John, don't! Don't hide behind sea chanteys and farmer prattle. Sweetheart, husband, shall thee not look at me, speak to me?"

He opened his mouth and closed it several times. A black beetle squashed under one of the chair legs.

She stood up. "I believe I'll go help Rachel in the shop. I've heard the bell tinkle several times. Is thee warm enough in the sun here? Does thee want a scarf? Best not rock that old chair, thee'll fall and hurt thyself."

"Except a man be born again," he said in the singsong of the Quaker who is moved to preach, "he cannot see the Kingdom of God. There are many bornings in a single lifetime, and every borning is accompanied by travail. I am grateful to the glorious son of God who hath shown grace to this sinner. I was a fountain of corruption, I knew all manner of sin. And so the Lord punished me. *Sed post tenebras, speramus lumen de lumine*. After the suffering, came the Light, and I was cleansed. The Lord said eat and I ate, for it is incumbent upon man to reverence life and to do all in his power to prolong it. Then the Lord in His great mercy did forgive me to the uttermost, and He created a great wave on which was I borne homeward." He stopped rocking. "I am come home, wife. Is that not enough?"

She slipped to her knees, held his hand to her cheek. "Aye, 'tis more than enough, 'tis a miracle, and I am grateful for thy return." But inside, the truthful scream: Don't preach in that singy voice, sanctimonious gibbery-gab. I've heard it all my life, never thought to hear it from thee! We're not dead, we're sitting in the noonday sun! On the grass is a bowl of peas I shelled for our dinner. Tonight there's an oyster party and I shall wear a lime-green petticoat. Samuel will be there and Zaccheus Macy, and not a few others who'll watch me out of the back of their heads. Little Kezia will fetch thee thy dinner and sit at thy knee. Can thee not revive thyself, summon a shadow of thy old style? If thee cannot enjoy, can thee not cease to fear me? Aloud she added, "All I ask is that thee trust in me. Talk to me. I would be friends again that we may comfort each other."

Stricken, she watched a tear form between the closed lids, trickle down the seamed cheek, and hang glistening on a white tuft of whiskers. The lump in her throat swelled till she thought she would choke. She dropped his hand, ran into the house. She took the stairs two at a time, threw herself across her bed, rammed her fist into the pillow. Poor *thing!* Poor old ball-less thing, he thought she wanted his cock. No matter what she said, he thought that and only that.

"I shall go stark staring mad if I don't get away," she told Dr. Tupper. "He fends me off till I could scream and claw. We are worse than estranged. My very shadow makes him cower, his flesh creeps at my touch."

"Well, take a journey. Do you both good. When home feels like a prison and you feel like an inmate, be an outmate, fleet away. You've nursed him faithfully for three months around the clock. You been leading an invalid's life and you ain't sick. Ain't no'thard o' sixty-five neither, and don't he know it."

"That," she said icily, "is not the rub."

" 'Tis not thy fret mayhap, but I dare say 'tis his. You're his wife."

"I might be his warder. He's so withdrawn, so changed."

"Not certain sure he's all that changed. Not so much given up as given in. To a passivity he's always had and considered unmanly. I've known John Coffin a long time. He it was who had to go and hunt the biggest fish, stay out the longest time, bring in the

richest catch, when all the time what he yearned to do
was set by the fire and toast his slippers. Come to himself the hard way, he has, but then, some never do.
My advice is give him a breathing spell. When the cat's
away, the mouse'll play. Let him play a while. With his
daughter and his twin sister. Their demands he can
meet."

"I make no demands!"

"No, no, *you* don't, but he does—of himself. And
is loath to fall short. Then there's this aspect. Little
Kezia's a wonder to him. Come home and find you've
sired a comely maiden—well, that's a wonder to a man.
I speak from personal experience. Fathers have a special feeling for daughters, you know—"

She chewed viciously at a thumbnail, ripping it off
from the quick. No, she didn't know, how could she?

"And daughters return the feeling, more often
than not. Some go overboard. Take Debbie's Christopher's firstborn. Twenty-two and eyes only for her
Dada. Mark me, she'll be a thornback all her born
days."

She started to protest. Little Kezia was but fifteen, hardly a candidate for spinsterhood. Still she
wasn't a young fifteen, nor an undeveloped fifteen, and
though she had many young friends, she had no swains
that Kezia knew of. And she did spring to serve her
father, thoughtful of him in many creative ways. "Happen I go, I'll take Little Kezia with me. She's never
been off-island, time she saw some sights, met some
foreigners."

"I shouldn't, not this trip," advised the doctor.
"Lose both his women at one stroke—that might jolt
the sick man, he might feel abandoned. There's Debbie,
but she's not under his roof, she's got her own man to
do for."

They parted in the marketplace. He chucked her
chin. "Don't take any wooden nutmegs."

She smiled vaguely. She was hearing other, older
words: "It's a one-headed, two-legged, five-fingered
maid no bigger'n a bass!" And now that little bass

needed a husband. Where to go for him? She wanted diversion, and she also needed to raise hard cash for a country seat at Quaise. If war came, Nantucket would be in a bad way to get supplies and provisions, vulnerable to the navies of both sides. It would be well to have a private bay for running her ships ashore. The cave there which had for so long been a love nest for her and Samuel ran inland the better part of a mile. Shored up with four-by-fours it would make an excellent storehouse for smuggled goods. She thought to build the 'summer villa' over its rear end, with perhaps a trapdoor under the hall. With this in mind, she'd been buying up parcels of Quaise Neck on the quiet. These and the parcel Uncle Samuel had left them would give her ownership of Quaise. But her purchases had drained her cash, and there were a few more lots still to acquire.

Boston was out of the question. The Port Bill had but lately been clapped on it, shutting it off from trade. Its people would be hard-pressed until it was lifted. The new designated trade center was Salem, but unfortunately the entire town was in Elias Derby's pocket, and she and that peacock did not get along. In New Hampshire and Rhode Island the currency was bad. New York was muggy at this time of year and she had but few notes outstanding there. Though it meant a longer journey, there was only one town where she could sell her oil, get sterling for her cargo and her notes, be well entertained, *and* find a suitable son-in-law. That was Philadelphia.

Cousin Benjamin Franklin was in England but there were a sight of 'wet' Quakers (wet as opposed to the dry stuffy variety) who would be pleased to put her up. The Pembertons, for example. Their mansion on Third and Chestnut streets had vastly impressed her—alleys of crushed clamshells, evergreens pruned into fanciful forms, a sundial that sparkled in a garden of stock and pinks and lilies—a veritable *rus in urbe*. And Israel Pemberton had been especially attentive to her last time she was there. He'd not laid a hand on her, but he wanted to, she could tell. Would he still find her attractive? Furthermore, unlike the Nantucketers who traditionally married each other, the Quaker aristocracy there, though endogamous, encouraged matrimonial ties in England and other colonies. In the summer season, there would be all manner of suburban sociables—fishing and boating parties, tea parties, cookouts, dances, games of battledore and shuttlecock, ninepins, hide-and-seek—ample opportunity for an overlook of the eligible bachelors. With a weather eye peeled and the grace of God given, she ought to have one stowed aboard on the return journey.

Eighteen

"Who is that woman, Israel, drinking tea with the white-haired man? She keeps staring at us."

He glanced over and nodded, showing white teeth, but his blue jaw was hardset. "Old Mistress Cadwalader, *the* Cadwaladers. She thrives on tittle-tattle, pay her no mind." And he went on talking, as he had all the week, of his wayward son.

It was as before. She was drawn to Israel because of his good looks, and there was no doubt in her mind he was also attracted to her, but they couldn't stand each other. Everything one said irritated the other, yet they took every opportunity to be alone together, and his wife gave them many. Of this tea, for example, she'd begged off. "I'm going to snatch forty winks. That wine at dinner has made me drowsy. Or mayhap the warm weather. Israel, why not take Kezia to see the Falls? The ride to the clubhouse is not half an hour. 'Tis Sixth Day so they'll be serving tea. But do be home in ample time to dress. We are expected at the Norrises' at eight."

Israel had changed little. Tall as a tree, hard-muscled despite a relatively soft life, high-colored complexion, black hair, a magnificent hawk nose and the bluest eyes she'd ever seen. She was particularly vulnerable to his planklike wrists and strong square hands, caring nothing for the qualities of his character —a kind of dynamism-in-ferment, an aura of authority, an acuminated commercial sense—that had earned him a fortune in addition to the one he had inherited, the deference of an entire city, and the title, 'King of the Quakers.' He was the only person of whom she was admittedly jealous. Not of Mary for being his wife, but of him. She believed she was astuter than he. If she had been born a man with his beauty and such a legacy, where might she not have gone?

Mrs. Cadwalader was nigh off her chair for leaning. Was it possible that to her old eyes their *tête-à-tête* looked like a scandal? Mischievously, Kezia put a languid hand over his clenched one that lay between their posset cups. Yes, Mistress Cadwalader watched. When her husband pressed the dish of lemons upon her, she waved it away and cupped her ear, tipping her bonnet askew. Kezia grew bored with the gambit, looked out the paneless window. The steaming greenery wafted clover blossom. A trout broke water, danced on his tail. On the apex of an evergreen a brown mocker sang, fluttered up and down with white flashings—a fat and saucy lunatic.

Should she not change her mind and stay another week? Everyone was urging her to. Why was she so much more popular in the cities she visited than in Sherburne? From the moment of arrival here, she'd had nothing but successes. Philadelphia was not free with its social favor, but once you broke the ice, you were thereafter roundly welcomed. Of course it did not hurt to be the kinswoman of Benjamin Franklin, whose importance grew annually—even though at the moment he was the subject of controversy in the colonies. Nor did it hurt to be the houseguest of the Pembertons. Her business exchanges had been quickly and profitably dispatched as a result. She'd got a good price for her oil, and for her spermaceti candles she'd been paid in pounds sterling. She'd also collected moneys owed her in hard cash which would go to the purchase of Quaise land.

Once her business was done, she was busied by day with shopping. The shops here were almost as fine as in London. Evenings, she was delightfully entertained in the homes of the elite. Every meal was festive, the company jolly and informed, and after supper, there was usually a harper or a fiddler or a singing quartet. One night she actually danced the Hornpipe with one of the dozens of marriageable young men. She wished she had brought Little Kezia with her. Come spring, she would. . . .

She has told the Pembertons and her ship's captain that she'll depart on the morrow. She is eager to return to John. Now that she's had a spell of refreshment, she feels in charge of herself again, competent to handle her household. Competent too to deal with Samuel. She is glad she talked Samuel out of coming here to be with her. She has decided to put an end to that affair. It was lovely while it lasted, but now it is time to set carnality aside; there is an ebb and a flow to life that must be respected. To go against its tide is to make oneself ludicrous, there is nothing worse than a kittenish matron. Besides there is too much risk. John, already crushed, would be annihilated by a scandal. She looks back at Israel and shines upon him the full melanic glitter of renunciation.

Israel is refueled by her gaze which he misinterprets as sympathetic interest. He goes on to tell of his wastrel son's latest scrape, must needs report it in exact detail. "I first got wind of it on Third Day, the day before thee put in. No, 'twas Second Day, I mind because—"

Looking Israel in the eye, brown to blue, she wonders if John will be pleased with the Chinese porcelain footbath she picked up for his bedchamber. She has also ordered to his measure a greatcoat mink-lined of all female skins—the male's are longer-lasting but heavier, and she would have the garment lie light on those frail shoulders. For Little Kezia, she has bought a whole new wardrobe, sprightly garments in the latest mode and of the finest quality. Dainty summer dresses of white lawn, winter ones of cashmere, mitts, fans, ribbons, shoes, even a hoop. The Philadelphia maids wear caushets to make their shapes appear straight up and down, but Kezia would not have her girl's bosom battened down.

She does enjoy choosing and bestowing gifts. For Samuel she has bought a pepper grater he can carry in his pocket. For her mother, a teethrake. (Ever since the robust Mister Pinkham died of a corrupted tooth, Abigail has been zealous about dental hygiene. She has also sold to many a dentifrice of her own invention—a mixture of cuttlebone, brown sugar, gunpowder, and saltpeter.) For Debbie, two Richardson novels, *Clarissa* and *Sir Charles Grandison,* which were but fifty cents apiece. For each of her sisters, neckatees, and for her brothers-in-law, muffs. Strings of rock candy for the nieces and nephews. For Rachel Bunker, three pairs of thread stockings from Germantown at a dollar a pair. (Mayhap one of those pairs should go to Debbie, the books were so cheap.) For Hagar, snuff and a pretty box to keep it in. Oh, yes, and the opium for Dr. Tupper, for which she'll not charge him—all those visits to John. For herself, enough new clothes to make even John sit up and take notice. And all of brave colors. The Norris women wear every color of the rainbow and gaudy shoes too, and no one in the Quaker sisterhood complains of *their* display. For the new clothes, two mahogany clothes presses, one for herself and one for Little Kezia.

And last but not least, a four-wheeled carriage with velvet seats and silk fringes. If her mother should reprove her, she is prepared: "In Philadelphia, there are eighty-five equipages, thirty-three of which are owned by Friends. These figures I obtained from the Stadt House. Does thee set thyself up as judge of thy Philadelphia brethren?"

"He knows I'll pay his debts—the disgrace—my credit and standing in the community. He counts upon this. I ask thee, Kezia, was ever Job so beset?"

" 'Tis the cross thee and Mary bear. In all other ways, thee are blessed. We all have some sorry things in our lives, Israel."

"Aye, thee has a shipwrecked husband, but believe me, Kezia, nothing is as heartbreaking as a bad seed."

"Do not despair of him. He'll find his way in his own time. Now, let be, grieve no more. Shall we not take a pretty walk? I am eager to behold the waterfall."

"Of course. What a dullard, ever recounting my woes. Thee go along. I would speak to the caretaker here about some maintenance matters. I'll catch thee up shortly. Take the Indian trail upstream. It parallels the river, thee cannot go astray."

On the way out, Kezia gave the inquisitive Mrs. Cadwalader a trullish look and was instantly sorry. They might meet tonight at the Norrises', and then would she not feel foolish?

Kezia meandered at a leisurely pace. She followed the path above the dappled bank, the river purling below her ear, and ahead, in a higher, invisible glade, she thought she heard the rush of the cataract. They said it frothed white as cow's milk over a palisade of limestone. How multiple were the wonders of God! How much nearer He seemed in a forest than in a meetinghouse. Here was mystery, beauty, a sense of antiquity, of animism. Nothing like Nantucket, whose bare face was open on all sides to wind and sea and sky.

The growth on the high side of the footpath was an herbalist's paradise. Cornelian cherry, witch hazel, creeping vinca. From time to time she bent to pick a sheaf of berries or a flower, an inveterate collector on beach and trail. She hopped over a fallen log, frog-leaped a boulder. She pretended to be a lone Indian scout in an olden time, her moccasins kicking up dust not yet trod by English, Swedish, or Dutch. A scout would be looking for signs of danger as he tracked. What would he notice? That was when she heard the preternatural quiet. Not a pigeon, no dog-day cicadas, no scampering chipmunk, only the plash of the river. Then she heard it—a hollow rattle—and stopped dead.

It might have been a hickory limb fallen across the path except that it was black and scale-patterned. Its blunt head was flared, showing pale chin skin, and its split charcoal tongue flicked in and out like the tip of a whip. One extruded eye was fixed upon a squirrel whose bushy tail arched above the slanted tree trunk. The squirrel began to chitter. And to run up the trunk and back down again, as if tied by a string to the poised head. Five times the little fool ran high enough to get away, each time it briefly held a position of alert arrest, then turned and ran down again. The fifth time the serpent coiled quickly, rearing a whitish blue belly, but did not strike.

Kezia had heard that reptiles could charm birds and mice and the larger rodents, but she had never seen nor quite believed it. Her breasts tingled, the base of her spine went cold, and up along her vertebrae she felt a quivering as of hackles. Like the men with the roosters at the cockfight in London, she had some deep kinship here, a mythic involvement. She hated the snake and loved the squirrel, and she was full of dread. She knew black snakes were not poisonous, but she also knew that they were so swift dogs rarely could catch them, and if one coiled about your chest, it could shut off your pipes. She stood absolutely still, and the breath she parted with would not have stirred ashes. She watched the snake who watched the squirrel who continued to behave like a maiden being wooed.

Her senses were sharpened, and she felt with certainty there was another watcher. Her ears picked up no sound behind that might have signified Israel's approach. Without batting an eye, she glanced around but detected no movement ahead or above or on either side of her. Perhaps the watcher was another animal or a bird, perhaps more than one woodland creature watched with her this *liebestodt* opera. A mournful, pathetic sound escaped the squirrel. Its head was so close to the snake's, they rather resembled each other, and the snake seemed to be smiling. The cry broke once more, high and helpless. Kezia stamped her foot, commanding aloud, "No!" and threw the bouquet she held at the squirrel, glancing hurriedly around for a stick.

Everything changed. The snake whirled to her, winding down like lightning. The squirrel ran away, as

if the string had broken. There was no stick, nor time
to get one. The snake was writhing toward her, head
up, with incredible speed. She fled down to the river,
feeling her hat go. The river was too shallow at that
point for swimming. It would slow her movement, but
not the snake's. If he caught her in the water, she'd
either be squeezed to death or drown. Uphill running
was too slow, she must make for the clubhouse via the
water's edge. Before she could turn to do so, she felt
the flat slippery cable wind her ankles, toppling her
face down in cool river mud. She felt the slither up
her calves. A high needle-thin pain in the back of her
knee told her the devil-tongue had penetrated her
oh-so-thinly-wrapped network of immaculate blood
vessels. The loathsome thing was sliding higher.

"Help!" she screamed.

"Courage!" called a man's voice, not Israel's.

She twisted her neck with a violent jerk and saw
a lad in white shirt and buff pants kneeling at her feet.
Out of the corner of her eye she saw the raised knife
point come down. The snake poured like oil from
her thighs. She saw it wriggle away in the grass. A
boot stamped on its shiny middle, and there were whizzing sounds as the knife cut through air. When the
chopped fillets continued to move, Kezia let her chin
fall to the mud and vomited into the river.

Retching, she heard him come back. She saw all
the colors, the red and black and silver of the knife, the
carmine on the white sleeve, the green of grass, the
brown mud, gray lichen on a fallen bough. She had no
power of movement. She could not raise her head nor
lift her arms to pull her petticoat down over her legs.
She could not close her legs which had fallen apart
when the snake left them. For an irrational moment
she waited for the knife to sink into her back. Then she
felt her apron whipped off her and saw the blue of it
darken in the river.

He dragged her prostrate form sideways against
his flank, bathed her face with the dripping fabric.
Even upside down, she saw he was fair.

"Sorry—but it was horrid—ugh!"

"There now. Rest easy. You're fine."

"He bit me in the knee. His saliva's in me."

"It might swell up—sting or itch—but 'tis not poison."

"I know. We have them too. They squeeze the breath out. It was crawling up—I thought sure—"

"Not this one. This rogue's done all he'll ever do."

"Oh, I cannot thank thee enough, friend. Ooh." A wave of nausea came again. That spiced milk punch, if only she'd had cold tea. But she would not foul upon him. Instead, she let herself slip away.

When she came to, his shirt was not white, it was unbleached, and instead of grass, a hard flange bit into the bite under her knee. The sun was hot and sticky, the cool breath of the river gone. There had been a man's hand on her bare breast, it had been withdrawn the instant her eyelids fluttered, but the sensation of contact lingered. She clutched her bodice, springing up, crying, "Put me down, let me go," though Israel was making no attempt to hold her. She looked down upon her muddy gown, her muddy slippers, felt her pate for the lost bonnet.

"Where is he—the young man?"

"He went off," said Israel.

"Who is he?"

"I don't know."

"Thee did not ask his name? I would thank him. I might have been suffocated unto death!"

"I thanked him. He told me what took place. He'd been fishing in the stream, upward from where he found thee." (What he'd *said* was he had had a leak and was lacing his smalls when he was drawn to the spot by the chittering.) "He could not believe it when thee made outcry. Had thee not, thee were in no jeopardy. I did not think to detain him, I was so set on carrying thee back and keeping my footing. Thee's got more flesh on thee than meets the eye, Kezia. But I jest. 'Twas a nasty experience, I ought not to have let thee go alone."

She felt unbearably cast down. How could he just go off?

"Letting thee wander through unfamiliar wild-wood—"

"Could've happened at home. We're overrun with snakes. Nantucket's soggy in the lowlands."

"Thy color's coming back, I'm glad to see."

"Fancy me fainting. Never did before." She yanked her sleeve back onto her shoulder, brushed at her petticoat, wrung out her hem and her hair, looked up at the lodge. "I do hope the Cadwaladers have departed. I shouldn't want to be seen like this, dirty as a sow."

"They've gone. And so have the help. And so shall we be, soon's I put this moistened tobacco on thy bite. To draw out the sting."

"Nay, nay, tis no more troublesome than a wasp bite. Don't fuss, Israel. I would see the falls. When we get back to thy plantation, I'll poultice it with a rag soaked in turpentine." Actually her whole leg was throbbing, but there was an off chance she'd find her rescuer.

"If thee'd prefer, thee may apply it thyself. I'll avert my eyes." He held out the wadded shreds on his palm.

"Nonsense, I'm not overly modest. It troubles me not, I say. Now come, lead the way. I don't want to miss a spectacle of nature. Throw that stuff away."

"Very well, if thee insists. 'Tis not much of walk, thee was almost to it. I vow, Kezia, I know not what to make of thee. There's not another woman I know would fight a snake to save a squirrel. Not at all sure thee's not a bit squirrelly thyself. Let's step lively, before the sun dips. Thee's not too wet? I'd not have thee take a chill."

He set a brisk pace on the trail. She followed close on his heels, scanning the banks.

"The cataracts of the Delaware near Trenton and hereabouts on this river render them useless in the conveyance of goods," Israel explained. "There is talk of making them navigable but I should rather hate to see—"

"Israel, we must find that young man. I'll not rest till I return proper thanks. He was so kind, so master brave."

"Hm."

"Thee'll inquire?"

"Certainly," he said without heart.

The river ran faster, louder, swirled to rapids. And disappeared. She made the turn and stood transfixed. White water cascaded from a height of some thirty feet, the roar of it filled her whole body, she felt its spray on her face.

"I've stood behind it," he shouted into her ear. "There's a kind of shelf—dry's a bone."

She kicked off her shoes and pulled off her stockings. Gripping where she could get purchase, she inched, limpetlike, along the jutting rock until she gained the ledge. At the middle of the ledge, she turned carefully, leaned back, stared through the green curtain.

"She-goat!" panted Israel, taking the hand she stretched out to him. "I was a boy when I last did this!"

It was like the green ice days that came to Nantucket in a record winter. Then the wind was frozen out of sound and the water was frozen out of sight and one could walk past Wauwinet to Coskata, feeling enclosed in a vast green glass bowl. Here one felt inside a bubble, half dark and half light, half solid, half aqueous, an unearthly place suspended between heaven and hell, and she a land mermaid with the rules to learn all over again.

She stroked her hair which ran like rockweed down her sodden clinging gown. A dream of violation stirred in her womb. She looked to see if Israel were changed, and he was. A film polished his hair and cheeks, wetted his red lips, and in his lightened eyes was the predatory look of terns when they came down in their black caps to melt and split the ice with their hot beaks. His kiss on her mouth was fierce, his strong tongue raced around her teeth. He flung her petticoat over her face, yanked loose her strung drawers, and grabbing a fistful of her bush, shook it hard as if it were wet. She was hot, weak, and loose-limbed when she felt his huge horn-hard cock go into her. It whirled about as had his great tongue and suddenly withdrew, spurting slime against her belly. His braced upper hand slipped, landed on her covered face, flattening her nose. She made a protesting sound, and it was quickly gone. Her skirt dropped into place as he scuttled off.

She stayed on a moment or two, wiping herself free of his juice with what was now but a damp sigh of a dress. She turned to exit, forgetting the dropped smalls which caught her ankles, and fell, sprawling on the verge. The heavy spray was cold and frightening on her back. She kicked off the drawers and watched the rapids suck them away. (There, Mrs. Cadwalader, is a bit of gossip for thee if thee be walking by the river.) Once out of the green habitat, back in the weird world of man, she squeezed out her hair and the hem of her dress as she seemed to have done often that day.

When she caught up to him on the path, he was banging his forehead against a barky willow that dropped toward the river. "What—Israel, has thee lost thy wits?" She pulled him away, turned him to her.

His eyes were blind as gray paint, and there was spittle in the corners of his mouth. He'd broken the skin of his forehead, there was blood on his scraped nose. He grabbed her wrists, held her fingernails to his cheeks. "Rend me, mark me, I deserve it, I did thee violence."

Sane or insane, she hated everything this man ever said. So theatrical. She said dryly, hoping to bring him to his senses, "I've not been stood up against a wall before but it does beat getting shot."

He did not even hear her. "I am wickeder than Cain. I have defiled thee, a guest in my house, woe is me, I am no better than the serpent." He tore off a willow switch, forced her fingers round it. "Take thy vengeance, I give thee leave. Castigate me till my visage runneth with blood."

"Oh, for pity's sake," she said, loathing him, and flung the switch away.

He picked it up and shook it in her face, "Then I'll mark thee, Jezebel, for thee it was bewitched me!" He grabbed her dress, already torn at the shoulder, and pulled it away from her breast. "I'll stripe thee till thy breasts pour like wine gourds. Thy buttocks shall spurt jets of blood—"

And mad enough to do it, she thought, struggling with him to stay clothed. She was as outclassed as the squirrel. The only upper hand she ever had of him was when she showed scorn. She went quite limp, waved aside the willow wand, saying, "Oh, come, Israel, what a to-do. I went first, thee but followed. What else, after all, is there to do behind a waterfall?"

The catharsis that should have come with ejaculation came now. His streaked forehead smoothed. He took long shuddering breaths. He closed his eyes, pinched the bone of his nose. When his eyes opened, they had regained color and sight. He grinned down at her.

"I vow, Kezia, thee hath the body of a woman but thee thinks like a man."

She gave him an implacable eye. "Is that so? In my view, men and women think alike." And tramped toward the lodge.

He hurried after. "What's with us, Kezia? Why can I never hit the right note with thee? Thee forgives an abominable assault, but not my mildest utterance. Why do I so vex thee? I meant it as a compliment."

"That's what vexed me," she retorted, striding on.

The fence behind the lodge held only their two mounts. Kezia remained sullen. He without saying anything conveyed an importunacy. It was in the way he handled the horses, gently untying them, slowly saddling them, handing her her reins.

"Forgive me, Kezia."

"Thee's forgiven."

"Then smile."

"I cannot."

"Look on me."

"I would not."

He sighed, made a cradle of his hand for her get-up foot. "What? Lost thy shoes?"

In a trice, their roles reversed. She was no longer the scolding mother but an errant child. "I forgot them."

"Where? I'll go fetch them."

"Nay, we'll be late. I have others."

"But that's waste. I'll not permit it. Where did thee leave them?"

"Oh, Israel, don't be tiresome. They're away down at the cataract. My bonnet's gone too—I know not where nor care. We're due at Fairhill at eight. Mary says 'tis halfway to Germantown. She said not to tarry."

But the mention of his wife worked an antithetical magic. He fondled her foot, ogled her. "Tell me, witch, how many men has thee known?"

She made a fist of her foot, kicked him hard under his ribcage, and then jabbed her bare heels into the horse's flanks. The beast broke into a lazy canter but she kept kicking and whipped the sides of his neck with loops of rein until she had him galloping. Then the road forked, and she was obliged to rein in, not knowing which direction to take.

Israel pulled up. "Kezia, I most humbly beg pardon. I don't know what comes over me. I've not been myself since I found thee in a faint."

His handsome face was flushed, one could drown in that deepwater gaze. He was, she reminded herself, not only her host but an invaluable business contact. She had no trouble bestowing a smile. "Think no more on't. Nothing has happened. All's as it was. Now which way do we go? I'm all at sea."

The carriage wound from the highway onto a wheel road through acres of tanglewood. Here and there grottoes of cold kissed her flushed cheek. Whether from reaction to the snake venom or in anticipation of the farewell party, she felt giddy, feverish—or was it the press of Israel's thigh bone?

There appeared against the coral-streaked sky a two-storied house with a cupola surmounted by a weather cock. It was of pink brick with white window sashes, bright green shutters, and blue mansard roof. The gardens were formal with white gravel walks and parterres. Surrounded by hoary thicket, Fairhill was like a many jeweled brooch in a richly wrought setting pinned to a homespun blouse.

"How charming!" exclaimed Kezia.

Mary nodded. "Isn't it? Everybody finds it so."

Israel said miffily, "Of course, this is their year-round residence. We purposely keep the Plantation rustic by way of contrast to our city mode of living."

They were received by a liveried doorman into a high-ceilinged foyer with a balustraded staircase and scenic paper mural. Their names were announced to the gathering in an exquisitely appointed drawing room of small but perfect proportions. Above the pianoforte, looking down with a cold and dubious eye, was a belted earl, presumably, but not necessarily in this land of new money, an ancestor. Despising herself for it, Kezia felt intimidated—not by the titled ancestry, but by the opulence. Wealth—even now that she had it herself—overimpressed her. Was it because her mother had ever inveighed against it? She wished she were purer, such shoddy values. Well, come, this was no time for self-vilification. There was a front to put up. Shoulders back, chin up and out, walk tall. At least she was not a ninny like these vapid young mothers comparing panadas. Or this knot of dowagers, fanning themselves, perceiving the need of sharp whippings for slow servants. She sailed past them to the men.

"Yes, there's unrest in Boston," Israel was saying to a rapt audience. Men always listened when Israel held forth; riches speak louder than words. "And some discontent in the back counties in the South, but when's there been a time without disturbances? No one can deny we are in a period of prosperity. The Tidewater tobacco crop's good, the Jerseys are growing an abundance of food. Rafts of fine white pine float down the Delaware. Our sheep are thick-fleeced, our pigs fat, and we've more venison than we know what to do with. We make our own bricks for the new houses going up. Why should England want to antagonize her most productive, most promising offspring; it behooves her to keep us quiet and happy. Mark me, my friends, men don't make war in time of plenty, and England knows it. Men fight for food, not for freedom."

Kezia felt a surge of pride in Israel. He was convincing, she alone had a tendency to underrate him. But then, with his next breath, he sounded odious to her.

"Men don't want freedom," Israel said. "They want a strong paternal government, same's women want from marriage."

Everyone laughed except Kezia, who not only frowned but also snorted.

Someone asked her impressions of their town. What did she like best? The great leafy trees. And the least? The slave mart. "An odd sight in a city whose name means Brotherly Love," she rapped out tartly.

The footman was announcing the old Cadwalader couple from the Fishing Club—and there between them stood her young knight!

He was even fairer right side up—tall, tawny, leonine of feature with drowsy green eyes. He was dressed, her noble Leo, in a gold-braided tricorn, buff-colored frock coat with black velvet collar, white cravat, white silk stockings, sealskin shoes—the last word.

"My dear young man! My very dear sir!" Kezia cried out, running across the room, arms outstretched. "Mr. Fanning? Did I hear the name aright? Oh, I so feared I'd lost thee for good and aye—that I'd not see thee more!"

He smiled delightedly and swung her hands. Could it be—? Where was the draggled, skinny, livid—? He wanted to shout. How beautiful—no idea you were—proud to have—

"Phineas!" Mrs. Cadwalader's chin skin shook above a collar of dirty silver lace. "Who's this? What's she to do with thee?"

The company was staring at them. He dropped her hands, stammered, "I—you see—this afternoon—I —I—" Then he saw Kezia's amused look, and recovered himself. Still blushing, he took back one of her hands, laid it across his forearm. "Cousin, may I present my Lady Guinevere to whom I played Launcelot this day?"

"Eh? Mistress Landslock? Where from?"

Israel stepped forward, made the proper introductions, and then gave an account to the company of Kezia's battle with a black snake. Anecdotes of encounters with vipers both poisonous and un took them well through the first course, *olla podrida,* a highly spiced soup to encourage wine-bibbing. There followed the usual Philadelphian banquet served on Crown Derby, though the host maintained they lived 'downright in the country way.' A baked fish with a caper sauce. Then ducks, baked ham, roasted beef. Hot buttered green asparagus, mushrooms, pickled samphire, sweet-and-sour purple cabbage. Five wines as well as porter and beer, though it was said there was less gout in Philadelphia than in England and all her colonies. For dessert, berry tarts, trifle, several cheeses, quiddanies, and a huge bowl of fruit—pears, peaches, cherries and raisins, and almonds already shelled.

Young Fanning was seated far below the salt, and

Kezia, as the guest of honor, above it, so it was not until the company removed to the drawing room for sugared coffee that she was able to bait her hook.

His parents, he said, resided on Long Island, and he was here on holiday visiting his cousins, the Cadwaladers.

"So thee's an islander too. Then thee must be a good sailor, eh?"

"The roar of the sea was my first lullaby. And I grew sea legs before I walked to school. But I don't care for seafaring as a way of life."

"What does thee fancy then?"

"The law. I have but lately returned from London where I studied at the Inns of Court."

"Oh, my, how enterprising! And did thee pass the bar?"

"Yes, I did. Not with any great distinction, but considering that I had my early education here in the colonies, I and my father are well satisfied. Now the problem is where to practice. I have been investigating the opportunities here."

"How old is thee, Phineas?"

"I'll soon be twenty-four."

"Indeed. Then I dare say thee's pledged?"

He blushed again but answered solemnly. "I cannot think of keeping a wife till I know how I may keep myself."

"Is thee set upon living in Philadelphia?"

"I am undecided. My cousin has had me talk with a friend of his, a most eminent barrister who two years ago gave up a lucrative practice to devote himself to religion. Unfortunately, I am too late to take over his work. He promises, however, to recommend me to some of his ex-clients."

"Thy cousins be Quakers, I understand."

"Yes."

"And thy persuasion?"

"Presbyterian, same's my parents."

Oh, well, she was virtually disowned anyway. She'd bought a spinet for Little Kezia to which the

Friends objected. They were always on her about some trifle or other. "Too bad we have so little time to talk. I find many things in thy religion that appeal to me over the Quaker. Politically, I dare say, we stand together. Thee's a Tory?"

"Indeed I am, ma'am."

"Do call me Kezia, Phineas. At home we go much by given names, old and young. Well now, what of the other law offices in Philadelphia? Has thee canvassed them?"

"Oh, there are many outstanding lawyers here. I've not spoken to them yet, though I mean to. But the young attorneys I've met have been rather discouraging."

"Perhaps they fear competition."

"Perhaps so, but I have the distinct feeling that Philadelphia is not beating the bushes for law clerks."

"In Sherburne," she said, "we've nary a one."

"What! Is it so?"

"Not a one, and the need grows daily."

"But is not Nantucket largely Quaker? And orthodox? And do not conservative Quakers still regard lawyers as did George Fox who saw all of us as black as our robes?"

She laughed. "Well, not as bad as all that. Quaker aye, more than two-thirds, and orthodox, very. Till recently most disputes were settled in Meeting, or at least such was the recommended procedure. But our whaling industry grows apace and with it the land industries that serve it. As a result, our economic tangles become more frequent and more complex. 'Tis my candid opinion a young lawyer would find a mort of work on our island. Why not ship out with me and give it a look-see? Thee'd lose nothing but time and at this point in thy career it would seem thee has it to spare."

The green eyes took fire. "No competitors," he mused.

"I could promise thee *my* legal work straightaway, and I have many close friends among our foremost merchants. The Rotches, Samuel Starbuck, Timothy

Folger, and others. I should put thee in the way of them."

"How kind you are."

"Not at all. I confess, Phineas, I feel much drawn to thee. Not just because of thy succor this afternoon. But some affinity. Does thee not sense it?"

His smile was so warm, so open, her heart leaped. He said, "I do."

"Of course, the living is primitive on Nantucket. We are whalers, coopers, yeoman, shepherds. We live simply, dress plain. Nothing as high-flown as London or Philadelphia society."

"I like simplicity. And I like islands. I'm used to coming home over water by the skin of my teeth and an extra inch of sail. It makes homecoming all the sweeter."

"Aye, we islanders are a separate order. And Nantucketers, I must warn thee, are separater than most. They're picky about foreigners, but I should act as thy buffer against that. Now, when I said primitive, thee must know we're not a typical backwater village. Our commerce is farflung. Europe, the Orient. We are not worldly in our ways, but we know the ways of the world."

"I suppose there's a lodging house in Sherburne?"

"Why, Phineas, thee should live under my roof. I've a most commodious house. There's a room for guests, thee'd be comfortable."

"Only if I could pay rent."

"Well, perhaps we could work out some sort of trade. Say, room and board for an equitable amount of legal service."

"Capital! But what of your family, madam? Kezia. Would not your husband find a boarder intrusive? And your children?"

"My husband is broken in health, Phineas, and considerably—ah—older. I have ever been in charge of our domestic affairs. Money matters as well, for he was a whalemaster and much at sea. So it is with many families on Nantucket, the women have the say of things. As for children, I've but one. A daughter."

She saw him stiffen. Leery, no doubt, of ambitious mothers.

"How old is she?"

"Fifteen last First Month."

She was amused to see his relief. "Oh, but a maid, that's well then," he said.

To Kezia's extreme annoyance, the host at this point struck a wall gong with a little mallet, held up his hand for silence, and introduced a Miss Drinker, who would favor them with a rendition of a piece from the *Well-Tempered Clavichord*. Kezia and Phineas, along with the rest, turned polite faces to the pianoforte. Israel, who had been glowering at them, looked pleased and crossed his long legs, knocking over a footstool. Old Mrs. Cadwalader cupped her ear. Into the quiet came surprisingly strong cadences considering the delicacy of Miss Drinker's hands and the paleness of her hair.

"I say, I am tempted," whispered Phineas. "When does your vessel leave?"

"On the morrow, but I could lay over if—"

"No, no need. I shall be there."

"We leave on the afternoon tide. My ship's the *Diana*. And look here, don't feel committed. Thee's but taking soundings."

Israel coughed and glared.

Kezia returned his look with defiance. 'Twas an entertainment, after all, not a Meeting. But listening, she was less sure. Bach's thesis seemed as romantic as any sermon: the world is an orderly place, life is not what it is but what it should be, man is created in God's image and if he tried, he could be divine. Selah.

Miss Drinker's head dropped over the keyboard, showing a tender nape with tendrils of gold.

The company clapped, but Phineas clapped loudest and longest, mouth smiling and agape. That settled it—the spinet stayed.

Late as it was, she brushed and plaited her hair, rinsed her mouth with watered essence of peppermint. She started to untie the bed draperies and then decided to leave them open, for her chamber under the eaves retained the day's heat. She threw herself naked atop the patchwork-quilt, listened to the sounds of the night: throb of cicadas, croak of bullfrog, and the running creek. Close to the house, a bough broke. There was no wind, a bough come to the end of its time. . . .

A moth flew at the candle. She waved it away but did not blow out the flame. She was too keyed up to sleep. Fancy completing her mission at the eleventh hour! Pray God young Fanning did not change his mind. How fortunate she had bought Little Kezia those beautiful new clothes! If only the child were a little more artful. But then, mind how pretty and provocative Damaris Worth had been and what did it get her but that ape, Edward Starbuck. With every child, she'd lost a tooth, some hair, she was nothing now but a tired ailing scold, and it was common knowledge that Edward Starbuck wenched with young black Juba in New Guinea. "Juba this and Juba that, Juba in a kettle of fat," sang his children's schoolmates on the sly. No secrets on Nantucket, not even from the young.

She yanked the pillow down under her neck. She still felt dizzied in spite of the ballast she'd put down. She hoped she'd not dream of snakes. The thought woke her bite but she would not permit herself to scratch it. Her Venus mount smarted from the hair-pulling, but not enough to get her up for a cool wet cloth. Besides, there was barely enough water left in the pitcher for the morrow's toilette. The water had to be carried up from the brook, and the staff of servants was small at the Plantation. Israel kept it not only rustic but Spartan. How jealously he had responded to her praise of Fairhill, what a transparent man he was! And yet—and yet he lit up a room as well as candles. Sarah Norris had not taken her eyes off him, though her own husband was very attractive. Did Mary Pemberton notice these goings-on? Did she care? Was she aware of Israel's attentions to Kezia? If she was, she certainly did not betray a suspicion. At times she even seemed to be throwing them together. Had Mary had her fill of that black swan's cock and his need to punish it? One never knew what went on behind a marriage. By the look of him, tonight, for instance, Israel was the soul of decorum, a pillar of respectability. But lah —take her Cousin Benjamin Franklin, was he not of the same cloth? All those mealy-mouthed maxims, that serene mien, who would believe that on her last visit to Philadelphia he'd chased her around his dining table and promised her shares in the Ohio land venture if she'd let him take her to bed. And Benjamin Franklin was not a man to give up easily. Kept sending her little gifts—the last, a pair of brass candlesticks from England. The note attached was signed 'your affectionate kinsman.' Oh, he was affectionate, right enough.

She heard a little sound. Her eyes flew to the door latch. It reared slowly. Her heart began to thud and she knew she'd been awaiting him. He closed the door with infinite care, his back to her. Then he turned, and threw off his nightcap, his gown, and took the bed in a leap. She lay wide-eyed under his dark wingspread. His cock pointed above her head and, in a brief sweep of hysteria, she thought of the wicked lampoon of Caldwell's *Navigator:* 'The angle of the dangle is equal to the heat of the meat.'

"I am at thy mercy," he growled softly, grinning. "My dumpling, Mistress Mary, sleeps lightly. Thee may ruin me with a single outcry. Wouldst have me go or stay?"

"If I let thee stay, shall thee go berserk again?"

He shrugged, his teeth blue-white in hell's-fire lips. "That is the chance we take. I never know."

It was no longer puzzling how Israel came by an uncontrollable son.

He made no move, awaiting her decision. She drew a fingertip over the scratch on his forehead. "Blow out the candle."

"Nay, I'll not blind thee again. This time thee'll watch."

She found the condition irresistible. That and the threat of his going daft. As he kissed the nipple of her breast, she whispered in his ear, "No need to up-anchor, love. Thee may let thy scupper run free."

The tag ends of a dream left her melancholy. Yet she remembered the vivid color. She'd been flying about, swooping, describing circles in the sky. She came to rest on one foot on a piling. A golden ship hove into view—a royal barge resplendent with red velvet sails and gold fringes. The parquet deck was carpeted in turkey. Her sister Mary, with a flap of wings, whizzed past her, squeaking, "My turn, my turn!" Kezia would have raced her to the proud vessel but her foot was stuck in pitch. Little Kezia, not more than two years old or three, stretched out baby arms, calling, "Mama, mama!" But Kezia was stuck fast and the gold ship sailed away. She opened her eyes. At first she could not figure out where she was. Then, as the dream fled, it came to her—the Plantation. Departure day! Phineas Fanning!

She flung back the thin patch-quilt and began to scoop up her clothes. She must be packed and dressed and breakfasted in time to ride into town with them. After Meeting, Israel had promised the carriage might stop for the fur-lined greatcoat. If the tailor was not done with it, she'd take it as it was and have it finished in Sherburne. She pressed her belongings down into the little pigskin trunk, threw her toiletries into a knapsack—hairbrush, hand-mirror, medicaments against sunburn, a variety of cosmetics. She put them and the bandbox outside her chamber door for the coachman to carry down. She wasted several minutes frantically searching for the seed-pearl brooch Lady Anne had given her. And found it when she moved the slop jar under her bed. She dressed quickly, investigating her bite as she drew on a stocking. The heat was gone from it and the redness fainter. She splashed the last of the

water on her face and hair, too late to brush it, she'd
packed the brush and lost her comb. She tied on her
cap, threw a cashmere pelisse over her arm. The day
was already warm, but she'd need the wrap later on the
water. She laughed at her silly dream. The *Diana*
waited upon her pleasure. She couldn't very well miss
her own boat.

Nineteen

"Thee tires of me," Samuel diagnosed dejectedly.

"I never needed thee more," she said, and meant it. The 'change' was upon her, and even though she had long been infecund, yet she was saddened by this sign of encroaching age. She had nightmares in which she pulled and pulled the afterbirth from her throat where it choked her, and often she woke from a girlhood dream hot with desire. Even today at the business conference in Will Rotch's offices, her parts had burned at the sight of Samuel's competent hands. She had talked of shipping and of war, but her body lay with him in Calcutta. She had tried unsuccessfully to give him up. Yet now when they would steal a few moments of love between day and dark, she could not take joy in it.

"Oh, Samuel, believe me, 'tis not me and thee, 'tis me and Little Kezia. This day we collided bow on. For the first time I saw hate in her eyes, heard rage in her voice, and I am withered from the blast. Fancy being hated by one's own child." By the babe she nearly died birthing. Had raised single-handed from the time Aunt Hannah passed on almost ten years ago. Now it was Dada this and Dada that, Father's house, Father's sheep, Father's fields, Father's fleet, as if John had been the dotingest of landlubber fathers.

His bones softened to enfold her. "What provoked her?"

Kezia frowned in an effort to give an unvarnished account. "Well, there's a do tonight at the Husseys'. All's I said was, 'May thee not meet Lucy Hammett at the Husseys'?' I spoke in a pleasant tone, I am ever at pains to spare the girl's sensibilities, though it takes monumental control. She so vexes me the way she behaves to Phineas. For nigh onto a year I've watched her vanish from the room whenever Phineas enters it. She rejects his every advance, bridles at his teases, acts altogether like a bad Indian. And what mealtimes would have been like without Phineas's extraordinary good humor, I shudder to think. John quiet and strange, Little Kezia mute and sullen, stuffing herself like a festal goose, never saying a bright thing, not even looking the lad in the eye. What use were all those Philadelphia dresses if she has to force herself into them like so much sausage meat?"

What Kezia had actually said was, "Must Lucy be glued to thy side wherever thee goes, whatever thee does?"

"Lucy's my best friend," Little Kezia had shot back.

"Well and good, but that doesn't mean thee must be with her every waken moment."

"Not must, would. I am happy when we're together. Thee ought to understand that. I heard Grandmother say time was when thee and Aunt Miriam couldn't be pried apart with a cold chisel."

"And see what it came to—naught but enmity."

"That's as may be but at the time—"

"At the *time,* I was already married and—"

"Hah. *There* it is. Why beat about the bush? Thee's afraid Phineas Fanning will wed another and thee fetched him here for *me.*"

"Suppose I did? Is it unnatural for a mother to put her daughter's interests foremost?"

"He's ten years older than I."

"What of it? Thy father's fifteen years older than I."

"Thee cannot brand him as thee would one of Dada's bull calves. If heifers give him the eye, thee can't blind them."

"Who eyes him? I am curious."

"Curiosity killed the cat."

That was sauce and it burned, but Kezia was

determined not to stoop to that childish level. She said, trying to sound amused, "And Phineas, whom does he eye?"

"If I knew I'd not tell thee!" cried the girl, and ran in to the keeping room where the clock chimed once. That was when Kezia should have tied on her bonnet and departed. Instead she dogged the girl's heels, saying, "No need. I know. Dinah Starbuck, Polly Brock——"

Little Kezia wheeled on her. "Fie, spy! Does thee keep a list? Here's more for it then: Sally Fitch, Betsy Calef——"

"He only likes Betsy because she plays the spinet. And she don't play as well as thee by half. I regret thee gave up the lessons. I've a good mind to fetch that spinet back from the Husseys."

"Thee may not! Dada gave his solemn word. He stood up in Meeting and said he had no hand in bringing the spinet into this house and would forbid it ever being used here. He promised the Friends not to displease them long's he was in his right mind."

"An interesting loophole," said Kezia icily. Told by this chit what she might and might not do! "Is he planning to go out of it?"

They stared at each other, each daring the other to admit that he often did.

Kezia was the one to back down. "Oh, fear not. I love thy father quite as much as thee does and would do nothing to discompose him. Any more than I'd discompose thee."

"But thee *does* discompose me! Time after time and I wish——"

Kezia reached back for the support of a chair arm. "I? Discompose thee? How? When?"

"The way thee treats Lucy for one thing. So coldly. She perceives thee has no liking for her."

"I've nothing against Lucy, nothing at all. Except that she's ever underfoot. And don't tell me she's not here more often since Phineas——"

"She's here for love of me," Little Kezia screamed. *"My* company! Can thee not credit a body would value me for myself alone?"

Did the cry have a familiar ring? Kezia never heard it. She drew herself up, exactly as her mother was wont to do. To get away from that statue of disapproval, Little Kezia ran up the stairs, and Kezia ran hard after, elbows akimbo to hold up her petticoat, never seeing Hagar in the hall door nor Patience ducking backward with her broom into John's chamber. "Dare to run out on me, my girl?"

"Then leave me be, can't thee? Have done!"

The door slammed.

Kezia shouted through it, "All's I want to know is, what's thee got against Phineas?"

The door flung open. "Thee!" And slammed again. And latched.

"Now what precisely did she mean by that, I'd like to know?" Kezia asked of Samuel.

"Mayhap they are not meant for each other, Kezia. The heart cannot be coerced."

"And I tell thee they are exactly right for each other. He's a comely, intelligent, warmhearted lad—he builds a fire one can draw up to. But he must needs be a hero, his pride is shaggy, and Little Kezia gives that kind of nourishment. She has no need to shine herself but she adores the shining person in a high place. A hero-worshiper. What better combination?"

"They're of different faiths."

"Well, what of that?"

" 'Tis not I who'd make objections. 'Tis thy mother."

"My mother! She made a thornback of Aunt Hannah. There's some gets one chance and one only. I wouldn't want Little Kezia passed by. What matter if a man's not born a Quaker long's he's wellborn? There's but one God for all. Besides, I shall cross that bridge when I come to it. And I'll not come to it if Lit-

tle Kezia keeps gorging herself like a greedy little beast.
That's John's side of the family. Look at Debbie, my
once beautiful Debbie. Isn't it a pity?"

"Now, now, Little Kezia's not out-sized. 'Tis not
unnatural at her age to be on the chubby side. And
there are men who favor a well-fleshed woman. I
don't happen to be one of them but—"

She could hear the amusement in his voice but
she did not leaven. "Thee's heard of hog-drunk? Well,
she's hog-fed."

"There are those who try to slake their miseries
with spiritous liquor. Maybe Little Kezia is trying to
quell hers with food. When her distress passes, her
appetite will lessen."

Her own disastrous incontinence with opiates
never crossed her mind. "Distress, my foot. Greed's
what. And I doubt thee'd be so easygoing if it were
thy daughter doing the eating."

"If God had seen fit to grant me a daughter, I
think I should have looked upon her with love and
understanding. It strikes me thee's as hard on the maid
as thy mother was on thee."

That did it—the last straw. Stung, she pointed
out his errors as a father, and they parted silent as
stones.

It was the dark side of dusk when Kezia arrived
home. John and someone had already supped. The remains were still on the table. Little Kezia and Phineas
were gone to the party. Through the doorway Kezia
could see Hagar chopping parsley by the light of the
candelabrum that had lit the supper. Hagar chopping
parsley was something to see—the several chins jumped
like blackberry jelly.

"Have you et? I've supper set by."

"Nay, and I'm starving. What's for supper?"

"Bluefish," said Hagar, throwing the name away.

"Blue? Why, it's ten years—not since the Indian
plague!"

"They come back. Mr. Tristram Starbuck caught
a mess of them, and Mistress Debbie fetched some

here. I filleted them and fried them light and crisp.
They had a feast, her and Cap'n John. Ate every last
morsel except the piece I saved out for you."

Kezia absently chewed a parsley stem. They rarely had a chance to dine alone, he and Debbie. What
did they talk about—the present or the past?

"And I baked green currant pie. Set down to the
dining table, Mistress. Or would you have it up in your
chamber? You're looking fashed. And you ought to
wear a leathern overskirt, your petticoat's dirtied."

"I shall have it here in the hall with thee, and
some of that wine too. Take down two cups—one for
thee."

On the wooden sink was a trencherful of her
favorite sweetmeats: candied orange peel and pickled
limes. She popped an orange peel into her mouth.
"Mmm. Hagar, thee spoils me."

"Not my doing. Little Kezia's. She made them this
afternoon."

A peace offering. Kezia sighed. "Did she tell thee
about it?"

"No need. I got ears."

"Does thee hold it against me?"

"No, but 'tis past believing how a woman smart
as you can be so wrongheaded with her onliest young
one."

"How'm I wrong?"

"Least said, soonest mended." Hagar flipped the
fish.

"Oh, speak out—thee's bursting too."

"Nosiree, not this old head."

"Hagar, I'm too fagged out to beg."

"Well then. I say let her be."

"I have. I've had lockjaw for nigh a year."

"And may have for another year, even two. But
she's smitten, I promise you that."

"She's hateful to him."

"That's the proof of the pudding. If she treated
him kindly, you'd have reason to fret."

The bluefish was white-fleshed, velvety, with a

delicate flavor that the minced parsley brought out. "This is delicious, Hagar. Is there a bit of lemon?"

"There, you got me agoing and I forgot." Hagar fetched a dish of quartered lemons. "Nobbut a few drops, mind. It don't take much to sour the sweetness."

"Sit down with me. Pour us more wine."

"Not me. I've had my wine and I've had my say." But she refilled the cups and sat down, helping herself to one of the lemon wedges, eating it rind and all.

"When I asked her what she had against him, she shouted, 'Thee!' That's what upset me. What can she mean?"

"Mean what she said. He and Little Kezia do fine when you're not about. Talk and laugh up a storm. Soon's you come in, it's all over. He starts abowing and ascraping, tells you this happened and that, what he done about it, and you tell him how clever he is and the two of you's off jawing and jabbering like you was both sitting on Altar Rock and Cap'n John and her's no more'n a couple of dandelion puffheads."

"I but try to fill the air. They talk so little and *say* so little when they talk. He's an educated man, graduated from the finest law school in Londontown, and accustomed to high society. I keep fearing he'll get bored and depart."

Hagar slipped off her shoes, took a pink-soled horny-heeled foot into her lap, pulled at the big toe to ease the bunion. "Can't pilot everybody's ship, Mistress. Wants to take off, he'll take off." She rolled a mouthful of wine from cheek to cheek. "My guess he's dropped anchor."

"Well, I didn't help matters today. Thee's got the right of that."

"How's the pie?"

Humble, Kezia thought to herself, but Hagar wouldn't understand. "Very good."

"Good's my sister Hepsy's?"

"Better."

"You mean it?"

"Would I say it if I did not?"

"Might. I expect I feel about Hepsy the way Little Kezia feels about you. Outdid."

When John's snoring ceased across the way, she heard the brook run and the harbor waters lapping, lapping. Somewhere a bell tinkled and fell silent, tinkled and fell with the rock of the tide like the voice of a complaining woman. Otherwise all was still. There was a bounty on dogs again so there was no barking, and the birds were asleep, all but the barn owls who gave out wide-spaced, low-throbbing hoots. So familiar, so intimate, so peaceful, the sounds one hears from one's bed, one's dear own bed. Hard to credit that thirty miles away Englishmen crouched behind cannon and musket, waiting to kill each other.

There they were now. Late enough. She lit her candle again, took it to the landing, called down softly lest she wake John.

"Daughter, is't thee?"

"Yes, Mama."

"What is the hour?"

"Half after ten. 'Twas a merry dance."

"Phineas?"

"Yes, Marmy."

His nickname for her—self-consciously devised because her given name seemed too familiar in the presence of her husband and daughter—and she'd come to like it.

"Help thyself in the kitchen. There's currant berry pie and sago cream."

"I thank you but I've had my fill."

"Little Kezia, I'd like a word with thee."

"Right away, Mama."

There was a scuffling and the low throaty warbles of wild pigeons. She went back to bed, leaving her door ajar.

"Mama?"

"Come in dear, come in. I would thank thee for the orange peels and the limes."

"I'm glad if thee liked them."

"Oh, I did. I do. I'd have eaten more but Hagar

stood over me, watching every mouthful of pie to see it well-received."

They laughed, and Kezia patted the bed at her knee. "Sit a spell. So it was jolly, eh?"

"Oh very. Cushing dances they were called. Sprightly."

"Well, good. Now, my dear, I've thought on the —ah—other matter, and I believe I have erred. I ought not try to pilot thy ship. I mind when I was thy age, I wanted to be an apothecary. I was fascinated by simples and mithridates and such. I thought to live in the great city of Boston, beholden to no man, independent and free. And now I perceive thee's like me. There are those of us who do not desire marriage and children—*kinder* and *kuchen* as the Pennsylvania Dutch call it—who seek professions rather. Thee and that journal thee's so entranced with. I was blind not to see it. I perceive now that writing might be thy call. And a noble calling it is. 'Writing is of all the arts the most useful to society—the soul of commerce, the picture of the past, the regulator of the future, and the messenger of thought.' Oh, Daughter, I should be so proud if thee become a great novelist—the first woman to follow in the footsteps of such geniuses as Smollett and Richardson! How stupid I was to try to push thee into matrimony. There are vaster worlds to—"

"But, Mama, I do want to get married and have children. I've no wish to write books. I only started the journal becasue thee gave me that stationery during inventory last year. I had no one to write to, so I took the notion people in some future time might wish to know how it was in ours."

"There, see? The picture of the past!"

"Not a picture, Mama. A record. Merely entries such as any keeper of accounts might make in a ledger book. I'm but a clerk using words instead of numbers."

"Thee's overly modest. I should love to see it. May I?"

"Oh, no, 'tis all blotted and full of misspellings and scratchouts. I mean to copy it and then thee may read in it. But, Mama, I do want to get married and soon. Phineas and I—oh, we have been such numskulls."

Only then did Kezia notice the wild wet look in her daughter's eyes. And about the mouth. So they had kissed. Hagar was right.

"I thought it was hopeless. All the girls prinking and preening before him. I thought he found me dull, when all the time he was but waiting for a sign. He thought I didn't fancy *him!*"

"I shouldn't wonder. Thee's been so graceless."

"Oh, I know, I *know*. But our set-to today—well, afters, I saw the light. When he came in at sunset, I was waiting for him under the window. I had changed my apron and my hair was smooth and wound into a knot. I behaved most cordially to him, offering him some of the sweets I had made—"

Hah! Not for her at all, for him.

"To which he replied he preferred the sweetness of the server to the served—and kissed my hand!"

"I hope he took no further liberties?"

"Well, yes. Tonight walking home, he slipped his arm around my waist. Oh, Mama, I was all of a tremble and tried to hold myself still. He said my hair smelt of orange blossoms, the wedding flower. Mama, I know not how to ask this, but if he should kiss me— mouth to mouth—is there a special way I must respond? Is it different when—?"

"Thee's never kissed a boy?"

"Nay, none ever asked. Nor tried to steal."

"Ah, well, there's no know-how, love. It just happens and 'tis wondrous sweet."

Little Kezia threw herself on her back and smiled at the rafters. "He said he was prepared to wait years."

"Well, now he needn't," Kezia said, observing the stubby brown hand, so like John's, and wondering that Phineas should have been moved to put his lips to it. "We can publish intentions as soon as thy father is told. And oh, my dearling, we shall make a great day of it. Thy grandmother may make complaint, but I know how to get round that. We'll have the entire family here for dinner midday—a feast to remember. We'll broach pipes of wine, we'll spit ducks and geese and hams and beeves. Then we'll bid them farewell and proceed, just the four of us, to Reverend Shaw's for the ceremony. And after we'll come back here to supper. We'll have an entertainment solely for young folk, with a fiddler for dancing—"

"Too lavish, people will talk."

"Talk? I want them to measure time by that day! My little girl, a bride!"

Unexpectedly, John opposed the union. Kezia argued without force, glad to see that inside that ruined carcass there was still a shred of man.

"She might lose him, he's a catch."

"Then she may marry within the true religion."

"Is persuasion more important than a good son-in-law?"

"Quakers also make good son-in-laws. He's not the only pebble on the beach."

"I thought thee liked him."

"I do. But she is young. If God wills the union, a period of consideration will not deter it."

"Very well, Husband, we shall abide by thy decree."

John's stand as paterfamilias and Kezia's acceptance of it was good medicine for him. Mentally he sharpened, had fewer lapses, physically he gained vigor. Encouraged by his improvement, Kezia told him of her Quaise project. She said nothing of the tunnel, he might turn foolish again and babble. But about the plan to build a country seat he was enthusiastic. "I mind we once dreamed of it. And Father ever favored real estate as investment. Especially if one could enjoy its use as it appreciated in value."

And so they purchased another fifty sheeps' lots which completed the accumulation of Quaise meadows. John accompanied her and Phineas to the signings, and in spite of the war-troubled waterways, they dispatched craft to York and Philadelphia for lumber along with stores such as flour, sugar, salt, tobacco—all in short supply on the increasingly beleaguered island. Their two square-riggers had been captured, the old salts had proved right, the *Gemini* and its sister ship, the *Gemini II,* were no speedsters. But they still owned two whaling sloops which recklessly plied from the Falklands to the South Seas for oil, and a brigantine which fetched merchandise from the capitals of Europe and foreign free ports such as Surinam, St. Eustatius, St. Pierre. Incredible as it seemed in a country fighting for its life, imported luxuries even at war-inflated prices were much in demand. Not, however, by the Nantucketers—they were feeling the pinch, for of all the colonists, they were in the most peculiar and most vulnerable position. Being two-thirds Quaker and thus principled against all violence, the town fathers had decreed a policy of strict neutrality. Without it they were doomed. With it they were mistrusted by both sides.

Since the natives were dependent upon the mainland for the very necessaries of life, even firewood, Kezia had purchased in Bedford two shaving mills—open schooners built of shallow draft for fast pickup and delivery along the Atlantic seaboard. Phineas usually captained these voyages, known as "Apple-tree runs," often without papers, for if stopped by British vessels their Falmouth (Massachusetts) permits made prize of them, and if their documents bore the crown's seal they were fair game for the Continentals.

With few exceptions, the Quakers were Tory in sympathy. They considered themselves Englishmen and the war a civil one. In their view those who fought the king were not patriots but traitors. The king's navy protected their ships; they were prospering in spite of taxes; they preferred the status quo, fearing to lose by change. They were of course the prosperous stable element of the populace who stood to lose by change. The poor on the other hand who could only gain by it and the hotheaded young who spoiled for heroics were inclined to be Whiggish. They and the handful of Congregationalists, particularly the ne'er-do-wells, resented the town edict forbidding the use of firearms. They stood on the beaches with the rest, watching the British and American ships fire upon each other outside their bar not to protect the island but to decide which of them should plunder it.

At sea the Nantucket vessels were defenseless against the men-of-war of both navies. It took a master navigator like Phineas Fanning to make it back home. Little Kezia studded her journal with such entries as, "P.F. arrived today with a load of provender after going through everything but death." Once he managed to outrun his pursuers by hogging the shaving mill. He took a saw to the main rail, the bulwarks, the plank-sheer, and made incisions on each side of the ship. Who but an islander born and bred would know that a weakened ship sailed faster than a sound one?

This was early in the rebellion that King George had been advised would be quickly put down. As it dragged on year after year and the Nantucketers continued to be harassed, as they lost men and property, suffered hunger and privation, division among themselves deepened. Miriam Pinkham's son had been overhauled by the British in a neutral vessel and he languished in some wretched prison ship. Kezia's sister Abbie Coffin's son was similarly taken and was impressed into the British navy. Who could blame such put-upon parents for turning against Empire? They became passionate Whigs, and whereas they had formerly nipped at Kezia they now clawed. "It has got so," Kezia sighed to Samuel, "one doesn't know from one day to the next who's friend and who's foe."

On a March night that presaged rain, the family, including Kezia's three sisters and their husbands, the Tristram Starbucks and the Richard Pinkhams, trooped to Kezia's mother's house to supper. Somewhat surprisingly, Phineas Fanning was also invited. Up to now the old lady had ignored the courtship. After two years of residence, she still referred to Phineas as 'the lodger.'

Kezia's nerves were frayed because she had just had a row with John, he having been quietly firm, she strident and unavailing. The end of the betrothal period was but two months hence, and so Kezia was moved to discuss with John her plans for the wedding. He agreed to the family dinner and the afternoon ceremony at the Reverend Shaw's, but he flatly refused to permit a dance for the young people in the house.

"Why? King David liked dancing very well and our Lord smiled on the feast of Cana."

"The Friends take exception to dancing."

"Phineas is not a Friend. Little Kezia will take his faith."

"But *I* am a Friend. Kindly suffer me to be master in my house. Or would thee like the loan of my breeches?"

"I wouldn't be caught dead in them."

"Or mayhap the loan of God's robes?"

"God knows they ill become *thee!*"

That sort of thing. Stupid bickering, born of controlled resentment, devoid of meaning, accomplishing nothing. So it was small wonder the oysters rankled in her gullet. After the meal, when they all moved near the fire for Abigail's reading of the Scriptures, Kezia could only hope her wambling stomach was less audible to others than to herself.

Abigail was over seventy. She projected an air of authority that gave no quarter to age—her daughters still thought of her as taller than they. Her hair was spun silver, her teeth perfect, her skin fair, her dress immaculate. She was a practiced reader and she gave a fiery rendition of Ezra rending his garments and pulling his hair from his beard until Shecaniah proposed putting away their foreign wives and children.

A loose shutter banged against the house. Abigail lowered her spectacles and said in her everyday voice, "The Lord has seen fit to send us a nor'wester." All eyes rolled to the windows and perceived that the rain was real as well as storied. "I had intended a more extensive reading but there's no sense in everybody getting soaked. I'll conclude with this portion from the Book of Nehemiah." She flipped forward a few pages, and her voice gained power as she read. "In those days I saw the Jews who had married women of Ashdod, Ammon and Moab. And half of their children spoke the language of Ashdod, and they could not speak the language of Judah." She looked up at John Coffin, reciting, "And I made them take oath in the name of God, saying 'Ye shall not give your daughters to their sons!' "

John blinked. And coughed. And hung his head.

Abigail switched her octagonal gaze to Kezia, who thereupon fell prey to a hot flash that soaked her hair under her cap and caused her garments to steam.

"I have no pleasure in thee," said the stern mother-voice. "I will accept no offering from thy hand. Thee will not listen so I will curse thy blessing . . . I will rebuke thy offspring and spread dung upon thy faces, the dung of thy offerings, and I will put thee out of my presence!"

The banging of the shutter went unheard as Phineas Fanning came under fire.

"The Lord will be a swift witness against adulterers!"

Phineas turned green. His hair seemed to tarnish, and his full lips were lavender and wrinkled.

"Abomination has been committed on our land," quoted Abigail, her finger waving at Phineas. "But behold, the day comes burning like an oven, when all the evildoers will be stubble. For those who fear and serve God, the sun of righteousness shall rise with healing in its wings. But the wicked will be ashes, and to them will be left neither root nor branch!"

Abigail snapped the book shut. A fine powder went up from the old pages. No one stirred. Rain catstepped the roof, tapped the panes. Abigail moved to the fireplace, took up a poker, and stabbed the logs, releasing a shower of sparks. The wind whistled down the chimney and breathed black. Live coals blew onto the hearth. Abigail replaced the poker and took out after the escaped coals with a reed broom. With her back to her family, she said, "Thee'd best shove off. Weather's getting heavy."

The men shuffled into the entry, showing slices of eye, handing out wraps. They said nothing, sensing that in some way this was a sorority fight. Abbie and Miriam rode the waves like proud ships, their necks long, their busts high, their eyes glittering. Kezia's face was carved jade. Mary and Judith looked unhappy. Debbie, alas for Debbie. When one reached that size one looked nothing but fat, just as octogenarians look nothing but old. But not to John. His eyes met his twin's and he found a sympathetic strength therein to which beauty holds no candle. Little Kezia's face was blotched and shiny, her hand pulling her affianced who lumbered after her as if his eyes had been put out. Primly, as if nothing untoward had taken place, as if no offense had been given or taken, Little Kezia thanked her grandmother for the supper, gave her the usual departure peck on the cheek, and accepted the mantle that Phineas pushed onto her shoulders. The others took decorous leave, shrouding themselves in outdoor garments. Someone opened the door and a wet wind came in like a hungry animal.

Kezia's cloak was the last on the rack. "Thee go along," she said to John who reached for it. "I'd have a word with my mother."

"It's going to storm, thee'll catch thy death," John protested, looking frightened. "See her on the morrow."

"I'm not made of sugar. I shan't melt. I'll not be long. Go."

There were looks, but when Kezia said, "Go," in that tone, no one gainsaid her.

Kezia closed the door on the last of the supper guests and returned to the keeping room. Her mother awaited her at the fireplace. They faced each other down, priestess and heretic.

"I'd have thee know, Mother, that I shall not soon forgive thee. I have long known thee hated me but I deem it cruel to have shamed Little Kezia and her young man. Calling them adulterers! Was it for this thee asked them to sup? Did thee fatten them up for the kill?"

"Kezia, thy rhetoric has ever been more eloquent than mine. I am a simple woman and I speak plain. There has never been out-marriage in our family. Nor on the Coffin side as I know's of. Thy husband is as upset over it as I. This unholy alliance is all thy doing. Thee brought him here. Thee encouraged the suit. Little Kezia is thy pawn as everybody knows. 'Tis too late to save thee, but I pray God 'tis not too late to save her. It is my duty to make her see the Light."

Their voices rose with their tempers.

"Thee and thy Light killed Aunt Hannah's chance for happiness."

"There be no happiness in hell, thou wanton! And now is thy issue cast out of heaven—"

"Enough! Revile me all thee will, but let not thy evil tongue besmirch my daughter!"

"If truth be evil, then is my tongue! For I say thy daughter has lain with her Gentile in the dark bowels of the earth."

A bolt of black lightning zigzagged through Kezia's body. Blurred her vision. Her open hand raised and came down. Not the face, she could not touch the bare skin, and not with force, she would not hurt. Her falling hand struck the covered shoulder. Three times she smote her mother, crying, "Evil! Evil! Evil!"

Abigail did not wince. Her lips thinned. She made a slow half-turn, proffering the other side.

Kezia clapped her uncrippled hand to her mouth and ran out the door.

Her mind took her first to the beach and then to the hills, but her feet took her home. The night ran with her like a lover, wept with her, stumbled with her, and when she fell flat on her face, lay down with her. Its running earth filled her wet mouth like a lover's tongue, licked her face and her hair, smeared her clothing, dug into the quicks of her nails. She swallowed mud, fed it to herself as an infant feeds on its own excrement, and sobbed aloud. "Mother, Mother, Mother."

Signs of the migraine brought her to her senses. She went into her house and cleaned herself and woke Little Kezia and took the girl into her bed.

"Little Kezia, be not afraid of me. No matter what thee has done or shall do, thee may count upon my love. Now, answer me true. Grandmother Pinkham said thee and Phineas have lain together out of door. Is this so?"

"Aye, Mama. Mind the day we went to the Polpis tavern with Lucy and Polly and Seth and the others? The wind came up strong while we supped and the tide was high, so we set back early for town. Phineas and I took the beach road home and there came a tremendous storm. The snow fell so thick, we thought it unsafe to go on. We decided to bed down— the mare, too—and wait for a break in the weather. We thought to huddle under a bank of sand. But up close we saw the bank was a reed-covered mouth, a cave, right below Father's land on Quaise Neck. We lay in the shelter where some Indian had stored hides and we covered with the deerskin from the calash. Oh, what a snug haven! But Mama, we did no wrong, we did but bundle. And at first light, when the storm abated, rode home."

"Why did thee not tell me?"

"Well, we were home betimes, no one was about. And then later, mind, there were shipwrecks among the vessels at the wharves? We—I had no idea we were seen."

There was no doubting Little Kezia's innocence, she was incapable of dissimulation. Indeed, Kezia had often remonstrated with her for wearing her heart on her sleeve. "What for does thee think God gave thee a rib cage?" Besides, was there not a pleased note in the maid's voice? Why, of course—she was proud to be one of Nantucket's secrets at last. Reputation did not matter, getting old enough to have one did.

They talked for two hours. Little Kezia was indignant at her grandmother's treatment of Phineas. John, too, she said, had found the readings regrettable. "Father was most comforting and supportive. He said we might publish intentions. This very day."

For it was day. The light of morning rain ran silver down the windowpanes.

"Today?" echoed Kezia. It was too soon. She was not ready. Too tired. Too upset. Getting sick. "Daughter, fetch me the carafe. I believe Hagar left some toddy in it. There is a thing I must tell thee."

She took several burning gulps. She drank till the rum spread through her chest, tingled between her loins, buzzed in her toes. The words came so simply she wondered she had stewed so long over it. "Certain of the Folger women, not all, grow an uncommon thick maidenhead. I myself did, and not having been forewarned in any way, my wedding night was a botch. In fact, I proved impenetrable. It was not until years later that Zaccheus Macy with one stroke of the knife—I never felt it, I vow, not so much as a pinprick—broke my hymen. That's why I did not have thee until late in life. Now the time's come to have thee examined to see if thee needs such a cut. Zaccheus Macy is trustworthy in every way. He'll apprize thy intended of the operation so there can be no doubt of thy purity."

"There's no need, Mama."

"No *what?*"

"My maidenhead's broke."

Four long brown braids wobbled in the light of two candleflames. Kezia thought, I am a pariah, the beldam spoke truth.

"When?" she asked carefully lest the pain on the left side of her head widen to include the whole and so increase the nausea. "When did he—did thee—?"

"This night. After Father gave us his blessing."

Strangely though the left side of her head held
the pain, the right side of her body was getting numb.
Ergo, it could not be a stroke. And—oh, God—for the
first time in half a year she felt pincer-contractions of
her uterus. Blast, she'd thought she was done with it.
She blinked her eyes and raised her eyebrows high as
they'd go, but there were still two Little Kezias.

"We must get thee wed at once. There must be
no delay."

"Do not fear, Mama. We took precaution."

"Listen to me, my poor goose, withdrawal's no
safe precaution."

"No, a surer way. Father once told Phineas of it.
Oh, not apurpose. 'Twas long before Father thought of
me as anywheres near old enough for Phineas. Two
years agone or more, a night when they spoke man to
man. 'Tis accomplished by means of a silk handkerchief." Little Kezia smiled dreamily at that innocent
maid who asked Phineas what he would like for his
birthday—some little gift—and he said a silk handkerchief. He was having a joke of her, but she didn't
know it. She bought him five.

"I've had too much to drink, child. I'm seeing
double. Quick, the bowl!"

Little Kezia ran for the washing basin. "Oh, Mama, have I—has this sickened thee?"

Emptied of Abigail's supper and the undigested
earth, Kezia spoke around the wet cloth with which
her daughter was sponging her face. "Nay, do not
blame thyself. I have had it before."

"But, Mama, it's black! Shall I not run for the
doctor?"

"Nay, 'tis part of it—the megrims. It passes. Fetch
Hagar. She knows what to do for me." She put out a
limp hand which was snatched and kissed.

"Mama, is thee too unwell to answer a question?"

Kezia almost smiled—the urgency of the young—
one could be dying. "Nay, ask it."

"Dada says Phineas must stay at Aunt Debbie's
till the wedding. He says once intentions are declared

the Book of Discipline says we may not dwell under
the same roof until—"

"Rubbish. Thee'll not pass Meeting in any case.
Outmarriage. I'll take the responsibility. Back to bed
now. Bless thee both. Fetch Hagar."

On April 5, 1777, at four of the afternoon, Little
Kezia Coffin and Phineas Fanning were married by
Reverend Bazaleel Shaw at his house. The Tuppers and
the Husseys were witnesses, fulfilling the tradition that
two 'judicious, grave and weighty men' stand beside the
groom and 'two such women' by the bride. Kezia, having been disowned by the Friends (over the spinet),
did not qualify, and John, as a Quaker, was not permitted to be present at a ceremony conducted by a
'hireling minister.' He stepped into the hall until called
back into the keeping room to partake of the votive
champagne and the wedding cake that Hagar had
baked and carried over under a white napkin and
stayed to serve.

The bride wore green damask and held a bouquet
of orange blossoms from the island of Catherine in
Brazil. Kezia wore garnet satin, but she looked sallow
and drawn. Following the migraine, she had contracted
and still had a bad cold. The orange blossoms made
her sneeze so they were left to dry out at the Shaws'
before being stored away in the keep chest.

At the front door, Mrs. Tupper took off her slip-
per and threw it after the bride, calling, "That you
may stroke down your man's head if he be unruly!"

Little Kezia threw it back. "I shan't need it and
thee does!" Thus the newly wed couple, arrived so
solemn, departed laughing—a good omen for increase.

There was a wedding supper at the Coffin home
for a hundred people, young and old. Not the memo-
rable one the mother of the bride had dreamed of, but
with the bite of war hard upon them that would
have been graceless, even if possible. As it was, there
were some who considered it to be an 'overallowance.'
Grandmother Pinkham stayed away, but all through
the town the young people breathed a sigh of relief.

Twenty

On a foggy morning in 1779, Kezia was writing letters in her chamber. Looking up from her bureau, she saw several vessels westward in the Sound.

She ran downstairs and out the front door, but she could not make out the ships' flags, and there was no crowd on the wharves. She was about to go back to her letter-writing when a 'dust-devil' appeared at her feet. She was superstitious now about eddies and whirlwinds, believing them to be embodiments of Shana. She took a spyglass up to the roofwalk, and there made out seven vessels under British colors. As she watched, five of the vessels anchored at Brant Point while two smaller craft sailed across the bar. She grabbed her bonnet and mantle and poked her head into the shop. "Rachel, something's up. There's British ships coming in. Alert Shongo. The rest of the men are gone with the master to Quaise. Shongo must stand guard over the house."

"Refugees or Rebels?"

"Refugees."

"Lord help us."

The Refugees were of all the raiders the most merciless. They were American Tories who had been dispossessed by the Rebels, their property and chattel confiscated or burned, their families scattered and in some cases injured or killed. Now, with letters of marque from the Crown, they wreaked their vengeful fury not only upon Whigs but upon 'soft' Tories, those who were still leading reasonably normal lives and getting along with their Whig neighbors. Crazed with outrage, the Rufugees burned and pillaged, and they did not scruple against pointblank shooting either.

"Best lock the store and run home, Rachel," advised Kezia.

Nay, my man's there, now he's out of work. I'll bide here. Those Sons of Baleal shall not have their way in this shop, not without they feel the butt of my broom."

"Well, then, I'm grateful. There's the sacks of salt just come in. Oh, and the bags of pieces of eight! Take them to bed, my bed. Get into one of my nightdresses, and sit with them under the covers. I'm off to see the lay of the land. If soldiers should come before I return, Hagar must say thee's sick. The louts'll not rout a sick woman from her bed."

"They'll have nothing from here if I have to pepper them with shot. I'll take the fowling piece to bed with me too."

"Good girl," laughed Kezia, and ran off, not noticing the flush that flooded the plain woman's face, smoothing out the premature wrinkles.

War had slowed but not stopped the pulse of Sherburne. The three wharves bustled, the shoreline stank of whale oil and drying cod and boiling tar. From the shops on the waterfront floated the volatile rhythms of hammers, looms, creaking machinery. The tin horns of the fishmongers criss-crossed the oysterman's hand-cupped call. "Oys, fresh oys, caught this morn, soon be gone, buy me oys, fine oys!" Counterpointing both were the chanteys of the crews as they hauled sheet and scraped bottoms, and a bass section was furnished by the rumble of hoofbeats on the planking and barrels drum-rolling down wooden ramps. Today a barrel had broken open and the smell of coffee wiped out the stink of blubber. Against the walls of ordinaries lounged sailors and no-good Indians and two drunks, their jibing and laughter ribboning out over the gray water. Even as Kezia ran, bonnet-strings aflap, the concert stilled, and from the shops poured leather-aproned craftsmen, journeymen in homespun blouses, waistcoated clerks. They fanned out in slowspreading fingers on the docks.

Will Rotch and Samuel Starbuck and several other men came hurrying out of the Rotch Market which had become the coffeehouse of the town where political issues were disputed and commercial news exchanged.

"Refugees," Kezia told them grimly.

Samuel took her elbow, seemingly to help her over the cobbles, actually to reassure and be reassured by the hold of her.

The two vessels made fast off North Wharf. Soldiers spilled over the sides and formed a line against the natives, the tips of their bayonets glinting in the light of the receding sky. Unwittingly some of the laborers stepped backward as from a wave that might wet their feet, but their eyes were as flinty as the steel of the weaponry. Then down leaped a Macaroni in gold-braided scarlet coat and a mariner's cuffs, lace at his throat, bows on his breeches, a cocked tricorn atop his long white curls. The drab islanders waited, blinking.

"I am Captain Leonard," bawled the dandy in a jarringly high voice. "We are come to ascertain the disposition of the people of this island. The British navy would know how you stand. Whether for king or for country."

"If that's all ye come for," someone yelled, "wherefore the guns?"

The fair face mottled. "I'll not deal with rabble nor put up with rousing. I am come from Newport under orders. If there is one among you who can provide us with local information, let him step forward."

Tiny gurgles of water sounded around the pilings. A hatch of sand flies flew up. The captain waved at them around his face. "We would molest no loyal citizens," he piped. "We come for Rebel goods. But if the Loyalists among you refuse to tell us who's who, you'll all suffer alike."

Will Rotch moved up front of the crowd.

"I am William Rotch," he said quietly, without touching his hat. "Quaker, merchant, resident of Sherburne. We are all kin and neighbors here. There be no informers—"

They could have no better spokesman. Will Rotch projected a candor and dignity before which hotheads fell back and partisans became men without a cause. It was not the first or last time Kezia was glad he was one her side. Her peripheral vision caught the creeping line of women and children on the beach some thee hundred feet away.

"—nor is there anything to inform. All here are pledged to neutrality. In principle we are against all violence, possessed of no arms, determined to harm no fellow man. We ask only to be allowed to go about our business in peace."

"To ask for peace in time of war is to shirk duty, Mr. Rotch. I too would have preferred to go about my business. The Rebels did not permit me, I was brutally robbed by those greedy Jonathans, as were many of us who are pledged to give them no quarter. My men are prepared to use these muskets. We come for Rebel goods and we intend to have them. There must be no assemblies. No interference. If you would save your townsmen grief, advise them to disperse, sir. Keep inside your doors. The faster we can work, the sooner we'll be gone."

Will Rotch turned about then and walked unhurriedly through the parting crowd. Samuel Starbuck fell in behind him and Kezia followed. They did not look back till they reached the Town Pump. The women and children had followed them and close behind were the men. The swivel guns mounted on the two ships were nosed at the town. Refugee guards were posted at intervals on the beach and all three wharves while soldiers looted the stores, throwing the merchandise out on the docks. As Will Rotch and Samuel and Kezia turned back to look, so did the rest of the people. What they saw evoked a low but rising growl.

Will Rotch, cupping his hands, addressed them.

"Friends, neighbors, let us keep our wits. With cannon and gunnery trained against us, what can we do to stop them? I say better loss of property than of life and limb." He had their faces then and he spoke a shade more softly. Voices carry when the bay is quiet. "If any of thee has a plan—one that does not involve our use of arms—thee'll find me willing to listen and to act. Meanwhile, let us continue peaceably onward to our homes."

The morning fog evaporated. The sky cleared to a baby blue and clusters of clouds rode it, so fat and fleecy they could have been plucked and floated in a bowl. The streets of Sherburne drowsed in the sunshine. Now and then a fragment of "Yankee Doodle" whistled upon the air, and once a musket went off, but no Nantucketer—English, Negro, or Indian—was to be seen. Mysteriously, like the dance of the honeybees, the events of the day were communicated from one dwelling to another. By sunset there was not a householder who did not know what had been taken. Fifty thousand dollars' worth in all. Out of Thomas Jenkins' warehouse alone, 260 barrels of sperm oil, 1800 lbs. of whalebone, 2300 wt. of iron, 1200 lbs. of coffee, 20,000 wt. of tobacco, and miscellaneous articles. Jenkins himself was not on the island at the time, but what could he have done if he were? Christopher Starbuck and Timothy Folger were on it and from their shop had been taken flour and tea and wool cloth estimated at eight hundred dollars. Shubael Coffin journeyed from his shop to his Quaise home with a springcart full of goods, but he couldn't take everything, and his shop was robbed of sundials, ax-helves, butter, quarter-glasses, woolen blankets, and candles. Kezia's brothers-in-law, Caleb Macy and William Starbuck, were cleaned out of their stock of shoes.

Over fences, through grapevines, from window to window, roof walk to roof hatch, they tried to calm or rile each other.

"Will Rotch had the right of it. 'Tis only money, not lives."

"Rotch—easy for him to talk. That rich, he don't know what's gone or what's got. Rest of us'll be on short allowance for quite a spell."

"Lay it to the Friends. 'Tis they who have rendered us defenseless. ¥ we'd declared allegiance, there'd be American vessels stationed here to protect us from marauders."

"Pretty hard to protect an island. The Americans don't have enough navy to protect the coast. Neither ships nor guns."

"Then we ought to have pledged to the Crown."

"Then we'd be a naval base—under constant fire."

"Well, this way, we're sitting ducks. Not even a breastworks alongshore to scare them off."

At three o'clock they had to laugh. The soldiers had moved up into the streets, guarding the entire marketplace. That bad boy, Peter Jennings, holding a live scrub bush up in front of himself, had crept close and thrown a rotten egg! Missed the fellow's eye but caught his Adam's apple. Stank to high heaven. Cursed worse'n a Barbados sailor. And did thee hear about that behemoth, Deborah Chase? She needed water, and though her Dada said her nay, she was bound and determined to fetch some from the Town Pump. Went out, bucket in each hand, and when a guard tried to force her back, she flung the bucket square in his face, knocking him senseless. Filled both pails. Homeward bound, she stepped over the prostrate man without spilling a drop. Wouldn't think she'd have any suitors, a girl that size. Little men wanted her bad, like climbing a mountain.

By four o'clock every native islander knew that Will Rotch, Samuel Starbuck, and Timothy Folger had treated with the Refugee guard at North Wharf and had been allowed to pass. The three men had rowed out to one of the vessels outside the bar. They were aboard till set of sun, and when they came back they were accompanied by Captain Leonard and some of his officers who then called upon Kezia.

To the Whigs, these transpirings looked suspicious if not damning. They've ratted, they concluded, the Tories scratch each other's backs. But the majority of the townsfolk believe in the honor of their foremost merchants. They believed that all four had stood firm in their refusal to name names.

Next morning Captain Leonard and the officers were seen entering Kezia's house. "That ties it," said the Whigs, "they're mates for certain sure." Said the others, "Nay, she's but laboring with them." Peepers observed the raiders breakfasting at Kezia's table. Eavesdroppers heard Kezia tell them she had had word in the night that a punitive expedition was en route from Boston. News of their attack had got to Falmouth, she claimed, and thence to the American Militia.

True or false, the rumor worked. The breakfast terminated at once. By nine A.M. the two vessels loaded with spoils filled away. A third vessel, taken in prize to haul more of the stacked loot, languished on an ebb tide in the unusually pacific bay. The prize was a brig, half-owned by Tom Jenkins, the same unfortunate absentee whose shop had been so thoroughly sacked. The coowners plumped hard for retaking their ship. Since she was manned by only five Refugees, they felt they could overpower the thieving crew by sheer numbers without a gun fired. Several young hotheads cheered the idea. "We're with ye! Let's swarm 'em, lads!"

Will Rotch held up his hand. "Wait, good neighbors! Wait! They have now got what they would take at this time. If we go after them, we'll have the seven men-of-war come back upon us. Let them go and I am willing to contribute to defray the loss of the stolen vessel *and* the stolen goods." He turned to those who were standing nearby in a huddle: Kezia, Samuel Starbuck, Timothy Folger, and Dr. Tupper. "Shall thee share this cost with me, my friends?"

The four heads nodded assent. It was not entirely altruistic, plunder of their shops would cost them a great deal more. Benjamin Tupper who owned half of his son-in-law's grog shop made more from its custom than from his doctoring.

At the chorus of boos, Kezia jumped up on a cask top. "What'll thee have—the loss of a brig or the loss of our town?" She pointed to a knot of young men. "Thee who'd be heroes—do thee mind what they did to the Vineyard?"

That proved to be the magic word. "The Vineyard, aye, the Vineyard," murmured the crowd. There a company of Refugees had razed the whole village to the ground. The protests, the shaking fists, suddenly turned against the spoiling young and the owners of the brig, who went off in a huff. The mob remained to watch the afternoon tide carry the brigantine serenely across the bar. They waited, squinting into the hazy fireball, till the other seven vessels up-anchored and stood out to sea.

As a result of this incident, Kezia along with Samuel Starbuck, Will Rotch, Benjamin Tupper, and Timothy Folger were duly called to stand trial before the General Court in Boston for the crime of high treason. The impeachment was brought by Thomas Jenkins, who formally accused them of aiding and abetting the enemy, encouraging depredations on Whig property, and publicly dissuading certain 'well-disposed inhabitants' from rescuing his stolen brig and the loot it carried. The punishment if found guilty was death.

For one reason and another, the trial was put off until late March 1780. On the twenty-second day of that month, the defendants, twelve witnesses, and the attorney Phineas Fanning arrived in Boston. They were wrought to a fine pitch, fearful of injustice at the hands of a Whig court. There was a week's delay in gathering a committee to judge their case. Phineas spent the time boning up in the Harvard Law Library in Cambridge, treason being far out of his line. Evenings, the defendants gathered at Captain Partridge's where Kezia and Phineas were staying. There they burned midnight oil, rehearsing their testimonies and their anxieties, while the witnesses went out on the town at their expense.

The night before the trial Dr. Tupper insisted upon standing them all to supper at the Sign of the Lamb. He expansively included Kezia's host and hostess, which brought the number of tabs to a very sporting twenty. The doctor's breezy confidence and openhandedness heartened everyone but Kezia. Tupper's disdain of the Rebels was legend, he'd been in and out of prison several times since the war, but what passed for courage struck her as suspiciously Dutch.

Doctors are generally conservative men, as was he. Or had been. She wondered that the others did not seem to notice the change in him. His second wife had died two-three years ago, and for a while he was inconsolable. Then his personality seemed to undergo alteration. Moreover he did not look well. He had ever been of a cinereous complexion; now he was moist and pink and the pupils of his eyes were constricted to pinpoints. This last was the clincher. It took one to know one.

"Mark me, Friends," said Tupper, wafting a lordly arm, "this whole affair will turn out a blank. Come, Tim, drink up. Have some more of this flip—great nightcap—puts lead in your pencil."

The flip was a mixture of rum, molasses, and beer, and was served hot. A sailor in Greenland waters might be able to put two leatherjacks of it away and stay on his feet, but Timothy Folger, no drinker, had just recovered from a bout of influenza and he was sitting near a roaring fire. As a result he had a bad night and could keep down only a meager breakfast. The good doctor prescribed several slugs of brandy to 'bring him up.'

Unfortunately, Timothy Folger was the first man called to the bar.

There was the usual sticky business of swearing on the Bible.

"Ronor," Timothy Folger said, swaying on his feet, "I be a Quaker and am forbid to take oaths. But my yea is my yea and my nay is my yea—that is, my yea is nay—"

The chairman rapped the titter down. "Is it not likewise forbidden to Quakers to partake immoderately of intoxicating liquors?"

There was laughter among the committee members which Timothy watched foolishly and then joined. As it subsided, he broke wind—a loud bubbling poop —and the committee har-hared. Will Rotch yanked Folger back to the bench by his coattails. The committee men kept rolling their eyes to the only woman present. Kezia hot-flashed from head to toe. And seethed. At Jenkins. At Timothy. At the committee. At men. Did they think farting was exclusive to their sex? She had a good mind to let one herself; gassy as she was, she could certainly improve upon Timothy's. That whey-faced clod-pate, he could cost them their lives. She cast a nervous glance over her shoulder at Dr. Tupper. His palms lay upturned on widely parted knees. His face was waxy and bland as a grapefruit. Her heart plunged. One rumpot and one hophead, God help them.

She leaned over and whispered to Samuel, "Don't let Tupper talk either. He's barmy."

Will Rotch was asking to be permitted to testify while Timothy Folger 'recovered his sense.' Permission was granted and the Bible again presented.

"If it please the court," said Rotch, seemingly unruffled though Kezia happened to know that in his perturbation at the accusation of treason, he had asked God to take his life, "I would remind them respectfully that it has been an accepted legal practice in both America and England for those of our faith to be allowed to make simple affirmation as to the truth of their statements and this I most solemnly do. I would further ask the court's forgiveness of Mr. Folger's incontinence. It is unwarranted, I grant thee, but also unwonted. He is a man of uttermost sobriety. I can vouch for him, as can the several witnesses present, for we have known him throughout our lives."

Will answered well to the charges against him, but he was, to Kezia's mind, pompous, weasely, long-winded. She listened, foot awaggle, bored and critical as a ticket-buyer. Suddenly the thought occurred to her that she might be the next called, and she went blank. Totally blank. Clean as a wiped slate. She could scarcely remember what she was here for. To plead for her life. But why? Who were these strangers who could decree whether she should go on living or be put to death? She looked at their faces for the first time, scrutinized them, one by one, and saw in each member of the committee the seven things the Lord hates: haughty eyes, a lying tongue, hands that shed innocent blood, a heart that devises wicked plans, feet that make haste to run to evil, a false witness that breathes out lies, a man who sows discord among brothers. How could one plead before such brutes? She found it hard to believe they were Englishmen. That one there on the end, with the sagging underlip, flat nose, popped fish's eyes, low-thatched forehead. Would God let such a man as he judge *Will Rotch?* That one pulling the hairs out of his eyebrows, and the third from the right rubbing the sneeze-snot from his nose with his sleeve—could the angels be on the side of louts like those? Was it possible that after fifty-six years of striving and scheming and struggling one's life could be snuffed out by idiots with thumbs?

Frantically, to remind herself that there was a little of God in every man, she tried to marshall some of Phineas's beautiful sentences. "Treason is at best a murky legal problem, doubly so in time of Revolution, which is a civil war and thus divisive of countrymen, neighbor, kin." "The laws are only as just as the society that makes them and the men who enforce them." Never mind the beautiful sentences. Maybe it was more important to listen. Know what was said so she would not repeat, see what was well received so she would know what tack to take.

"—before I step down, sirs, I beg leave to ask one question of the plaintiff."

Will Rotch's sincerity had worked its accustomed magic. The chairman purred, "By all means, Mr. Rotch, by all means."

"Tom Jenkins, it is bruited about that I offered thee money if thee would withdraw thy complaint. Now I would have thee tell this court—have I ever done so?"

Kezia's heart plunged with sick force into her bowels. She it was who had tried to buy Jenkins off, though she had not even told Samuel. She had counted five hundred pounds well spent to buy herself peace of mind. The crafty scoundrel thereupon demanded a thousand and now she wished she had paid it.

Jenkins was a rangy, leathery man with a wolfish face. He was always angry, given to harangues so infused with ire they were almost incoherent. She sat coiled, trying to make sense out of his splenic barks.

"—they promised to restitute each of us and well they should for they stood solid behind Mister Rotch and Mistress Coffin who talked the crowd into standing by like a bunch of do-nothings. Besides the loss of the vessel, I was cleaned out of every last article in my store. The twenty-five hundred pounds paid jointly by Rotch, Starbuck, Tupper, and Mistress Coffin—Folger welshed—don't defray my loss since half the moneys went to those that had moieties of the said brig."

Through the gibber she perceived that he was not going to reveal the bribe. Was it not too late then to meet his price? She'd talk it over this night with Samuel and Phineas. Will needn't know. Samuel might even be willing to put up the other five. No, she must not tell Samuel nor even Phineas. She must go it alone. It was the only sure way. And it was her way.

The voices droned on. Witnesses were called up and stepped down. Timothy slept. Tupper stared beatifically into space. Kezia who longed to lean against Samuel's dear body moved an inch farther away from him on the bench. She suddenly realized she was famished. It had been a long day. She whispered to Samuel who pulled out the silver turnip-shaped watch she had bought him in London. Five o'clock. Another day's grace before she had to testify. She would have roast beef and ale. Too bad the Whigs had taken over The Bunch of Grapes—it was by far the best tavern in the town.

She was stark naked when a noise on the window drew her head. She saw in its frame the blur of a hatted canine face. She pulled the patch coverlet quickly about her Indian fashion, as Jenkins raised the sash and threw a long booted leg over the sill. Her room was at the back of the house, so low-ceilinged under the slanted roof that Jenkins could only just stand up. When she saw the elongated fangs, she realized she had never before seen him smile.

"Sorry to startle you, Mistress Coffin."

"See here, Jenkins! How dare thee—"

"Soft, soft, woman. You wouldn't rouse your landlord, would ye now? The look of things is all against you."

"Thomas Jenkins, state thy business and get thee hence." Shivering in the wind that blew cold and raw off the harbor, she clutched the quilt tight about her.

"Have no fear, mistress. I be bent on business not pleasure. I would split the difference in the sums of money mentioned between us previously."

"Seven-fifty?"

"Make it seven seventy-five."

The chiseler! "What? No shillings, no pence?"

"None of your lip now. Take it or leave it."

She hesitated. "Thee'd withdraw the charges in their entirety?"

"On the morrow. First off."

Oh, not to have to testify! The smile was to herself but his eyes changed. He lunged toward her. Her gut lurched.

Behind him, the curtains blew apart and another boot appeared. A hand showed—*Samuel?* And then the familiar beefy torso and the blessed hatless head. He leaped once, grabbed Jenkins around the throat with one arm, and punched his lower back with the other. Jenkins grunted, and his head reared as Samuel's hold tightened. The snared man grunted again and again as Samuel shoved his fist hard into the kidney.

"Enough!" Kezia whispered hoarsely. "He must be able to walk from here. Let him be while yet he stands!"

"Scum! Vermin!" hissed Samuel softly through clenched teeth, and he punched him twice more. But he had heard Kezia and he heeded her. He jackknifed the thin body, knocking Jenkins's nose hard against his bony knees, and threw him out of the window. "Decamp, buss-beggar!" Samuel growled, leaning out the window. "And hand up me hat, or I'll be down to get it."

The beaver hat sailed over Samuel's bent body and plopped on the rag rug. Outside, there was a small howl of pain and then a hobbled run of heels on the cobblestones. Samuel closed the window. He picked up his hat and rubbed the fur the right way—they were, after all, not young nor new lovers, and a good hat was a good hat. He blew out the candle. She recalled his jealous nature, and feeling guilty in spite of her innocence, she said, "He was after a bribe."

"Cold as a witch's tits in here. I wouldn't live on Boston Harbor for money." He tucked her in bed, quickly peeled his clothes and slid in beside her. She alternately clung to and repulsed him.

"Does thee not want me?"

"The Partridges—"

"A pox on the Partridges."

"And Phineas across the corridor."

"Fie on Phineas."

She giggled.

"Ssh! Damme, thee's a very eel. Be good, love, let me love thee quiet or we'll wake the whole house."

"Thee and Jenkins, a fine pair of blackmailers." And then, relaxing, "Oh, my love, my love, I thought 'twas over between us."

"Never. Not in this life."

"We may soon be in the next."

"Is it jokes thee would make or love? Can't do both and I'm not in a humor for laughing."

In a very few moments neither was she. She put her arms around his neck and swung into his lap. His cock lay hard between her buttocks. She opened her legs to let his hand in and gave herself up to physical sensation. He entered her sooner than she'd have him, she was not fully lubricated, and it was quickly over. Their bodies were not the powerful machines they had been, and they were out of practice.

He would have risen but she held him fast. "Do not leave me. I am afraid."

"No one heard us."

"Of dying, silly."

"Oh, that. I too."

They clung to each other, nestling, taking comfort from their warm touching skins. He said, " 'Tis heartening to know Jenkins was willing to sell out. Mayhap he knows something we don't."

"The witnesses have not borne him out. Nevertheless, I should have bought him off had thee not come. How'd thee know to?"

"I saw him leave a tavern in the town. I followed. I was going to thrash him, the rat. I never dreamed he was on his way here."

"Samuel, shall they vote against us?"

"Honey, thy guess is as good as mine. Anyway, we'll have our answer all too soon. Thee's the last. They'll call thee on the morrow. Look, love, thee must be beautiful as well as eloquent. Wear thy Sunday best, use every trick. And do not give in to dander. No matter how vexed. Understand?"

"I shan't, but oh it's galling to be at the mercy of louts."

"A colonel, senators, congressmen—hardly louts, my dear. And I for one believe they seek to be fair."

"Would I did! It has been my experience that the bandaged eyes of justice ever have peepholes and its scales, more often than not, a make-weight candle."

"Then if thee can't believe in thy fellowmen, believe in the Lord. There's a bit of the Lord in each of
them. Center down on that, never mind how smart they
are or how they part their hair."

"Unless I think them stupid or ugly, I'll take fright
of them. My tongue will cleave to my jaws."

"Stuff and nonsense. Thee's stronger than that.
Thee but scares thyself, ever thy own worst enemy.
Look here, lass, thee's sharp as a tack and thee's passing fair. Make the most of both, I caution thee. They'll
be soft with a woman."

"Fair no more. Old," she said, thinking of her
dry hole.

He chuckled softly. "Well, they be not young."

She feinted at his chin. Her fist froze as, outside
their door, another opened. And still another. Then
through the closed window came the thin but clear
sound of piss.

"Phineas!"

"Too lazy to walk to the Necessary."

"I'd not either. 'Tis cold and damp. Trying to
rain."

"Thee's a broody hen. Let anyone dare say a word
against him and——"

She stopped his mouth with her hand.

Two doors closed softly, first one, then another.
No sound of latching. Her body eased. Well, they had
stolen one more time. She said in a wash of relief,
"Samuel, I do love thee."

He was silent for so long, she prodded him.
"Nothing to say to that?"

"I'm speechless. I have waited too long to hear it.
I mind the time—long ago, we were but children—
thee said thee loved John more than me or thee. It cut
me to ribbons."

It was difficult to remember the John she had been
in love with. Had she loved him? She knew she had
feared him. And somehow that fear had made him
irresistible, she didn't know why. She no longer enjoyed

fear. She said, "Life changes people. John is changed and so am I."

"But why did thee say it tonight for the first time? Because I am all that lies between thee and the hustings?"

She said, playing with his ear, "Love is love. Why sift it for lumps?"

"Aye, well, if it comes to that, I'm fond of thy lumps too," and kissed her breast.

They talked of the trial.

"I was so proud of thy testimony yesterday. Thee spoke as stirring as a politician. 'Thee ask if we be traitors and I ask traitor to whom?' " she quoted. " 'To God whose law says thou shalt not kill? To the king who provides letters of marque that his navy may prey upon us? To our countrymen who tell us we are too far away to be put under their protection? This case ought to be tried on Nantucket where every house has a view of the warships in the harbor. Both the king's men and the Continentals take our bread, our firewood, our oil, salt, wool, tools—all manner of necessaries which we have collected at great risk of property and life. The fighting men need stores, they say. But what of the raids on our houses? Of what use to warriors are our stocks, tables, chairs, old rugs, chests of drawers? That is looting, gentlemen, wanton and malicious. How do we explain to our young men as we stand by and watch this thievery, our hands at our sides? It is hard, uncommon hard, to be called cowards by our sons and traitors by our countrymen. To sit fairly in judgment upon us, it behooves thee, gentlemen, to translate thy minds and hearts to our situation. Pinch thyself to know how the pinched do feel.' "

He was so still, she then pinched him. "Rapt is thee? Vain of thy words, eh? Well, I can't say's I blame thee. Takes a good mind to make a speech like that."

"And a better one to repeat it after a single hearing."

"Oh, Samuel, what if it's all for naught? What if we go bright as new guineas to our death?"

"Trust on the Lord."

"What if they bring up the smuggling?"

"They won't. That's not at issue."

"But if they should?"

"Deny it. Up and down."

"And what shall the Lord say to perjury?"

"The Lord is all-knowing, all-merciful, all-understanding. Look here, we are not criminals. We have attempted to supply people's needs and wants. By our labors and our risks we have gained a livelihood. I should have preferred to be law-abiding at all times, but the trade laws have been despotic and impractical. I should have preferred to see these corrected by reason rather than by bloodshed, but American impatience has prevailed. The matter is out of our hands, we must protect ourselves as best we can. This is our duty to our families, to each other and to ourselves. We do no one a service by playing into the hands of the enemy."

The heart of white pine had spoken. What Doubting Thomas could argue with such rectitude? She sighed and burrowed deep into his side.

"Sleep here with me," she begged. "I'll wake thee before first light."

"What of the Partridges? Phineas?"

"A pox on them."

He laughed and hugged her. "I believe I've made a woman of thee at last, Kezia. Thee admits to needing a helpmeet."

As they filed into the courtroom at nine o'clock of a rainy morning, Phineas gave Kezia some last-minute tutoring.

"Mind, Marmy, the law clearly states that no person shall be convicted of treason unless on the testimony of two witnesses to the same overt act. Not one of the hostile witnesses was on the island at the time. What they can offer is hearsay, no more, and hearsay is not evidence."

"Oh, God help me, my mind is a sieve, Phineas. How I wish thee could speak for me."

"If needs be, I can. But since it has been agreed among you to speak for yourselves, you must give it a try. You'll feel better once you're called. Sometimes being nervous improves the performance."

She straightened her hat. "How do I look?"

"Ravishing. Exactly as you did the night you proposed to me."

"I *what?*"

"On behalf of your daughter."

He was trying to give her back to herself and she played the game as a sick person goes along with the nurse's 'we.' "Rascal," she said, slapping his hand.

"I shall never forget you that night. You wore yellow and pink, and those eyes—!"

His transparency was touching. "Bless thee, Phineas, my good, dear son."

He turned up her mitted hands and kissed the fingertips. The palms of the mitts had been cut out to secrete hand-printed cards cueing the speech he had written for her which she had committed to memory before a mirror.

Samuel came up, flushed, sweating, his eyes ringed with brown shadows. "Mind what's at stake. Don't spit in their eye, for God's sake."

"Oh, Samuel, stop, thee's making me nervier." But he was not. His nervousness was making her calm.

Timothy wrung her hand. Tupper kissed her cheek. Will Rotch put his hands on her shoulders. "Thee's not alone, Kezia. We are together in this every step of the way. And God is with us."

"I know. Fear not. My mind is quiet and well-ordered. Phineas's instruction is with me." And winked at Phineas.

She had a sudden urge to go to the Necessary, but it was too late. The chairman was in the doorway, spreading his cloaked arms, shaking his feathers like a wet eagle-hawk. He took his seat at the center of the table, struck the gavel three times.

Kezia took the oath in a water-clear voice. She felt as if she were attending a play she had seen several times. The actors were as familiar as kin and today she was one of them, not only audience but participant. They looked almost pleasant this morn, fresh-shaven, rested. All except Jenkins, for whose shining blue-green cheekbone and swollen red nose which had bled into and all but closed his eyes she felt a kind of once-removed pity, a pity not for the man but for the fragility of the human body.

"Mistress Coffin, how do you plead to the charge that you pointed out to the enemy for plunder the store of Thomas Jenkins?"

"I deny it unconditionally, your honor."

"Then it is your word against his. Do you have any means of proving your denial?"

It was the hot flash that undid her. It broke her concentration. Before she should go blank or tongue-tied, she replied in her haughtiest voice, "The burden of proof is upon the plaintiff, is it not? And he must have two witnesses who bear out his contention—is that not so? Of all the witnesses summoned, the only ones who have borne out his charges were off the island at the time of Captain Leonard's invasion. Therefore their testimony is hearsay and hearsay is inadmissible in a trial of treason." Ha! She glanced at Phineas for approval, but he was shaking his head in vigorous negative, and the chairman looked vexed. Her head swam. What wrong had she spoken?

"Mistress Coffin, you need not instruct the committee in the law," said the chairman sternly. "We should appreciate your restricting yourself to answering the questions put to you."

To her horror, she began to cry. She looked imploringly at Phineas who leaped to his feet. As through doors, like last night's pissing, she heard his pleas, watched his blurred lion's mane flow about his shoulders. There was proof . . . he could attest . . . she was but distressed, unaccustomed to courtroom procedure. If he could be sworn in . . . relevant testimony . . . her

behalf. He took the oath: Whole truth, nothing but. . . .
She clenched her back teeth, curled her toes, sniffed
fiercely. She would not touch her cheeks, let them dry,
damn her tears.

"Your honor, I was present in the Coffin House in
Sherburne on the night of April 5, 1779. Captain Leonard and some of his aides called upon my mother-in-law
for the stated purpose of enlisting her aid in the seizens
of Rebel—ah, Whig—ah, *Continental* properties."

"Where was Mister Coffin at this time?"

"He had retired, sir. He is not a well man. He
customarily retires betimes and this was about nine
o'clock."

"I see. And what did Mistress Coffin reply?"

"She refused to cooperate in any way. Her exact
words were uttered with asperity. She said, 'I do not
rat on my neighbors, Captain Leonard.' He then threatened that her shop would be raided in reprisal. At this
she terminated the conference."

"How did she do that?"

"She stood up and showed them the door. They
were in the house but a few minutes."

Stephen Hussey, a witness, corroborated Phineas's
estimate of the length of the visit. He and his wife had
seen the Refugee contingent enter the Coffin House at
nine and saw them come out some five or ten minutes
later.

The interlude had given Kezia time to compose
herself. She felt much better. The worst had happened
—she had blubbered. Short of wetting her drawers, she
thought wryly, she could fall no lower, therefore the
only way to go was up—and up, with the grace of God,
she would go.

The chairman offered her the privilege of sitting
down during her examination. It was clear she was going to be treated as a woman instead of an equal. She
decided to follow Samuel's advice and make the most
of it. She gave the chairman a melting look. "I appreciate thy gallant indulgence, General, but my heart is too
full. I fear my tongue would be incapable of utterance

whilst I sat." She took a lace handkerchief from her sleeve and dabbed her cheeks.

The chairman who was only a colonel rubbed the back of his neck. He hawked his throat and lowered the pitch of his voice. "Did you or did you not on the morning of April 6, 1779, entertain certain Refugee officers at breakfast?"

"I am not sure I entertained them, General. I did feed them."

There was a low rumble—not quite chuckling, more an amused murmur.

The chairman rapped his gavel once lightly. "But they did not quarter themselves in your home. They came at your invitation?"

"They did. But I did not purpose to comfort them, your honor. I invited them to get rid of them. To make them leave our town. At that breakfast I conveyed to them the news that the American Militia was en route from Boston."

"And from whom did you receive this intelligence?"

"I—uh—from no one. I invented it."

The laughter, totally unexpected, broke over her with the shock of a salt wave. As it foamed, she looked from the guffawing, thigh-slapping judges to the delighted faces of her friends, and power flooded her like light. Then she realized that there *was* light and she was standing in it. It clothed her, energized her. She looked to its source—the east windows. The shower had stopped and the sun was out. It shone on the black trees and paled their tight green buds. She looked down at the brown tips of her moiré shoes, and lo, they winked blearily back at her. She held out her hands and the nails glazed with the white of a blood-spotted egg (didn't do to eat them, but didn't do to waste them either) sparkled as if baked in a kiln. The sapphire taffeta of her skirt rippled like pond water in a land breeze. There was no doubting it, the light was heaven-sent for her benefit. Her bedazzled glance fell on Thomas Jenkins. He alone was unsmiling, his bat-

tered visage a lesson to liars. Seeing him thus, she suddenly felt a righteousness that she had never felt before.
Feelings of guilt and rage and fear and despair were
well-known to her but the feeling of righteousness was
new, intoxicating, strengthening, cleansing as the light
in which she stood.

"This wicked man," she quoted, pointing a finger
at the would-be extortionist, rapist, assassin, "watches
the righteous and seeks to slay them, but the Lord will
not abandon them to his power, or let them be condemned when they are brought to trial." The words,
soaked up over a lifetime of nightly Scripture readings,
poured in a steady gold-struck stream from her immaculate heart. "The wicked man plots against the
righteous and gnashes his teeth at them. The wicked
draws his sword and bends his bow to slay those who
walk uprightly, but his sword shall enter his own heart
and his bow shall be broken, for the Lord upholds the
righteous. The Lord knows the blameless, and they
are not put to shame in evil times. The wicked takes
and cannot pay back, but the righteous are generous
and give." She departed from text and inserted a perti-
nent example: "They give out of their own pocket for
the good of others—damages in the amount of thousands of pounds which the Refugees should rightly
have paid. Yet this greedy knave would have still more
restitution and our lives in the bargain.

"It has fallen to thee, good senators and congressmen, to sit upon us in judgment. We have made
our defense truthfully. All we ask is that thee do thy
office justly." She almost put out her hand, in a gesture
of simple pleading, but, remembering the cue cards, she
clasped them to her bosom instead. "Would thee deliver us unto the will of a man who bears false witness
and—but look at him, gentlemen—brawls by night?
Who seeks not justice but personal profit? Thee must
give answer to that and the answer must come from thy
souls. Mind thee well, my countrymen, if our innocence
do not protect us and our lives should be taken, our
blood will be required at thy hands."

She bowed her head.

There was a moment of silence.

"No further questions, Mistress Coffin. You may step down."

She sat close to Samuel, her legs tightly wound, her hands still clasped, suppressing a fit of shakes that came not from cold or fear but exhilaration.

Samuel moved his foot till his shoe touched hers.

Jenkins shambled up and offered to withdraw his complaint. He was excused to put this request in writing. The committee adjourned to submit in writing their willingness to accept the complainant's withdrawal. The upshot was that all were set free.

Sheep-shearing that June was not festive. Nine tenths of the island's flock had been lost to the severe winter. The Nantucketers were on the whole stoical. Better sheep than ships, they said, better sheep than men. In spite of the intermittent gunfire in their harbor, in spite of the continued looting of their shops and warehouses and homes, life went its homely way. Phineas lost a brother, gained another son. Damaris Starbuck, once the prettiest girl in Sherburne, died. A whale landed on the beach at Siasconsett and a thousand people of all ages came to see it. A muskmelon raised on Tuckernuck weighing sixteen pounds was put on exhibit at Meeting. Phineas went to Muskeget to get hay and Little Kezia gathered currants to make wine. One night the Fannings danced to fiddle music till two in the morning.

Off-island, the Revolution, like the earth, was revolving. The Americans with the aid of the French fleet took Newport. Major André, the handsome young Royalist who talked Benedict Arnold into changing sides, was hanged as a spy. The British and the Tories were defeated at King's Mountain, South Carolina. By 1781, when Cornwallis surrendered Yorktown to Washington and Lafayette, the tide turned.

Twenty-One

The onset of peace was as slow and painful as had
been the onset of war. Of Nantucket's whaling fleet that
had numbered upward of one hundred fifty vessels,
only two or three old hulks remained. With the death
of its whaling, the subsidiary industries—the rope
walks, the cooperages, the sail-rigging lofts—were
obliged to close down. Its manhood was decimated,
leaving five hundred widows and orphans on the town
dole. Some men were killed in action; some perished
in prison ships; some were simply missing, probably
suffering in wretched foreign jails. Some returned des-
titute, crippled, bitter against whichever side had overhauled their neutral sloops and impressed them into
service. More than two hundred had fought and died
in the Rebel cause, notably under John Paul Jones, and
were promptly disowned by the Friends for shouldering
arms.

Brutalized by the years of dealing and dodging
bloodshed, unemployed, bored, depressed, the veterans
prowled the streets like a pack of lions. In spite of a
night patrol of sixty-four volunteers, the rebellious
young men set fire to barns, shops, and storehouses;
broke into homes, beating up householders to steal as
little as four shillings' worth of green corn or sundry
silk handkerchiefs or a razor. In this distressed and
turbulent condition the town of Sherburne continued
well into 1784, three years after Cornwallis's capitu-
lation.

As for Kezia, she was wiped out. Her ships were
captured or lost, her shop looted. Greed operated freely
under the guise of patriotism, and as a proclaimed
Tory, Kezia was helpless to prevent her real estate

properties from being confiscated. Even her cattle went under the hammer. Forewarned that her Quaise estate would be seized, she had had time to sell off what goods and oil she had stored in the tunnel, but the money she received in payment she had laid by till war's end, by which time it was worth nothing. ("Not worth a Continental," as the phrase still goes.) Nevertheless she did not permit herself to despair. The Samuel Starbucks, the William Rotches, all the Tories throughout the new country were in the same boat. And some worse off. She still had a roof over her head—her somewhat rundown but extremely comfortable townhouse. As long as the sun shines, one does not ask for the moon.

She and John were dining quietly one clear day in December 1783 when she heard the jangle of cowbells she had hung on the front door.

Hagar plodded from the hall past her into the entry.

"Do not open till thee asks who 'tis and what's about," Kezia ordered sharply.

"I know, I know," muttered Hagar. "Told me often enough."

She watched Hagar peep through the newly installed glass side-light which was low enough to see out and too high, since the landing outside was a step lower than the threshold, to see in.

"What do you purpose?" called Hagar.

Kezia could not make out the reply but the rumble was male and plural. She looked quickly to John. He was sipping beer, not in the least curious, the house had long been a matriarchy.

"There's two of them," Hagar turned to announce. "Come to check the fireplaces for foul chimney hearts."

"Did thee recognize them?"

"Barnards."

"Matt Barnard's one of our fire wardens. Very well. Let them in."

Hagar obeyed, first unlatching, then flinging open the door. Four men, the two she'd seen on the stoop and one from each side of the two-sided stairway, rushed in. They brushed by Hagar, clumped into the dining room. The sheriff barely glanced at John, strode to Kezia, waving a paper. The other three men hulked by the sideboard, dripping slush onto the hooked rug and the polished black pine that bordered it. The well-known phrases filled the room like choking smoke, turbanning her head tightly, stopping up her nose, tickling her dry throat.

"I, as sheriff of our county Nantucket, empowered by the Commonwealth of Massachusetts, with these my deputies do hereby—"

She pushed the rattling document fiercely away.

"Did recover judgment against John Coffin wherefore the complainant . . ."

Thoughts scurried about like headless mice, their tails lashing the delicate membrane behind her eyes. Remain composed, but think, think! What to do? Who could help?

"In the amount of seven hundred dollars—"

"Seven hundred dollars?" she screamed. "Robbers, dolts! Know not that this house and furnishings are valued at five times that?"

"Commanded to attach these goods and chattles and lands . . ."

She threw the porringer. "Get out of here, toads! Decamp or I'll—"

The sheriff's inexorable baritone continued as a glob of custard oozed off the broad brim of his hat onto his sealskin shoulder. "In execution of which order for evictment . . ." He dodged a mug, a spoon. "Do now seize and possess these domains as herein described."

John rose deliberately from the table, wiped his mouth, rolled up his napkin, and put it in the whale-bone ring. Then he walked to the entry and took down his fur-lined greatcoat.

"Husband, stay! If thee makes thyself a sheep, the wolf is ready!"

He might have been deaf. Having missed the first
button, the buttoning stayed wrong. He tied a wool scarf
about his neck. He put on his beaver hat, sat on the
bench under the stairs to pull on his boots. His hat fell
off and he picked it up and screwed it low on his ears.
He pulled on his mittens and walked out, leaving the
door lapsed.

"Hagar, fetch Shongo!" Kezia ordered, clutching
the ends of the chair arms. "Fetch every hand! Have
them arm with shovels, axes, pitchforks, anything in
the barn. I want these skunks driven out of my house!"

Hagar went out back and the three statues beyond
the sideboard came to life. They squared their shoulders, took wider stances. One, who had been leaning
on his ancient bell-mouthed firelock, took it up and
pointed it at the hall door.

"Take example from thy husband, woman,"
growled the sheriff. "Top thy boom!"

"I'll see thee in Jericho first!"

"Lend me a hand here, Matt," said the sheriff.
"Let the harpy squawk. We have our duty."

The two men tried to hoist her up by her upper
arms.

"Lay not thy hands on me, whoresons!" She spat
in Matthew Barnard's face, clawed the sheriff's cheek.

"Take her up chair and all," barked the sheriff,
whose cheek divulged three welts, one beading slowly.
"Watch it now, don't dump her, she'll sue. Hellcat's in
the courtroom every day." He dodged her blow. It
glanced off his nose. "Steady on, watch the wet flooring!"

As they took her past the sideboard, she put out
an arm, curved it around Aunt Miriam's punchbowl,
sweeping it behind her. The flint glass exploded. It
prickled the back of her neck. There were tinkles and
sighs as well as thuds. That would be the set of goblets
Cousin Benjamin Franklin had sent her.

The crowd in the street stood four deep. Kezia,
squinting into the bright day, observed the grim faces;

they'd been jollier at the street hangings in London. Men and women stood in the snow, holding their babies over their shoulders. There were staring children of all ages; they were always brought to fires, public whippings, funerals and the like, it was a vivid way to instill apprehension of misdoing and death and hellfire. John stood in their forefront, his breath going up in fumes. He looked small and slimsy, a sparrow among vultures, and she felt disgraced by the way his coat was buttoned up.

They set her down in the middle of the street, facing her Christian door. She wore no kerchief—she'd spilled beer and whipped it off, it was still on the dining room floor—and the wintry air laid a heavy hand on her chest, and clammy fingers pressed the glands of her neck. She held her head high to escape the fingers but then she felt the snow come up through the soles of her silk slippers. A cloak was put around her shoulders. Hagar. But her teeth locked as if a rusty nail had infected her. She forced her jaws apart. "Stop snuffling, has thee no pride? Get thee to the Fannings."

"Cursed be the tents of the wicked!" called a woman from the sidelines.

That was all they needed, a cue. There were jeers and catcalls, and the more daring threw out sentences like savins on a bonfire.

"Where's your fat old King George now, Mistress Traitor?"

"Comeuppance! Teach Coffins to put themself above—"

"Boot's on the other leg now!"

The first snowball caught her under the ear. She turned sharply in the direction from which it came and took another on the nose. One burned her eye. Unexpectedly, the town's bad boy jumped the snowballers. "Belay, ye cowards—smite a woman, will ye?" They rolled about in the slush, pummeling, yelling. The forbidden words *arse, shit, bugger* drew growly laughter from the men and titters from the girls.

Phineas came running. He wore his yellow-green face with the purple lips. "My God, Marmy, what broil is this?"

"They've seized the house—thrown us out of it— with everything still in it, even the remains of our dinner!"

In the crook of Debbie's arm, John whimpered.

Phineas high-hurdled the white railing, pounded with both fists on the door till there was blood on the paneled cross. He leaned to look into the keeping room window. When he saw the men sprawled in chairs, lounging under the house flag, drinking by the fire, he put his fist through the window.

The front door opened.

"Watch it, son, or thee'll be in jail. Destroying private property."

"You watch it or you'll be in there with me. *Confiscating* private property—namely, booze."

"What do you want here, Mr. Fanning?"

"Entrance. To recover personal papers, divers documents."

"All is impounded. Those are our orders."

"Look here, you coldhearted officious—! You can't put these old people out in the street!"

She could not believe her ears. Surely he meant John. But he said people. "These old people." She was an old person. Phineas saw her so. The night they'd met at Fairhill, she'd been eaten up with jealousy of Little Kezia who was going to have him. Not that she did not wish the best for her daughter but that her own marriage had been so wanting. If she had felt trepanned then when she was still beautiful, still rich, desired, respected, what was she to feel now—a has-been, a never-was, missed the boat? Mayhap there was no boat to catch. Maybe one *was* the boat and one just pissed along willy-nilly, burned by sun, buffeted by wind, steering an instinctive, totally insignificant course by uncaring stars, destination death.

The sound of a child whooping pulled her back

from cosmos to microcosm. There was an epidemic in the town and she'd been fearful for her grandchildren, dosing them with horehound potions whenever Little Kezia turned her back, Little Kezia set little store by medicines. Now, over the hideously grating whoop, she heard Billy say, "I want a chair, too. I want to sit in the street like Gramama!" That brought her to her feet.

"Come, Billy, let us go home to Mama. This is no place—"

She took the child's hand, and a snowball, meant for her, knocked his hat off. He began to cry. Suddenly, as if he had not only eyes but also wings in his back, Phineas was in the street, cudgeling the culprit's ears. Then the bullyboy's father assailed Phineas, and soon, like the boil of a pond under onslaught of rain, fights broke out all about. It might have been a Donnybrook, but down from Centre Street bore Samuel Starbuck and Captain Moores in their sea clothes. Moores was the current town hero. The first man to sail into English port flying the new American flag. The two captains held up their hands, bellowing orders as if the street were a shipdeck and the citizenry mutineers. The spectators felt suddenly not like a pack of anonymous wolves, which had been exciting, but like naughty children, which was demeaning. They quieted sullenly. Disentangling themselves, they were again individuals and families, responsible for their conduct. They melted away. Kezia, too, walked off, holding tightly to Billy's hand. She had said not a word to Moores, dared not look at Samuel, but at the corner, she saw them and Phineas being let into her house.

The Fannings were living in a house loaned to them by her brother Daniel who had removed to Slocum's River. They and her sisters and Debbie each offered to take her and John in. She chose to live with Debbie. By sunset, Phineas, Samuel Starbuck, and Samuel's son, Samuel, Jr., delivered there the Coffins' papers, clothing, medicaments, oddments both valued and worthless—whatever could be hastily scooped out of drawers, off tables, even off the walls. Indeed, as Kezia remarked to Debbie, one good seizen and a body didn't need a fire.

Everyone talked of migration. Samuel Starbuck pleaded with Kezia to join him in a removal to Nova Scotia where the governor, commissioned by the king and Parliament, offered restitutional aid to Loyalists. Kezia steadily refused. "I would not leave my family, Samuel. Phineas will not come and John cannot." Besides, she was determined to stay and fight to recover the properties that were her children's and her grandchildren's rightful heritage. "Phineas," she'd told her son-in-law, " 'tis well we have an attorney in the family. I want thee to keep these cases in the court long's I live."

The day before Samuel Starbuck was to sail for the new land, Fools' Day actually, 1786, Kezia and he cohabited without taking a stitch off in a sheepfold at Capaum where the first town of Sherburne had been raised by the Forefathers. Afterward they nestled in each other's arms on a spread piece of old sail. A white nanny goat came to the sunken doorway. They threw a pebble at her to shoo her off. An afternoon breeze came up and the candleberries knocked the roof.

"I must go, love. I would give Debbie a hand with the supper."

He held her down. "Not till thee says thee'll sail with me in the vanguard."

She reached up and touched his cheeks. "Dear Samuel, I cannot leave. I cannot."

He drew her hands from his face, folded them on her breast. "Nay, not while Debbie and John live. 'Tis a strange coil, thee and them. Passing strange."

Stranger even then he guessed. John had developed a penchant for stealing Debbie's things: a pitcher, a purse, a shell, a silver thimble. Like a magpie, he'd collect them all week, and then on First Day Debbie would find them returned in a pile on her chest of drawers or on her bed, and a thing of his own might be added: a candle, his quill pen, his whalebone letter opener. Poor John, there was little enough he had left to give her. And Debbie, who did the cooking—all their childhood favorites: jugged hare, Indian pudding, Jerusalem artichokes, pork cake—had herself lost taste for food. The pounds were falling off her, she was beautiful again, it pleasured Kezia just to look at her, she wanted to stroke her. Perhaps her mother had been right, perhaps it had been Debbie she'd cared for above all others and married John because he was her image. And then there was the other symbiotic relationship—Tristram's to John, but only requited when Debbie was inaccessible. Once when John was helping Debbie skim milk in the buttery, he didn't answer Tristram's call. "Where in tarn's he gone to?" asked Tristram of Kezia who was sanding the floor, and she kept her tongue in her cheek. Why? There was a rivalry between her and Tristram as of siblings for parental favoritism. A strange coil indeed . . .

She suddenly felt Samuel stiffen against her.

"Hark, hear that stepping?" he whispered.

"The he-goat come for the nanny." But she whispered too.

A broad-brim appeared in the frame of the paneless window. "Ho-ho!" said Christopher Starbuck, leering, and loped away.

They stood up hurriedly, brushing each other off, Kezia moaning aloud the while. "Of all people. He hates me, ever has! He'll give testimony, I know it! And I've no money now to buy them off. Nor has thee. I shall be whipped—at my age. Oh, God, the shame! My children, John! And the little ones, my grandchildren. Aunt to eighty-one nieces and nephews! Samuel, I'll take my life before I let—"

He grabbed her, stopped her mouth with his upside-down hand. "Keep still. No harm shall come to thee. Did I not promise it?" To her bewilderment, a smile glinted in his eye. "Now thee'll *have* to come with me to Nova Scotia. At once. Before the blab."

Twenty-Two

"I wish I'd never come! I loathe it here! 'Tis a mull, the entire affair. The governor's promises were all cry and no wool. Nova Scotia's dismal and cold, I can scarcely get going of a morning."

"*Thee* has a good stock of health—my rheumatism's killing! The governor gave us Dartmouth and the wherewithal to build—"

Kezia didn't want Samuel to have rheumatism, she wanted him to be strong, indestructible. She went on angrily. "Everything makeshift and crude. Less than twenty houses for forty families. Ever running out of the simplest provisions—sugar, salt, tea, coffee, butter. Butter's needed to keep the brain alert. As for the people, a drearier little band of emigrants I cannot imagine. The self-same Friends—Folgers, Bunkers, Barnards, Macys, Coffins, Paddacks, Rays, Colemans—I liked not at home nor they me, and disappointment's not improved us."

"Verily, thee is a spoiled woman. Impatient, intolerant, intractable—"

They were in his ship's quarters. She had come with a batch of gooseberry jelly to wish him Godspeed for he was sailing out on the afternoon tide to hunt whales. It was the only place that afforded them privacy. At his home were his wife and his sons' families, whereas she lived next her busybody cousins, the Timothy Folgers. If Nantucket were a leaky vessel, then Dartmouth, Nova Scotia, was a cracked pitcher.

"Complaining of a shortage of butter! Two years agone at St. John's, newcomes sipped water from cavities in the rocks and subsisted on snails."

She flung her knuckles at his paunch. "Eating better than snails at the Starbucks', hm? Or is thee over-fond of thy wife's cooking?"

His fist went up. He shook it in her face. Badgered leader of the diaspora, blamed for everything that went wrong, suspected of skimming cream off the top, he was in no frame of mind to take teasing. "Vexing bitch, 'tis no wonder thee's misliked hereabout!" They hated her because again she'd built the grandest house and gone heavily into debt doing it. But when he saw her face, though she tossed her head, saying, "I care not for a fig for their liking!" he was sorry he'd hurt her. He patted her, took her on his knee. "They're just jealous, pet. But, mark me, this is not Nantucket where lambs and pigs wander through an empty jail. Men have died in Halifax prison. People have been incarcerated for owing less than five pounds. If I had the money, I'd pay thy debts, but I'm barely supporting my family. Thee owes everyone—the butcher, the baker, carpenters—"

She stroked his thinning biscuit-colored hair. "I know, I know. Don't think it doesn't gally me. Several tradesmen have come round nasty of late, threatening to have me served. But, Samuel, thee perceives the house is not large for show, 'tis for John and the Fannings. They'll come, I know they will. They'll have to. Phineas's law practice hardly exists. Not just because he's been a Tory but because Nantucket's industry is scuttled. No one can afford to pay attorneys. They've gone back to settling disputes at Meeting. And as his earnings wane, his cost waxes. Five children and Little Kezia thinks she is fruiting again. I invested in this chandlery so that Phineas should have a business here. How could I know I'd have a competitor in Halifax? And *he* has the wherewithal to advertise in the *Nova Scotia Gazette*. He undercuts my prices and he bad-mouths the quality of my product. Nevertheless, rot his soul, by summer's end, I'll have a shipment for exportation. If I can but hold my creditors off till then, I'll have clear sailing."

Dangerous optimism. Before the day's sunset, two

constables appeared at her South Street door with a writ of *capias ad satisfaciendum*. They gave her five minutes to collect a few necessaries. She thanked them with icy calm and offered them chairs in the keeping room. Debtors' prison! Oh, God, was she to be spared nothing? She thought of the fat white lice in the hair she'd shaved off John. "I regret I have no wine to offer, gentlemen, nor rum neither. Thy country has taught me the meaning of short allowance."

They were young men, abashed, and they stood mum, disdaining the chairs, their arms folded over their chests.

She went about her bedchamber, selecting warm garments in spite of the season, prisons were notoriously damp and cold. She shivered in a cold flash—the menopause was still upon her. She thought she was clearheaded, but later she found things she'd no idea she'd taken. A little flask of infusion of willow bark in csae of 'jail fever.' Lady Anne's gold brooch. She found the latter and a guinea in her back hair when she took off her bonnet in the cell.

It was while she was on the pot in her bedchamber that she realized no one in the settlement would notice her absence. Samuel was gone. She had told her cousins she was going to Barrington to visit the Richard Pinkhams. And she had so purposed. Both to dodge her creditors and to see if she could borrow money. She had loaned money to them in her palmy days and never been repaid.

"May I apprize my kinfolk next door of my whereabouts?" she asked when she came downstairs.

"Sorry, mistress. We're too long gone already. Come along quiet now. If you make no fuss, there'll be no need for fetters."

Fetters! The young jackanapes. She was no criminal, for mercy's sake. Debt was not felony or murder. "Where do thee take me?"

"Hollis Street."

Her heart slid steeply into her pelvis. Debbie's

grandson, taken from a Rebel ship, had died in the Hollis Street prison.

The brawny, clod-faced warder asked, "Have you been inoculated for the smallpox?"

"Nay."

She had, in New York, but she lied in his despite.

"Then you'll be better off in 'solitary.' 'Tis pestilential in the old jail. Lady like you, you'll be glad of the consideration. I'll remove you when 'tis wholesome."

Even though she heard the unctuous bid for a gratuity, her heart swelled with thankfulness. Privacy, blessed privacy, she thought. But she proved wrong. A person confined alone loses a little identity each day. She came down with grippe and lost even more, retaining shreds of a past self. There was no present time at all until she woke to a mulatto girl's face and felt a cool wet cloth pressed to her forehead. She asked on the off-chance the girl had some laudanum, "Has thee nepenthe for me, Daughter?"

"Olady's comin round. Sweatin good."

Kezia looked further to see who else—and there was a man. Very black, slight, eating of her daily bread—the slice of sky. He did not turn to see.

"What is thee called?"

"Amy."

The girl's hands were lined with pink velvet. Kezia looked up into the mild, popped eyes, brown pebbles rolling in a bluish white Nile. "Thee is kind, Amy."

"Hush," the girl said, giving her water off a spoon. Now how did she come by a spoon in this spare dungeon? It hurt to swallow, but Kezia smiled at a thought: John feared unmanliness above all things, and lo, castrated is he. I did fear ejectment and entrapment, and lo, I have won myself both.

She woke again. The girl came at once to her side. Must be able to hear the flutter of eyelids.

"Some better?"

"My bones feel crushed. And I thirst."

The girl fed her two spoonfuls of a cold white bland but nasty soup. Mashed lice? She swallowed without pain.

When next she opened her eyes, sunlight striped the bottom of her blanket. And there came the lice soup, she must have the noisiest eyelids in town!

"I am Kezia Coffin of Nantucket." But it felt like a lie, as if her claim to the name had gone down with the punch bowl. A woman 'without a country, a worm despised of the people.'

"Aye, we saw you in the great house in Philadelphy where George and I were slave. You been awful sick. You be well by um by."

Kezia smiled through tears. If she could lift her arms, she would hug the girl.

When Kezia was well, she talked and talked, she could not stop talking. George mostly lay or stood, eating up the half-foot of sky, drinking in the half-foot of air, he neither talked nor listened. But Amy listened. They were husband and wife. He was broody, high-strung, undecided whether to bend or break. She was sweet and stupid, big-boned, with calf eyes and a mouth sculpted for a face five times the size. Kezia poured the story of her life into those bovine eyes as if sanity depended upon it. Everything, down to the last detail, smiting her mother, her wedding night, her drug addiction. She told Amy the name of every man she had ever lain with. Amy listened with scrupulous wonder, but she told Kezia nothing, not even the name of her master.

"Blast and damn thee, Amy Williams. I have told thee my life secrets and thee tells me nothing. Would thee not be my friend?"

Amy glanced at the narrow form of her sleeping husband on his pallet under the clerestory. She looked from side to side and over her shoulder as if there were more than just the three of them. She licked her lips with a pale tongue and whispered hoarsely. "In Philadelphy my master he back-scuttle me. I never told nobody in this world." Having presented Kezia with the gift of her shame, she looked again at her husband's inert form. "Tore me up. 'Tis why I don't get with child, or so I believe."

Anywhere, any other time, Kezia would be appalled at the overpayment she had extorted. As it was, she accepted the anguished revelation as a proper token of fealty and was prepared to reward it with a protection as invalid as the tears of a crying drunkard.

"Does thee fear thy husband?" she demanded, ready to do battle.

"George? Lordy, no. George good as gold, but we have much trouble. His nerves is raggedy."

"What are thee in for?"

"Not me. George. I go where he go. He stole money. From the Overseer of the Poor. Eight pound."

At last Amy began to talk. And Kezia listened. The tale was one of thousands, by its very wholesaleness it lacked luster. When in 1779 a proclamation offered freedom to Negroes who would shoulder arms against the Rebels, George Williams joined up, and Amy followed his military corps from camp to camp. After the war, compensation was made by Britain to their former owners, and some three thousand Negro Loyalists were evacuated to Nova Scotia, New Brunswick, and northern Canada. Those who survived the journey were segregated in a ghetto, Birchtown, off Cape Sable, and then abandoned. No pay, no work, no provisions, no promised land-grants. The ghetto had steadily deteriorated. Weakened by a stomach ulcer, full of rage, out of work, out of hope, George had tried to steal enough for passage back to America.

"When is thy trial?"

"Nobody say. Just hale George and when I won't leave him, cart us both away and clap us in jail."

The time had come to give up the guinea. And the brooch.

"I shall help thee. Once I get out, I'll get thee out."

Kezia wrote to Governor Parr enclosing the brooch "which might go some way toward bailing me

out that I may apply to kin and friends in Dartmouth
for a temporary loan. Incarcerated, I am in no position
to manage my chandlery so that I may accumulate the
funds with which to pay my creditors. Indeed I am,
through my detention here, running up additional bills
for room and board." She also wrote to Samuel, mark-
ing the letter 'Personal,' which proved to be a mistake.
And she wrote to Little Kezia and Phineas.

The warder, rewarded by the guinea, did as he
was told. Unfortunately, he caught the governor as he
was walking with the collector up the steps to the
courthouse. Governor Parr tore open the envelope
forthwith, and when the costly pin fell out, he turned
red and did not deign to read the note. "Some petitioner
evidently thinks to bribe me," he said, tossing away
the balled paper. "I've no sympathy for those who
would corrupt officials to gain their ends. Here, put it
in the treasury with the tithes—whatever it brings in,"
and handed over the bauble.

Abigail Starbuck not only was piqued by the label
of privacy, but she recognized Kezia's handwriting.
She opened the letter, read it, made a feline hissing
sound, and burned it in the fireplace.

In the little cell appetites are hearty whether the
fish is bad or fresh. The barley bread is devoured with
coffee-flavored water each morning. All three talk
now, not compulsively but with the intimacy of a close-
knit family—one-word jokes, nicknames for things
and routines, sometimes a kind of code like school-
children use to emphasize their separateness from the
larger world. Now and then, a hue and cry from the
larger prison below increases their smugness and allegiance. The emotional balance of the triangle is constantly shifting. It is always two against one but the
pairs change. Most often it is Kezia and George versus
Amy. During this alignment, the talk is of escape,
methods of, materials used for. Often it is the two
women against the man. For some hours after the mar-

rieds have had sexual intercourse, it is Kezia who is shut out—teased, mocked, ignored.

Rats, fleas, and roaches are constant and therefore of no moment, but from certain insects they know which month it is. June beetles. July mosquitoes and daddy-longlegs. Toward the end of August when the night air has a nip in it, small vicious spiders and earwigs which in the instant before death give off a spiteful brown stink.

"All you high-and-mighty talk of setting fire," Amy says, near tears at having been odd man out overlong. "George ain't yet got his bonds off. Onliest thing to do is wrench him free of them fetters." They all look at George's handcuff. It was rough on the inside, and so now between it and his raw skin there is a wad of Kezia's linen underskirt. "When the warder fetch in the breakfast, bounce them chains off his head and walk on out."

George and Kezia look at each other. They begin to laugh. The slow one has outsmarted them both. Kezia hugs Amy. The delicate seesaw of love wobbles into perfect horizontal balance—they are a threesome, and light floods the cell. It is precisely at this moment that the warder approaches. Their fellowship freezes. Have they laughed too loudly? Will he vent his need to bully? Torture at last?

"Gentleman in the corridor waits on you, mistress. He has paid you up in full. You're sprung."

Kezia's heart sinks. Now? At once? Leave this warm umbrageous microcosm, rich with the smells of excrement, the sound of piss, snores, ablutions, orgastic groans, belches, farts (they are much troubled with gas pains, especially Kezia), scratchings, pickings of scabs? Once George yelled, "Say something, don't stand there looking!" and he fetched Amy a smart slap across the face with first the pink of his hand and then the black. Kezia felt a surge of satisfaction, identifying with George as if they were male siblings, there was something maddening about Amy's dumb bestial patience. Amy cried out and George sought the slit of air, and Amy crept to Kezia's breast. Kezia rocked her, murmuring, "Hush, he didn't mean to hurt thee. There, love, don't cry. He's not angry with thee but with himself. This place. This world. He's so helpless. We're so powerless." The girl quieted almost at once, and George turned back from the window and they all smiled deeply at one another. That moment and this last, thinks Kezia, contain all the fellowship ever I wanted. Now, the "gentleman" (Samuel? Back so soon?) would express her from this womb, turn her out onto that perilous track where the name of the game was virtue, the goal heaven, and you played it with money?

"God keep you," says George, as they hug farewell. So thin, these two, their bones slip like sticks in mud in each other's embrace.

"Going to miss you, missus," mourns Amy, laying her cheek on Kezia's.

The fellowship is already ebbing. 'Missus.' They have been calling her 'Kezia.'

"I shall return," says Kezia fiercely. "If not on the morrow, then the day after. At breakfast hour. Amy's plan. I shall come equipped for it. Be of good cheer."

When she saw Samuel standing there—rosy, portly, impeccable—an implosion of love and gratitude nearly felled her. But as he squeezed her against his chest and hard paunch, his questions and explanations and kisses flew about her head like a covey of birds that finally annoyed her. "What happened? Good Lord, thee's a shambles! Why did thee not contact the folks in Dartmouth and get help? How long's thee been here? Did thee treat thee well, feed thee? Thee's so gaunt, so gray."

She pulled away. His hysterical concern was sufficiently grating, must he also tell her how ugly—? She affected a light voice that soon went quavery. "Lah, Samuel, thee's been slow enough coming. Almost gave thee up for lost. Has thee been astern of a tortoise?"

"Slow! I've been to the South Seas! I've just pulled into Halifax Harbor. Ran every step from the dock."

"Thee's not been to thy home, then? How'd thee know where I was?"

"I was in Nantucket on end-of-voyage business. Little Kezia brought me thy letter. I sailed out of Great Harbor first tide out of the same day. Never was there a slower voyage. Such calms as thee'd not credit in northern seas. We were fortunate to make two miles an hour."

She almost told him she'd written him in Dartmouth, but she thought better of it. He was head of a family of three generations now, she would not put them asunder.

Back of the jailhouse, she kept his pace down the grassy slope, reliving the time she'd climbed it. How long ago that seemed. And, in another way, but yesterday. It was actually—half of May, June, July, August—three and a half months.

"I must smell like old haddock. And look like death." Her hand went to her matted hair. She'd forgotten she had hair, let alone considered its coifing. Freedom has its own enslavements.

"Thee does want washing," he said, and was glad she could still laugh.

He left her to a toilette in his quarters. A ship's cabin had never looked so palatial, nor so forbiddingly clean. She handed her clothes to him through a crack in the door, including the bonnet. "Throw them overboard. Fleas are the least of it."

She came topside in the cabin boy's clothes and his captain's cap.

"Well, look at thee," he said, his eyes soft, merry. "Thee's dropped ten years." He dared not hug her in sight of the crew, but he held her arms, his face close, an inch from kissing her forehead. "Now that's more like it. Thee smells good enough to drink."

"Not surprising. I splashed with perry."

The light hurt her eyes, but the fresh air was

heavenly, she could not drink it in fast enough, she swallowed it in gluttonous gulps.

"I'm beholden to thee, Samuel."

He smiled wryly. "Nothing at all. But I accept the thanks. Thee has never been wont to spoil me with endearments."

"Thee was home, Sherburne. Was it pleasant?"

"Very. More so than I preferred to remember."

"Did thee see John?"

"Aye."

"He's well?"

"Aging, I'd say, but content to be living with Debbie and Tristram."

"Did he ask for me?"

"Uh, not in so many words, my dear. He's quite senile."

"And my children? And grandchildren?"

"All in the pink."

"Shall they come to Nova Scotia?"

"They're not yet of a mind to but I think they might be persuaded. Phineas's law practice is not flourishing. The Whigs are still very hostile. But he's managing a livelihood—with a little codfishing and some 'running' on the side. Oh, here. A letter from thy mother."

Kezia took it but did not open it. She stared out at the water. "Poor John. I know now a little of his suffering. I thought of him often in that lousetrap."

"Aye, prison's against nature. And for but overspending, it's excessive punishment. There ought to be bankruptcy laws."

She began to shiver in the breeze. They returned to his quarters. He poured them wine and brought out biscuits.

" 'Tis a dream from start to finish. I can't sort out the real from the fancied. Ah, Samuel, I thought thee'd done with me."

"Thee has hardly been my rod and staff in my time of need," he growled bitterly.

Kezia broke the seal on her mother's envelope.

"Dear Daughter Kezia," ran the shaky script, "My time is nigh. I shall journey shortly to the Promised Land. That old ful Tupper treets me Chearful but no man can pul the wul over my Eys. Therefor I make this effort to convey to thee my forgiveness for exercising me by thy wilfulness. I pray for thy Reformance, and thy Return to the True Religion of Light. Except thee Repent, I and thee shall not meet again. Yrs. in Christ, Abigail Folger Pinkham."

For just a second she caught it: that she made her mother feel in the wrong too, that the guilt was mutual. And then, because there was no mention of love, anger scathed her. Tears of anger filled her eyes. But soon she began to laugh. Sixty-five years old and still crying for her mother.

"I'd not have more wine were I thee," Samuel cautioned. "Nor biscuits either. Never surprise the stomach. My daughter-in-law Lucretia shall bring thee some tastes of our supper."

She paid no attention, gobbled the biscuits, drank the wine like cold tea, and threw up into his washing basin.

"There now," she gasped, fainting back on his arm, "I must look myself again."

He held her close. "The same thorny blowfish, prison's done thee no good at all."

The transition was too swift. It was like coming out of the opium world without the sobering bridge of withdrawal symptoms. Her house looked immaculate, enormous, luxurious, and felt—empty. Everything in it was strange to her and a little inimical. Things that should have been light were heavy and fell from her hands. The sight of her provisions—salted meats, pickles, jams, strings of dried apples—turned her stomach. Friendlier was the furry green mold on a fresh cucumber that was left out on the drainboard. Before throwing it away, she picked off the mold and pressed it to a gleeting spider bite on her calf.

Her chamber was as she had left it, her last piss

turned hard and dark in the pot and the room smelling
like a long unopened drawer. Before she dealt with the
pot, she looked at herself in the mirror and was appalled. Her hair was no longer salt-and-pepper nor
silver like her mother's but a dull mouse gray. There
were purse wrinkles all around her mouth, pads of
flesh on either side of her jaw, deep frown ruts between
her eyes. Her neck was scrawny, the skin slack. A face
only the Williamses could love. She longed for them,
but as she made her second toilette of the day, any joy
she might have taken in the hot water, the fragrant
salves and London soap, the unbarred window, the
clean, elevated, soft bed, was spoiled by the thought
of her promise to rescue them. A wild promise, a
mountain of impossibility. How would she get across
the harbor? She was too weak to row; even carrying
hot water up the stairs had taxed her. Samuel? No, she
would not involve him. He'd be no party to the plan in
any case. She saw him stuffed tight into his fine wools,
heard him bawl, "What? Has thee lost thy wits? I
might try to get clemency for them, but I am not
pleased to spend my leeway with the governor on
petty thieves. And I disapprove interfering with the
wheels of justice."

What would the world do without young people?
It would surely come to a standstill. Lucretia, when she
came, was romantical about the project. "Leave everything to me," she said. "We shall sleep but a few hours.
I shall rouse thee. I have this gift, I can wake myself to
the dot of time. I shall tell Samuel Junior I stayed the
night because thee was twadgetty—thy first night
home, and all."

They worked the details out over supper of which
Kezia could swallow but a few bites.

"But the warder," Lucretia said. "Might he not
recognize thee? Then he'd know just where to come
for the escapers. And thee'd be locked up again as the
accomplice." She tapped her teeth, frowning. "Aunt
Kezia, has thee any corks?"

"Aye. One in a jug of molasses, another in a jug of cider, I believe. 'Tis long since I beheld my larder."

"Well, we could plug the jugs with rags and burn the cork to blacken thy face. Thee could go with a basket of food, as a neighbor or kin. Ah, thee's so frightfully thin—mayhap a bit of padding—"

Nervy as the discussion made her, Kezia had to laugh. "Dear Lucretia, thee treats the whole operation more as a prank than derring-do. But I draw the line at blackface and I'll not dress up like a sore finger. We're getting absurd. We must keep cool heads."

"Cool heads get a deal of credit that belongs to cold feet. What of the Boston Tea Party—Englishmen in feathers and paint!"

But they overslept themselves. They were awakened by Kezia's next-door neighbors, Lucretia's parents, the Timothy Folgers, who brought over breakfast porridge. And all through the day came callers with provender and sympathy and belated offers of money.

"I thank thee but one creditor is enough and I soon hope to have none. Samuel Starbuck has kindly lent me the wherewithal to start up my chandlery again."

Worn out with the unwonted socializing, Kezia slept through yet another night. But at cockcrow the day following, she and Lucretia were on the bay in Kezia's dory. Lucretia rowed through scarves of fog with Kezia as navigator. Lucretia had dressed as a lad in her brother's garments. "Then if we're stopped while I'm rowing the prisoners, I shall say I but ferried thee for a pittance," Lucretia explained gaily. Kezia did not demur. She was too fluttery to trust her judgment, though she saw no more harm in this bit of playacting than safeguard. And she envied the girl's high spirits, remembering the pleasure she had taken in masquerading as a dandy for the cockfights in London. For herself, she relied solely upon bribery. From the money Samuel had loaned her she had taken a five-pound note. In a hamper she carried a crock of butter, some gooseberry jam, and two loaves of fresh-baked bread with which she had been gifted yesterday, and in her reticule, a solid brass pestle, a small hacksaw and a link cutter which Lucretia had filched from her father's set of tools in the barn.

As she cautioned Lucretia, now larboard, now starboard, Kezia prayed that God succor her endeavor. And that she behave valorously. "If thou faint in the day of adversity, thy strength is small." In spite of all her glib fantastic talk in the prison, she had no clear plan. She hoped to so dazzle the warder with the whopping tip that he would lead her forthwith to the cell to deliver to her friends the supplementary food. While he bent to the lock, she'd bash his head with the pestle, not to kill, but to stun. (Oh, God save her from a killing blow!) George's fetters could be quickly bit through with the pincers or, failing that, the saw. Then, as Amy had imagined, they could 'walk on out.' Lucretia would be waiting in the dory below to row them across to Mill Cove. Kezia had yesterday learned her cousin Francis Coffin's vessel, the *Hibernia,* was up-anchoring on this day's noontide. (That was one good thing that came from gamming with neighbors, one learned what was going on.) She had no doubt her cousin would agree to carry the hapless couple to Nantucket. Phineas and Little Kezia and Hagar could be counted upon to take it from there.

The warder was new.

"Whoever they were, they have gone," he said. "The solitary cell wants cleaning. There were some black folk, but no more. Might be removed below to the old jail. Or you might inquire at the courthouse— the trial may have come up."

There were no Williamses on the warder's list of inmates in the old jail.

The clerk of the courthouse, however, had not only heard the name Williams, he had, he said, recorded their sentence.

"When?"

"Yesterday. Afternoon session."

"Does thee know what the sentence was?"

"I do. I heard the verdict, I was the scribe. George Williams was fined fifteen pounds and court costs plus forty lashes on the bare back with the cat-o-nine-tails. Unable to pay the fine, the couple was indentured to a family in Londontown. The ship being ready to embark, they were stowed in the hold, the lashes to be delivered aboard ship at the captain's discretion."

Kezia turned slowly, feeling punched. But then she came back, eyes ablaze, and shook her finger at the clerk. "George Williams fought for the king! Seven years! He was entitled to the initials U.E.L. after his name. United Empire Loyalists. Him and all his descendants. That ought rightly to have been taken into consideration."

"Look you, ma'am, I did not pronounce sentence, I merely recorded—"

"Indentured, thee says! They were *free,* I tell thee. Freed by the law of the Crown! I never heard a grosser miscarriage of justice!"

He jumped up, grabbed her elbow, and hustled her roughly through the open door. "The man was a thief. There were witnesses. It was a fair trial. And you'd best shut your peep, old lady, or you'll find yourself behind bars!"

A day and a night. They had made all the difference between a life of dignity and a life of slavery for her two dear friends. The delay on her part had been sheer cowardice, she could see that now. As John suffered in the night for his cannibalism, so she would henceforth relive this bitter regret. In her span of error and mistiming it was the one thing she would never forgive herself.

Out of prison, Kezia set about wangling the compensation Britain had promised her loyal subjects. Without it, the chandlery must founder. Armed with a hidebound volume of copies of deeds of purchase and sale plus notarized affidavits of loss of ships and cargo and stock in trade—over fifty transactions in all, ranging over the past eleven years, furnished her by the diligent Phineas—she spent her days in the commissioners' offices. And when they sneaked out of back doors, she found them in their homes. Even the news of her mother's death did not pull her foot off the slow treadle of Empire bureaucracy.

And then one day in the midst of her negotiations, she came to Samuel Starbuck and begged him to carry her home. "John's dying," she said, "I must go to him."

"Thee's had word?"

"No, but I feel it. In the bones of my heart."

"What? Not even wait for thy due reparations? Let all that work—thousands of dollars—go for an elfish notion?"

" 'Tis no notion. I'm certain sure."

"But what of thy chandlery? Thy house?"

"Lucretia and Samuel Junior need a home of their own, Samuel, and Lucretia would be pleased to live next door to her parents. The Halifax chandlers, Cochran and Sons, are eager to buy me out. Thee'll handle these matters for me, love, shall thee not? I would fain embark on the morrow."

"But thy things—furniture, clothing—thee can't just up and—"

"My clothes will fill but a single chest. And Lucretia would admire to have the furnishings. Don't make a fuss, Samuel, there's a dear."

They sailed out of Mill Cove the next day, July 19, 1788.

When they reached Nantucket, they learned that John Coffin had died at sunrise of that date, attended by his twin sister and his daughter. His first love and the last. Kezia's jealousy sank fangs. Yet and still, she was glad they were with him at the Haulover. Sometimes the pattern of things had a grace to it, a rightness, haphazard though it might appear.

Twenty-Three

For some days Samuel Starbuck lay over in Sherburne, loath to leave Kezia in so low a state. She would not get out of her bed in the borning chamber of the house the Fannings had rented. She ate little, drank much, wept not at all. When anyone came to labor with her—Debbie, Phineas, Little Kezia, her sisters, himself—she turned her face to the wall. At length, he decided to leave her to heaven, he had his own family and pressing business matters to attend to.

"Thee grieves not for thy husband," he told the back of her head, "but for the young bride he takes with him to the grave. I am not jealous of that grief, believe me. Our time is done. We must think now of our children and our children's children. It is for them I would see thee hoist thy topping lift, old mate. Shall thee not look me eye to eye and tell me thee'll try? The plucky maid I fell in love with, shall thee not show her to me ere I go?" Not a move in the hump under the coverlet. He sighed and rose and put his hand on her mussy gray hair. "Kezia, is there no word thee'd speak to me? Not even farewell?"

How can you tell a faithful lover that the light in your life has gone out with another man? She put her hand out back of her and let him clasp it. And when he lay a kiss in the palm, she closed her fingers over the kiss.

But he had reached her. That night John appeared to her in a dream, saying, "Our seed shall not beg bread, they shall inherit the land and dwell therein." And the next day Phineas came to her in some excitement with a piece of research he'd done on the law.

"Listen carefully, Marmy. Open your mind to

369

what I have to say: At Common Law a wife is entitled
upon her husband's death to a life estate in one-third of
any real property of which he was seized during their
marriage. In sales, whether voluntary or forced, a husband cannot transfer his real estate so as to cut off his
wife's right of dower unless the deed specifically so
states and the wife's signature is affixed and duly witnessed. Now hear this, Grandmama: I have reviewed
all the records of your deeds, and except in a few early
transactions made before the war, the dower rights are
unassigned."

Kezia turned to him and leaned on an elbow,
covering her slack bosom with the quilt. "Tell me all
that again, Son. Say it slow."

For ten years Kezia pursued her dower rights in
the Courts of Common Pleas up and down the Atlantic seaboard as relentlessly, as dauntlessly, as her
brethren pursued whales. Eventually, she hit a school
and sank harpoons.

By this time the Whigs were the Republican
party and the Tories Federalists, but all, all were
Americans, and none more so than Kezia who rejoiced when John Adams succeeded Washington as
President of these United States. Now a new group sat
in the judges' seats, younger men unaffected by the
prejudices of a war twenty years ago. And just as their
faces were new to Kezia, so was hers to them. They
saw not an obsessive suer but a determined widow with
a valid legal complaint. They listened and they decreed. One by one in the town of Nantucket (the
name of Sherburne was dropped in 1795), the defendants went down before the bench. She retrieved a
thousand pounds cash for looted merchandise and falsi-
fied debts. In real estate she was awarded her meadows
at Pocomo, Shimmo, Shawkemo, both Monomoys, her
warehouse at Brant Point, acreage adjacent to the rope
walks, twenty-six sheep and eight cows as well as pas-
turage on Tuckernuck Island. But her sweetest victory
was over Josiah Barker—he who had had her carried

out of her house into the street. From him she was
assigned a third of her Wesco land including the townhouse and the outbuildings along the creek. Barker
appealed the verdict in the Court of Boston where
the decision was upheld.

But as much as Kezia hated losing, neither did
she love winning. She found herself patting Josiah Barker's shoulder as they descended the courthouse steps.
"Cheer up, friend," she said to the grim-faced old
man, "none of us gets to keep things very long."

The thought did not charm him. He shook his
cane at her. "You die hard, Kezia. They'll have a hard
time laying your ghost."

On a March evening in 1798, Kezia sat, straight
as a spindle, in a wooden armchair by the fire, drinking
a good Spanish sherry with her son-in-law. Her dark
eyes were ringed with fatigue but there was a shine in
them and her cheeks were flushed. They had that afternoon won another dower case, an acre and four rods at
the lime kiln from her brother-in-law William Coffin.
She still had on her calash. Her bombazine 'round
gown' was new and black (she had worn no color
since she was widowed), the severity relieved by a
cloud of white neckerchief. From her glossy petticoat
peeped modish sandals with black rosettes. (High heels
and buckles were out—one kept one's flag up.)

"I cannot tell thee what it means to me to have
regained the townhouse, dear Phineas. To walk by my
buildings and be shut out of living in them put a thorn
in my side. Now we must buy back the Quaise properties from the house to the beach. I want my grandchildren to have a snug winter home and to look forward to summers in the country. The islander has a
shallow root system at best, it must be counteracted by
tradition and strong family ties. By fond memories of
youth."

"That kind of money's a ways off."

"Maybe so, but it will come. These several re-
coveries have set the precedent, and with thy genius, I

doubt not the rest of what's due us shall be forthcoming."

"I hope so. For your sake. For myself and Little Kezia, home's wherever you and the children are."

He put his hand on her shoulder and she leaned her head to press it. "Aye, I can see that. Thee's more contented than I ever was." She sighed. "I would Little Kezia were here this night to share today's triumph. She's been in Boston nigh on to six weeks."

"She went on your business, Marmy," he reminded her gently. "I look for her in the next day or so. May I pour you more sherry?"

"I'll do it," she said, groaning as she rose. "This sciatica. Well, at seventy-five, that's little to complain of. Aye, 'tis a good union, thee and Little Kezia. I knew it should be."

"You did, didn't you? And we give you full marks for the match. You and the snake."

"That was no snake, my lad, that was the long arm of Providence. Ahoy, what's this?" On the dresser next to the decanter stood a small glass vial. She lifted the stopper and sniffed. That unmistakable smell—like a busy wharf on a close summer day. What was so painful that she took to it? What so promising that she fought free of it?

"Oh, that? A potion Dr. Tupper gave me. I forgot it. I had the headache yesterday, but it went away. If I'd taken the stuff I'd have credited it with a cure."

"Old Tupper's too free entirely with his prescriptions. Thee'd do better to call young Dr. Easton when thee needs physicking. This is laudanum, tincture of opium, and opium breeds a craving. It ought not to be left about. The children might get hold of it."

Phineas nodded. He got up to throw another log on the fire.

Once, she thought, just this once, this potion, and not again. She'd earned the respite, a small indulgence. Oh, that airy feeling, so careless! And she so tired, so lonely, in spite of the children. She missed her peers. No, that wasn't it, she had her sisters. She missed the ones she had loved. Love lasts, lovers don't, as Grandmother Wilcox used to say. She could now bear even Debbie's passing if she just had Samuel. But Samuel was resettled with his tribe in Wales, they scarcely corresponded anymore. Hagar was with them. Unable to pay her wages, she had sent Hagar to them. Now she had money again, might she not get Hagar back? She would be company.

"Marmy?"

"Mmm?"

Besides, look at Benjamin Tupper. Three grains a day every day for over twenty years. Said there was a whole coterie of takers, seemed to be hinting she might hook in with them. "Heave to, Ben," she'd told him. "I was for a decade of my prime years the vacuum that nature abhors. Tempt me not, I'd not waste my last ones." But of course it would be different now. She was knowledgeable about the pitfalls, she could restrict the dose—

"Marmy!"

She started. "Yes, dear?"

"Are you quite well?"

"Certainly. Why?"

"Woolgathering, then."

"Well, I was thinking, Phineas. I'm fair sick of mucking about courthouses. Now the drift is our way, I think thee might take the wheel."

"I can't quite see you as a homebody."

"Well, I might start up the school again," and as she said it, she meant to. "Little Kezia would assist me. And this time I'd have black and Indian children as well. I often think on my prison friends, the Williamses. If they'd been literate, they might have—"

"Colored scholars? You'll meet head winds. Gospelizing them's one thing, educating them's another. Folks'll say—"

"Let them. Public mouth's nothing to me. It has chewed me up and spat me out oft before. Where's thee going, Phineas?"

"To your sister Judy's," he said, buttoning up his

reefer. "I thought you heard me. She's giving the children supper, mind? And I said you looked so fashed, I thought I'd tarry there for a bite, save you the bother."

Kezia stretched her neck this way and that. "I'll not say nay. Judith ever has something tasty on the hob. For myself, I shall warm up the breakfast porridge and so to bed."

The minute he left she fleeted to the dresser. She emptied the contents of the vial into her winecup and added sherry to the brim. She took the potion to the settle under the window and took off her hat, setting it down beside her. She sat sipping, watching the dusk gather. The hawthorn bush swayed in an offshore wind. Peace settled about her shoulders like cashmere. The trouble was she tried too hard, ran too fast. And for what? No more than the birds and the bees who woke each morning to seek food all day to take them to another nightfall. Pretty cup. Porcelain. My, all the fine things she'd had and lost . . .

Phineas was back in a trice.

"Forget something, Son?"

He laughed. "I didn't forget them. They begged to spend the night with their cousins. They talked me round. Why do you sit in the dark? It's melancholy."

"I and the dark are old friends."

He lit two candles. They sprang to light—huge yellow teardrops.

"I'll wager you've not supped," he said.

"Just setting. Adream."

"Aren't you hungry?"

"Aye. Ravenous, now I think of it."

"Then aloft with you, woman. You're frazzled, anyone can see that. I'll bring you some porridge. Call it a day."

"Sufficient unto the day is the goodness thereof!" She giggled. How witty!

"So tired you're getting silly. Now, go along. Up to bed with thee. Whoops, watch it!"

She'd meant to set the drained cup down but the table was farther away than it looked. The pieces winked wisely, tinkled, slow-falling in the rainbowed light. She brushed china dust off her hat, bent to pick up a shard.

"Don't bother. I'll sweep up." He offered her one of the candlesticks.

She shook her head. "I've one in my chamber." She glided past him into the entry. She could smell the oil of cedar on the winding stairs—the leased house would be returned a sight cleaner than it had been received. She slid her palm along the rope handrail. Now where—? Ah, yes, her mother's house. Burned her hand running down, late to breakfast on sheep-washing day, hair in a ribbon for John.

Her scream fell like a star, and she after it. It was the sound she had come in on, and, except for the parting utterance of regard for her daughter, it was that body's last.

So is it written in Kezia Fanning's diary which is kept in the Peter Folger Museum at Nantucket.

ABOUT THE AUTHOR

DIANA GAINES, author of five novels including *Dangerous Climate* and *Marry in Anger,* spent five years writing *Nantucket Woman.* She attended Smith College and graduated from the University of Chicago, Phi Beta Kappa. She is now an active golfer and fisherman, as is her husband, Henry L. Jaffe, M.D. They live in Pacific Palisades and Palm Springs, California.

RELAX!
SIT DOWN
and Catch Up On Your Reading!

Bantam Book Catalog

Here's your up-to-the-minute listing of every book currently available from Bantam.

This easy-to-use catalog is divided into categories and contains over 1400 titles by your favorite authors.

So don't delay—take advantage of this special opportunity to increase your reading pleasure.

Just send us your name and address and 25¢ (to help defray postage and handling costs).